I0762121

lost in the affair

new york times bestselling author

E.K. BLAIR

LOST IN THE AFFAIR

Editor: Lisa Baker, Adept Edits and Ashley Williams
Cover Designer: Emily Wittig Designs
Interior Designer: Champagne Book Design

ISBN: 978-0-9963970-7-0

Credit: Penguin Random House LLC, "Corelli's Mandolin" by Louis de Bernières

Names and locations have been changed to protect the identity of Anonymous, but the story is true.

ACCLAIM FOR E.K. BLAIR'S
LOST IN THE AFFAIR

"You want something to shake you up? You want to read a raw reality "love story"? This is the one. "It's the most real, distressing, shocking train-wrecks of a love story I've ever read. But a love story, it is. I think." ***-Maryse Black, Maryse's Book Blog***

"*Lost in the Affair* at times reads as a scathing critique of the illusion and escapism the entire romance industry provides. It begs the question as to whether or not these created fictional spaces can become dangerous portholes into delusional perceptions about reality. Blair heroically weaves a page-turning novel every writer, reader, agent, publicist and publisher in the romance industry will scramble to read." ***-New York Daily News***

"Minds blown! Addictive doesn't begin to describe it! E.K. Blair perfectly captured the potency of the story and the characters in a raw, revealing, gripping, shocking and scandalous guilty pleasure which left our emotions in disarray. One thing's for sure, it will have readers talking long after turning the last page!" ***-Totally Booked***

"It's insane, intense, inappropriate—all the things that a *True Hollywood Story* episode would have." ***-All Romance Reviews***

"E.K. Blair wrote the hell out of this book!" ***-Must Read Books or Die***

"Lost in the Affair is unlike anything I have ever read. Shocking. Scandalous. Real. Raw. You have to read it to believe it." ***-Kim Karr, New York Times Bestselling Author***

"As always, E.K. Blair's brand of intricately woven prose allows the literary darkness to shine through and Holy. Sweet. Hell! it's shining bright throughout *Lost in the Affair*. Blair's best work to date and a top read of 2016!" ***-Read and Share Book Reviews***

"Best Book of the Year!!!" ***-Just Me & My Kindle***

"Unique. Raw. Gasp-worthy. So different from every other book I've read this year. E.K. Blair is fearless." ***-Alessandra Torre, New York Times Bestselling Author***

"*Lost in the Affair* is a compelling and addictive account of a woman who craves attention. It's beautifully written—a sensational narrative—by E.K, who does a sterling job re-telling this extraordinary confession." ***-Ellesea Loves Reading***

"Real and gritty. Ugly and truthful. EK's best writing to date. A heroine that is neither bland nor boring, but shamefully relatable." ***-Tarryn Fisher, New York Times Bestselling Author***

"*Lost in the Affair* is an emotional and highly addicting read. A truly shocking and intense page-turner I could not put down." ***-SL Scott, New York Times Bestselling Author***

dedication

To anyone who's ever fucked up

lost in the affair

part one

"Chaos is an angel who fell in love with a demon."

~Christopher Poindexter

chapter one

THE DREADFUL SOUND OF MY ALARM WAKES ME FROM A DREAM I WASN'T READY to leave just yet. Giggling from my girls echoes through the door of my bedroom as I blink my eyes open, holding on to the vanishing visions before lucidity erases them entirely. I stretch my arms and legs as I breathe in the scent of pancakes and bacon, the aperitif of familiarity and comfort.

Tossing the blankets aside, I leave slumber's fantasies on the pillow and get out of bed. When I slip on my robe, I head out to the kitchen for some much-needed coffee.

"Look who's awake, girls," my husband announces as he flips pancakes onto the kids' plates.

They give me a fleeting acknowledgment as Landon sets their breakfast on the table. While they stuff their mouths, I focus on making my cup of coffee.

"How late were you up last night?"

Stirring the creamer into my mug, I look over to my husband of eight years and respond, "A little after two."

"What kept you up so late this time? A fighter? A pilot? A billionaire with a dark past who finally met the one woman that would change him forever?" He laughs as he says this, and I can't fight the urge to bust out laughing too. Because he's spot on. "You read such garbage, you know?"

"Hey!" I chastise through my own fit of giggles. "I write that stuff too."

"So what was it, huh?" he continues to tease.

With a toying glare, I admit, "The billionaire with a dark past."

"Knew it! You like 'em rich and filthy, which is why you married me."

"Are you stashing money I don't know about?" I joke as he begins to wash the dishes. Looking over to our girls, Emily and Jill, I tell them, "Hurry up. We're leaving in fifteen minutes."

They shove their last bites in their mouths, jump out of their chairs, and run up the stairs.

"Get back here and clear the table," I call out, trying not to sound too naggy, and then grab my coffee before heading back into my bedroom to throw myself together.

I'm in the middle of brushing my teeth when Landon walks into the bathroom.

"Don't forget that I'm working late tonight. Damon and I are testing out a few new recipes for the menu," he says and then hops into the shower.

Landon is the sous-chef at Chin-Chin, an upscale French steak and seafood restaurant in the heart of Boston. We met when I was in college at Boston University, where I majored in film and television studies. During my third year, I took an internship in the props department at FOX25, Boston's local news station. At the time, Landon was a young, up-and-coming chef and had landed a guest spot for a demonstration segment on the morning show.

"That guy was so hot."

"I wonder if he's single?" Brooke, my best friend who also interns, says as we are down in the kitchen, cleaning all the dishes from the segment.

"I doubt it. He's probably banging some blue-eyed, blonde tart who drinks spritzers."

Brooke narrows her eyes at me. "You just pretty much described me."

I laugh and shake my head at her as I continue to wash the pans and plates while she dries.

"Excuse me."

Brooke and I turn around to see the hot chef standing in the doorway.

"I think you accidentally took my knife case," he says.

"Oh . . . I'm so sorry." I take my hands out of the soapy water, dry them

off, and walk over to the cart that we loaded all the props onto. Kneeling down, I find his knives on the bottom rack. When I move to stand, he steps beside me, and I stumble on my feet, hitting my head on the cart and knocking over a few ramekins of sauce onto my top.

"Crap."

"Oh shit. I'm so sorry," he says, grabbing ahold of my arm and helping me up.

Looking down at my blouse, which is now covered in oil and teriyaki sauce, I lie and tell him, "It's okay." When I shift my eyes up, I can see the embarrassment on his perfect face.

"That top is ruined."

"Yeah, well, I guess I'll just have to go shopping then."

"Let me make it up to you."

"That's not necessary."

"No, it's not," he says. "But it would make me feel like less of a dick."

"It's really— "

"Stop being shy and let him make it up to you," Brooke calls out from across the room, her words blemishing my face in my own embarrassment.

With a smirk on his face, he asks, "What's your name?"

"Tori."

He holds out his hand to me, and when I slip mine into his, he says, "I'm Landon."

His eyes are deep brown, nearly the same color as his hair, which is cut short and gelled. He's clean-shaven with a preppy look to him that makes the all-American statement.

"What's your number so I can call you to make plans?"

He pulls out his cell and adds my number before slipping it back into his pants pocket. When he reaches down to pick up the case with his knives, my cell buzzes with an incoming text.

Unknown: Sorry about the shirt.

When I look up to him, he's smiling. "Had to make sure you weren't trying to blow me off with a fake number."

He takes the case from my hands and drops his voice when he says, "I'll call you later."

I watch him as he walks out of the kitchen, and as soon as he's gone, Brooke squeals, "Oh, my God! He was totally flirting with you."

Shoving my cell back in my pocket, I roll my eyes and walk over to the sink. "Flirting? He wants to take me on a date because he ruined my shirt, Brooke. That's not flirting, that's pity."

"Well, you better take it, whatever it is because you need to get laid."

I yank the bowl she's holding from her hands. "What's that supposed to mean?"

"You're uptight, Tori."

"Aren't I allowed to be?"

Brooke dries her hands, and when she sets the towel down, she looks at me with compassion. "Of course you're allowed. But it's been months. Don't you think you should start putting yourself out there?"

"I am out there." My defense is weak at best. We both know I'm hiding.

"You're a terrible liar. Look, Trey was a grade-A dick, but not every guy is like that."

Pain grows thick in my chest, building pressure around my heart that I will to dissolve. I wonder how much longer this will last. She's right, it's been nearly seven months since I broke up with Trey. We'd dated since high school—I gave him four years of my life, and I thought he was the one. But it turned out, I was just lying to myself. I was blinded by familiarity.

From early on, Trey had been physical with me. What started out as meek pushes and shoves eventually morphed into slaps and punches. But I stayed with him because I loved him. At least, I thought I did. I now know differently. I'd convinced myself that if I just loved him a little harder, if I behaved a little better, that he'd stop.

No one knew what was happening behind closed doors—we hid it well. It wasn't until Brooke ditched her blind date one night and returned to our dorm room much earlier than expected that she walked in on Trey hammering his fist into my back. That was the moment my world fell from its axis. Our dark secret of abuse and lies had been discovered by the one woman who would fight harder than Trey ever could. The only difference—she fought for *me, not against me.*

"If he calls, take the pity date."

I swallow past the memories and nod my head. "Fine. I'll take the pity date . . . if he even calls."

"Girls, come on! We're gonna be late!"

While Landon finishes up in the shower, I run around the house like a crazy lady with her head chopped off. Typical weekday morning.

"Mom, I can't find my other shoe," Emily hollers from her bedroom.

"Well, if you'd put your things where they belong, it wouldn't be lost."

I grab a to-go mug from the kitchen and quickly brew another cup of coffee before remembering I never went through the girls' school folders last night. *Shit!*

"Jill! Em! I need your backpacks!"

Jill walks into the kitchen with her folder already out and is followed by Emily who has one shoe on.

"Mom, did you find my shoe?"

"I don't have time to find your shoe. We should already be in the car and—"

"Found it!" Jill announces into the chaos of the room with her arm shoved under the sofa.

With fast hands, I clean out their folders, sign their daily planners, and pull out a note from Jill's teacher, requesting me to come in on Friday to volunteer in the classroom.

Just because I work from home doesn't mean I'm not busy, Mrs. Briman.

Shoving the folders into their backpacks, I dump an obscene amount of creamer into my coffee, screw on the lid, and grab my keys.

"Let's go."

The kids run out to get into the car as I shout, "I love you, babe!"

"Hey, while you're out, we need more toilet paper."

Love you too.

After I drop off the kids and run by the store, I head back home and am just in time to see Landon's car pulling out of the driveway. We both stop and roll down our windows.

"Remember, I'll be home later than usual," he tells me.

"That's fine. I have a lot of stuff to do before my trip this weekend."

"Well, if you're not too tired, maybe we can spend some time together when I get home."

That's code for sex.

"Maybe."

"Just pretend I'm that billionaire in the book that kept you up all night."

I laugh and drive into the garage at the same time he smiles and heads down the street.

Walking into the house, I embrace the silence and solitude. When Jill was born six years ago, I decided to take a short leave of absence and then return to my job as creative director at FOX25. But before I reached the end of my leave, I found out I was pregnant with Emily.

After I resigned, my life became focused on the kids and Landon. Though I was happy and content for a while, those feelings eventually waned, and I began itching to have something of my own again. So, in the evenings after everyone was asleep, I stayed up and wrote. I didn't know what I was writing. There was no plan. I simply enjoyed getting lost in a world that had nothing to do with changing diapers, folding laundry, and cooking dinners. I took parts of my past and present and twisted them into a work of fiction, and pretty soon, it turned into a novel.

I remember calling Brooke, who lives only a short drive from Belmont, where I live. She has a beautiful home with her husband and son, Ryder. I told her about the book and began sending her chapters to read. She humors me, even though her tastes in books are anything other than the steamy romances I write.

Writing became my obsession. I couldn't wait for everyone to go to bed so I could get back to my self-created chimera. I'd be lying if I said I didn't sometimes fantasize about the male lead in my book while Landon and I were having sex. During the day I was mom and wife, and at night, I was something else entirely. I created a world where laundry didn't exist, sex wasn't something I had to schedule, and there were no children in the background throwing fits. Before I knew it, four months had passed and I had a finished book.

After college, Brooke went on to work for a multimedia entertainment agency, and with her knowledge, she guided me to the world of self-publishing. Together, we found a designer to create a cover for the book, we hired an editing company, and next thing I knew, the book was published online for anyone to download and read. I even had a company produce paperback books that people could buy.

And they did.

People actually bought the book. Lots of people. The reviews were wonderful, and after two weeks, the book hit the *New York Times* bestsellers chart! It was a whirlwind when I started getting emails from literary agents who wanted to represent me. Landon and Brooke helped me decide which agency to go with, and once the contract was signed, my book was sent to the top publishing houses in New York City. By the end of the year, my book was no longer self-published; instead, it was being published by none other than Simon & Schuster.

My life changed overnight—literally—and Landon was so proud and supported me wholeheartedly. All of a sudden, I wasn't just a stay-at-home mom, but a published, bestselling author. I even hired Brooke as my full-time assistant, which I have way too much fun with.

It's been three years since the release of my first book, and I've published several more since then. I've written a number of typical, alpha male-driven romances; it's time to do something different though. But for the past two weeks, I write and delete, write and delete, write and delete. I'm driving myself crazy. I made the decision to take a break from writing until next week. I'm scheduled to appear at a book signing this weekend in Las Vegas, and a few of my friends who are also authors will be in attendance as well. I plan to let loose and not even think about this book until I get back.

chapter two

"I AM SO EXHAUSTED," LANDON SIGHS AS HE KICKS OFF HIS SHOES AND THEN falls back onto the bed. "But I have some news for you."

After pulling my suitcase from the closet, I set it next to Landon and open it. "What's the news?"

"Damon got a call from the *New York Times*."

I stop in my tracks with a handful of clothes in my arms and look at him as he tries to play it cool. "The *New York Times*?"

He nods, and I toss the clothes on the bed. My jaw drops before repeating with growing elation. "The freakin' *New York Times*? Oh, my God, Landon!"

His smile grows, and I jump onto the bed, taking his face in my hands. "This is amazing."

I straddle him when he sits up, and with his arms wrapped around my waist, he laughs under his breath at my display of excitement. "They're sending a critic to do a write-up. If he likes the food, this could be huge for the restaurant."

"What do you mean 'if'? Of course he'll like the food; you and Damon are amazing chefs." I lean in and kiss my husband, who has worked so hard to finally be in the position to garner national recognition. "I am so proud of you, babe. So, when does this happen?"

"In two weeks."

"That soon?"

"I'll be working a lot more until then."

"Of course. Do you need me to find someone to help out with the kids this weekend while I'm in Vegas?"

"I was going to call my brother to see if he and Marcia can help out," he says as he runs his hands through my hair.

On a faint whisper, I tell him again, "I'm so proud of you," and then press my lips to his in a slow kiss. His hands drop to my hips, tugging me closer, and I moan into his mouth as the friction between my legs sparks a trill through my body.

"Yoohoo! Tori?" Brooke's sing-song voice announces from my cell's speaker-phone through the app we use to communicate.

"Ignore it," Landon mumbles against my lips as we continue to kiss.

He grabs my breasts over my shirt, squeezing them as he runs his lips down my neck.

Sensual warmth spreads through my body, building the ache between my thighs, and I grind my hips over his lap. Sparks of pent-up heat sizzle through me, and my body begs for more.

"Tor, I need to go over the itinerary with you. Oh, also, you had a few last-minute preorder requests, so I'm going to pack some extra books. I also called the hotel to confirm the package deliveries and—"

Landon drops his hands from me, and I groan in frustration.

"Let me talk to her really quick and then I'll turn off the phone," I tell him while Brooke continues to ramble on in the background.

He releases a hard breath when I get off the bed.

"Hey, I'm here," I tell her through the speaker.

Landon hates that we use this app, since it's pretty much a walkie-talkie and he has to listen to us gab.

"Did you get my last message?"

"We all got it, Brooke," Landon calls out so she can hear.

"Hi, Landon. Why do you sound so crotchety?"

"No reason, aside from the fact that I was just about to get laid."

I shoot Landon an exaggerated look of mortification and mouth the words *Oh, my God!* to him. He responds with an amused grin. He loves embarrassing me.

"Sexxxxy!" she teases.

"You two are so ridiculous. Can we get back to what you need to talk to me about?"

Brooke goes on to discuss the details of the Vegas trip while I continue to pack my suitcase. Every now and then, I look over to Landon, who is now lost in sorting through emails on his phone. The conversation with Brooke lasts much longer than expected, and after I have myself completely packed and my luggage is in the trunk of my car, I return to the bedroom to find Landon sound asleep.

"Brooke, I gotta go," I tell her in a quiet voice. "I'll message you when I'm on my way to the airport tomorrow."

I turn my phone on silent and check the time. Guilt rears its head when I realize I've been talking to Brooke for over an hour. When I slip into bed, I look at the face I fell in love with thirteen years ago as the moon casts its glow across the room. We were so young when we met; it seems like a lifetime ago.

"You love him?" Brooke asks as I rifle through my closet in search of my blue chiffon swing top.

"What? It's only been three months."

"Yeah, so . . .?"

"Here it is," I murmur as I pull the top off the hanger and slip it over my head.

"You're with him a lot. Don't think I don't know you've been staying up until all hours of the night texting him."

"We really need to get an apartment so I can have my own room," I respond as I continue to get ready for my date tonight.

"So, do you love him?"

"I don't know," I tell her while applying some gloss to my lips. "I'm just now getting used to him."

"What does that mean?"

Turning from the mirror, I look at Brooke, who's sitting in the middle of her twin bed. "He's nice. Like, really nice."

"And?"

"I didn't like it at first. I guess I was just so used to how Trey treated me that when Landon would do or say sweet things to me, it used to turn me off. In a weird way, it made me feel smothered and icky."

"Why didn't you ever say anything to me?"

I shrug my shoulders, walk over to the edge of my bed, and sit down before admitting, "I don't know. I guess I was embarrassed. I mean, what was I going to say to you, 'I don't like him because he's perfect and nice and it makes me feel gross'?"

"That's exactly what you should have said to me." She shifts to sit on the edge of her bed so we are face to face. "Do you still feel that way?"

"No."

"What are you texting about in the middle of the night?" she teases, and I quickly respond.

"None of your business, you little perv."

Her face lights up. "Let me read!"

"God, no!"

"Come on."

"You are so nosey, you know that?"

"Yes, I am well aware. So, are you going to let me read?"

"Absolutely not," I say, and before she can continue her begging, my phone buzzes with an incoming call from Landon.

"I'm downstairs in the lobby."

"Okay, I'll be right down."

I grab my purse and give myself one last lookover before turning back to Brooke, saying, "Stay out of trouble while I'm gone, will ya?"

"Never," she responds with a smile as she gets off her bed and walks toward me. "You're right. Landon is nothing like Trey, which is why he's perfect for you."

I look at my best friend and then pull her in for a hug. "Thank you."

When I make my way to the dorm's lobby, I see Landon sitting on one of the couches. He looks amazing in his dark-wash jeans and charcoal button-down. His hair is styled perfectly—not a strand out of place. He stands as I walk over to him, and the smile he wears so beautifully releases a flutter inside me.

"You look amazing," he says before giving me a soft kiss to my lips.

Even though we've been seeing each other for a few months now, we've been taking things really slow—slower than most girls my age would. Our physical relationship has been very PG-13, aside from the late-night dirty texting. I'm fairly reserved, I always have been, but then again, I've only ever been with one guy.

As we walk out of the building, I catch a few girls giving Landon a gawking eye. He looks down at me and jokes, "Maybe I should've done the whole college thing. Apparently, I'm a stud."

I playfully jab his ribs and laugh along with him. His humor is one of his best traits.

He takes me to The Barking Crab where we sit on a wooden picnic table along the water and enjoy lobster and a bucket of crab legs. We take our time, talking and enjoying the sunset before we head to his place. Landon lives in the heart of Boston in an amazing warehouse loft with exposed brick and hardwood floors. I flop down on the leather sofa while Landon grabs some wood and gets the fireplace going.

My eyes are on his as he walks toward me and joins me on the couch. The sight of him releasing a swarm of sharp-winged butterflies in my stomach. With his arm slung over my shoulders, he tucks a lock of my long brunette hair behind my ear.

"You're so beautiful," he says softly, and the compliment makes me blush.

I run my hand along his clean-shaven jawline. The only light in the room coming from the flickering flames of the fire. My heartbeat kicks up when he moves in and kisses me. His lips are warm against mine, and I immediately soften against him. He shifts over me and lays me down on my back, my legs opening for him to settle himself between.

His kisses are soft and slow, deliberate with every brushing sweep of his tongue along mine. My mouth is marked by his taste, and I want to lose myself completely with him, but I'm unable to. The thought of letting myself go scares me, as it does every time I find myself in moments like this. I want him badly, but I know all too well how quickly a person can change their colors, and I'm scared I'm just setting myself up to get hurt again.

Landon begins moving his body over mine, and I instantly tighten my grip on his hips, attempting to halt him. He catches my signal and slows himself down. My face is hot when he drags his lips from mine, taking his sweet taste from my needy mouth. When I open my eyes, he's looking down at me.

Slightly embarrassed, I whisper bashfully, "I'm sorry."

"Is it me?"

His question catches me off guard. "What?"

"Every time I try to touch more of you, you push me away."

"I didn't mean—"

"Don't apologize," he says, his voice a rasp of a whisper. "I just want to know what it is that's making you hesitate with me."

I release a heavy sigh and push myself to sit up, but I don't speak. I'm not quite sure how to express what I'm feeling.

"Can I admit something to you?" he asks, taking a little of the pressure from me. When I nod, he runs his hand through my hair and cups my cheek before saying, "I'm falling for you. I have been for a while now. I've been trying to rein it in because I can feel you're holding something back. I just want to know what it is."

"Landon . . ." I begin, but lose my words as his seep into my heart. His honesty pushes me to want to give mine in return, but I'm worried my words might hurt him, so I tell him that. "I'm afraid I'll hurt you."

"You won't," he assures.

I close my eyes and drop my head for a moment before looking back at him and revealing, "You're right. I'm scared."

"Why?"

The fire crackles loudly through the silence in the room as I take my time to gather my thoughts enough to answer him without sounding like I'm stumbling nervously over my words.

"There's only been one other guy before you," I tell him when I feel my palms beginning to sweat, but he only holds my hands tighter. "He, umm . . ." I hesitate. "He . . ."

"You can tell me anything."

My eyes fall from his, and I stare at our hands when I tell him, "He hit me."

I hear him let go of a hard breath as his hands constrict on mine.

"It didn't start out like that. Everything was perfect at first, but then

. . . I don't know, somewhere along the way he changed." When I finally get the courage to look at Landon, I see the anger in his eyes. "I'm sorry. I didn't mean to make you mad."

"No," he interjects. "I'm not mad at you. I'm mad at what that asshole did to you."

"I would do things that would anger him and—"

"Baby."

"He would yell at me and throw me around. He'd punch me and slap me—"

Landon takes my face and angles it up to him. "Is that what you're afraid of? That I'd hit you?" He speaks with fervency, asserting, "I would never lay a hand on you. That guy was a sick fuck for thinking it was okay to touch you like that. But I'm not him, and I'll do whatever it takes to prove to you that you can trust me to take care of you."

"I have a lot of strong feelings for you, Landon. I'm just scared to give in to those feelings just to wind up getting hurt."

"So you're scared it might not work out?"

"Yes."

"Not everything comes to an end, you know? But what I'm feeling for you, I don't want to hide from that. Everything inside me is screaming to fall in love with you."

"What if loving me isn't as good as what you're hoping for?"

"What if it is?" he counters. "What if loving you changes the trajectory of both our lives for the better?" He takes my hand and presses it against his chest, adding, "But what about you? Are you *willing to love* me*?"*

The sincerity in his voice begs for affirmation, and if there were any man to take this chance with, I know deep inside that it's Landon.

"You don't ever have to be afraid when you're with me."

So without the protection of guarantees, I trust in his words, and tell him, "If you're willing, I'm willing."

He sits back and pulls me on top of him. His hands wrap around my hips, and with mine gripped on to the back of the couch, I drop my armor. I reach down and pull his one hand up to me and rest it on my breast. "Touch me."

Gently, he squeezes me in his hand as I watch him, and his eyes never leave mine when he sits up and sucks my nipple, which is still covered by my lace bra and thin chiffon blouse. The sensation ignites me, and I drop my head back. He keeps his mouth on me as the dampness from his tongue seeps through the delicate fabrics, wetting my pert nipple.

Emotions swarm, a plethora of them, but I choose to hone in on the ones that bring me comfort. The patience Landon has exuded these past few months says a lot about who he is as a man. Never pushing, only ever taking each moment for what it is and allowing us to bond as friends.

And now . . . now I give in to what I've been wanting but have been too scared.

I unbutton his shirt and push it back, sliding it over his shoulders and down his arms. His skin is smooth under my touch as I run my hands around his back and up his neck, burying my fingers in his hair. Landon's head falls back onto the cushion, and he stares up at me. His face glows in the firelight.

"I never wanted anything as much as I want you," he says deeply, and his words elicit my need to be closer to him.

Taking the hem of my top in my hands, I slip it over my head and drop it to the floor next to his shirt with my bra to follow next. Exposed to him for the first time, he looks at my body for a moment before shifting his eyes back to mine.

His breathing is just as heavy.

He touches me.

Skin to skin.

My body melts in a frisson of passion.

He picks me up and lays me down on my back. His eyes speak for him, asking a silent 'is this okay?', and when I nod, his hands grip the waistband of my pants before sliding them down along with my panties. He keeps his pants, but he spreads my legs and lies between them. With my fingers digging into his shoulders, he slides his tongue over my nipple and then sucks it into his hot mouth. He moves from one breast to the other as he drags his hand down between my thighs. Watching me intently, a sexy smirk graces his lips when his fingers slide between my folds and find my clit.

"Oh, God," I moan as I open my legs wider.

Already wet with desire for him, I can feel him use my arousal to coat his fingers as he rolls them over my clit, driving my body to bow up to him.

"Open your eyes," he says, and I do. "Does my touch hurt you?"

I shake my head.

"Does it feel good?"

"Yes," I breathe on a broken pant.

"Don't ever be scared of my touch," he says before sliding his fingers inside me.

"Landon."

My eyes fall shut as he continues to touch me so intimately, but it's not enough.

I want more.

Need more.

I reach down with greed and unfasten his pants. He helps my eager hands and removes the rest of his clothes. Once he slides on the condom, I pull him down to me and kiss him. He holds himself against me, and I lose my control. Needing him to be mine, I arch my back at the same time he pushes himself inside me, melding our bodies completely.

chapter three

This is where my life takes a shift. It's only a momentary shift, but one I've come to yearn for. When I step onto the plane, I'm no longer Tori Garrison, I'm Madilyn Kline. It's always a breath of fresh air when I can leave Tori, wife and mother, behind and become this pseudo-self I've created. Madilyn is perceived by my fans as a seductive woman who radiates confidence and sexuality. But she's fictional, just like the characters in my books. I'm a far cry from the sexually confident woman the world thinks I am. Sure, I write explicit stories of love and romance, but my sex life is nothing like that in my books.

The only person in my inner circle who is privy to both women is Brooke. She sees all of me. She always has.

Brooke eyes me mischievously when I walk into our dorm room wearing the same clothes I wore last night. Heat burns my cheeks as I open my closet, attempting to avoid looking at her all-too-knowing stare, and strip off my clothes in exchange for the comfort of pajamas.

Once changed, I hop onto my bed and slip under the covers.

"Late night?" Brooke inquires with a sly tone to her voice.

It's the first time I've gone on a date with Landon and have not returned in the same night. I can't help the slight timidity I feel, and I cannot control myself when I break out into uncomfortable laughter, pulling the sheets over my head.

"You're such a slut," she teases through her own fit of giggles and throws a pillow at me. "Tell me every last detail."

Tossing the sheets off my heated face, I look over to Brooke, who's sitting on her bed with a bad case of ratty bedhead and a cup of coffee in her hand.

"I'm tired," I tell her and try to push off the conversation. "Can we talk after I get some sleep?"

"Umm . . . no. You can sleep after you tell me what it was you were doing all night when you were supposed to be here studying with me for our midterm."

"I'm sorry. I lost track of . . ." I stumble off and grin wildly, "well, everything."

"I bet you did. Now spill it. You had sex with him, didn't you?"

My smile is obnoxiously big.

"I knew it! Damn, I'm jealous of you. That guy is so hot. Oh, my God," she rambles. "How was it? I bet it was amazing. I mean, with a guy like that, it has to be mind blowing."

"Brooke!" My voice is playful as I scold her.

"Okay, I'm sorry." She sets her coffee mug on the nightstand between our beds and does her best to compose herself. "Seriously though. How are you? I mean, this is a big step for you."

I straighten up as the joking subsides and a more serious tone takes hold of our conversation. "I told him about Trey."

"You hadn't told him yet?"

I shake my head. "I didn't really know how. It finally came out last night, and then . . . I don't know, maybe it was all the emotion that drove me to sleep with him. Telling him and then hearing his response . . . His words were perfect, Brooke. I guess it was just everything about that moment."

"How do you feel about it now?"

"Last night I felt needy for him after revealing that, but when I woke up this morning . . . with him . . . it felt right."

"I'm glad you told him and opened yourself up. It must feel like a weight off your shoulders," she says warmheartedly, and I agree, saying, "Yeah. I was being standoffish with him. I knew he could tell I was keeping him at arm's length. And now that he knows why, he's put me

at ease and has given me the reassurance I've been needing but was too scared to ask for."

"He seems like a good guy."

"He is," I respond, and when she picks up her coffee mug, I see the shift in her demeanor.

"Now tell me, what was the sex like?" I burst out laughing and cover my face with a pillow as she goes on, "I bet he's the intense type."

"Stop!"

"A dirty talker."

"Brooke!" I shriek through a fit of hilarity.

"A bed breaker."

"Anything to drink?" the stewardess asks as she stands with her hair in a perfect low bun, flawless makeup, and a smile way too big for it being so early in the morning.

"Vodka cranberry."

I look over to Brooke, who stole the window seat from me. "It's eight in the morning."

"Make that two vodka cranberries."

I shake my head and tell the stewardess, "An orange juice will be fine."

"With a side of vodka." When I look to Brooke, she simply smiles innocently and says, "Come on. This Vegas signing only happens once a year. Lighten up."

"Do you remember what happened last year?"

"How could I forget the guys from the Thunder from Down Under. Seeing them practically molest you on stage will go down as one of the highlights of my life!"

"So humiliating."

"Humiliating? The look on your face told a different story," she says with a devilish smirk. "To everyone in the audience, it looked like you were enjoying every second of that guy grinding up on you."

"I had way too much to drink. I blame the alcohol."

"Did you ever tell Landon?"

"No. He'd be pissed if he ever found out," I say a pitch too loudly.

"Did you ever tell Chris how you made that stripper pole your bitch that night at the club?"

"Of course I did." Our drinks come, and after we dump the mini bottles of vodka into our juices, she adds, "He's been jealous of that pole ever since."

We hold up our cups, and I toast, "To Vegas."

Once we land, collect our luggage, and make it to the hotel on the strip, we head up to our room and settle in. Brooke is immediately on the phone with the bellhop to have all the boxes she shipped to the hotel brought up to our room. As soon as they are delivered, I help Brooke organize the books that fans preordered. We bundle them, slap sticky notes with names on them onto the covers, and check them off the spreadsheet. We then verify the boxes filled with the swag she purchased: bookmarks, bracelets, magnets, and everything else readers gravitate to.

A knock on our door pulls me away from the pile of books surrounding us on the floor, and when I open it, I'm thrilled to see my friend, Erin, another author who will be attending this event.

We squeal and hug like giddy schoolgirls. When I started in this line of work, my friends faded away and I cemented myself to other authors. Writing is a very isolating job. When I'm deep in the writing process, I tend to shut everyone out. Most of my friends took it personally, but it wasn't intentional on my part. It was just a gradual drift. Now, the majority of my friends are other authors, because we totally understand the lifestyle and are much more forgiving than those outside of this "sorority." The one downside: the only time we get to see each other is if we happen to be at the same book signing.

"I'm so glad you're here, Madilyn," Erin says as we break our hug. We all address each other by our pen names. I know Erin's real name, but never once have I thought about actually referring to her by anything other than her pseudonym. It's an unspoken respect we authors give one another.

Erin turns to Brooke to share an embrace as well. Brooke has been with me since day one. There isn't a book signing she hasn't attended with me, so all my friends are her friends too. I'm so lucky she's been able to be a part of this whole experience with me. But I notice Erin's assistant isn't with her, and ask, "Where's Jen?"

Brooke's head whips around in my direction with her rictus mouth. "How do you not know?"

I look between the two of them. "Know what?"

"Well, I only heard this through the gossip of a couple of the other authors that were at the last book signing in Dallas, but Erin would be the one to ask and confirm."

"Why does no one tell me anything?" I accuse.

"Girl, it's all drama in my camp," Erin tells me.

"What happened?"

"So, remember last month in Dallas when we all went out after the signing to the Trophy Room Bar?"

"How could I forget? Brooke got me drunk on tequila, and before I knew it, I was riding the mechanical bull."

"You owned that bull," Brooke jokes.

"Well, Jen also got drunk and decided to sneak out with Gabe."

"Your cover model?"

"Yep."

Erin has used Gabe for the covers of her latest series. The fans go crazy for him when she brings him along to the book signings. Not all events will allow cover models, but Dallas did, and this signing here in Vegas will be loaded with them as well. It's really not my thing. Most of them are just fame whores, but Gabe is a good guy and has always been the epitome of humility.

"Anyway," Erin continues, "I didn't know she had left with him until I got back to our hotel room."

"No!"

"Oh, yeah," she says with an exaggerated nod. "He had her bent over on her knees, butt naked, pounding her from behind."

"Holy shit!"

Brooke and I explode in laughter, and then Erin adds, "On my bed, mind you!"

"Is that the story you heard, Brooke?"

She looks at me and nods. "Mmm hmm. Apparently, Jen told someone with a blabby mouth because a group of authors were talking about it over breakfast in the hotel restaurant the next morning."

"Where the hell was I?"

"Sleeping off your hangover."

"Well, now she's too mortified to see him, so she stayed home," Erin tells us.

"Did you say anything to Gabe?"

"I asked him what happened, and he just said they were both drunk and one thing led to another. He told me he called her, but she declined the call, and he wound up apologizing to her on her voicemail." She shrugs her shoulders and says, "I mean, they're both single, so it's whatever. It doesn't bother me as long as they can still act professional. I think it'll be fine; she's just embarrassed. It'll all blow over with time."

"What does he look like naked?"

"You'll have to excuse Brooke; she was drinking on the plane."

"Don't make excuses for her. We all know she would ask that same question even if she were stone sober."

We decide to spend the rest of the day shopping, and after a good night's rest, we are up early eating room service and getting ready for the signing. The event coordinator sent up volunteers to pick up all the boxes from our room so they can get my table set up for me. It's always hectic getting ready for these events. I'll be signing books for the next five hours and taking countless photos. So, I take my time applying my makeup, making sure to put on enough of it so it doesn't wear off halfway through the day. I enjoy it though, because my life as Tori basically consists of yoga pants, no makeup, and my hair up in a knot.

"Are you ready?" Brooke asks as she applies a touch of mascara to her lashes.

"Almost." I scramble around the room, slip on a pair of heels, and give myself one last look before grabbing my cell.

Before we can reach the ballroom where the signing is being held, we must first walk through the throng of fans that are already waiting.

If only they could have a back entrance for the authors. It's uncomfortable to watch everyone stare as I walk by. Not to mention the times when I have to use the restroom and there are fans in there who can hear me as I pee.

Maybe it's just me, but nonetheless, it's awkward.

Before the doors open to the readers, Gabe comes over to my table to say hello. I can't blame Brooke for wanting to know what he looks like naked. He's young, fit, and sexy as hell. But I'm well aware he probably just views me as a middle-aged housewife. I'm creeping close to mid-thirties, and I do what I can to stay in shape and stay young, but having kids has a way of physically—and mentally—aging you.

"How are you?" I ask after we hug.

"I'm good."

His muscles aren't too obscene like some of the other models here, which to me, makes him all that more attractive. He wears a slim-fitting shirt and his hair is unruly, but I know he spent a good amount of time styling it to look that way.

"You look like you're firming up," he says as he looks me up and down.

"I've been doing those new workouts you showed me."

"It's paying off," he tells me and then peers over my shoulder. "What's that shit-eating grin all about?"

"You know what it's about," Brooke says with mild flirtation.

"Ignore her."

"You women gossip too much."

"She's just jealous it was Erin who walked in on you and not her."

Gabe looks down at me and, with a hushed voice, admits, "I didn't mean for that to be a one-time thing, you know?"

"Did you tell her that?"

"She won't take my calls, and it isn't really something I want to tell her over voicemail."

"Give her time. She's just a little embarrassed."

Gabe joins Erin at her table and the doors open up. Since I just released a book last month, my line is consistently long. I try not to look up at the sea of people in this room, as it tends to overwhelm me, so I stay focused on the fans that are right in front of me. I smile and autograph books to the point of hand cramps. Getting to meet the readers who enjoy my books is what makes this job so rewarding. It's thrilling to see their excitement.

Tori doesn't exist in this moment, it's all Madilyn—sizzling hot author.

Loading the dishwasher and washing her husband's underwear isn't a part of Madilyn's life. No. When I'm her, I'm the woman who's free from being tied down to family obligations. I'm the woman who can let loose, take shots, and ride a mechanical bull. I'm the woman who can laugh while being dry humped by a male stripper as an audience cheers. This is my escape; these are my moments of freedom. I love my home life, but I love this life too.

"I'm drained," I moan as I kick off my heels and fall onto the bed.

"Don't get too comfortable. I was talking to a few of the girls and told them we would meet them down in the lounge for cocktails and dinner."

"How long do we have?"

"Thirty minutes," Brooke responds.

I rest my head on the pillow and watch mindlessly as Brooke counts the money I made from book sales and separates her cut from the pile of bills. She then packs the leftover swag before freshening up her makeup.

Soon, I'm joining her. With a quick change of clothes and a mist of perfume, we are out the door. The girls are already at the table and waiting for us when we arrive. We drink and gab as only authors do. It's a lot of gossip and sex talk. Most of these women have loud and strong personalities, so I tend to sit back and take it all in as they go back and forth.

"Congratulations on your last book, Madilyn," Amy, the author sitting next to me says.

"Thank you."

"Didn't it hit the *New York Times*?"

"Yeah." I respond excitedly.

"How do you keep the momentum?" she asks, garnering the attention of a few of the other girls at the table.

"I honestly don't know."

"What are you working on now?" another author asks me.

"Good question. I'm having a case of writer's block. I need to find some inspiration, so I've been listening to a lot of music, but nothing is sparking."

The waiter delivers another round of drinks, and as I take a sip of my lemon drop martini, Kristen, another *New York Times* bestselling author says to the whole group, "You want to know where I go for inspiration?" When eyes turn to her, she sets down her glass of wine and continues. "There's this fetish website another author told me about."

"FetLife?" Amy asks.

"That's the one. Have you been on there?"

Amy nods and a few of the other girls announce they've gone on it too.

"I'm seriously the last to know about everything," I whine in jest. "So what do you do on this website?"

Kristen looks at me from the other end of the table. "It's kind of like Facebook for the freaky. Don't get me wrong, there's light stuff on there as well, but it's a lot of different people who have various fetishes from polygamy, BDSM, swingers, group sex, voyeurism, foot worship, to adult babies and shit like that."

"What the fuck is an adult baby?" Brooke asks as I laugh and then take another drink.

"You know, people who wear diapers and act like they're a baby."

"People are into that? Like, sexually?" I ask in disbelief.

"It's a real thing," Amy confirms. "That site has so much stuff I've never even heard of. But you can join groups and message people. I had to do that for one of the books I wrote."

"The threesome one?"

"Yes. I wound up in a group chat with this triad. They were actually really nice and forthcoming, allowing me to ask questions and stuff."

"That book was so hot," I tell her and then turn to Brooke, knowing she doesn't read any of these books, and boast, "Seriously, you should read it. It was off the charts when it comes to erotica."

We continue to chat books when our food arrives, and once we are done, Erin suggests we hit up one of the night clubs. Everyone is game, so we hail a cab and make our way to a club filled with some of the hottest people I've ever seen. Brooke and I take a couple shots before hitting the dance floor. We dance with each other, dance with random guys, dance with the other girls, all the while laughing, drinking, and living it up until the early hours of the morning.

The sun is on the horizon as we load into a taxi van and head back to our hotel so we can get a few hours of sleep before we have to pack and fly home. With booze on our breath, we all say goodbye until we see each other at the next signing. I spend the next few hours as Madilyn passed out in my bed and then guzzling countless Gatorades in the airport while I hide my bloodshot eyes behind my sunglasses.

"Another awesome Vegas trip."

I look over to Brooke and smile. "I couldn't agree more."

chapter four

It's edging close to midnight as I pull the car into the garage. When I grab my luggage from the trunk and head into the house, irritation slaps me across the face the moment I flick on the lights. The girls' books and art supplies are strewn across the living room, and the kitchen sink is filled with dirty dishes.

Goodbye Madilyn; hello Tori.

A glow peeks under the bottom of my bedroom door, and I do my best to bite against the bitter taste of annoyance as I walk in and see Landon lying in bed, watching television.

"Welcome home," he says. "How was your trip?"

"Fine," I snip as I wheel my luggage into the closet.

"Everything okay?"

"Just perfect."

I unzip the suitcase and toss my dirty clothes in the laundry basket.

"What's going on?" Landon questions when he walks into the closet.

I throw another wad of clothes into the basket and then straighten myself, planting my hands on my hips. "You couldn't have tried to clean up before I got home?" My voice is belittling, I know. But I'm tired, hungover, and battling a piercing headache.

"By the time I got the girls to bed, I was drained."

"You look pretty damn relaxed if you ask me. Here it is, midnight, and you're chilling in front of the television when you knew I'd be dead to the world when I got home," I nag, sounding like the acerbic housewife I swore I'd never be. "And now, instead of going to bed, I have to clean that shit up."

Landon's face hardens and his words are clipped when he bites back at my sour mood. "I'll clean it in the morning."

"I don't want to wake up to that mess."

"Then I'll clean it before you get up. What's the big deal?"

"The big deal is that this place was clean when I left, and I shouldn't have to come home to a mess after a long weekend."

"I wish I had your life, Tor. No, really, I do. It must be rough to have to leave your family for a couple days to party it up in Vegas."

His pugnacious mood rankles my nerves even more. "I can't help that my job looks different than yours, but don't you dare forget that it is indeed a job that affords us the lifestyle we have." I immediately regret the low blow I just served him, but before I can apologize, he throws the animosity right back at me.

"And who afforded you the luxury to discover this new career of yours? Don't forget I solely supported this family for years while you stayed at home and didn't work. I bust my fucking ass for you and the girls," he snaps. "But you don't see that because you're blinded by a few dirty dishes in the goddamn sink."

"I never said you didn't bust your ass at work."

"Dammit, Tori. I've been killing myself working all these extra hours. Cut me a little slack."

We come to a deadlock as we both stand and glare at each other. These spats aren't out of the norm for us when we are both drained. Landon hates fighting—I do too—but I also think it's normal for couples who have been together as long as we have to get into arguments. At least that's what I tell myself: that we are just like everyone else.

"Welcome home, dear. I'm going to bed," he says listlessly before turning his back to me and walking to the bedroom.

I let go of a heavy sigh wrapped in disappointment. All I wanted was to come home to a clean house and happy husband—you know what I mean, the fantasy we create in our minds, and when it doesn't go our way, we are left with the disillusionment of reality.

I slip on a pair of pajamas and leave my suitcase lying open in the middle of the closet when I go upstairs to check on the girls. I walk into

Emily's room where she's wriggled her way down beneath her blanket. I pull it back and give her a kiss on the forehead. My little four-year-old baby is growing so fast. Faster than what I'm ready for. I stroke my fingers through her blonde hair and give her one more kiss.

When I walk into Jill's room, my big first grader, I sit on the edge of her bed and stare down at my first born. Her face is thinning out of the rounded baby cheeks she once had. My little lady won't even let me call her my baby anymore. I think back to the day this angel pie made me a mommy for the first time.

"Landon," I call out from the bathtub where I've been soaking for the past hour. "I need help."

"Coming."

I'm two days overdue and beyond the point of wanting to die. Every bone and tendon in my body is constantly on fire with pain. I've been spending most of my time trying to soothe the aches, but the warm water only attempts to assuage.

"Are you feeling any better?" Landon asks when he walks into the bathroom.

"I feel like it's getting worse. It's all through my back."

He reaches down, and I grab on to him as he helps me to my feet. I wait for him to hand me a towel, and when I start drying off, I notice him staring at my body.

"What?"

"You want me to clean you up down there?"

I follow his eyes, which are zoned between my legs, and huff, "Are you kidding me right now?"

"Come on, babe."

"I gave up shaving down there two weeks ago."

He laughs. "I can tell."

"Don't be an ass."

I wrap the towel around my chest and hold Landon's hand as he helps me step out of the tub, all the while, finding humor in the fact that my lady parts have gone National Geographic.

"You've got a lot of nerve teasing me when I'm this hormonal," I tell

him as I give his ribs a jab, and when I do, I instantly feel a weird pop in my belly.

"Oh, shit!"

"What?"

With a look of shock on his face, Landon steps back from me. "I think you pissed yourself, babe."

As if this pregnancy hasn't robbed my sex appeal enough. But when I look down at the puddle of fluid I'm standing in, I realize it's not pee.

"I think my water just broke."

Landon's face drops, and I've never seen such alarm in his eyes.

"Landon?" He doesn't respond as he stares at me. "Are you okay?"

In a flash, he jumps into motion like a maniac and rushes out of the bathroom, leaving me standing here, dripping wet, wearing only a towel.

"Holy shit. Shit. Shit." He continues to ramble incoherent obscenities as he runs around the house.

I hear drawers opening and closing, along with cabinets and doors, and I have no clue what the hell he is doing. I proceed to drop my towel and grab a couple more to soak up the mess on the floor. I then do my best to clean myself up before slipping on a pair of underwear.

Landon then zips through the bathroom in a mild panic. "Where the hell is the hospital bag?"

"It's in the closet, and can you please calm down?"

He turns to face me, and nearly yells, "You're having a baby!" as if I had no clue. He then freezes for a second before grabbing my face and elating with utter joy, "We're having a baby!" He wraps his arms around me, radiating with excitement, and when he draws back, I look into the eyes of my husband who's about to become a daddy.

"I'm scared," I admit. "I don't think I'm ready for this."

He cups my cheeks and dips his head so he can meet my eyes straight on and assures, "You've got this. You're the strongest woman I know, and I have no doubts you're going to kick this motherhood gig in the ass."

"Promise me something?"

"Anything."

"Promise me we won't become those cliché parents who wear cheesy matching outfits for family portraits."

"Those people make me sick, you know that."

"One more thing," I say as I stand in front of him with only a pair of panties on and my belly nudging up against his toned abs. "Promise me you won't change the way you look at me."

"I'll never look at you and not be reminded of how lucky I am to have you. You're so damn sexy, and your being a mom isn't going to change that. I love you most and more," he tells me intently. "Now come on and get dressed."

Our sweet moment quickly evaporates as Landon tosses clothes at me to put on. I move as quickly as I can, but not quick enough for my husband as he runs circles around me and texts family that the baby is on its way.

By the time he fastens my seatbelt, the pain wrapping around my back begins to intensify. My hand flies to Landon's, and I squeeze tightly.

"You okay?"

"Mmm mmm," I sound through my lips as I try to hold my breath.

"Don't hold your breath; it'll only make the pain worse."

I trust him and take in a deep breath through my nose and release it through my mouth. I do this three or four times before I tell him, "Call Brooke."

"I already did. She's meeting us at the hospital."

Landon keeps his hand locked to mine as he weaves through traffic. I close my eyes and try to focus on anything besides my back pain. Soon enough, we arrive at the hospital and are placed in a delivery room. The nurses hook me up to the monitors, and as much as I don't want to be pregnant anymore, the fear of how this baby is going to change our world scares me. It's only ever been me and Landon. I can't even imagine what it's going to be like with three of us.

"I got here as soon as I could," Brooke announces when she barges into the room, but I'm in too much pain to talk.

She goes to Landon, allowing me time to breathe through the contraction that just hit me.

"How are you doing?" she asks him after giving him a hug.

"Anxious. The nurses just checked her and she's dilated to five already."

"Do you need anything? I can grab you a coffee or something."

"Thanks, but I'm fine," he tells her. "Where's Chris?"

"He's stuck in a meeting. He said he'll call as soon as he's free."

A wave of nausea hits hard. "Landon, something doesn't feel right."

I grab my belly and tears spring from my eyes as a blast of pain shoots through my stomach. I'm loud when I scream out, and he takes my hand in his.

"It's okay," Brooke soothes as she stands on my other side and places a cold washcloth on my forehead.

Landon calls the nurse, and when she comes into the room, I cry out, "Please, stop the pain."

She quickly checks me, and when I look down at her from between my legs, she gives me the worst news ever. "Too late for an epidural, dear. You're ready to start pushing."

Fear ignites like a wild fire in my chest, and I panic. "Landon, I can't do this without an epidural. Please, do something."

His face mirrors mine when he looks up, and then I hear Brooke hollering at one of the nurses that is now in my room.

"You need to call the anesthesiologist now. There is no way she's having that baby without drugs."

"Your friend doesn't have a choice."

"Oh, God! I need to push," I cry.

Everything moves in hypervelocity as I grab on to my husband. He's right by my side, kissing my head and repeating over and over how much he loves me. In a whirlwind, the doctor rushes in. Brooke holds my one leg as a nurse holds the other, and with Landon's forehead pressed against mine, I bear down and push through the scorching pain, screaming with tears falling down my face.

It all happens so fast, and now, as I lie in the hospital bed, I look over to Landon who's holding our baby girl. He looks familiar and different at the same time, and it's astounding. Before my eyes, I watch my loving husband change into an adoring daddy. She's wrapped in a soft pink blanket, bundled up and snug in Landon's strong arms. I see him soften instantly as he looks down at our daughter and runs the tip of his nose over her forehead, and when he looks at me, his eyes are rimmed in teary joy.

He joins me on the bed and settles baby Jill into my arms. "I can't stop looking at her."

"It seems like a dream," I tell him. "How is it possible that we were able to make something so perfect?"

"Because," he says as he lifts my chin, "she's a part of you."

"And you."

His lips drop onto mine, and we kiss slowly in this quiet moment above the new love of our lives. My chest aches in a pleasurable pain as my heart grows. Tears dampen my cheeks, and when Jill coos in my arms, our kiss is fractured by my breathy giggle.

"I swear to both of you girls, no man will ever love you like I do," he vows. "I never knew life could be so good to me, and it's all because of you, Tori."

Landon bands his arms around me and Jill as I continue to weep. I rest my head against him as he comforts me like no other man has ever done before. An overwhelming sense of peace consumes me, and I bask in the euphoric bliss I didn't know existed until this very moment.

I can't even remember our life before our girls. I'm sure it was less stressful and more spontaneous, but I wouldn't want to go back. Sure, the daily cycle can become monotonous, but I guess that's what being a grown-up is. Brooke's life with her husband and son is the same, but we love that our families have adapted to the uneventful routine of life.

Another reason why I love my job is it provides me an escape. And after the spat Landon and I just had, I need an escape.

I lean down and give my Jilly-bug a kiss, tucking the blanket in around her before shutting the door behind me. Making my way downstairs, I get my laptop and settle myself on the couch. I kill time by scrolling through my social media pages, replying to posts fans have tagged me in and a few of the endless private messages. I do my best to keep up so readers don't think I'm being rude and ignoring them, but there's just no way I can get to every single message without it taking over every minute of my day.

While I'm scrolling through my newsfeed, I come across a status update from Kristen. Our conversation at dinner last night plays back in my head, and I try to remember that website she told me about. It takes me a minute to remember and I type "FetLife" into the search engine. I click on the first link that pops up, which takes me straight to the site, but I'm blocked from exploring unless I create an account.

Not sure about what I'm going to come across, I decide to make a vague account, filling out only the required info. I leave no description of who I am, but I'm forced to list at least one fetish. Scrolling through the selections they offer, I'm shocked by how many there are and how many I've never heard of in my life. I may write sexually charged books, but apparently I'm not as educated as I thought.

Needing access to this site, I decide to select the one that's most familiar to me, but also the one that is far from my personality. What do I care? I mark my fetish as "submissive." There's no requirement to upload a profile pic, so I don't. Clicking "submit," I create the account and now have access.

The site is a tad confusing as I fumble around. With a click here and a click there, I find myself on random forum threads. There are lots of explicit photos as I scroll through the feeds. When I pass one that shows a man's fist being crammed into a woman's vagina, I look in horrid disbelief.

Fucking gross!

Who the hell would be into that? And why? I swear I feel phantom pains in my own vagina just by looking at the picture. I wonder what kind of messed up childhood these people had to wind up having such questionable sexual desires. It's so weird.

I exit the page and shut down the Internet. I'm much too tired to be seeing shit like this. Knowing I have to be up early to drop the girls off at school, I close my laptop and go to bed, unfortunately with lingering images of perverseness running through my head.

Curling behind Landon, I regret fighting with him earlier. He has been working such long hours lately, and I shouldn't have come down on him like I did. His body stirs, and when he rolls over, I whisper, "I love you."

He pulls me into his arms and tucks my head under his chin. His body is hot against mine, and I cuddle into him.

"I'm sorry."

"I'm sorry too, babe," he murmurs in a sleepy rasp before drifting back to sleep.

chapter five

By the time my alarm goes off and I roll out of bed, the kitchen is clean and the girls are already dressed for school.

"What's going on?"

"I told you I'd do the dishes in the morning, and it's morning." He stands with humorous pride with a dish towel slung over his one shoulder. "Coffee?"

"Please." I walk over to Emily and Jill and shower them in kisses and hugs. "Mommy missed you two so much. Were you girls good for Daddy while I was gone?"

"Super good," Emily says in her sweet four-year-old voice. "Daddy let us have a floor picnic in the living room last night and we watched Cinderella."

"Wow." My voice rises in enthusiasm. "You must have been really good."

"Emily tried flushing one of my Barbie heads down the toilet and made it overflow," Jill tattles.

"It was an accident! Daddy, tell her it was an accident."

"How do you accidentally flush a Barbie head down the toilet, Emily?" I question while trying to hide my smile, but she just stares at me, dumbfounded, and shrugs her shoulders.

"I thought we were over this incident," Landon interjects. "I rescued the head and attached it back to the body. The toilet it fine. There's nothing more to discuss aside from the fact that neither of you have brushed your teeth yet, so hurry up before we're late for school."

Both of them run and clomp up the stairs as Landon hands me my cup of coffee, but before I take a sip, I set it on the counter.

"I'm really sorry about last night. I was tired and bitchy, and I took it out on you."

"I'm over it. Don't worry about it," he placates. "I'm under a lot of stress, but I don't want you to mistake that for a lack of caring. By the time I get home, I can barely even focus because I'm so drained."

"I know you are. And I know my traveling this weekend put a lot more weight on you."

He kisses me when I slip my arms around his waist.

"Please tell me you and Brooke at least had a good time in Vegas while I was fishing out the decapitated head from the toilet," he laughs.

"We did. It was a good trip." I turn, pick up my mug, and take a sip at the same time the girls come bolting down the stairs.

"I'm going to take them to school and then head to the restaurant. I won't be home till late. Damon wants to run a couple new recipes and sample them on the menu tonight and then tweak them according to the feedback."

"Okay, well, try to have a good day." I walk over and hand the girls their backpacks, and before the door is closed behind them, my cell phone rings. I run to the bedroom and grab the phone to see it's my editor from the publishing house. "Hello?"

"Madilyn, it's Tabitha."

"Hi, how are you?"

"I'm good. Look, we need to talk deadlines, but first I want to congratulate you on hitting the *New York Times* again last week. I'm keeping an eye on sales, and with luck, I think you might find yourself on that list for a third week. I have marketing getting some advertisements ready to go up onto Goodreads, and Target has already agreed to move the book to an endcap for more visibility."

"That's great. Thank you. I still can't believe it's doing so well," I respond as I head back into the kitchen for my coffee.

"It is, and with that being said, it's important we get the ball rolling on your next project. Look, I've granted you leniency with time because

I know you've been struggling creatively, but you are under contract for three more books. I'm going to need a minimum of an outline by Friday. If you can get me a few chapters by then as well, even better."

Tabitha's urgency awakens the anxiety in me. She's right. My name is hotter than it's ever been, and I can't allow that to fade if I want to stay relevant. The industry is cutthroat these days with the influx of people who are now self-publishing. I know this because I'm what's considered a hybrid; I'm both traditionally published and self-published, thanks to the non-compete clause my agent fought against.

"No problem. I'll get to work today. I understand timing is everything, so as soon as I get the summary done, I'll email it to you so you can review while I work on hammering out some chapters."

"Good. We'd like to aim to have the book on shelves within the next five months, so we are pushing a tight deadline. Get working on it and I will email you today or tomorrow with hard deadline dates for each stage."

"Thanks, Tabitha. I'll talk to you later."

With an exhale, I plop down on the sofa and kick my feet up onto the coffee table. There have been a few fleeting ideas that have come to me in the past few days, but nothing that's anywhere near fleshed out enough to write a summary for. I swipe my phone and open the app to voice chat with Brooke.

"Brooke, you there?"

While I wait for her to respond, I take the pad of paper that's on the coffee table and jot down a few notes. This is the first book I have to develop under a time crunch. Up until the last contract, I've pitched story concepts to the publisher that they have liked and contracted me for. But with this contract, not only did they take the two-book series I pitched them, but they also wanted three more books beyond that. Now that we are at that point, I feel more pressure than ever since I normally wait until a story naturally comes to me before I start writing. Now I have to manufacture a story without allowing it to form organically. I know this is how most authors in the traditional world operate, and I'm sure I can do it too. It's just new and uncomfortable.

"I'm here. What's up?"

"Tabitha just called."

"Uh oh. Are you in trouble?" she teases.

"I could be," I tell her. "I have to have a summary for the next book to her by Friday, and she is pushing for me to also have chapters for her. So I need your help."

"Of course. What can I do?"

"Well, I have a few ideas I want to run by you and get your opinion. I know you're more of a murder mystery girl, but I need to get some direction here."

"Tell me what you have."

"Okay, well, what if I did a student/teacher type th—"

"No," she interrupts. "There's too much of that out there and it isn't *you*. It would just get lost in the sea of other books just like that. You need something more original."

"Oookay. Well, you shot that one down fast." I laugh as I cross that idea off the list.

"Sorry, but you asked for honesty. Next."

"Military. I was thinking maybe the husband gets wounded at war and is now disabled. It takes a toll on the wife and—"

"And she falls in love with one of his combat brothers while turning to him for support."

"What the hell, Brooke?"

"It's been done a thousand times. And what do you know about the military anyway?"

"Well . . . nothing, but that's why I have you."

With a sarcastic moan, she says, "As if the workload you give me isn't full enough, you want me researching military shit? Pass. Next."

"Oh, my God. I want to slap you so bad."

"I bet you do, hooker." Her response is followed by a loud, bellowing laugh.

Going to my next idea, I read, "A girl who winds up in a mental institution for some reason I can come up with later. But she should be young, fourteen or so. Her therapist is the crazy one and winds up developing a very unhealthy attraction to her. Fast forward, she's a young adult and that therapist from her past is obsessed with her. I don't know where the story goes, but I can develop one around that premise."

There's a pause as I cringe at what her response will be, and then she says, "I like that."

"Seriously?"

"Yeah. But you can't make it sleazy and slutty. I mean, obviously he's gotta be psychotic . . . like clinically diagnosable."

"Yeah, yeah. Totally. It would be a dark story."

As I sit here, ideas spark in my head faster than I can talk. "Brooke, I'll talk to you later. My mind is running a million miles an hour now."

"Okay, well, message me if you need me."

Tossing my phone aside, I open my laptop and type out all my thoughts as they come to me. It's amazing how sometimes talking things out with someone is all it takes to get the creative juices flowing. The more I type, the more excited about the story I become. Random scenes play in my head, and I write them out so I don't run the risk of losing any of these ideas.

Time passes as I lose myself to this developing storyline, and when I come to a standstill, I see two hours have gone by. I've written four pages of notes as it pertains to the plot, scenes, and different characters along with their names, traits, and background details. Mindlessly, I pick up my mug, take a sip, and immediately spit the cold, stale coffee back into the cup.

"Oh, gross," I mumble and then walk over to the sink to wash out the mug so I can make another cup of fresh coffee.

Returning to my laptop, I save the document and open my email to send it to Brooke, as I do with everything I write. She will typically read what I send in the evenings once she has her son put to bed, and then she will message me to discuss. Doing this helps me stay on track and it's always good to get a second opinion.

Once the document is sent, I scroll through the mass of emails that came through while I was in Vegas. There are over a hundred of them, so I flag the important ones I need to come back to and delete all the random ones. As I'm going through, I stop when I see several in a row from FetLife.

I click on the first one to see I've received a private message from someone on that site. The other two emails are also notifications of users who have sent me messages. It's a little strange that anyone would message me since I provided no personal information, not even a photo. For all they know, I could be a wretched, morbidly obese woman who has a bad case of acne.

I stare at the message in the email I have open.

ALEC107: Why so secretive?

Curiosity gets the best of me, and I click the link, which takes me to the login screen on the website. I enter my username and password, and when I hit the submit button, I'm directed into a private chat room where I can respond. I notice the message was sent to me at five o'clock this morning from the timestamp.

My fingers hover over the keyboard as I think of a reply. This should be easy, considering I'm a best-selling author and all, but I'm unsure of what to say, so I just type the first thing that comes to me.

ANONYMOUS: Secretive?

I watch the screen for a minute, and then open another window to check my social media sites. As I'm reading a message concerning a book signing I've been asked to attend, an alert dings from the private chat.

ALEC107: No picture. Not a member of any groups. No information. All I know is that you're a 32-year-old submissive female who lives in Boston. I question the accuracy of that though.

Before I respond, I notice the small photo next to his profile name and click on it. A new window pops up and I'm taken to his profile page. His photo is a candid shot of him standing on a pier. I doubt it's even him, because no one that good-looking would be on a site like this. He probably just catfished the photo, but I'll pretend it's him instead of the troll I'm sure he really is.

I then read his profile stats:

Gender: Male

Ethnicity: Caucasian

Age: 41

Hometown: Boston, MA

Fetishes: Breath Play (giving), Impact Play (giving), Munch, Play Parties, Rough Sex, Sensory Deprivation (giving), Swinging, Subspace (giving), Topspace (receiving), Voyeurism

Holy shit! I don't even know what half of those things are. I click back to his photo, and I know this can't be him because he looks way too normal to be into this kind of stuff. Hell, not that I live under a rock or anything, but I always associated this kind of stuff with movies and books—never with real life. At least not the life I've been living.

ANONYMOUS: It was late when I made the profile. I was tired.

While I wait for him to message me back, I go back to his profile to read through his list of fetishes again, but he's quick to reply.

ALEC107: What made you join this site? Looking for like-minded people? Looking for a play partner?

ANONYMOUS: A play partner?

ALEC107: You're a submissive, correct?

I wonder if I should play along or just fess up to the fact that I'm simply a curious intruder.

ALEC107: Do you have any other fetishes?

Knowing he'll probably bust me due to my lack of knowledge, I decide to go with the truth.

ANONYMOUS: Umm . . . actually, I'm not a submissive. And I don't have any fetishes.

ALEC107: So why are you here?

ANONYMOUS: I don't really know. Curious, I guess.

ALEC107: You do know that you could've simply selected "Vanilla" instead of "Submissive." It's an option.

I'm an idiot.

ANONYMOUS: Oh. Apparently I didn't scroll down enough to see it was there. So, are you a dom?

ALEC107: No, doll. I'm not a Dom. And I can see you're pretty

green, because if I were a Dom, I would have your ass for not capitalizing the "D."

ANONYMOUS: My ass? Doubtful. Can I ask you a question?

ALEC107: Sure.

ANONYMOUS: I looked at your list of fetishes on your profile, and assuming you aren't randomly selecting choices like I did, what is "Munch?"

ALEC107: What do you think it is?

ANONYMOUS: Umm . . .

ALEC107: Don't be shy.

ANONYMOUS: If I'm wrong, don't laugh.

ALEC107: Promise.

ANONYMOUS: Ass eating?

I immediately cover my face with my hands and start laughing, wondering if I'm right.

ALEC107: No. Sorry to disappoint you, but I'm not into "ass eating" as you call it. Have you ever tried it?

ANONYMOUS: OMG! NO! That's so gross!

ALEC107: How do you know it's gross if you've never tried it? You might like it.

ANONYMOUS: Have you tried it?

ALEC107: Yes.

ANONYMOUS: And?

ALEC107: As a receiver, it didn't do much for me. As a giver, it got me hard to see how much pleasure she got from it.

His candid response takes me aback. I never talk about this stuff with anyone other than Brooke, but it's always jokes and laughter. Nothing serious. I may write in a sexually straightforward way, but that's make-believe. Plus, there's safety in anonymity, and since I hide behind my pen name, I feel a sense of freedom.

ANONYMOUS: So, are you going to tell me what "munch" is?

ALEC107: It's a small social gathering of friends who share some of the same fetishes. We meet for coffee or dinner. It's low-pressure. You tend to see a lot of newbies, as yourself, at munch gatherings.

ANONYMOUS: I'm not a newbie.

ALEC107: No? I thought you said you were curious.

ANONYMOUS: I mean, I am. But only to broaden my knowledge, not to actually do anything.

ALEC107: Are you scared to try something new?

ANONYMOUS: No. It's just not my thing.

ALEC107: How do you know? Don't be so quick to think you know what you like and what you don't like. Have you ever been spanked?

ANONYMOUS: That's a pretty personal question.

ALEC107: I'll go with something easy then . . . what's your name?

ANONYMOUS: Tori.

"Shit!" I mutter to myself the moment I send the message and realize I probably shouldn't have given him my real name.

ALEC107: Is that short for Victoria?

ANONYMOUS: Yes, but no one aside from my grandmother calls me that.

ALEC107: I'm surprised.

ANONYMOUS: Why?

ALEC107: It's a beautiful name.

Is he flirting?

ANONYMOUS: So, Alec . . . what do you do for a job since it's the middle of the day and you're chatting online with a stranger.

ALEC107: I'm a partner at an advertising firm in the city. And you're not a stranger, Victoria. I know you're a 32-year-old who lives in Boston and isn't into eating ass. We're practically friends. ;)

ANONYMOUS: Well, if that's your basis of a friendship . . . LOL!

ALEC107: And what is it that you do for work since you're chatting online in the middle of the day too?

Finding no harm in telling him my job since Tori has no link to my pen name, I go ahead and reply.

ANONYMOUS: I'm a writer.

ALEC107: What kind of writer?

ANONYMOUS: An author. I write fiction, mainly romance.
ALEC107: Anything I would know?
ANONYMOUS: Maybe, maybe not.
ALEC107: Again, you're being secretive.
ANONYMOUS: I'm being cautious. You see, I have different standards of friendship than you do, and to me, you're a stranger. If I were to tell you what books I've written, you could easily Google me.
ALEC107: And you don't want me to Google you? Why? Are you ugly?
ANONYMOUS: No. At least I don't think I'm ugly. I'm just private. Not secretive . . . private. There's a difference.
ALEC107: I can respect that. Most women who get on this site usually put everything out there without regard for their safety. I like that you're protecting yourself. But I can't help but wonder what you look like. It doesn't seem fair since I'm sure you've already looked at my profile picture.
ANONYMOUS: You mean your fake photo?
ALEC107: Fake?
ANONYMOUS: There's no way that's you.
ALEC107: And why is that?
ANONYMOUS: Because that guy in the photo is hot and pretty normal looking.
ALEC107: And what am I? Abnormal because I have different sexual preferences than you do?
ANONYMOUS: I didn't mean it like that. I'm sorry. That sounded extremely judgmental and that wasn't what I meant.
ALEC107: What is normal? Are you normal?
ANONYMOUS: No. It's just that . . . I don't know. I guess I have you stereotyped, if I'm being completely honest. In fact, you're easy to talk to, which I didn't expect. Again, preconceived perception and all. I didn't mean to offend you.
ALEC107: I appreciate your honesty. You admitted to being vanilla,

which is far from my world, but just because we are different doesn't mean one of us is normal and the other abnormal.

ANONYMOUS: I agree.

I stew in my foot-in-mouth moment, and after a long pause, he finally messages back.

ALEC107: So . . . you think I'm hot?

Oh, God. I can't believe I said that. But for all I know, it could still be a fake picture.

ANONYMOUS: No. I said the guy in the photo was hot. How do I know that's even you?

Another long pause.

ANONYMOUS: Are you there?

No response. After another minute passes, I'm about to exit out of the chat room when I see he's sent a file that I need to download.

ALEC107: Open it.

I click on the file icon, and as soon as it downloads, a photo appears on my screen of the same guy that's in his profile picture. But, he proves himself to be legit as he's holding a piece of paper with today's date on it along with a note that reads: To my new friend, Victoria, who doesn't like ass eating.

Holy shit! It's really him. He wears a big smile on his face that crinkles in shallow wrinkles at the corners of his blue eyes. His hair is a dark brown that's graying throughout. He's wearing a suit, but I know he's in shape from the photo of him on the pier where he's wearing shorts and a T-shirt.

ANONYMOUS: I guess you weren't lying.

ALEC107: Now it's your turn?

ANONYMOUS: I'm not sending you a picture of me.

ALEC107: Okay then. Let me ask you something. Do you drink coffee?

ANONYMOUS: Yes. Why?

ALEC107: I drink mine black with two sugars. None of that sugar substitute bullshit. Real sugar.

What a weird thing to even say.

ANONYMOUS: Why do I care how you take your coffee?
ALEC107: That's up to you whether you care or not. I have a client meeting I have to get to. It was nice talking with you, Victoria.

Before I can send my reply, his status switches to "offline."

"That was fucking weird."

chapter six

It's been two days since I've spent any time with Landon. The food critic from the *Times* willf be at the restaurant next week and he and Damon have been working on perfecting a couple new items to be added to the menu. They've also hired an interior designer to make some tweaks to the entrance and main dining area. With his busy schedule and me trying to get my editor some chapters, the only time we see each other is in passing each morning. After taking care of the girls all evening, I've been going to bed earlier than usual and am asleep before Landon gets home.

I was able to talk Brooke into watching the kids tonight so I could meet Landon for dinner. Mid-week is typically slow at the restaurant, so even though he's at work, we will still be able to spend some time together. It's not often that I drive into the city, mostly because Boston has the most screwed up streets I've ever seen, and I never fail to get myself turned around and going in the wrong direction. But I'm a sure shot when it comes to Damon's restaurant, and when I pull up, the valet is right there to open up my door.

"Mrs. Garrison, good to see you," Mark, a student at Boston University who has worked here for the past two years, greets.

"You too. How's school going?"

"It's going," he groans with a hint of a smile. "Only one more semester until I graduate."

He slips into my car, and after I congratulate him, he shuts the door and drives off. Walking into the restaurant, I'm greeted by the hostess, who then leads me to the lounge area and seats me at the bar before going to get Landon.

"Tori," Chelsea says from behind the bar. "Landon said you'd be coming up, but I didn't believe him."

"I know. I've been really busy lately." There was a time when I used to come around more often, but with the girls and my busy travel schedule, it's been months since I've been here.

Chelsea sets a cocktail napkin in front of me. "The usual?"

"Please."

I watch her as she makes my drink, looking fabulous in a black shift dress and high heels. She's tall and fit with bright blonde hair that makes me miss being in my mid-twenties. What I wouldn't give to have perky boobs and a face free from emerging wrinkles. Most of the time I feel young, but when I'm around girls like her, I feel old.

"So . . ." she says, stringing out the word as she sets down the lemon drop martini. "I finally got around to reading your last book."

I pick up the glass and take a sip.

"All I can say is Landon hit the jackpot with you."

I practically choke as I swallow the alcohol and try not to laugh. "Don't believe everything you read."

She laughs quietly and shakes her head, saying, "I mean, I thought I was kinky, but you have me beat by a long shot."

I laugh along with her as I take another sip and will the vodka to curb my embarrassment. If she only knew how boring my sex life actually is. Landon and I are anything but kinky. We are so predictable, going through the same routine of motions each time we have sex. It's pretty standard and boring, but what can you expect after being with someone for as long as we've been? I'd never admit that to anyone aside from Brooke, so I go along with Chelsea's illusion of me and instead of denying, I opt for coy silence.

"Hi, honey. I hope you weren't waiting long," Landon says before giving me a sweeping kiss.

"I just got here," I respond.

Chelsea gives me a wink before walking away to serve an older couple at the other side of the bar.

"What's that about?"

"She read my latest book and now worships me as a sexual goddess," I quip.

He laughs it off.

"How were the girls when you picked them up from school?"

"Good," I respond as we go into our usual line of questioning and conversation, which is just as predictable as our sex life. Next, he's going to ask me about work.

"Did you get a lot of work done today?"

"I got in around three thousand words."

"That's good," he says.

"How has your day been?"

"Not too bad."

We continue with our idle chitchat when one of the servers brings us our food, which Landon had previously told the kitchen to prepare for us.

"You know, I was thinking. We should get away, just the two of us."

"When? You're always traveling," he says before taking a bite of his swordfish.

"Why don't you come with me to one of the signings and we can extend our stay?"

"That sounds doable," he responds halfheartedly as he takes another bite.

I reach out and touch his arm to get his attention, and when he looks at me, I stress, "I'm serious, Landon. We need to take some time for us. Lately, it's been nothing but kids and work."

He pushes his plate out of the way and takes my hand in his. "You look amazing," he says as he looks at me—his first real look since I got here, finally slowing down enough to notice the navy, pencil-skirt dress and strappy nude heels I'm wearing.

His eyes are shadowed in exhaustion as he sits here in his white chef coat, and I see how worn down he is. "You've been working so much lately," I tell him softly. "I miss you."

"I just need to get through next week and then I'll be home more."

"You need to take care of yourself."

He cradles my cheeks in his hands as we face each other. "Do you know how much I love you?"

I nod.

"I'm sorry I haven't been home much, but don't doubt that you and the girls are my life."

"I've never doubted you—"

"Excuse me, chef," Chelsea interrupts. "Damon is on the phone for you."

"I'll be right back."

I watch Landon as he walks into the back and then turn to my dinner that I've hardly touched. His words echo in my head, and as sweet as they are, they are said all too often. The thing is, if it isn't his work pulling him away, then it's mine. We are both filled with excuses and apologies and words to soothe, but we've yet to find ourselves on the same page in life. I tell myself that maybe it's supposed to be this way, that this is adulthood. I'm not foolish enough to believe life can ever go back to the way it used to be when we first met, but I guess I never thought the spark that once lived within me would die such an early death.

I make attempts to reignite us. Like tonight, wearing a pair of designer heels that are much too expensive, slipping into this dress that covers a sexy black lace thong, and taking my time to apply the perfect smoky eye. But he didn't even notice until I forced him to look at me. Maybe the spark within him has burned out as well. Maybe it's an inevitable part of marriage, and all those couples who claim to still have the wild burning fire are full of shit.

Landon reemerges from the back. "I'm sorry. I have to cut this short and get back to work."

"We haven't even finished our food." I try my best to contain my annoyance, but my voice pitches regardless.

"I'm not that hungry anyway."

He's totally missed the point.

"Take your time and enjoy your dinner. I'll be home around midnight."

And with that, he gives me a kiss and returns to the kitchen, leaving me to finish our date on my own.

"Another martini?" Chelsea asks as she clears Landon's dishes.

"Thanks, but I should get going."

On the drive home, I turn up the music and blast it through the speakers to help alleviate my sour mood. The hassle of having Brooke watch the kids, the effort I put into my appearance, and the hope of having a nice dinner with my husband now feel like an utter waste.

"How was your date?" Brooke asks from the couch in the living room when I walk into the house.

I kick off my heels before falling back onto a chair with an annoyed huff.

"What happened?"

"He ditched me halfway through dinner and left me sitting there like a desperate housewife."

"Why?"

"I didn't bother asking." Brooke doesn't respond, but I can feel her eyes on me, and after a beat passes, I look over to her and ask, "Do you think I need Botox?"

"Girl, you started needing it last year," she jokes and then shifts to a more serious tone. "What's going on?"

Slumped down in the chair, I roll my head to look at her, and admit, "It's been almost a month."

"Oh." Her voice is a mixture of surprise and sympathy. Or maybe it's pity. "And you think it's because he doesn't find you attractive?"

"Hell if I know."

"Don't do this to yourself. You're both so busy. It's not surprising that you're going through a dry spell. Everyone does."

"Even you?"

"Tori, life isn't like the books you write. I mean, maybe it is at first, but you and Landon have been together forever. You can't expect to be jumping each other's bones five times a day. You have kids, jobs, and a crazy travel schedule. Life is messy, and you can't compare reality to fiction because you'll always wind up disappointed." She then stands and grabs her purse.

"You're leaving?"

"I need to be up early in the morning. Ryder's school is having a special donut breakfast for the parents and I can't be showing up in my gym clothes next to all those fancy working moms in their stylish clothes and perfectly manicured fingernails," she says with snarky attitude. "Plus, you need to spend some quality time with your vibrator tonight."

"Why do I bother confiding in you?"

"Because you love my honesty."

I stand and walk Brooke to the door. "Thanks for watching the kids tonight."

"Any time."

When I'm showered and in my pajamas, I skip the vibrator and crawl into bed with my laptop. I open up my manuscript to do a quick read through, but it doesn't take long for me to get sidetracked, and soon I'm cleaning out my download folder. I go through and click open the files I don't recognize, and before I know it, I come across the photo Alec sent me the other day.

After our conversation ended so weirdly, I never messaged him back. I've been so wrapped up in writing that I haven't even checked my personal email account to see if he's sent me a message. So when I log out of my author email and log into my personal account, I scroll through to find that I have no waiting messages.

I decide to kill a little time and see if he's online, because I can't deny that he's entertaining to talk to. I sign in to my FetLife account and go to the private message page to find that his icon is lit up green, signifying his online status. I scroll back through our previous conversation before deciding to send a message.

ANONYMOUS: You there?

His response comes a couple minutes later.

ALEC107: I was wondering if I'd hear from you again.

ANONYMOUS: I've been busy. Deadlines and all.

ALEC107: Writing?

ANONYMOUS: Yes.

ALEC107: Anything good?

ANONYMOUS: Of course. I'm writing it, so it's all good! LOL!

ALEC107: When are you going to tell me the name you write under so I can have the pleasure of reading some of your work?

ANONYMOUS: Why do you want to read my work?

ALEC107: For the same reason you decided to message me tonight.

ANONYMOUS: Which is?

ALEC107: Curiosity.

ANONYMOUS: You think I'm curious about you?

ALEC107: How many times have you thought about me in the past few days since we last spoke?

I hesitate before responding because I'm not sure how to. If I tell him the truth, he might assume something it's not. Because I have thought about him, but only from the natural, human instinct one experiences when they come into contact with someone new. And yeah, I am curious about him, who wouldn't be? He's a total mystery and completely opposite of who I am when it comes to intimate lifestyle.

ANONYMOUS: I've thought about you at least once, which is why we're talking.

ALEC107: Are you embarrassed to admit the truth, that I've crossed your mind every day, multiple times?

ANONYMOUS: Are you wanting me to feed your ego or something?

ALEC107: Just wanting the truth.

ANONYMOUS: Ask me something else then.

ALEC107: You ever been married?

He catches me off guard at the mere assumption that I'm currently single, but then again, he did find me on a fetish website. To him, I can be anything . . . anyone. A smile crawls onto my lips as I think about what type of game I want to play here. I'm a blank canvas that I can paint however I desire. For the first time ever, I get to be the character in my own fantasy land.

ANONYMOUS: No. I've never been married. You?

ALEC107: No.

ANONYMOUS: Wow. 41 years old and never married. That must mean one thing.

ALEC107: ???

ANONYMOUS: You're stubborn and set in your ways.

ALEC107: I could say the same about you. 32 and never married.

ANONYMOUS: Touché. Kids?

ALEC107: No. You?

ANONYMOUS: No.

I lie as my kids are actually sound asleep upstairs in their beds.

ALEC107: Do you want any?

ANONYMOUS: If I met the right man, yes. What about you?

ALEC107: I've always wanted kids. But I'm 41, single, and apparently stubborn, so I'm doubtful it'll happen. ;)

His humor makes me laugh, and I play into my act when I respond.

ANONYMOUS: Maybe we are destined to be forever alone.

ALEC107: Are you lonely?

ANONYMOUS: At times . . . yes.

My words are truth. Most people associate loneliness with being alone, but no matter how full my life is, there are times when I do feel very isolated. Just like tonight. This house may be filled with love and happiness, the pictures on the walls prove my full life, but here I am in the silence—lonely.

ALEC107: When was the last time you were with someone?

I think for a moment about how I want to answer.

ANONYMOUS: Almost a year since my last relationship.

ALEC107: I meant sexually.

ANONYMOUS: You're invasive with your questions. Why on earth would I tell you when the last time I had sex was?

ALEC107: Why not?

ANONYMOUS: When was the last time you had sex?

ALEC107: Yesterday.

ANONYMOUS: Yesterday? I thought you were single.

ALEC107: I am.

ANONYMOUS: So you just have random sex?

ALEC107: Yes. But you should know that if you've read my profile.

I click on his picture, which takes me to his profile so I can re-read. I come across *Play Parties* and *Swinging* noted on his list of fetishes and then click back to our message screen.

ANONYMOUS: Swinging? I though that was married couples swapping partners with other married couples.

ALEC107: It can be, but not typically.

ANONYMOUS: And what exactly are Play Parties? Is that part of the whole "swinging" thing?

ALEC107: Yes and no. It's a mixture of couples and also singles who like to have sex while people watch.

ANONYMOUS: Do you know these people you hook up with?

ALEC107: Not all the time. Boston is a large city with lots of play clubs, so while I usually go for anonymity, I do occasionally find myself with a repeat.

I sit back against the headboard of my bed and stare at his message—stunned. I never thought of myself as a lily-white traditionalist, but now I question how sheltered I am. The fact that I've lived here my whole life and have never even known that these clubs existed. Again, I just assumed this was something left for the movies and for books to titillate hidden fantasies that we all have. And here I am, talking to a living, breathing person who walks in the darkness that intrigues me and inspires the stories I write. This guy embodies all that I try to convey on the pages of my books. No longer do I have to guess at the type of man who indulges in this lifestyle. I'm talking to the real thing. Kristen was right when she told me about this site—it's a great place for research.

ALEC107: Are you okay?

ANONYMOUS: Yes. Just digesting. To be honest with you, I didn't know these places actually existed. I know that makes me sound naïve.

ALEC107: You're not naïve, Victoria.

ANONYMOUS: Can I ask you something personal?

ALEC107: Only if I can ask something personal in return.

ANONYMOUS: I feel like I'm being setup, but I'll take the bait. So, my question: Why do you like unattached sex with random people?

As I wait for his response to come through, I think about the cliché reasons that I often write about and also what my other author friends write. It's usually a man with a dark past: abuse, death of a loved one, or just your typical bad boy. In books, there is always a reason for the behavior and there's always a girl that cures said behavior, and by the time you reach the ending, the guy is monogamous and head over heels in love.

ALEC107: For as far back as I can remember, I've had a copious sex drive. When I was young and discovered masturbation, I couldn't get enough. I would jerk off every morning in the shower before school and often at night too. As I grew older, I never found myself in many relationships, and after a few failed ones, I found it easier to leave the strings cut from sexual partners. I want sex without expectations of preconceived standards most traditional women have of the men they sleep with. Sex is just that—sex. It's a basic animal instinct that society has built a hedge of morals and values around. But it's just sex. If I wanted true intimacy, then I would be in a relationship. Until I find a woman worthy of the stress relationships bring, I just want to indulge in my lascivious ways, get off, and go home.

And there it is—an unapologetic explanation without an underlying tragic past. A man who likes casual sex because he just does.

ANONYMOUS: Do you even want a relationship or are you content with your life as it is now?
ALEC107: I'm very content with my life. I'm not out purposely seeking a relationship, but if I found the right woman, I wouldn't be opposed to settling down with her. Like I said before, I've always wanted children, so of course I want to eventually find myself in a relationship. I just don't believe that's something one can achieve with the mindset that we can actively make happen. I prefer a more organic approach.
ANONYMOUS: What will be, will be.
ALEC107: Exactly.
ANONYMOUS: I can appreciate that.
ALEC107: My turn to ask the question.
ANONYMOUS: Go easy on me.

I smile in anticipation of what he will want to know about me, and when his question pops up on the screen, I instantly blush.

ALEC107: When was the last time you touched yourself?
ANONYMOUS: OMG! NO! You can't ask me that.
ALEC107: I can, and I did. Fair is fair. You know it was just yesterday when I last had sex, and I'll give you one more: it was this morning when I last jerked off.
ANONYMOUS: You are more open with divulging that stuff than me.
ALEC107: Why are you so shy? According to you, we aren't even friends, only strangers. No need to hide. So tell me.
ANONYMOUS: Why do you want to know?
ALEC107: The same reason you wanted to know about me. Curiosity. Plus, I like making you squirm.
ANONYMOUS: What makes you think I'm squirming?
ALEC107: Because I've made you uncomfortable. Don't lie. You're squirming, aren't you?

I shake my head with a nervous giggle as I type my response.

ANONYMOUS: Fine. Yes. Your question made me squirm.
ALEC107: Do you use toys or your fingers?

ANONYMOUS: Seriously?!

ALEC107: You're making me laugh.

My hands hover over the keyboard, and I tell myself that he's right. I'm just a stranger. He doesn't know me, and what he does know isn't even the whole truth. But I choose to give him an honest answer, because what does it matter anyway—I'm just having fun.

ANONYMOUS: Last week.

ALEC107: How?

ANONYMOUS: I used my vibrator. There. I answered you. My turn. With these clubs you go to, are you worried about diseases? I mean, can anyone off the street go to these places?

ALEC107: I always use protection, and no, you have to be a member to get into the clubs I go to. Of course there are clubs that anyone can go to, but who would want to?

ANONYMOUS: Does it cost money?

ALEC107: There's a membership fee and required STD testing that you must abide by, along with club standards and rules. It's a very clean and safe environment. You should come if you are interested. Members can bring a guest, but they aren't allowed to participate with anyone aside from the member that brought them. It's simply a way for someone new to see what it's all about before joining.

I can't believe these places actually exist and that he talks so casually about them as if it's no big deal. I know I shouldn't be shocked, but I am.

ANONYMOUS: I don't even know who you are and you're inviting me to join you at a sex club.

ALEC107: I'm not inviting you so I can have sex with you. Only because I'd rather you go with someone who's safe and won't take advantage of the situation. But if you prefer, why don't you meet me for coffee?

ANONYMOUS: You say you're safe, but I don't know that.

ALEC107: Okay, then. Why don't you call me next time you want to talk? Is that slow enough for your liking? ;) 857-222-3535

And, just like our last conversation, his status goes to "offline" before

I can even respond. I sit back, thoroughly entertained by our chat as I stare at his phone number, curious about what this guy's voice even sounds like.

Closing my laptop, I set it on the nightstand and turn off the lamp before slinking down into the covers and lingering in the high that comes along when meeting someone new and intriguing. Someone so different, so straightforward, and yet, so much more mysterious than anyone I've ever met. I replay our conversation in my head as I drift and eventually fall asleep.

Warmth cocoons me from behind. A heavy hand wraps around my shoulder and pulls me onto my back. I reach up my hand to run it along smooth, bare skin, never opening my eyes because there's no need. His touch, his smell, it's undeniable. I'm half-awake, half-asleep, as I maze around in my obscure state of mind. With my eyes still closed, I feel Landon's hand slip under my shirt and graze along the swell of my breast, his palm brushing over my nipple, hardening it as I sway my body up to his.

He's entirely naked above me, and when he knees my legs open, he presses his hard cock against my hottest part that yearns for the animalistic pleasure Alec was telling me about earlier tonight. I need to get lost in a place where nothing exists but pure ecstasy.

I lift my hips when Landon slips his fingers under the hem of my panties. I can feel how wet I am as he pulls them down my legs. Quickly, I peel off my shirt, grab the shaft of him, and guide him inside me. I'm eager and selfish and horny as I urge him to move fast and hard. His mouth runs along my neck, kissing me between his heavy breaths and moans.

Keeping my eyes closed, Landon is no longer my husband, he's an obscurity as I lose myself in a rhapsody of hedonism I imagine Alec's world to be. I roll on top of the fictive stranger, reach my arms over to the headboard, and hold on as I thrust my hips back and forth. I break our routine of choreographed sex and selfishly take control.

"Damn, Tori. You're so wet," the man below me groans as I rise and fall over his cock.

Sweat beads at the nape of my neck while I drive my body higher and higher. I throw my head back when I feel the swelling of his cock inside of me, and I grind down harder. My movements grow more rigid as I reach my peak, and when he cums, I slip off the cliff's edge and explode in mid-air as I fall wildly out of control. Sparks of fire shoot through me, leaving a sizzle in their wake as I ride out my orgasm.

Never opening my eyes, I drop my head down to his chest, and with a deep breath, I take in the scent of my husband—a stranger no more.

He wraps his arms around me, both our bodies covered in a sheen of sweat. "That was unexpected," he murmurs on staggered breaths. "What came over you?"

Through my pants and heavily beating heart, I finally open my eyes and look into his sated ones. "I don't know. It's been a while for us . . . I guess I needed that more than I thought."

Landon rolls us over onto our sides and kisses my damp forehead. "I'm sorry I've been so distracted lately."

"Don't be. I understand."

"I love you most and more," he tells me when he tucks my head under his chin.

Nuzzling into his chest, I breathe in his scent once more. "I love you too."

chapter seven

Four days ago, I called Alec for the first time. I thought it would be weird, but just like our private message conversations, it felt effortless. So much so, that we wound up talking on the phone that first day for nearly five hours straight. Needless to say, I haven't been getting much writing done because we've been talking on the phone every day since.

I've found myself opening up to him more quickly than I do most people when striking up friendships. But we only communicate through text and phone calls, so all we have are words to fill our time. It's inevitable that we would learn about each other faster than if we were spending time together in person. Not that he hasn't asked, but I always decline, mostly because I've created myself as a lie. Not entirely though. I guess the only real lies are that I'm single with no kids. Everything else I've told him has been factual. But those two details aren't minor—they're the monumental threads that weave soul to flesh and make me who I am. It's not like I lied about something trivial and meaningless, and for that fact, I just don't feel like there is any point in taking this any further than our texts and phone calls.

In the past week, I've learned about his family and upbringing. He's shared stories of growing up the youngest among three brothers who are now all married with children, all of which still live nearby. The adoration he has for his nieces and nephews is apparent in the way he speaks of them, and I don't doubt that he wishes to have children of his own. He also shared with me how the death of his father a few years back forever changed the dynamics of his family.

I too opened up to him about my family. The divorce of my parents when I was only three years old, my older brother marrying and starting a new life with his wife, and the isolation I've always felt. He knows my family is distant, that aside from holidays and birthdays, there's no real communication between us. To my surprise, I even found myself telling him something I never talk to anyone about. I got swept away in the ease of our conversation and told him about the day my mother died. I couldn't remember the last time I had talked about her to anyone, but for some reason I told Alec.

"She died in the morning and no one even bothered to tell me," I weep.

"No one told you?"

"No. It was evening, and I had dropped by the house to visit her. The street was lined with cars. Everyone knew . . . everyone but me."

"How old were you?"

"Twenty-two," I respond. "I was her only daughter and no one gave a shit about me to tell me when they had told everyone else. I'll never forgive my family for that."

"You shouldn't. They don't deserve your forgiveness. What they did was fucked up and you have every right to hate them," he insists fervently.

He sat there on the phone with me while I cried. You'd think it would be awkward to cry on the phone to some stranger, but I the obscurity between us made it easier. We have this barrier between us that grants a protective shield, just like when I write. Hiding behind a keyboard makes me brave. I can say anything, be anything.

"You're up early," Landon says when he walks out of the bedroom.

Settled on the couch with my cup of coffee and laptop, I'm still in my running gear. "I decided to wake up early and get my run out of the way."

Landon rummages around the kitchen as I check my email. I see I have a private message waiting on me, which surprises me since Alec and I haven't been using FetLife to communicate now that we have each other's cell phone numbers. I click on the link, which directs me to the site's login screen.

"What on earth are you looking at?" Landon questions as he looks over my shoulder from behind the couch and sees a woman tied up and bound to a St. Andrew's Cross.

"Research, dear," I tease.

"What the hell is this new book about?"

I laugh and lean my head back to look up at him. "Do you really want to know?"

He kisses my forehead and then flirts his words, suggesting, "Instead of telling, maybe you can show me later tonight. I'll be more than happy to help you *research*."

"You? I've been with you for over thirteen years, Landon."

"And?"

"And you are nothing like this."

"I could be," he says as he walks back into the kitchen, and I brush off his words with a giggle.

ALEC107: Dropped my phone in the parking garage after work, and the fucker no longer works. Wanted to let you know in case you call or text and get no answer from me. Should have a new phone this afternoon.

ANONYMOUS: I assumed a man like you wouldn't have clumsy hands. I feel sorry for all your conquests. LOL!

After I send my response, I close the lid to the laptop and join Landon in the kitchen.

"Today is the big day," I say. "Are you nervous?"

He sets his coffee mug down, and when he turns to me, I wrap my arms around his waist.

"Very. I tossed and turned all night."

"So, you're saying I wasn't able to satisfy you," I murmur seductively with a grin.

"Oh, you definitely satisfied me." He then leans down and nuzzles his kisses into the crook of my neck. "You are more than welcome to do that to me every night."

"That's so romantic," I joke. "Sure, you just lie there while I do all the work."

His laugh is loud as he pulls away and slaps my ass playfully. "That's right, babe!"

I pick up my coffee, take a seat at the bar top, and watch as Landon resumes his normal morning routine of fixing the girls a hot breakfast. He pulls out ingredients from the pantry and fridge.

"How is Damon feeling about today?"

"About the same as I am. When it comes to the *Times* it only takes one review to make or break you. It can go either way," he says with his back to me as he cracks open an egg. "We've worked so hard getting this restaurant up and running."

"And you've been successful every step of the way. The two of you know what you're doing and you're great at it." When Landon turns to wash his hands in the sink in front of me, I look him in the eyes and affirm, "You've got this, babe. You're an amazing chef."

Wiping his hands dry, he smiles at me. "I don't know what I would do without you. All the late nights and endless weekends I put in at the restaurant and you're always there to support me and take care of the girls. I don't tell you enough how much I appreciate all that you do."

"We're a team," I tell him, feeling guilty for complaining about him to Brooke last night. I should try harder not to dwell on how mundane life has become and focus more on all the good things I have. After all, Brooke is right. I, along with most of the women who read my books, have conditioned my mind to what love should be but isn't. This is real life, and it's not perfectly passionate and spontaneous and without flaws. I'm the first to admit that there have been times that I wished Landon acted and behaved in a certain way that reflects the men I read and write about. But when that's the world I spend my days in, it's easy to lose sight.

Once the girls wake up, the morning moves at lightning speed, as it always does. By the time I drop them off at school and get back home, Landon is already gone. I shoot him a quick text to wish him luck before my phone rings with an incoming call from my editor.

"I read the chapters you sent me, and I love the direction you're moving in. An email is being sent with the deadlines. You need to look over it, insert your electronic signature, and send it back by the end of today."

"Thanks, Tabitha. I'll go check my email now."

I give the dates a quick lookover, and although the deadlines are hard and fast, I shouldn't have any problems meeting the requirements. I sign the form and email it back. I then take a chunk of time to talk to Brooke before opening up my manuscript and getting to work.

Finding my groove comes easily today. Three hours have passed, and I've already hit twenty-five hundred words, which for me is above my average word count for an entire day. I'm in the pocket, actuality has dissolved into a faraway shadow, and I'm immersed in a story so rich and fleshed out that it becomes my reality. I laugh and cry as my fingers skitter across the keys, experiencing every emotion my characters do. But as deep in as I am, I can easily be yanked out with the slightest distraction, and right now, that's coming from the chime on my cell phone from an incoming text.

I force out another paragraph before grabbing my phone.

Alec: Thinking about you.

His flirtatious words cause something inside me to stir—a warmth I'm not used to feeling, but it intoxicates. I can't remember the last time anyone has flirted with me. I'm smiling as I quickly save the progress on my manuscript. I close the top and slide it off my lap, returning to my phone with a slight enthusiasm.

Me: Did you get a new phone?

Alec: I did. But it's missing one important thing.

Me: And what's that?

Alec: A photo of you. We've been talking for a week now, and I still have no clue what you look like. With the amount of

information we've shared with each other, I wouldn't assume us strangers anymore.

Me: I went for a run this morning and have yet to take a shower. I look like shit.

Alec: So you're concerned about what I might think about you?

His words imply that I want to look good for him, and when I think about it for a moment, he's right. Why do I care? I shouldn't, and I shouldn't lead him to believe that I do. I open the camera on my phone, hold out my arm, and snap a shot of me smiling. I don't feel as awkward about sending him my photo as I did earlier this week. Even though we've only been talking for a short time, some of our conversations have run deep. When I text him the photo, I can't help but scrutinize it—my messy bun, my every flaw free from the camouflage of makeup.

Alec: Who's catfishing who now?

Me: Please. If I wanted to catfish you, I wouldn't have sent you that messy picture.

Alec: Messy wouldn't be the word I would use to describe you.

Me: What word would you use then?

Alec: Beautiful.

His single word elicits a smile, and I respond teasingly.

Me: I think your old age is impairing your vision, but thank you anyway.

Being nearly ten years older than me when Landon is only two years older is noticeable. Alec wears his age in a way I find extremely attractive. It's not only etched in his face and the gray in his hair, it's also in the way he talks and his life experiences he's shared with me. With Landon, we're equals, discovering life together, teaching each other. But when I think of Alec, the dynamics are different. He doesn't feel like my peer, like my equal. There's a divide: I'm young and less ripe, and he's the opposite. He's the teacher and I'm the student. This imbalance appeals to me and has a way of making me feel little next to him. As if I could stand still and know he would lead the way because he's more experienced—seemingly paternal in a way.

Alec: Have you ever dated someone my age?

Me: No. Only guys around my age.

I don't bother to ask him the question in return. He's told me his lifestyle, I'm well-aware he's been with all ages.

Alec: Does it bother you?

Me: No.

My phone suddenly vibrates in my hand with Alec's incoming call.

"Aren't you supposed to be working?" I scold in jest when I answer.

"I could ask you the same thing." His voice is low with the right amount of masculine rasp and no hint of a Boston accent. It's a voice that matches his photo. "I took the rest of the day off. I'm at home."

"I know you live in Boston proper, but what part is it that you call home?"

"Back Bay area. I live in a studio loft next to Charles River."

"Right across from Cambridge," I note. "My assistant lives there." There's a noisy rustling in the phone. "What are you doing?"

"Lying down. What are you doing?"

"In the middle of the day? Must be nice."

"You never take an afternoon off to relax?"

He asks this question assuming my lies as truth, that I'm single and free of children. I honestly can't remember the last time I took an afternoon nap.

"Take a break from writing," he says on a laid-back sigh, and I imagine him settling into his bed.

I hesitate but then decide to set work aside for once and do something out of my norm. "Okay. I guess I'll be lazy too."

I set the phone down on the bed and take off my shoes, socks, and running pants, and when I slip under the covers and lie down, I grab the phone and exaggerate my words as I stretch out my legs, saying, "It feels so good to lie down."

His laugh is throaty, and I join in when I note the awkwardness of the situation.

"This is a bit strange."

"It wouldn't have to be, but you seem to have something against meeting me for coffee," he says, his voice growing lighter as he relaxes more. "Why are you so hesitant to meet me?"

Because I've lied to you about who I am.

I dodge his question entirely, tuck myself deeper under the sheets, and ask, "You do this often?"

"What? Lie in bed with a woman over the phone? No. But you're a peculiar one, so I'll take what I can get."

"Hmmm," I breathe into the phone as I close my eyes, sinking into the mattress and enjoying the reprieve.

Neither one of us speaks as time passes. His breaths begin to lull me into placidity as I rest on each of his inhales and exhales.

"Victoria."

My only response is a gentle hum.

"Touch yourself."

My eyes pop open and the stillness in the air disappears.

"What?"

"Touch yourself," he repeats.

His request throws me for a spin and a nervous giggle slips out before I tell him, "No."

I can hear the smile on his lips when he questions, "Why not?"

"Because that's weird."

"Why?"

"Because it just is." I push myself up and lean against the headboard. "I don't even know you."

"That excuse no longer works. We spend hours on the phone every day talking to each other. You know a lot more about me than most, and I'll bet that I know more about you than most."

He makes a point in that I have shared with him parts of myself and my past that I normally keep private.

"Put your hand between your legs," he pushes, and I resist again. "Tell me what you're wearing."

"Alec."

"You touch yourself anyway. Why not do it with me?"

Closing my eyes, I fight the urge to laugh him off and change the subject. The idea of doing something that's outside of my comfort zone is a titillating thought, but it isn't me. Sure, I used to dirty text Landon when we first started dating, but we never had phone sex.

"I'm looking at the photo you sent me," he says, but I don't respond as I contemplate my next move.

It's not like I even know this man. Yes, we've been talking a lot, but I don't know him in the flesh, and I never will. I'm nothing more than a lie to him. As real as it may feel, it simply isn't. It's a game. It's fun. It's anything but real.

"The thought of you lying next to me has me hard right now."

His voice breaks my reluctance for a moment, and I do what I can to push myself to do something I would never do in real life. Because this isn't real. It's simply a false perception of reality I've created for my entertainment.

I shift back down under the sheets, and when I glide my hand down the length of my body, I silently repeat to myself that this isn't real.

This isn't real, Tori.

This isn't real.

This isn't real.

This isn't . . .

"Are you touching yourself?"

"Yes," I breathe, when my hand finds itself over the top of my panties.

Alec releases a heady moan that ignites a spark of arousal as visions of him stroking himself play in my head.

"Take your finger and roll it over your clit."

I shift my panties to the side and emit little ragged gasps as I follow his instruction. Every touch has my whole body tingling in excitement as I ride on this fantasy come to life.

"Tell me how it feels, Victoria."

"Please. Don't make me talk," I plead, because I'm not sure I can even conjure up anything that would sound remotely sexy in this moment.

"Fuck, you have me so hard right now."

His voice pushes me even more, intensifying my pleasure. "Oh, God." I lift my hips and shove my panties down my legs, slipping one foot out and letting them dangle on the ankle of my other. When I hear Alec's breathing falter, I slip a finger inside and use my arousal to continue stroking my clit. Without much thought, I voice aloud, "I'm so wet," as I writhe under my own touch.

"If I were there, I'd have my tongue buried so deep inside that sweet pussy of yours."

"Shit," my voice pitches. Never in my life have words spoken gotten me off. Every time he talks, my body reacts instinctively, amplifying the noise in the room as I breathe louder.

Alec's words crack as he continues to talk, and we both lose ourselves. "I'd spread your legs open and fuck your wet pussy with my cock."

"Alec," I pant.

"Say it again."

"Alec," I nearly whimper.

"Let me hear you cum, baby," he urges on a strained voice.

I take my fingers from my swollen clit and shove them inside me, pumping hard as I throw myself over the edge. My orgasm ruptures from the inside out, literally curling my toes as I mewl in pure ecstasy along with Alec. His strong groans fill my ear as I ride out the pleasure for as long as I can, not wanting it to subside any time soon.

My hand slows as I drift back down, still hanging on to each one of Alec's heavy breaths.

"Can you go again?" he asks, feeding into the greed that has taken over me.

Unable to speak, I moan to suggest I'm not ready to stop just yet.

"That's it. Keep touching yourself. Don't stop."

With my eyes still closed, I fade into the haze of ravishment as I work my body to another climax. Every filthy word Alec speaks drives me harder and faster. Sweat builds in the creases behind my knees and along my neck.

"Think about my hard cock pounding into you, coating my dick in your cum. My mouth sucking on your nipples as I thrust harder and harder. Massaging your clit with my thumb—"

"I'm cumming again," I belt out as a second wave crashes down over me, splitting me wide open.

"That's it. Let me hear you," Alec encourages, and I completely let go of all restraint and moan loudly into the phone as I slip off the edge and drown in the crashing waves of pleasure.

No longer do I identify with Tori, but rather, Victoria. Alec has always referred to me as the latter, and the distinction helps to separate the two identities. I never thought I was the phone sex type, but suddenly, I'm acutely aware of the nefarious greed inside of me that has just been unlocked, and I want to keep going.

Instead of feeding the hunger within, I refrain from touching myself to allow my body to come down from this unimaginable high. When the cloud of delirium evaporates and clarity sets in, embarrassment finds me.

Oh, my God! I just got myself off with this random person.

Heat of another nature creeps up my neck, and I hold my breath as I cover my face, but the scent on my hand mortifies me even more.

"You sound so hot when you cum."

As soon as he speaks, I want to hang up, crawl under the bed entirely, and pretend none of this ever happened.

What the fuck do I even say?

I'm a stone statue, unable to move, as if he'd be able to detect my presence if I do. Like a child who hides under a blanket and believes themselves to be invisible. But I know better, which makes it all the worse.

“Say something, Victoria.”

Scooting back to sit up, I respond coyly, “I don’t know what to say right now.”

“Did you like that?” he questions in a way that feels as if he’s holding my hand to guide me to talk.

“Yes.”

“You’ve never done that before, have you?”

“No.” My answers are pathetically short.

“Are you embarrassed?”

“A little . . .” I lie and then admit, “a lot.”

“Tell me why.”

“Because, I’ve never met you, but you now know how I sound when . . .”

“When you cum?” he finishes for me.

“Yes.”

“And to you, that should be private? More private than my hearing how you sound when you cry?”

“Well . . . yeah.”

“I don’t understand your reasoning. In order to cry, you have to expose the wounds in your heart. But sex, it’s just an act that doesn’t require such depth of vulnerability. What we just did was entirely free of emotion. Just two people who wanted to get off. But when you cried and told me about your mother, that was nothing but blood-filled pain and sadness.”

He makes a point and skews my perception of what constitutes intimacy. And he’s right, I was more unveiled to him the other day than what I am right now, and yet, it’s right now that I feel too exposed.

“This is what I mean about you being conditioned by society telling you how to think, act, and feel. Maybe there’s a possibility you’re more like me than you think.”

“Maybe.” I think about his words and allow them to idle for a while. This man is nothing like Landon. Everything about him is a contradiction to everything I know and am used to. The allure that draws me to talk to him day after day is this idea of what I could be because of him. That maybe the areas in my life I'm unsatisfied with are the result of my thinking and behaving the way he suggests society has ingrained in me.

"Have you ever tried letting go of your ideas of what's normal and acceptable?"

"No. I mean, I feel like I make decisions for me, but I also take into consideration how others will think and feel."

"When I asked you to touch yourself, you said no. But then you went against what you considered weird, and now how do you feel?"

Without thinking, I tell him honestly, "I feel good. I mean, afterward I felt embarrassed, but now—"

"Now you're ready for round three?" he teases.

"More like a shower. I was a mess after my run, and now I'm just disgusting."

"You also need to get back to work. I'll talk to you later."

After we hang up, my phone displays five notifications of missed messages from Brooke. I look at the time and can't believe I was on the phone with him for over two hours.

When I open up the messaging app, I tell Brooke, "Hey, sorry I missed your messages. I'm about to hop in the shower, but I was wondering if you could come over tonight around eight thirty, after I put the girls down. Landon has the food critic coming tonight so he will be working really late, and there's something I need to tell you."

chapter eight

"SO WHAT IS SO IMPORTANT THAT YOU COULDN'T JUST TELL ME OVER THE phone?" Brooke asks when I walk down the stairs after putting the girls down to bed.

"This calls for wine." I go straight to the kitchen and pull a bottle of white out of the fridge. I walk back into the living room and hand Brooke a glass before sitting next to her and taking a big gulp of my chardonnay. She watches me with curiosity, and when I swallow down the alcohol, I make my confession. "I had phone sex today."

She looks at me like I'm an idiot, and her brows cinch together as she mocks me, saying, "Wow. Good for you. You finally got to first base with your husband."

"Cute," I snark. "But it wasn't with Landon."

Her eyes shoot open. "What?"

I take another drink.

"Hold up. Rewind," she says. "Who the hell did you have phone sex with?"

"Remember in Vegas when we were all hanging out and Kristen mentioned that website she uses for research? The fetish one?"

"Yeah."

"Well . . . I've been talking to a guy I met on there. We've actually been talking a lot . . . like every day for hours. And when we aren't talking, we're texting." I watch her as she takes a sip of her wine, her eyes never leaving mine, and then continue. "He's so different than us, Brooke. I mean, everything about how he views people and the world. Every conversation I have with him is so interesting."

"Blah blah," she says as she wags her hand. "Get to the part where these interesting, philosophical conversations turn into phone sex."

"Well, obviously I met him through that fetish site, and I've been asking him a lot of questions about the things he's into and stuff, and I don't know, I'm not even sure how it happened, but before I knew it, we were . . . well . . . you know!"

"No. I don't know. I've been sitting at home all day cleaning and being a mom while you're over here having phone sex with some dude you met on a fetish site. I expect full details because apparently your life is way more interesting than mine."

"What do you want to know?"

"First off, what does this guy look like? Have you even seen a picture of him?"

I grab my laptop, quickly log in to my account, and pull up his profile picture.

"He looks suspect, Tori. That guy looks way too normal."

I laugh. "That's exactly what I said too, but then he sent me this other photo when I questioned him." I then open the picture of him holding the piece of paper with my name on it, and when Brooke looks at it, she bursts out laughing.

"You're not into ass eating? I totally pegged you as an ass muncher."

"That's so gross."

"So that's the guy?"

I nod. "His name is Alec. He lives across the river from you."

"He looks older," she notes.

"He's forty-one."

"Yum!"

"I know, right? When did older guys with graying hair become so sexy?"

She closes the lid to the laptop and says, "When we started getting older." Brooke folds her legs underneath her and then pulls one of the throw blankets over her lap, making herself comfortable before asking, "So, what's this guy like?"

"Honestly . . . he's addicting. Maybe it's just because he's someone new and it's exciting to get to know him, but he's also very blunt. He has no reservations when it comes to talking about sex. He speaks of it so casually and openly."

I continue to tell her about his fetishes, his family, and the dirty things he says to me. We're like two teenage girls, gossiping and giggling as I divulge all I can about Alec. She gets swept away in the allure just as easily as I do every time Alec is on my mind—which is often. She even opens the laptop back up just so she can drool over his photo. When I finish off my glass of wine, I add, "He's seriously like nothing I've ever experienced in a person before."

"But what about Landon?" she questions, her tone sobering.

"It's not like I'm hanging out with him. I'll never meet the guy. I'm just having a little fun," I tell her. "I mean, guys turn to other women to get off when they watch porn, so . . ."

"So Alec is your version of porn?"

Shrugging my shoulders with a light smirk on my face, I say, "Men are visual, women are emotional. So yeah, he's porn."

"Well, I can see why he's addicting. Maybe I should create an account on that site and get my own Alec." And just as she says this, my phone chimes with an incoming text.

Alec: Miss you.

I smile and then hold the phone out so she can read the text. "All throughout the day, either I'm texting or he is."

"'Miss you'?" she questions suspiciously.

"It's just something we say. It's either 'Miss you' or 'Thinking about you' and stuff like that."

"So basically you guys are like infatuated high schoolers on a hormone overload?"

"Pretty much," I agree and then text him back.

Me: Miss you too.

Alec: What are you doing?

Me: Hanging out with my girlfriend, chitchatting, and drinking wine.

Alec: Any interesting topics?

"What's he saying?" Brooke questions and then scoots against me so she can read the text exchange.

"Should I tell him he's the topic?"

"Totally," she eagerly encourages, and as I type my response, I tell her, "We're acting like children, you know?"

Me: Nothing too interesting. You might have come up once.

"We act like kids because something exciting is finally happening in our predictable lives," she responds when I send the text to Alec.

Alec: What did you tell her?

Me: That you're an elderly, foul-mouthed sexual deviant. LOL!

Alec: This elderly man just might sit you on his lap and feed you a lollipop.

Brooke and I nearly belly-over with laughter.

"Why does something so perverted come across as sexy?" she questions.

"I don't know. Half the shit he says to me should be icky, but coming from him, it never feels that way."

Me: Brooke thinks you're sexy.

"Oh, my God! You did *not* just send that?"

I continue to laugh. "Relax, he has no idea who I am. He doesn't even know my last name. Plus, he thinks I'm single with no kids."

"What? Does he know what you do for a living?"

"Yes, but I haven't told him my pen name." She looks at me with her mouth ajar, and I attest, "I'm just having fun."

Alec: Sexy, huh? Way to stroke my ego. I'll just have to tuck her into my back pocket.

"He can tuck me in other places as well," she quips with a wink.

Me: If she's in your back pocket, where am I?

Alec: Where do you want to be?

"Yeah, Tori. Tell him where you want to be."

"You're worse than he is," I jokingly chastise.

Brooke and I continue to goof around while texting Alec. We are just two girls teasing around with a boy, the way young adolescents would do. We may be women in our thirties, but girls will be girls no matter what age they are. At least that's how we function, which is why we have always been such good friends. Brooke totally gets me where others might look down their noses at me for acting immature.

Alec: I need to get going. You girls enjoy the rest of your night.

Me: Where are you off to?

Alec: A party.

A pang of something needles me. I'm unable to put a word to it, but it's a multitude of pieces of shock, jealousy, surprise, let down, inferiority, irritation, hurt, and insecurity that make up this raw emotion that pricks me. Maybe it's the denial I have about this guy who seems so genuine and nice. I know this part about him, but from everything we've talked about and his personality, it's so difficult for me to see him as this emotionless man that can go and sleep with random people. A man who doesn't care to even get to know these people he's doing this with. To me, the type of man who does that should come across as an insincere asshole, which is nothing like who Alec is to me. Alec spends hours on end talking to me and texting. He asks me questions and takes the time to answer mine.

"A party?" Brooke questions, and I explain to her what Alec told me about the exclusive sex club scene he's a part of. She listens in astonishment, the same way I did when Alec first told me about it. "But you said he got off on the phone with you today, and he still needs more? Is he like an addict or something?"

"I asked him if he was, but he assured me he wasn't," I explain. "He said he has a high sex drive but he gets off more on the thrill of sex with strangers, with watching people have sex, and with people watching him."

Alec: Are you still there?

Me: Yeah, sorry.

I respond when I realize the length of pause I took, and then the phone rings with his call.

"Hey."

"Is everything okay?"

I note the softness to his voice, a contradiction to his normal husky tone.

"Yes." Brooke then stands to excuse herself to the restroom, and I begin to ramble, "I just didn't know how to respond, and then Brooke asked what you meant by 'party' and I tried explaining to her what you had told me about it."

"Does it bother you?"

"No," I answer, but it feels like a lie. He doesn't say anything, and when the silence grows, I falter a little, saying "I don't know. I mean . . . maybe it does a little."

"Why?"

I deflect off my unsettled feelings and put it on him. "I guess it worries me, the fact that you're spreading yourself around. Aren't you worried?"

"Everything in life comes with risks, Victoria. But this is a calculated risk. I'm safe, my partners are safe, everyone is tested. It's not as if we are meeting up in sketchy underground clubs."

"No?"

"No."

"Then where?"

"Different places," he tells me. "Tonight I'll be at the XV Beacon."

"The XV?" I question because the XV Beacon is a luxury boutique hotel in the heart of Boston. It caters to the sophisticated and distinguished and has a rich history in the city. "That hotel doesn't seem like the one to accommodate a sex party."

"You'd be surprised, my dear. In fact, the Gilbert Stuart suite is host to our gathering twice a year."

"And they allow that?"

"A person of the 'they' you refer to is a member. So, yes, they allow. It's not like what you are imagining though. We aren't getting trashed off booze and drugs and having obscenely loud fuckapades."

An uncomfortable giggle slips past my lips because I have no idea what these parties are like.

"But I don't want to make you feel uncomfortable, and when you went quiet on me, I was worried I had done just that."

"It's just weird. Not you, just . . . I guess it's because I don't know that side of you. I mean, you've told me, but our interactions have painted you in a particular light, so it's hard for me to imagine you otherwise."

"Does it bother you?"

Nothing he does should bother me. He owes me nothing, and it would be foolish of me to assume that he should.

"No. I have no right to judge you. It's not like you ever hid this from me. You've been transparent from our very first conversation."

He takes a pause, and I can hear the clinking of keys and a car door shutting. A few more long seconds of nothingness pass before he finally speaks.

"It's something I need."

"I know," I murmur. "I didn't mean to make you feel like you had to defend who you are to me. I'm sorry."

He starts his car. "I'll talk to you later."

Setting my phone down, my mind runs wild with thoughts of what tonight would look like if I were a fly on the wall in that suite. How many people? What do they look like? Do they talk before they fuck? Will Alec be having sex or just getting himself off while watching others? I even wonder about the little things. What kind of car does he drive? What is he wearing? I tell myself these are normal thoughts to have about a picture I've never seen and have to create in my head to form a semblance of understanding.

When Brooke returns from the bathroom, I tell her my thoughts as she sits and listens. She assures me it's normal to be curious and that she's curious as well.

"He'll be at the XV," I tell her. "What if I went too?"

"Can you even do that?"

"No, I'm not saying go to the party. That wouldn't even be possible. But what if I went to see if I can catch a glimpse of him walking into the building?"

"Like a stalker?" she teases before smiling and enticing, "You totally should."

"You think so?"

"If it weren't for the kids, I would totally go with you. Yes. Go."

The mystery of who this guy is runs rampant, increasing my curiosity, and when I see the excitement in my best friend's eyes, I get the courage I need to go and check out this stranger I've come to know.

"You don't mind staying here with the girls?"

"Not at all."

I leap off the couch to grab my purse and keys. "I won't be gone long," I call out from over my shoulder as I rush to the garage.

Driving through the night and into the city, I go a little faster than the speed limit, hoping I can beat him there. He's battling city traffic for his whole drive, whereas I'm only battling it for part of mine.

My heart races, and my palms sweat as I grip the steering wheel. I feel as if I'm on a crazy adventure.

I kind of am though.

This whole week has been crazy. It's strange to think about how much I've come to know this guy in a matter of days. But Brooke was spot-on—it should be no surprise that I'm as enamored as I am. Alec is the wild card in my predictable life. He's thrown my daily routine off-kilter, and for me, it's exciting when I don't know what to expect.

So I drive.

Headlights pass me by in a city so alive with people. I wind through the zigzag streets as my car's GPS gives me directions, and I soon find myself pulling up along the curb across the street from the entrance to the hotel. Sky-high buildings line the narrow city street, and when I turn my car off, I scan the area, but Alec isn't among any of the people walking along the sidewalk.

The valet is in mere reach of me. I watch as cars pull up and the attendants open the doors to reveal the passengers. One by one, but none are Alec until a dark silver SUV pulls up. I inch my head closer to my car door window as he walks over to the valet stand to say something to one of the attendants. Finally, some of my questions have answers.

I know what kind of car he drives, and I know what he's wearing. A navy, collared, button-down shirt, which is tucked into a pair of dark gray slacks. I didn't expect to him to be so pulled together, but he is, and that esoteric pang returns in my chest.

Up until this moment, he's been someone I've created in my head—a fictitious character that lives inside my phone and on the computer, but now, seeing him, he's no longer imaginary.

He's real.

Stepping out of the safety of the phone and into reality, he never truly existed until now. Because it's now that I can see him, and if I were standing next to him and took a breath, he'd have a scent. And if I touched him, he'd have temperature.

I slouch down in my seat as I continue to watch his every move. The night's shadow reveals a slightly unshaven jawline and perfectly styled hair that's a tad long on top, not the tightly clipped style Landon has.

He turns to walk away from the valet cart, but he quickly stops in his tracks when his eyes find me. I freeze.

Fuck!

I'm paralyzed in mortification, holding my breath and wondering if he can even see me well enough to know if it's me or just some random person. He stands and stares right at me while he slips his valet ticket into his wallet and then shoves it into his back pants pocket. Only seconds pass, but it feels like minutes, possibly hours as I listen to the thumping of my heart against my chest. I notice the side of his mouth lift in a sly smirk before he opens the door and walks into the hotel.

As soon as he's out of sight, I release the breath I've been holding on to and drop my head into my hands, muttering to myself, "Oh, my God. Oh, my God."

He totally knew it was me, and now I look like some desperate stalker, which is exactly what I didn't want to look like. And what the hell was that look on his face? He must think I'm as pathetic as I feel right now. I cannot believe I am doing a drive-by this late at night on a guy I don't even know. I'm a thirty-two-year-old woman acting like a complete idiot. There is no way he's going to talk to me now that he's caught me spying on him. I mean, who does this?

I'll tell you who . . . me. A middle-aged housewife who was desperate for a little bit of fun.

Not five minutes after I return home does Landon walk in. My heartbeat spikes even further through the adrenaline rushing through me, and the heat of fear flushes my face when he looks at me.

Can he see I've just done something wrong?

Was it even wrong? I mean, it's not like I met Alec face to face, talked to him, or even got close enough to touch him. No. All I did was park across the street and watch him. Just a girl having a little fun—innocent fun—that's all.

When Brooke heads out, I use the high I'm still riding on and sling my arms around Landon's neck, asking, "How did it go?"

"It couldn't have gone better."

"How long until the review comes out?"

"Possibly next week."

I follow him as he walks into the bathroom and watch him undress before he steps inside the shower. With the excitement from tonight still coursing through me, I strip my clothes off and join him in the shower. He's been working so hard lately and has been under an exorbitant amount of stress, so I offer him some much-needed relief.

"Not tonight," he says when I run my hands up his chest, not even giving himself a chance to get in the mood. "I've got nothing left in me after the long day I've had."

I could push him, but I don't want to irritate him, so I step out of the shower to allow him time to unwind.

Landon joins me in bed a while later and falls asleep instantly.

I roll onto my side, away from him, and allow the thoughts of the crazy day I had to keep me awake. My mind drifts to the phone sex, to chatting with Brooke, to sneaking around in the city, to seeing Alec, and then ending at Alec's cryptic smirk.

That damn smirk.

What was the thought behind it?

I replay it over and over in my head. The way he looked at me, the way he smiled. I then go back to our phone call before I decided to go see him. I could tell by the concern in his voice that he didn't want to make me feel uncomfortable with the fact that he would be fucking random women tonight.

But then that look in his eye and that damn smirk . . . I can't stop thinking about it.

I grow even more restless the more I allow my mind to fester over all this. I reach for my phone on my nightstand and flick the switch to silence it. Looking over my shoulder, I see Landon has rolled over with his back facing me. His breaths are slow and deep as he sleeps, and when I roll back over, I cautiously type out my text and send it to Alec.

Me: Are you awake?

Staring at the screen, it eventually fades to black, and I can't help but wonder if he's still at the party. If he's having sex while his phone is buzzing from the pocket of his pants that are lying on the floor. But I wonder no more when my phone lights up with a text from him, reviving me instantly.

Alec: Why are you up so late?

Me: Can't sleep.

I wonder who's going to be the first to mention the elephant in the room, and when he doesn't message me back, I bite the bullet.

Me: I'm sorry about tonight.

Alec: Sorry? For what?

Is he really going to torture me by making me spell it out for him? Can't we both be coy, acknowledge my idiocy, and move on, never making a mention of it again?

Me: For coming to see you.

Alec: Tell me why you came.

In my exhaustion, lying in the warmth of my bed where I had two orgasms with him earlier, I throw the lies out the window and confess.

Me: I guess I wanted to know you were real.

Alec: I'm not real to you?

Me: You are now.

Alec: I've always been real, Victoria.

Landon shifts, and I turn around to make sure he's still asleep before returning to my phone.

Me: Can I ask you something?

Alec: Anything.

Me: You saw me watching you and you gave me a look . . . a smirk. Why?

Alec: Because you came to me.

My eyes absorb those five words until they swim out of focus and the pang I felt earlier returns.

Alec: Come to me again.

Me: It's late. And I'm nervous.

Alec: I'll wait then. I don't want you to be scared with me.

Me: You're just so different than what I'm used to.

Alec: And how do you think I feel? You're nothing like what I'm used to either. Your views, your modesty, your resistance, your values. I share your same hesitations.

Me: I guess I never saw it from your standpoint.

Alec: Let's talk more tomorrow. It's late and you need to sleep.

Me: Good night.

Alec: Good night, Victoria.

Setting my phone back on my nightstand, I close my eyes, but sleep refuses to find me as I wonder what it is I'm doing with this game I've created with Alec.

chapter nine

Brooke and I pile into the back of her husband's Escalade with the kids. It's a tradition with our two families that we visit the Belkin Family Farm at the peak of autumn every year. Landon was the first to bring me here back when we were dating, and I fell in love with it. It wasn't until Brooke and Chris had their son that we all started going together.

The three kids situate themselves in the very back while Brooke and I buckle into the second row bucket seats. The guys are up front, chatting about the New England Patriots game last week, oblivious to the mayhem of laughter as Emily and Jill play with Ryder. We head south, and the drive takes a little over a half-hour before we arrive at the 180-acre farm, which boasts train rides, hay pyramids, farm animals, mazes, hay rides, face painting, and more. It's enough to keep the kids entertained for the whole day, but the main reason for our visits each year is the apple, pear, and pumpkin picking.

"You have no idea how good it feels to finally have a day off," Landon tells me as we walk hand in hand.

I look to him as the kids run around in excitement, trying to decide what they want to do first, and smile. "Remember the first time you brought me here?"

"How could I forget? That group of kids caught us kissing with my hand up your shirt while we were in the orchards."

My head falls against his arm as I recall the squealing and laughter that erupted as Landon groped me. He thought we'd be well hidden among the plum trees, since their picking season had already passed, but a group of wanderers found us. I was flushed with embarrassment but Landon laughed it off. Those memories feel like a lifetime ago. No longer are we two young kids making out in the orchard. We are now husband and wife—parents—who are consumed by busy and stressful careers and who are, more often than not, passersby in the early mornings and late nights. Sure, we had spontaneous sex the other night, but that was a rare occurrence.

I can't remember the last time we spent a day like this as a family, so I do my best to focus on Landon and the girls, but thoughts of Alec creep in when I least expect them to. The girls get their faces painted, Brooke and I laugh as they jump wildly in the bounce houses, and I cuddle into Landon's arms as we go on a hay ride. Hours pass, and yet fleeting thoughts of Alec infiltrate moments where he shouldn't belong. I tell myself it's because this is the first day since we crossed paths that we haven't talked. It feels strange when every day this week has been consumed with him. We can barely go twenty minutes without, at the very least, sending a text. And now that Landon has a day off, I'm no longer afforded the luxury of time to converse with my new *friend*.

"I didn't take my birth control pill this morning," Brooke tells me quietly as we stand among a mass of Fuji trees.

My eyes widen when I look at the huge smile on her face. "So you're going for baby number two?"

"Chris has been asking for a while, and I don't know, when I woke up this morning it finally felt right."

I look over to our husbands: Landon has Jill on his shoulders so she can reach the apples toward the top of one of the trees, and Chris is watching his son as Emily helps him pick apples from the lower branches.

"Chris is a great dad," I note to which Brooke responds, "They both are."

And they are. We are two very lucky girls who have found husbands who are wonderful, hands-on fathers. I've never doubted Landon in our marriage, and I still don't, but even as I watch him, there's a needling inside of me that's creating an unfamiliar friction in my stomach.

It's an uneasy feeling I can't rid myself of—a noose that restricts me from reveling in the joy I should be feeling in this moment. So, I turn to Brooke, as if she's my security blanket, and focus on her.

"I am so happy for you," I tell her honestly.

"Thank you."

We continue to stroll through the rows of trees, filling our buckets with several varieties of apples. And when we are overflowing, Landon and Chris head over to the Cider Taproom to grab a couple beers while Brooke and I take the kids to bag up the fruit. The day begins to fade into evening, and when exhaustion kicks in, we load up our apples and the pumpkins and head back.

The kids fall asleep instantly, and with the guys sitting up front, I debate pulling out my phone and texting Alec, but I refrain. Anticipation grows as I think about when I'll be able to talk to him again, and then I mentally scold myself, asking why I'm so needy to talk to him. I tell my conscience that he's like a new toy, and today was the first day it's been taken away, so naturally I just want to have it back—to play.

By the time we get home, it's past eight, and when I ask Landon what we are going to do for dinner, he looks at me, utterly drained and says, "There is no way I'm cooking."

"I don't blame you," I laugh. I know the last thing he wants to do after preparing for the *Times* food critic is cook. A surge of deceit awakens in me when I see an opportunity to indulge in my new obsession and offer, "Why don't I call in an order at that little Italian restaurant down the street. If you'll get the girls showered and in bed, I'll go grab dinner for us."

"What about the kids?"

"Just give them a Lunchable or something quick," I tell him as I grab the keys to my car and head out.

As I pull out of the driveway, I'm already placing my dinner order, but it's the second call that causes my heart to pump small doses of adrenaline through my veins. When I hit the first red stoplight is when Alec answers and all the anxiety within me begins to sedate.

"Hey you."

"Hi," I respond, smiling without delay.

"Can you hold on for just a moment?"

"Sure." The light turns green, and I start driving while I listen to muffled voices followed by a door shutting and then silence.

"Okay, I'm back."

"If this is a bad time, I can let you go."

"No," he says. "I'm over at my brother's house and my nieces were singing along to some Disney movie, so I stepped outside where it's quiet."

I pull into the lot of the restaurant, park away from all the other cars, and kill the engine.

"What are you doing, Victoria?"

Releasing a heavy breath of tension, I close my eyes and lean my head back as thoughts tumble around. Confliction and contentment battle for the upper hand, but neither is victor. This has always been innocent fun—just harmless entertainment—but this isn't benign if I'm hiding out in the shadows of a parking lot just to talk to Alec.

"What are you thinking about?" Alec's voice is silk, slipping through the phone and caressing my ear softly.

"You." I shouldn't be so honest. I should lie. I should hang up. I should go home.

"I've been thinking about you too."

Don't say that, Alec. Don't encourage me.

"You have?"

"I told my sister-in-law about you tonight."

"What did you say?"

"Nothing much," he tells me. "Only that I met a girl who's piqued my interest."

"Alec . . ." I murmur breathlessly around the flutter he invokes.

"Talk to me."

"This isn't me," I admit. "I don't act this way with anyone."

"How do you mean?"

"I'm not a needy person. But with you . . . if I'm not talking to you, I'm thinking about you. You're probably the most intense person I've ever met. You're all-consuming—addicting—and I don't know what to do with that because it brings out this neediness inside me that's never been there before." My words fall freely from my lips as I make my confessions. "I feel a little crazy here because we've only been talking for a week and I'm so unsure of everything I used to be so certain of."

"Does that scare you?"

"Yeah . . . it does. And I'm not one who scares easily, which is why I feel so thrown off by you."

He doesn't respond immediately, but when he does, his words surprise me when he says, "You scare me too."

My laugh is one of nervousness and not of amusement. "How on earth do I scare you?"

"Because I'm not needy either, but I can't stop thinking about you. You're nothing like the women I go for. You're the opposite of what attracts me, and yet, the attraction I have for you is profound and difficult for me to understand."

"This is crazy."

"Why?"

"Because," I say as I lean forward and rest my head on the steering wheel. "Because this is really fast. Too fast."

"Look, I like you. But if this is too much for you, then we can end it now."

The thought of walking away doesn't sit right with me. I'm still curious about him. There's still so much left for me to explore and learn from him. I'm just not ready to close the door on him just yet.

"No. I don't want to end this. Today just shook me up a little bit. I didn't expect to feel this pull. I mean, I should be able to go a day without talking to you. I hate feeling this way because it makes me feel like a little weak girl."

"I like that you feel weak for me."

I shake my head, laugh under my breath, and tease, "You only like it because it feeds that big ass ego of yours."

"I made you smile though, didn't I?"

And he did, but I still feel so torn when I shouldn't. There's nothing

I should be conflicted about. I mean, I've never even met this guy, so why do I even feel like this? Why am I even here?

I need to get home.

"Can we talk later?"

"We can talk whenever you want. I'll be here at my brother's for another hour or so, and then I'll be home."

"I'm sorry for calling you like this and being so emotional."

"Don't ever be sorry for calling me. If you need to talk, I want you talking to *me*," he states. "And it's okay that you're feeling emotional—you're human."

"Thanks for listening to me."

After we hang up, I run inside and pick up dinner before heading back home. The weight I felt earlier is no longer there. I got my Alec fix, and when I return home, Landon and I sit down at the dining table and eat our dinner. We speak briefly about our day and then resume our meal in silence. I begin to think that if it were Alec sitting across from me, our food would probably go cold because we wouldn't be able to stop talking. Landon and I used to be that way. We could talk for hours on end, but somewhere along the way, we've stopped talking.

"Remember when we used to stay up all night talking on the phone?" I ask between bites.

"Mmm hmm." He nods as he chews his food.

"I miss talking to you." My words catch his attention, and after he takes a swallow, he says, "What do you mean? We talk all the time."

"I mean talk about something other than kids and work."

"Tor, that's our life right now. If we aren't consumed with the kids, then we're consumed with our jobs. There's very little time left in between."

I set my fork down and look over to all the buckets of apples that are sitting on the large kitchen island. I know Landon is going to wash them and create a whole menu on how he plans on using them, but I take this as an opportunity.

"Can I help you with whatever you're planning on doing with the apples?"

"Really?" His eyes light in surprise because this is the first year I've offered to help him. "But you hate to cook."

"Well, it's about time I try something new then. And maybe it will give us something to talk about," I tell him with a wink, but it feels like a farce.

As we sit here and eat the rest of our dinner in silence, my mind drifts back to the early years and how it used to be. I blindly thought we'd never change, that we'd never lose the spark, that we'd never run out of things to say, and that we'd never be able to keep our hands off each other. I miss the newness and the excitement that comes along with it, and I wish I knew how to get it back.

chapter ten

I SMILE NERVOUSLY AS I LOOK INTO HIS DARK BLUE EYES, BUT HIS LIPS DON'T RESEMBLE mine because his nerves don't taunt him like mine do. He's spent the past ten minutes or so trying to convince me to move the computer back so he can see all of me, which is now completely naked, but I'm much too modest to expose my body to him—a body that wears the marks of bearing two children.

"Let me see you, Victoria," he says as he looks intently at me through the screen of my laptop.

Biting my lip, I shake my head with a coy, "No."

"Why are you afraid to show me your body?"

I cover my face with my hands and laugh nervously.

"Look at me."

Dropping my hands, I tilt my head over to my laptop, which sits on the bed next to my face. Alec picks up his computer and sets it on a desk or nightstand, angling it to focus on the bed. I can't look away as my skin prickles in excitement when I see his fully naked body walk over and sit down on his bed with his back reclining against the leather headboard.

Every inch of his body is mine to look at now that we are video chatting. His lightly tanned skin is smooth over his long athletic cuts of muscle. He doesn't look into the camera when he takes his one hand and grips it firmly around the base of his erection. He stares at himself as he pulls his hand up around the tip and slides it down. Heavy breaths roll through my body as I slide my hands over my breasts while I take in the images of him pleasuring himself.

His head turns toward me and looks at me straight on. "You like watching me touch myself?"

"Mmm hmm," I moan, pinching my nipples between my fingers.

"Lick your fingers and rub your clit."

I slip my fingers into my mouth, spread my legs, and drop my hand down to my core. The first touch sparks a shock of heat through me and my body jerks upward. "Oh, God." I plant my feet flat on the mattress and continue to tease myself.

"Look into the camera," he says, and when I drop my head back to the side to look at him, he widens his legs and is now pumping his cock with more force. The muscles in his arms constrict as heat crawls up his neck. "Tell me how wet you are."

I avoid talking because it's not something I ever do during sex, and it feels awkward. So instead, I slip a finger inside of me, moaning out in desire as I close my eyes and imagine it's his cock filling me.

"Look into the camera," he repeats, directing my attention back to him. "Tell me how wet you are. Talk to me," he continues to press through his staggering breaths as he jerks off.

Swallowing against my dry throat, I muster up a tiny shred of boldness and speak. "I'm insanely wet for you, Alec."

My words elicit a low growl from him, enticing me as I lift my hips against my hand, grinding my clit and shoving a second finger inside myself.

"I'd like to taste that pussy of yours."

"Yes," I breathe as my body begins to climb. I writhe, tangling the sheets beneath me as I roll around in reckless passion.

"Have my cock nestled deep inside you, to feel how tightly you fit around me."

His words spur me, growing me even more wet as we both watch each other through the computer.

"You want to feel my cock in that wet cunt of yours?"

"Fuck," I mewl in response to his filthy mouth, losing all control. "Yes. I want to feel you so bad."

"Say it."

"I want you, Alec."

Our eyes remain locked as we spit our explicit desires, overtaken by rapturous heat. Everything around me fades into delirium as I focus solely on Alec. His face contorts at the same time I feel the bites of ecstasy on my overly sensitive skin.

"Don't let yourself go yet," he demands. "I want you to watch me cum."

I slow myself, withholding the orgasm that's building in my bloodstream. I watch as Alec's hand moves in rigid, erratic strokes along his thick cock while he stares at me intently. He bears down, gritting his teeth, and then grunts as he goes. His abs constrict tightly as streams of cum shoot onto his stomach. Every sound coming out of him dissolves all my restraint, and I don't even wait for him to tell me to continue when I shove my fingers back into my pussy.

I never stop watching him as I eagerly work my body up to the knife's edge, taking my other hand and rolling my fingers over my clit. My thighs quiver as my climax builds painfully slow and then erupts out of nowhere. The pleasure is beyond containment, and I pinch my eyes shut as I grind my hips into my hand, arousal coating my fingers as my body sweats through quakes of head-to-toe euphoria.

The moment the feeling begins to subside, I grow needy for more, fiending for the next fix like some insatiable junkie. Maybe I am. And there's no doubt that Alec is my enabler as he encourages, "Don't stop, Victoria. I want to watch you again."

He drapes a sheet over his legs, grabs his computer, and sets it on his lap. His face is all that fills the screen as he watches me. I glance to the corner of the video chat box to see that no longer am I hidden from view as I've shifted farther away from the camera, revealing everything down to my hips. But I don't care anymore, because I'm no longer me as I rub my clit and squeeze my breast.

"Talk to me, Alec," I blindly request, craving his dirty words, words no man has ever used with me before. "Give me your voice."

"Fuck, you look so hot right now." His voice is low and guttural, coated thickly in voracity. "My cock is still rock hard. Watching you, listening to your sex-filled pants, if I were there I'd flip you on your stomach, yank your ass up in the air, and pound my dick inside your pussy."

"Yes."

"You'd like that, wouldn't you?"

"Mmmm."

"You're not so vanilla, are you, Victoria? You like imagining me fucking you like an animal, don't you?" he taunts, and in this moment, if he were in this bed with me, I'd let him do just about anything to my body because I'm suspended so far above reality that I'm someone else entirely.

"Yes."

"You like the thought of me fucking you like a dog?"

"Shit," I blurt when my body peaks again.

My eyes fall shut as I ride out another intense climax while Alec continues his affliction of words. "I'd then shove my thumb into your ass, filling both your holes. I'd love to see how you'd squirm under my touch."

I'm completely under his spell as his foul words fill the air around me, filtering in through my erotic moans. Alec never stops talking as I float through orgasm after orgasm, feeding my outrageous appetite. I never knew I was so starved until now—I could go all day.

Alec is a whole new experience, nothing like what I've ever had before. He's unfiltered and raw, debasing me with his words that should offend me but don't. Instead, they intoxicate me and leave me wanting more.

My body collapses in a heap of sweaty, tingly mush. I roll onto my side, facing the computer screen, and attempt to catch my breath. My damp temple lies on my arm while I, once again, look into Alec's midnight blue eyes.

As I fall back down to reality, I fight the nervous giggle that threatens to escape. "That was slightly embarrassing," I mutter as I cover my naked body with a sheet.

"There's nothing to be embarrassed about. You're so fucking sexy."

"No."

"If I tell you something, no matter what it is, don't reject it as if it's meaningless."

Propping my head onto my hand, I stare at him, mesmerized in a way I can't explain.

"What are you doing to me?" I ask, not really expecting him to respond, but he does.

"I should ask you the same thing," he says. "What are you doing tomorrow?"

"I need to work. I haven't written in over a week because you have me so distracted."

"Let me distract you for one more day. Meet me tomorrow morning for a cup of coffee."

The mere idea excites me, but I know I can't. The moment I meet him is the moment this all becomes real, and I can't let that happen. I've already pushed my limit of fun with this guy, and if I meet him, I'm doing nothing but leading him on.

"Stop thinking and say yes."

"Alec . . ."

"Pavement Coffeehouse on Commonwealth. Ten o'clock."

The moment the words are out of his mouth, his lips flick in a subtle smile, and then he disconnects our video chat.

As I close the lid to the computer, my heart jumps out of my chest when I hear the door leading out to the garage open.

Holy fuck!

I bolt out of bed, sling the comforter over the messy sheets, grab my clothes, and run into the bathroom.

"Tor," Landon calls out as I throw my clothes on in a hurried panic.

"Going to the bathroom. Be out in a sec," I holler.

Shit!

After I zip my pants, I flush the unused toilet and open the door before quickly washing the sex off my hands with some fragranced soap.

"Nice hair," Landon jokes when he walks into the bathroom, and I respond, "Lazy morning."

I pump a little lotion into my hands, further hiding the scent of deceit as my pulse races wildly under my skin.

"What have you been doing?"

"Nothing much," I delude. "Just lying around, but I'm about to get to work. What are you doing home in the middle of the day?"

He then holds out the newspaper I didn't even notice he was holding. "The review is out."

His smile gives everything away.

"Gimme," I say and then snatch the paper out of his hands. I thumb through until I find the review. "Oh, my God!" I squeal and then read aloud, "Four stars. *New York Times* Critics' Pick. Chin-Chin is a radical reimagining of the grand style of French dining." Looking at Landon, his face is filled with elation, and I couldn't be more proud of him. "Congratulations, babe. This is just . . ." I look back down at the article and then to him again, "This is just so amazing."

"The phone has been ringing off the hook all morning. Our reservations are booked five weeks out. If this continues, we'll be booked through the holidays."

"You're kidding?"

"This is it, babe," he says with an exultant smile, cradling my cheeks in his hands. "This is what we've been working so hard for."

"I can't believe it. I mean, I knew you and Damon were worthy of it. I just . . ." Every word falls short of what I'm trying to express. Before I even met Landon on the set of FOX25, food has been his passion. He's dedicated his life to it, and now he's getting the recognition he deserves. He's incredibly talented, and he and Damon, the executive chef, are a force to be reckoned with. The time away from me and the girls was never in vain, it was always for *this*.

He kisses me, lips upon mine, and I can taste his mirth as it fills my mouth. Warmth spreads through my chest, and with my arms wrapped around his waist, I soften into his firm grip on me as we both revel in this monumental achievement.

Our kiss grows more intimate, his hands roam down to my ass, and my vision blurs.

"I only have a short while until I have to get back to the restaurant," his lips mumble over mine.

Taking advantage of this rare moment of sexual spontaneity between us, my fingers work fast to unbutton his shirt. Still reeling from the four orgasms I just had, I don't even dare to hesitate with Landon as I temper the swelling of guilt.

We stumble into the bedroom while peeling off each other's clothing, and when we edge up to the bed, Landon reaches down and pulls back the comforter to reveal the mess of sheets beneath right before we fall down onto the mattress.

Landon props up on his arms with a sly smile. "What were you doing in this bed to tear it all up?"

I can feel my heart in my throat and I wonder if he can see right through me. Suddenly, this game with Alec is no longer a game. The truth slaps me across the face, leaving a ridiculing sting as its reminder that what I did with Alec was not as innocent as I've been leading myself to believe.

"Were you touching yourself?"

I give him a coquettish nod, and it clearly delights him, so I feed him more to cover my disgrace, telling him, "I've been missing you."

"What did you think about?"

"The time we made love in the back seat of your car." My lie comes much too easily.

He leans down to kiss my neck, and after a deep inhale, says, "I can smell your cum on the sheets. You have no idea how much that turns me on."

What have I done?

He takes my nipple into his mouth and slides his tongue over the tight flesh before sucking it. Rolling him onto his back, I attempt to rid myself of the shame as I throw my entire body into making love with him. As if the harder I fuck him, the more it erases what I've just done.

Closing my eyes, I bring his hands up to my breasts and encourage him to touch me as I moan loudly. I rock my hips into him, thrusting his cock deeper inside me and then I reach down with my hand to massage my clit.

"Damn, Tori," Landon breathes, and when I look down at him, he's watching me play with myself. I feel him thicken inside me, and he takes my hips in his hands and maneuvers me up and down over him at the same time he drives himself into me.

Stroking my clit faster, Landon's voice amplifies as he inches closer. I don't stop touching myself as I lean over so he can nip and suck on my nipples. I bounce my ass up and down until he loses control and bucks into me, filling me with his cum, groaning out his orgasm as I grind myself on top of him, cumming yet again.

My body falls, draping over his, and Landon bands his arms tightly around me. We remain like this for a while, with no words spoken, until he softens inside me. I roll off of him, feeling the ache between my legs, and I know I need to end this little stint with Alec before it goes any further.

"You're amazing, you know that?"

"Only because of you," I tell him.

We lie in bed for a little while longer, touching and kissing before he has to get back to work.

"I'll be home in time to have dinner with you and the girls tonight," he tells me as I walk him to the door.

I congratulate him again, and as soon as his car is out of sight, I take a quick shower, throw on some fresh clothes, and drive as fast as I can to Brooke's house, all while thoughts of me getting off with Alec and then my husband play through my head like a fucked-up Lifetime movie.

chapter eleven

"I'M SO STUPID," I UTTER THE MOMENT BROOKE OPENS HER FRONT DOOR TO FIND me standing on her porch.

She reaches out for me and leads me inside. "What happened?"

Shaking my head in disappointment, I tell her, "Things got really fucked up today." We walk into her living room and take a seat on the couch. "It never felt like I was doing anything wrong until today."

"You mean with Alec?"

"God, this is embarrassing." I lower my head, pressing my palms against my forehead before looking up at Brooke and admitting, "We had cyber sex through video chat today."

"You saw him getting off?"

I nod.

"And he watched you?"

"Yes. But that's not all. Landon came home right after. If he would've come home a couple minutes sooner . . . fuck."

She reaches for my hands that are knotted together. "What happened?"

"After I threw my clothes back on?" I respond in humorless humor. "He was so excited because the *Times* review came out today, and we wound up having sex in the same bed I just got off on with another guy. Landon actually smelled me on the sheets."

"Shit."

"I know," I screech in humiliation. "I lied and told him I was missing him this morning and was touching myself."

"Tori," she says in disbelief as she sits back.

"I need this to be over."

"I agree. I mean, it was funny at first, but if Landon found out, he'd—"

"I know. He'd be so pissed," I interject. "I just don't know how to end it. I mean, I feel bad because I've completely led this guy on. He even told his sister-in-law about me."

"It's only been a week. You don't think he has feelings for you, do you?"

"I do."

"Really?"

"I mean, it's so much more than our dirty calls. We talk for hours every single day. We've had so many deep conversations and light-hearted ones as well. So yeah, I think he has feelings for me. He even told me he did."

"Oh, my God," she exhales as she rakes her hands through her hair. "And what about you? Do you have feelings for him?"

I immediately shake my head, as if what she's inferring is completely insane. "I don't even know him."

"You're contradicting yourself. You know that, right? Because you just told me about how much you two talk and how deep your conversations are."

"But I've never spent any time with him." My words are a lame defense she sees through.

"I'm your best friend, Tori. Don't bullshit me."

I already know the answer though. I knew it before she even asked me, but I'm afraid if I say it out loud I'll give it life, and I can't do that. So I lie. "I mean, as a human, yeah, I care about not hurting his feelings because of my deception. He thinks he has a chance with me, but he has no idea I'm married with a family."

"So what are you going to do?"

"I don't know. I mean, do I just stop talking to him and avoid his calls, or do I tell him the truth before disappearing on him?"

"You're treading dangerous waters. Whatever you do, you need to do it now before this goes too far."

Confliction torments my conscience. On one hand, I know I need to end this and now, but on the other, I don't want to. I like Alec. I like talking to him, because he makes me feel so many things—he's exciting, he's unpredictable, and he brings out a side of me I've never known until now. I find myself looking at Landon and wishing he were more like Alec. More crass, more alive, more thrilling. The thing is, maybe Landon and I aren't as good as what I thought, because if we were, then why am I being drawn elsewhere? Through Alec, I'm starting to see the flaws in Landon—I'm starting to see the cracks in my marriage.

But I can't be the one to take a cleaver to our relationship, because I love Landon, because I love our family.

"Can I use your computer?"

"It's in Chris's office," Brooke tells me.

"Give me a moment, okay?"

"Take your time."

I make my way up the stairs and into the office. Sitting down at the desk, I look at the framed photos of Brooke's happy family and wonder how, in a matter of a few days, my happiness fell askew. As much as I hate the thought of no longer talking to Alec, I know it has to end because there is nowhere for this friendship to go.

After I log into my email account, I begin typing.

I've made a mistake, I write. *Everything I've ever told you has been the truth, everything except for two.* The words come easily through my fingers but pain my heart as my eyes prick with tears. I wipe them away as they fall down my cheeks, and I can't believe how difficult this is to do. I can't believe how much this is affecting me.

I never thought I could grow so attached to a person in a matter of a week, but you are like nothing I've ever experienced, so I guess I shouldn't be surprised that I feel the way I do—but I am surprised.

You've asked about my pen name many times, and I was always too afraid to reveal it to you because all it would take was one Google search for you to know my two lies. But these are the two reasons why I can no longer talk to you, why I probably should have never talked to you in the first place.

I am so sorry, Alec.

I never meant to lead you on. I'm a selfish woman.

My author name is Madilyn Kline. You can read my bio on my website and on Amazon. That bio will tell you the truth to my lies and expose me for the awful person I am.

Shame carves its way down my face and drips from my chin as I finish the email. Once done, I text Alec, fighting myself with every letter I type.

Me: Can you send me your email address?

His response comes immediately.

Alec: Why do you need my email?

Me: I need to send you something.

His next response doesn't come so quickly. Tears paint the passing seconds, and his next text breaks a piece of my heart.

Alec: Don't you dare send me a fucking Dear John letter.

But that's exactly what I'm sending, and it hurts me to know that even he can feel it.

Me: Just send me your email.

And he does.

And I type it in.

And I hit send before I talk myself out of it.

And I drop my head into my hands.

And I cry.

Why am I crying? Why does this feel like I'm losing something special? Why did I get so attached?

"You fell for him, didn't you?"

I look up to see Brooke standing in the doorway, and a second later she blurs behind my heart's ache.

"I don't know how this happened," I cry. "I love Landon. I do. I promise you, I love him."

"He's a good man."

"I know." I turn to look out the window as emotions run rampant, and I begin to laugh through the sadness. "I feel so stupid, crying over a guy I never even met. It's pathetic."

"It's not," she says as she walks over to me and leans against the desk. "You got lost in a fantasy, and fantasies have a way of playing tricks on our hearts. This guy made you feel something, and you clung to it like most would because it's new and exciting. Even I got swept away for a fleeting moment when you were telling me all about him. I had my own moment of weakness, and I'm sorry. I know I probably encouraged you when I shouldn't have. I wasn't a good friend."

"You didn't do anything wrong. I encouraged myself. But it never felt wrong until this afternoon when Alec and Landon collided within minutes of each other. Suddenly I was sneaking around and lying to Landon."

"Don't beat yourself up, Tori. You lost yourself for a moment, and like you said, it's not like you ever met the guy. It was one week of fun and a lot of orgasms," she says with a slip of laughter, which I slip into right along with her. "Did you call him?"

"No. I sent him an email," I tell her. "I wonder how pissed he's going to be when he finds out I have a family."

"Why did you tell him that? Why didn't you just say you're not interested anymore and that it's over?"

I shrug my shoulders. "Because I felt like he deserved the truth." I then turn from the window to face her. "I told him my pen name."

Her face drops.

"You don't want this to end, do you?"

"Yes," I mutter. "It's over."

"Then why did you give him a way to forever find you? Hmm? By giving him that name, you just gave him open access to you."

I'm like an alcoholic. I know I need to walk away and be done, but for some reason, I leave gaps along the way to recovery because although my mind knows what's best for me, my heart tells me something different.

"Be done with this," she says intently, "before something bad happens."

"Can I stay here for a while? I'm not ready to go home just yet."

"Of course. I'll go make us some coffee."

I pick up my cell and text Landon to see if he can pick up the girls from school. When he responds that he can, I tuck the phone into my pocket and head downstairs. I spend the rest of the afternoon allowing Brooke to distract me, but it's in vain as I sneak glimpses at my phone to see if Alec has responded to my email or has texted me. So far, nothing. He should know by now the liar I am, and the thought that I might never hear from him again punctures my heart.

Eventually the sun descends, Chris comes home from work, and Brooke cooks her family dinner, all the while I do my best to fake a smile and good conversation. As I sit on the couch and watch the evening news, my phone buzzes from my pocket. The vibration of what could be spikes my heart to thump in rapid succession. But two words is all it takes to kill the beats into paralysis.

Alec: Damn you.

I've been waiting for hours, wondering if I'd ever get a reaction to the email, and here it is. I'm consumed with a million thoughts as I stare down at my phone, and when I finally pull myself away, I see Brooke staring at me from the kitchen. My face heats as hidden sadness resurfaces, and I can't let Chris see me this vulnerable.

"I'll be right back," I say before I stand, grab my coat, and step out onto the back porch.

Me: I'm so sorry.

It's a lame response, but I don't know what else to say.

Alec: A wife?

Me: Yes.

Alec: A mother?

Me: Yes.

He then sends a photo text of a picture of me with some random fan that he must have found on the Internet. *He's been researching me.*

Me: I am so sorry I lied.

Alec: What the fuck are you doing? Are you looking for an affair or just looking to fuck with someone's feelings?

Me: Neither. I never meant for any of this to happen. I was only on that fetish site for research. I never expected anyone to message me, but it happened, and I'm so sorry.

Confliction multiplies as I try to remedy this situation when I know I shouldn't. I should ignore these texts. I should block his number. But I'm losing control as I attempt to convince him I'm not the bad person he thinks I am.

Alec: What do you want?

Me: I don't know.

Alec: Are you happy with your husband?

Delete this conversation, Tori. Don't respond. Don't lead him on. Just end it.

Me: I don't know.

What the hell am I doing?

The bitter cold seeps into my pores as I wait for a response—for anything—but nothing comes. Shivers eventually take over and I give up, doing everything I can to hold myself together when I walk back inside.

"I should get going," I announce.

"It was good seeing you, Tor," Chris says from the dining table. "Tell Landon I said hi."

"I will."

I give Ryder, their son, a hug and a kiss and then walk with Brooke to the front door.

"You'll feel better tomorrow," she assures along with a hug. "Go home, take a bath, and try to clear your head, okay?"

I nod, swallowing painfully through the knot in my throat as I fight back tears. She sees through me though.

"Don't beat yourself up. You're going to be fine. Call or text me if you need anything."

"Am I being stupid?"

"No. You're being human."

"Don't tell Chris."

"Never. You know what you tell me is ours and no one else's."

I take another hug and then hop in my car. Nothing can vanquish his response as it replays in my head again and again.

Damn you.

Why do those words punch my gut every time I think about them? I wish it were as easy as soaking in a bath to take this all away. I wish I never set up that stupid account. I wish so many useless wishes as I drive through Cambridge and into Belmont, and as if it was scripted perfectly, the moment I pull into my driveway, my phone buzzes.

Alec sends another photo he pulled from the Internet.

Alec: Fucking beautiful.

His words have a way of erasing reality, and I smile. It's unreal how fast my mood shifts, how powerful he is to do that. I park the car and text him back.

Me: You should hate me.

Alec: I should.

I then turn off my phone before walking in to the house because I can't guarantee my reaction if he were to text while I'm with Landon. When I walk in, I spot Landon sitting on the couch with my laptop open.

"Hey, babe," I say as casually as possible, as if it is simply any other day, but he doesn't respond. "Did you already put the girls down?"

"Yes."

"You okay?" I question as he closes the lid to the computer.

He then stands and walks into our bedroom, my stomach flipping with each step he takes.

What if he suspects something?

Paranoia claims me as her bitch as I follow to find him pacing across the room, so I do what I can to act normal, to act as if I haven't been crying over another man, to act as if I'm not the asshole I'm proving myself to be. I walk over to him and run my hands along his chest to insinuate I'm in the mood for sex, but he grabs my wrists and pushes me away.

My conscience taunts me, and I grow even more worried.

"What's wrong, honey?"

His eyes are dead, stopping all my blood flow, and I panic.

"Landon?"

"I know everything." His voice is ice cold as he looks at me like I'm a disgusting piece of shit, and I don't even bother trying to lie my way out of this.

"Please," I say as calmly as I possibly can. "It's not what you're thinking."

"You don't know what I'm fucking thinking!" he shouts as he swings his arm across the dresser, sending picture frames that hold images of our love and devotion to the floor, shattering the glass against the hard wood.

"I'll tell you everything, Landon. I love you so much—"

"I read your texts to him," he seethes. "I needed to use your laptop, and there they were on your iMessages. I guess you forgot that those come through on your computer."

Oh, my God.

"I read them all, even the ones he just sent."

"No. Please, I just . . . It isn't what you're thinking." Words tumble out through the stampede of hysteria.

"Shut the fuck up before I really lose my shit on you," he yells with clenched fists. I've never seen this side of Landon in my life and it's terrifying. "I then wondered if you told Brooke, and when I checked your texts to her, I find out the lying whore you are."

"I can explain—"

"What? That you weren't having phone sex with that motherfucker? Fuck you!" He then rips the comforter off the bed. "Your cum is all over the goddamn sheets. You weren't thinking about me, were you, Tor?"

His voice is pure acid dripping into my splintering heart as I stand here completely helpless.

"Don't even try to lie because I saw that you had a two-hour video chat with him right before I came home this afternoon. So what was that, you felt guilty so you fucked me? On top of the cum from—"

"Please," I sob. "It wasn't real. I never even met the guy."

"No?" He grabs my shoulders and pushes me back against the wall. His eyes slay me with the fury in them. "I want to know everything."

"Okay," I tremble out.

"Did he watch you?"

"Yes."

His jaw ticks. "Did he talk dirty to you?"

"Yes."

"And you?"

"A little."

"Did you watch him?"

"Yes."

He squeezes my shoulders tighter, painfully bruising me as tears fall freely down my face. With clenched teeth, he goes on, asking, "Did you cum?"

"Yes," I confess, each one breaking his heart along with my own.

"Did he see your naked body?"

"Only my breasts."

His eyes pinch shut, and when they open again, his words drip utter heart-fracturing agony when he asks, "Did he see your face when you came?"

"Landon, don't—"

"Tell me!" he grits through his teeth, shaking my shoulders in his death grip.

My eyes fall shut, pushing out more tears, and I can't bear to look at him when I tell him the truth. "Yes."

"That was mine!" He slams my body against the wall before letting go of me as if I'm poisonous. Maybe I am. "I fucking hate you!"

"No," I wail. "You're mad, but you don't hate me."

He leans forward, getting in my face, and spews his words, "Fuck you, whore!"

And no sooner is he walking away from me and into the closet. When I see him pull out a suitcase, I panic.

"What are you doing?"

"I'm leaving. I can't even fucking look at you right now."

"Don't leave. Please. We can talk, I can explain—"

"I don't want to hear your voice," he says as he starts opening and closing drawers, filling the luggage with his belongings. "I should've known this would happen. You're always living in fucking la-la land with those fucking books you read and write. You're so fucking pathetic. All you authors do is sit around and write your fucking porn that you get off to. It's always bothered me, but you were happy and successful, so I kept my mouth shut. But you go to these book signings with all those cover models and loser housewives wetting their panties over them. It's a fucking joke! You're a fucking joke, you know that?" I sit on the edge of the bed and watch him as he yells his hate at me. I can't even fight him on his words because I deserve anything he wants to say to me at this point. I've broken him. I've broken the one man who trusted me not to break him. "The life you live in as an author is nothing but lies. The men you create, the men you read, it's all bullshit. I never understood your need for it when you have me. I guess I was never good enough, was I?"

"You are. It had nothing to do with you."

"All you authors are just self-centered pieces of shit that hold no value on the true relationships you have, so you create your versions of perfection that no man can ever live up to. It's embarrassing that my friends can see on your social media these signings you go to with half-naked men. It's disgusting and so fucking desperate." He throws his words at me, hoping each of them stabs me in my heart. "Turn the tables," he continues. "How would you feel if I went to a work convention and there were half-naked women in bikinis flaunting around? They have nothing to do with my job as a chef, just like those guys have nothing to do with your job as a writer. It's just a cheap ploy those women use to sell books, and it's so futile. This whole world of yours is just a pitiful cry for attention."

"I made a huge mistake, Landon. I'm so sorry, but I ended it—"

"Then why were you texting him in our driveway just now? I watched them pop up on your computer while I was watching you through the window!"

"I swear to you, it's over. Please. Don't leave."

He goes into the bathroom, grabs his toiletries, and tosses them into the bag before zipping it up.

"I always told you that if you ever cheated on me that I would divorce you."

"No!" I cry, falling to my knees at his feet. "I never met him, I swear. I love *you*! You can't leave me. You can't walk out on the girls!"

"Don't you dare throw my daughters in my face. You made this choice when you spread your legs for that fucker, so why don't you shove your face in your cum-covered sheets and cry your fake ass to sleep."

My chest heaves as I struggle to breathe through my sobs. I can't move while I watch my love walk out on me.

"You want to know the sad part?" he says before he leaves. "You didn't even care enough about me to say goodbye before you found someone else."

The slamming of the door obliterates every one of my hopes and dreams. Everything I know is ripped away, and all I can do is lie on the floor and cry through the torturous agony I brought upon myself, along with the realization that I just royally destroyed my marriage—my whole life.

My husband just left me.

What have I done?

chapter twelve

TIME IS A VILLAIN—MY VILLAIN. EVERY SECOND PASSES BY PAINFULLY, GRANTING me no reprieve as they multiply into minutes—hours—days. I beg and beg through text because he refuses to call me.

Me: I'm so sorry.

No response.

Me: Please, come home.

No response.

Me: I swear I'll love you harder—better.

No response.

Me: I never meant to hurt you. You're every part of me and I can't lose you.

No response.

There's no saving myself in this; he holds the power; he holds the future of us.

The waiting is the worst.

I cry and cry and then hold myself together as best as I can when the girls are around, fighting back the burning heartache that scorches every ventricle—every nerve ending, only to break down in heaving sobs the moment I'm alone again.

I've never known a pain like this. I never knew such pain existed, but it does, and I did it to myself. You would think a torture like this would come with a warning, instead it disguised itself and lurked in the stygian corners, waiting for its chance to attack.

It's been six days since Landon left me. He refuses to tell me where he's staying, refuses to hear my voice, refuses to come home. I told the girls he had to go away unexpectedly for business, and they accepted the lie without question. It kills me to think of what their reaction would be if they knew the truth. They'd hate me for tearing up this family—a family that had no reason for being torn apart.

Landon says I cheated. He uses the word "affair." Outwardly I own it, but internally, what I did doesn't feel like an affair. Did I lie? Yes. Did I do something I wasn't supposed to do? Yes. Did I have an affair? I don't know.

I wish he would just come home. Call me. Let me know if I ruined us or if we have a chance. He's only sent one text since he left: *I don't know if I can ever trust you again.*

And then there's Alec. He emailed me yesterday, the first communication since my world crumbled beneath me. I didn't respond, but a part of me wanted to—still wants to.

What the hell is wrong with me?

Headlights pierce through the windows when Brooke pulls into the driveway. She's been the sturdy rope I cling to. She calls me every morning, encouraging me to get out of bed, to shower, to eat, but I can't because every movement reminds me that I'm alone, and that it's all my fault.

"You look like shit," she says gently with a smile, and I wonder if I'll ever smile again.

Before I can speak, my eyes well up and tears spill over. Brooke hugs me, and the touch punctures the wound within.

"I'm such an idiot," I weep.

"Stop." Her voice is scolding. We walk into my bedroom so we don't wake the girls, and when we take a seat on the bed, she reminds me, as she does every day, "You're not an idiot. You made a bad choice, but that doesn't make you a bad person."

"What I did was horrible and I—"

"You're right. It was. But you're a good person. We all make stupid, horrible choices, but that doesn't make us horrible people."

"I don't think he's coming back, Brooke."

She crosses her legs in front of her, knee to knee with me. “He’s not going to leave you.”

“You don’t know that,” I rebut. “He’s so mad. He hates me.”

“He doesn’t hate you. He’s mad. You gotta give him time to calm down. But I don’t see him walking away from his kids. You talked to some guy for a week. A *week*. You never met him, never touched him. This could be much worse.”

We have this same conversation every day: me scared he won’t come back, Brooke saying whatever she can to give me hope.

“I need to ask you something though,” she adds, her eyes pinned to mine, marking her seriousness. “And I want you to be honest with yourself.”

I nod.

“We all move through our actions for a reason. I don’t believe they can be deduced to happenstance. I know that you got swept away and everything spun out of control before you knew it, but I want you to think about the why. Why did it happen? Why didn’t you feel it was wrong? Why was it so easy for you to get lost?”

I drop my head as guilt festers.

“I know you feel like shit, but I wouldn’t be a good friend if I didn’t ask. I think it’s something you should spend some time reflecting on.”

“What are you trying to say?”

She pauses, takes hold of my hands, and responds, “Maybe you were looking for a way out.”

“Out of my marriage? I love my family.”

“You’re feeling distraught and scared. The thought of your marriage ending, no matter what the reason, is devastating. But if you can step away from those emotions, then maybe you can dissect why this happened.”

Buried feelings do have a way of manifesting themselves through our actions; I’m smart enough to know that, but surely I would be aware if I wanted out of my marriage. Surely I would be aware if I was falling out of love with my love. Surely I would know all this, right?

"Tell me honestly, what was it that attracted you to Alec?" Brooke questions.

"I don't know . . . everything, I guess."

"Be specific."

"Maybe you're right," I suggest. "Maybe I was so drawn to him because my tastes have changed. That can happen, right? I mean, people can change. Maybe I changed and didn't know it because I'm in my comfort zone with Landon. He's my life, and maybe I lost sight that there's life beyond our own together." I surprise myself as I talk, saying things I never thought I'd say, because I never knew they were even there. "My life has become routine and predictable. I married Landon in my twenties. I was so young to be making such a huge life choice. And now I'm older and . . ." More tears slip out as I feel the truth crawling her way out of me. And I'm scared. I'm so scared to let her free because what if truth takes away all the years I've spent building this life for myself.

"We all change, but the question is, have you and Landon been changing together?"

I shake my head, my gut ripping itself into shreds. "No." Realization hits hard. "I do my job, and he does his. I don't really include him in my writing world, but I know I've changed because of it. I spent so many years being a wife and a mom, but my success has taken me away from that. I'm more confident. I'm more independent."

"You've always clung to Landon for guidance and stability," she says.

"I don't feel like that anymore."

"Maybe it was Alec's freedom that drew you in. He's single with nothing tying him down."

I've always been tied down. I met Landon at such a young age, settled down, and made a family with him. I never had what Alec has—ultimate freedom to do and be whomever and whatever he wants. It's always been defined for me—wife and mother. Those are my two roles. But what if there's more for me out there? What if what makes me happy has changed through the years? And what if . . . what if Landon can't be what I'm wanting him to be?

"I'm not trying to put any ideas into your head," she tells me. "I just think it's time for you to start questioning this situation you're in right now. If you can identify the issue, then maybe you and Landon have a better shot at working this out, or maybe not. I don't know. But I love you and I love Landon. I will always stand for your marriage and support that, but no matter what happens, I have your back."

After Brooke left last night, I couldn't sleep. I spent the whole night questioning myself, Landon, our marriage. Brooke was right. There's a reason why all this is happening. Perhaps this newfound career of mine has birthed a need for freedom within me. A freedom I never had the opportunity to indulge in when I was younger because I was always tied down.

As I was getting the girls ready for school this morning, I thought about what my life would look like as a single mother of two. I went through the motions as if I were that woman.

It's not to say that I don't love my life—I do. I love my little girls more than anything, and the thought of them not having their father in their lives every single day tears me apart. It kills me. They don't deserve that, and Landon doesn't deserve that. But the urge to seek self-gratification is powerful.

Ever since I got back from dropping Emily and Jill off at school, I've been staring at my phone.

Contemplating.

Second-guessing.

Fantasizing about what my life *could* be.

"Victoria," he says after I dial his number. His voice rich with concern. "Are you okay?"

"No."

He releases a sigh, and I immediately cry.

"My husband left me. He knows about you. He found our texts and read them all."

"I figured," he says. "He called me the other night."

"What?" I panic.

"Don't worry, I didn't say anything when I answered and heard a man's voice. I assumed it was him."

"Oh, my God. I'm so sorry."

"Don't be. I would never tell that man anything about us. I'm not some twenty-year-old, trying to prove something, so I don't want you worrying about that."

Silence spans between us as my tears continue to fall, but I don't know if they're falling for Alec or for Landon, and that alone makes me feel like the biggest piece of shit alive.

"I've missed you," he finally says.

"I'm so sorry I lied to you."

"Tell me why you're calling me."

Leaning back on the couch, I run my hand through my hair, and close my eyes. "I don't know. I couldn't stop thinking about you, but at the same time, I'm so confused."

"Do you love your husband?"

"I thought I did, but maybe not if I'm sitting here thinking about you."

"How long have you been married?"

"Eight years."

"Don't cry," he whispers, and I feel like a fool. "Look, I'm no expert or anything, but I do know that I've come to like you and care about you. With that said, I think what you're going through is common. I think most marriages go through these things."

"I just don't know what to do because I still want to talk to you."

"You need to do what's best for your family."

His words are salt and the thought of this being our last time to talk upsets me even more.

I now know these tears belong to Alec.

"Who are you talking to?"

I jump off the couch the moment I hear his voice, and I disconnect the call. I must've been so wrapped up in my head that I didn't hear Landon walking through the front door.

"Who were you talking to?" he repeats, and my first instinct is to lie, to tell him anything but the truth.

He would only catch me though. All he would have to do is look at my phone and see the same number he called the other night. So with my heart in my throat, I give up the fight and confess the truth.

"Him."

"Are you fucking kidding me?"

"I'm sorry."

"You've been begging me to come home, telling me you want *me*, and you're still fucking talking to him?" His voice is pure gravel as he shouts at me. "What are you thinking?"

"I don't know."

He takes a step toward me, fists clenched. "I came here so we could talk. It's what you've been pleading for."

I shake my head slowly—defeated, and take a seat on the couch as I cry.

"What are you doing to us?" he says on a fractured voice.

I want to tell him something to soothe him, but it would be a lie, so I take a hard swallow and open my heart to him, giving him the ugly truth.

"I don't know if there is an *us*."

When I say the words, I see a shift in his eyes as worry coats them.

I lower my head because I can't bear to see him like this, but I go on, saying, "I was in shock when you first left, but I've been thinking about us, and now I'm not sure what I want."

"You want out?"

"I don't know, but I do know that I don't feel like I'm done talking with Alec. And when you leave, I'm going to call him back."

With apprehension, I open my eyes and look up to my husband as tears fall from his face. It could be the realization that he no longer holds the power of the future of our marriage, but my husband is not a man who cries—ever, and to know it's by my hand that he's cracking is the worst feeling ever.

"What did I do? Tell me what I can do," he pleads.

"I don't know."

"I don't want to lose my family," he says, a sudden one-eighty shift, and I can tell he's feeling the same out-of-control panic I did when he left me.

"I don't want to lie to you anymore."

"Who is this guy? What is it he's giving you that I don't? You met him on that fetish site, right? So what is it? What fetishes is he into that you want a part of?"

"It's not his fetishes," I tell him as he stares down at me in utter helplessness. "He's just . . . I don't know . . . just completely different than who we are."

"And what? You no longer like who we are?"

"We've grown apart, Landon."

"Says who?"

I shrug my shoulders and drop my head again. When his next words come, they slay me entirely.

"Fine. If this is what you need, I'll give it to you. You can call him, meet him, fuck him, just promise me, for God's sake, come back to me when you're done." His voice cracks, exposing the wretched agony from his soul, and I cradle my head in my hands and sob.

I cry so loud that I don't even hear the door close when he leaves.

What have I done to this man?

I pick up the phone just like I said I would, and make my call.

"Is everything okay?"

"I can't do this," I wail. "I can't do this to my husband."

"You need to think about *you*, Victoria. What is it that *you* want?"

"You should hate me. You shouldn't take my calls. I lied to you. I lied to my husband. I'm a horrible person."

"I'm mad at you for lying to me, but I don't hate you, and I don't want to stop talking to you."

"I'm a piece of shit, just admit it," I tell him through my tears because I'm not strong enough to walk away.

I can't fool him though, and he calls me on my game. "This isn't going to work on me. If you want *me* to be the one to end this, I won't. I know what you're doing, and I won't do it."

"Why?"

"You know why. It's the reason why you can't stay away from me."

The fact that he's now chasing me makes this all the harder to do, but I can't continue to hurt my husband. He doesn't deserve any of this.

"Tell me goodbye."

"No," he states adamantly.

"I owe it to my husband to try to work this out, but I don't know if this is fixable."

"If not, you have my number."

I take in a deep breath, right my back, and wipe the tears from my cheeks, but my voice breaks anyway when I say, "Goodbye, Alec," and then hang up.

part two

"If you ever want your soul to dance in the clouds, you will at some point have to juggle lightning and taste the thunder."

~Christopher Poindexter

chapter one

THEY SAY TIME HEALS ALL WOUNDS.

Don't believe them.

It's been three months since my world fell apart. Three months since I broke my husband. Three months since I forever changed my marriage.

Landon tells me that we can never be what we once were because he no longer has the blind trust he once had in me.

It took him four weeks to come back home after he found out about Alec. I should've been ecstatic about having Landon back, but I wasn't. Maybe I was scared of how we would get along under the same roof. Or maybe I got used to being alone, got used to the idea of being free, got used to the idea that perhaps there could be something better for me out there.

When I was alone, it's was amazing how much thinking I did.

I thought about Landon.

I thought about me.

I thought about why I did what I did.

I thought *Did I get married too young? Did I cheat myself out of losing control and going wild when I was in college? Did I make a mistake by following the timetable of what society makes us believe is appropriate: college, marriage, kids?*

I thought until I drove myself crazy with confusion. And when that happened, I thought about Alec.

I still think about him.

Time hasn't weakened my memory of him.

The therapist Landon and I have been seeing since he came home told me it would take time to get over the loss of Alec. He told Landon that, as unfair as it seems, he would need to extend me patience to mourn the loss of Alec. I felt guilty to expect Landon to offer me that. I'm the bad guy. I don't deserve my husband's patience, but he's given it to me anyway. And our therapist was right—even though I only knew Alec for a week, I did mourn the loss of him.

I'm still mourning.

I still want to call him.

I think about it constantly.

Every time Landon and I fight, which is pretty often these days, my first thought is to run to Alec. It's not that I fell for him—I know I didn't. I'm smart enough to see now that what I fell for was the fantasy of him. I used him to bring that fantasy to life because for some reason I was desperate for it. I needed it. Needed the excitement, the allure, the temptation. With Alec, I felt alive, so I used him to sustain the euphoria.

Once during a private session, my therapist told me Alec was able to release endorphins into my bloodstream. The more we discussed it, the more I agreed. Every time I talked to Alec, I would get a drug-like rush—a high. I was instantly addicted to the feeling, which explains my constant craving. All it would take was a simple text from him, and I'd light up with excitement. But the craving is still there, something I refuse to mention to my therapist because I don't want to create any more friction in my marriage, so I hide it.

We go to therapy every week.

I sit there.

I listen.

I say all the right things, most of them lies.

And then I get in my car and daydream about Alec.

I'm starting to think the therapy is why I can't eradicate him from my head. Alec won't die because of all the endless talking about what I did with him and exploring all the whys.

But it isn't just the talking, it's the complete loss of trust. Landon is constantly suspicious of who I'm talking to, who I'm texting, where I'm going when I get into my car, and what I'm doing all day while he's at work. He's now linked all our phones and computers to the same account so he can monitor my calls, texts, and even my location through a GPS app he's installed on his phone. He can pinpoint my location and track my every move through my cell—and he does.

I'm a prisoner in my own world.

I know I deserve it, but that doesn't mean I like it. I don't. I hate it. It makes me want to run away even more. Makes me crave freedom over and above what I used to.

If there were ever issues in our marriage before, they couldn't come close to how many we have now. And the lack of trust has driven the biggest wedge of all between us.

This is another reason why I lie in therapy. I need the trust back, all the while knowing I'm the last person Landon should trust. But I want his trust to do untrustworthy things.

I miss my drug.

I miss my high.

I miss Alec.

I'm constantly wondering where it would've gone if Landon had never found out. It's like watching the most incredible movie ever, and right before I hit the peak of the plot, the electricity goes out and never comes back on. And there I am, left on this high I can't find my way down from, forever wondering what happens next. So I create my own version of the story. I keep it alive in my head, unable to let it go because it's constantly tormenting me. It's a story left unfinished. That's what Alec is to me.

I know I'm a horrible person. Every day I can feel myself growing more and more selfish. But every day, I can also feel myself growing more and more resentful of Landon. And again, I'm completely aware that this is all my fault. I created this world I now inhabit. A world of lies and mistrust.

I hate it.

I hate living this way.

"I hate this part of your job," Landon says from the bed as he watches me pack. "And the fact that you're going alone—"

"What am I supposed to do? Brooke is in her first trimester and has been extremely sick. There's no way she can make this trip."

"I know, but it doesn't help with my anxiety."

Because of my betrayal, Landon is in a constant state of worry, fearing his world could come crashing down again at any moment. I do what I can to assure him while I silence the devil inside me that's eager to come out and play. Landon has so many restless nights, so much stress, so much uncertainty.

"It's a quick trip. In on Friday, out on Sunday," I tell him before walking into the closet to pick out some shoes.

"Are there going to be male models at this signing?"

I walk back to my suitcase, which is sitting on the bed next to him. "Yes."

He huffs in frustration, leaning back against the headboard.

"Landon, try to use this as an opportunity to build some trust in me."

"I'm trying to do what Dr. Lapinski told me to do. I'm trying to give you my trust, but it's not easy."

"You have nothing to worry about. I love you," I assure him, and at least that's the truth. No matter what we are going through, I do still love my husband. I then try to lighten the mood and tease, "Plus, those twenty-something-year-old models can get any hottie of their choosing, so why would they choose a middle-aged housewife with stretch marks?"

"That's your defense?"

I shrug my shoulders playfully.

"I just heard Brooke gossiping to you the other day about some author having sex with her cover model and leaving her husband and kids, so don't pretend that it's so far out of the realm of possibilities."

He's right. This job of mine, this author world, it's filled with so much scandal. So many women losing themselves to the same thing that caused me to slip—fantasy.

I take a seat next to him and run my hand along his jawline, attempting to soothe him. "I made a mistake that I won't ever make again. And I am so sorry. But I love you, and I know you won't believe me when I say it, but I'm going to say it anyway: you can trust me."

More lies.

He cups my face in his hands, his eyes full of unease. "Just come home as fast as you can."

I press my lips to his and wish for all this to disappear, but I can't go back. I can't change what I did. So I temper my guilty heart by having sex with him. It's a lame attempt at normalcy in a marriage that's anything but.

I arrive in Austin, and it's nice to see my friends that I haven't seen in a while. After everything that happened, Landon had me cancel several of my signings, but this Austin signing is such a huge event that I couldn't miss it. Plus, after three months, it's time to get back to my schedule and not back out of any more events.

When we pull up to the hotel and unload our luggage, we head inside to check in. Even though Brooke couldn't come with me, she didn't fail to make sure she took care of everything. She booked the hotel, did my preorders, shipped everything I could possibly need to the hotel, and even found me a replacement assistant for the event.

"You're all set," the clerk from the reservation counter says as she hands me my room key. "I'll have the bellhop deliver your boxes to your room shortly."

"Thank you. Could you also have him deliver this suitcase? I'd like to grab a drink at the bar before heading up to my room."

"Of course."

As soon as I walk over to the expansive lounge area, I spot Erin and her cover model, Gabe, sitting at the bar. Gabe is one of the very few models who will be attending this event, which is on the classier side of book signings. No shirts will be removed or anything of that nature, unlike the Vegas event I last saw Gabe at, which is known for its wild antics. The host for Vegas is the polar opposite of the host for Austin—both insanely sweet in their own right.

"Erin," I say excitedly when I approach, and she leaps off her barstool to give me a hug.

"I didn't expect to see you here after you cancelled your last signing."

"I'm here. Life has just been crazy and the winter has been brutal on my girls. They got sick and my husband couldn't take off work." I tell her the same lie Brooke told the last event host I had to cancel on. I then turn to Gabe. "How have you been?"

"Good," he says before giving me a hug as well.

I look around, and then ask the dreaded question, "Is Jen here?"

"She's up in the room taking a nap," Erin tells me, and when I look over to Gabe, I ask, "I take it you worked everything out?"

He sits back down, and I join them.

"I took your advice and gave her time to come around."

"And?"

"I was just honest. Told her how I felt about her, and we've been seeing each other ever since."

"Are you serious? That's wonderful! I'm so happy for you," I exclaim. "How is that working out with the two of you living in different states?"

"It's not ideal, but we're making it work. I actually flew her to L.A. after Christmas."

"That sounds kind of serious."

"He's so smitten with her," Erin teases, embarrassing Gabe.

"Well, I think it's sweet," I tell him. "I'm glad it's working out for you."

"Thanks, Madilyn."

"Wait," Erin blurts. "Where's Brooke?"

"At home, barfing her insides out." I laugh when her face contorts in disgust. "She's pregnant."

"I guess I've lost my party buddy, but good for her."

"Oh, she'll be back to her old self after the baby is born. You haven't lost her for good."

We continue to catch up, and when I finish my drink, I head to my hotel room. A stack of boxes is waiting for me to organize, but after the long flight, I'm drained. I toss my purse onto the bed and flop down next to it. I'm not used to coming to signings alone and wish Brooke were here. But even with her gone, I'm still happy to be away from all the stress and tension back home.

I startle when the hotel phone rings loudly.

"Hello?"

"This is the front desk calling to confirm your luggage has been delivered to your room."

"Yes, it has. Thank you."

I hang up the phone and look for a way to turn down the obnoxiously loud ringer. That's when treachery creeps in.

I know I shouldn't be having the thoughts I'm having, but I am, and before I know it, they're racing out of control as my body begins to react in excitement.

This phone is untraceable.

I reach for my cell, pop off the case, and pull out the small folded piece of paper I hid in there that has Alec's phone number. I was afraid I'd forget it, so I've always kept it like a druggie's secret stash they smuggle into rehab.

I'm already hitting my high and I haven't even called him, but knowing I can is enough to spark the live wire inside me.

Just one call, Tori. Landon will never know.

I pick up the receiver, fingers shaking, and with each number I dial I know I should hang up, burn his number, and get the fuck out of this room. But I don't, because I know how good this call is going to feel.

The moment I hear his unmistakable voice, it all comes rushing back. Every vein weaving under my flesh tingles.

"It's me," I murmur when he answers, and I swear my heart is about to break one of my ribs, it's pounding so hard.

"Victoria?"

"Yes."

"I didn't think I'd ever hear from you again."

And suddenly, all the turmoil of these past few months rolls in like a tidal wave, crashing down upon the relief of finally being able to have a shred of freedom. Emotions slip out and fall down my face. I'm at a loss for words as I try not to completely lose it. But the moment I sniff, he catches it.

"Are you crying?"

"I'm sorry."

"Tell me why you're crying," he requests, his voice soft and smooth.

"I don't know," I tell him. "I've wanted to call you, I just couldn't."

"Why?"

"Because my husband watches my every move."

"When you never responded to my texts, I figured you didn't want to talk to me."

"You texted me? When? I never got them." I reach for my cell and scroll through my texts, but there's nothing. I then open my settings to find that Landon must've gotten into my phone, because Alec's phone number is on my blocked list. "He blocked you."

"Where are you calling me from?"

"I'm in Austin for a book signing. I'm on the hotel phone in my room."

Tears continue to quietly slip out.

"I'm sorry," I tell him after a long span of silence. "I'm sorry I lied to you."

He still doesn't respond.

"Are you mad at me?"

"I'm mad that you didn't give me a choice," he says. "If you would've told me from the beginning that you were married with kids, then I could've made the choice whether or not to pursue you, but you didn't give me that. Instead, I blindly fell for a woman who was already taken."

"And what about now?"

"I can't get you out of my thoughts. I still want that cup of coffee with you."

"But I'm married."

"Are you sure about that? Maybe on paper you are, but are you married in your heart? Because you're crying on the phone with a man that's not your husband."

"I don't know what I am anymore. I mean, I don't even know you. I've tricked myself into believing I do because I've spent the last three months creating you in my head. It's not who you really are though. I don't know who you really are."

"Then come find out."

"Alec . . ."

"All I'm asking for is to meet for coffee. Where's the harm in that? You can go to a coffee shop and I'll just happen to be there," he suggests as if meeting him wouldn't be a betrayal to my husband. It would be, and we both know it.

"Say I did meet you, and in a perfect world, things worked out, what about the fact I have two kids?"

"I love that you're a mom. Like I said before, I want kids."

His words are what every woman who fears walking away from a marriage would want to hear, and even though they're too perfect, I allow myself the comfort to get lost in them.

"But do you want a woman who would chase a man while she's married to another?"

"Like I said, you took that choice away from me when you allowed me to fall for the lie," he maintains. "Tell me something, are you happy?"

"No."

"Do you love him?"

"That's not an easy question to answer. I mean, things aren't what they used to be, but we've built a life together. We have a family."

"Don't let the idea that you owe him something because of the years you have invested cloud what it means to love someone. Love is not the same as obligation."

I lie down and rest my head on the pillow. "It's not so simple," I quietly weep. "I have two little girls I have to think about."

"Tell me about your girls," he says, and I do.

He continues to ask questions about them as time passes. My tears wane as our conversation drifts on, and before I know it, I'm unbuttoning my pants without his solicitation.

"Talk to me, Alec," I say thickly, needing his brazen words that I've been deprived of.

"What do you want me to say?"

"You know what I want you to say," I tell him as I slip my hand between my legs.

The sound of his belt buckle coming undone sends my system into overdrive.

"Tell me you've missed me," he urges, and I'm so weak for this attention that I give into his request without hindrance.

"I've missed you."

"Do you think about me when you get off?"

"Yes."

"Don't lie to me," he scolds.

"Even with my husband, it's the thought of *you* that makes me cum." And it's true for the most part. There's so much discord with Landon that when we're having sex, I'm imagining someone else, most often Alec. I know that makes me a shit person, but it's the truth.

"Fuck, that makes me so hard."

And that's it, I'm completely lost again, throwing my body into a raging orgasm with Alec as we get ourselves off with each other. But this time, I don't have to worry about Landon coming home from work early, so I take advantage and give into the gluttony of it all. We get off, talk, get off, and then talk some more. We go for hours like this, but it's still not enough to sate me. When exhaustion finally hits and the sun has set, I'm about to doze off when Alec takes full advantage.

"Tell me you'll meet me when you get back to Boston."

Numb and mindless, I respond, "Okay, Alec. We'll do this your way."

"Tell me," he pushes.

"I'll meet you."

chapter two

She appears the same to me when I look at her, but I know she no longer is. She's someone I don't know, but she stares back at me with mythomane in her eyes, which harbor compulsive lies and marrow-deep fantasy. She blinks nervously. I've been warned to stay away from morally wicked women my whole life, but there's something about her that makes me want to be her.

I pick up my lipstick and watch as she mirrors every single movement of mine, pressing her lips together to set the blushed bee's wax. Is her heart wildly out of control like mine? Is she scared like me? Nervous like me? Excited like me? Deplorable like me?

Alec: 11:00

His text marks the timestamp in which I will break yet another binding promise to Landon, further destroying our marriage.

Me: 11:00

I respond, confirming our nefarious coffee date.

I set down the disposable phone I bought after seeing the horrendously expensive hotel bill this past weekend. Thank God that charge is on my business account that Landon doesn't have access to. Now I can call and text Alec as much as I want without Landon being able to track me.

I grab my keys and walk out of this house that Landon and I have created as our home. With each step, with each breath, I'm selfishly pissing all over everything I vowed to love and cherish. I know I shouldn't be doing this, but the simple, self-gratifying reality is—I want to. I want to see Alec and talk to him face to face. I want to experience him in person. Just the thought of sitting next to him sparks an adrenaline rush in me that clouds my judgment even more.

No longer am I living in the gray.

No.

This is black and white. This is right and wrong. This is now a deeply carved line in stone that I'm about to cross.

It was one thing to unconsciously fall into something over the phone, but this is something else entirely. This is a conscious decision I'm making, knowing damn well the repercussions if I get caught. But I won't get caught. I've thought this out, made my plan, secured my safety in this situation. I have made sure that any incoming phone calls on my cell will be forwarded to my untraceable phone. And as far as Landon tracking me, I drive to CambridgeSide Galleria, make my way into Macy's and drop my silenced phone down into the center of a large, round clothing rack. Now if Landon tracks me, he'll simply think I'm spending the day shopping.

With each move I make, my nerves spike in fear, but it's not enough to stop me. When I get back to my car, I take a deep breath and then shift into drive. My stomach is one big knot, my palms sweat, and my heart ricochets against my chest.

I'm detestable, a married woman going to meet another man.

I'm not myself.

I'm the reflection in the mirror.

I'm her—*Victoria.*

Pulling into the parking lot, I scan the cars to see if he's already here, and when I spot the silver SUV I saw the night at the hotel, I park beside it.

Don't do this, Tori. Toss the affair phone and go back home.

You feel that, Victoria? You feel the rush?

This is dangerous. Landon will divorce you if he finds out.

This is the thrill of a lifetime. Don't turn back now. You've simply been standing in line, but now it's time to jump on the ride of your life.

You'll lose everything. This is a stupid cheap thrill with scathing consequences.

I open my car door and step out into the freezing damp air of Boston's winter. I'm numb. I don't even feel myself as I walk to the entrance.

Turn around, Tori.

God, this is electrifying!

Don't open the door. It's not too late to turn around and run.

I walk in and spot him sitting next to a fogged window, but I don't take another step. I can't.

He then shifts and turns his head in my direction.

We lock eyes.

My heart thrums, my skin tingles, my hands fidget.

The corner of his mouth pulls into a subtle smile, and when he lifts his chin to acknowledge me, my limbs thaw and, step by step, I walk toward my life's game changer. It's a magnetism that pulls me, an unknown force that's always been there, taking me hostage, but in no way do I want to fight myself from him—only toward him.

He stands, moving with such ease. "You came."

"You didn't think I would?"

Moving behind me, he takes the collar of my coat in his hands—fingers ghosting along my neck—and slips it off my shoulders. I turn to face him, my nervous smile meeting his confident one. He doesn't speak, and when he motions for me to take a seat, I do.

"Are you nervous?"

"A little," I admit, my hands still jittery.

He sits back, relaxing into his seat, never taking his eyes off me, and suddenly I'm self-conscious. I chastise myself for not checking my face and hair before getting out of the car. Alec takes his time as he examines me, his certitude a stark contrast to my anxiety, but I feign calm.

"Coffee?"

I nod and watch as he slips his hand under his suit coat and pulls out a credit card. He holds it out for me between his two fingers.

"You remember how I take my coffee, don't you?"

I look to his hand that's holding the card and think back to our very first conversation. Be it that it was three months ago, it shocks me that in fact I do remember, but if I admit that, is he going to think I'm some desperate woman? I mean, who would remember such a trivial thing after so much time had passed?

He withdraws his hand and turns in his chair to grab his coat that's draped over it.

"What are you doing?"

"Leaving," he says coolly.

"Why?"

"I told you it was your decision whether or not you cared to remember how I took my coffee. I would've thought, with everything that's on the line between us, you would've remembered."

Irritation flares. "Do you remember every little thing I've told you?"

"Yes, Victoria. I do."

"Really?" I shoot back with a slightly patronizing tone.

He turns back around, rests his forearms on the table, and leans in toward me. "Go ahead. Ask me anything."

I go for something as equally trivial. "What's my favorite movie?"

"*Crash*," he responds quickly, and then grows cavalier, adding to prove his point, "You graduated from Boston University, your brother's wife's name is Claire, you're a runner, and you suffer from nightmares about your mother faking her death as a way to abandon you."

I don't react as I sit here, stunned that he would recall all that after so many months have elapsed.

"So tell me, was I wrong to care enough to remember all that when you never asked me to?"

I shake my head, miffed. "Give me your credit card," I request before I run the risk of him leaving after all I've jeopardized to come here.

When he holds it back out for me, I take it and walk over to the counter to place the order. I fight the urge to look at him. While I wait for the barista to make our drinks, I don't know whether to be irked or amused at his little game. As if this isn't awkward enough.

"Here you go," I say when I return and set Alec's mug on the table. "Black with two sugars."

I sit down and take a slow sip of my coffee.

"Tell me why you're nervous."

I set my mug down and take a moment before responding. "Because this isn't me. Because I don't do things like this."

"Like what? Meet a friend for coffee?"

"You know this is a lot more than just coffee, Alec."

"This is whatever you want it to be. I'm not forcing you to do anything you don't want to do."

"This is my choice, I know. But at the same time, it isn't."

"How so?"

"You don't make it easy to stay away," I tell him. "I know I shouldn't be here. I know this is wrong, but you make it to where I don't care."

"Then tell me . . . Where *should* you be?"

"Home."

"Then why aren't you?"

Sadness thickens, and I take a deep breath. "Because I'm no longer happy there." I aimlessly fiddle with my mug, watching my nervous fingers, and when I look at Alec, I say what I've been terrified to say. "I don't think I love my husband anymore."

He extends his hand across the small table and wraps it around mine. The single touch is enough to awaken all my senses with a spine-tingling charge. But the core of me is in agony because of this. Because everything in my life seems to be spiraling out of control. Landon and I fight more than we ever did before. He's always accusing and suspecting the worst of me. And what's so fucked up is that I know he has every right to be that way, but I still loathe him for it. I'm bitter and angry, and it seems to get worse with every day that passes.

"And what about this?" he questions.

"This is confusing. I can't deny that I'm drawn to you in a way I've never felt before. Like I've told you, you're intense and all-consuming."

He takes his hand from mine and then stands to walk over to my side of the table. The heat from his body warms me wholly when he sits next to me. For months I've thought about what it would feel like to be this close to him, so when he wraps his arm around my shoulders, it's a toxic shock to my system.

He leans in, and with a hushed voice, says, "I care about you; I don't want you to think I don't. The last thing I want to do is pressure you, but it's hard for me not to want to sway you in my direction."

"I'm already swaying," I whisper before he brushes his thumb along my cheekbone. I haven't felt the touch of another man since I met Landon thirteen years ago, and I wonder if Alec can hear my erratic breathing.

"I'm nothing like you," he warns.

"I know."

But maybe this is what I need. Maybe I'm no longer interested in the familiar, in the safe, or in the comfort. Maybe I've outgrown my preference for standard. And maybe if I cross this line and explore this other way of life and this other way of thinking, I could be happier. Maybe I'm about to find out who I was always meant to be.

He slowly traces his thumb from my cheek, down my jaw, and to my chin. He tilts my head back but doesn't make another move. As I look into the midnight blue eyes of this man who's almost ten years older than me, I feel small—almost child-like—next to his confident demeanor. It's a feeling I'm not used to, but a feeling I like.

A menagerie of emotions collides inside of me, but lust, desire, and the curiosity of the unknown are the ones that tangle around my heart like a noose, and when they begin to strangle, I peer into Alec's eyes and give him the approving nod I know he's waiting for.

I inhale the spice of his scent, and my eyes fall shut when he drops his lips to mine and kisses me slowly. I hesitate for a moment when the stun hits me that I'm kissing a man that's not my husband, but the feeling fades as quickly as it appeared. My mouth gently moves with his, and everything about the way this man kisses is different than Landon. With such a slow moving kiss, there's a verve in it that feeds the endorphins that are bursting in my chest.

No longer am I a woman embarking on an affair in the middle of a coffee shop. I'm somewhere else, suspended above gravity in a world where nothing exists but me, and Alec, and this amazing high. When Alec pulls back, dragging his lips from mine, I already know that not even I can save myself from this as my appetite for more grows painfully ravenous.

"How do you feel now?"

"Happy," I tell him and then drop my head with a sigh of embarrassment.

"I want you."

I lift my head back up, and with apprehension in my eyes, tell him, "I don't know how to do this."

"I don't expect it to be easy, but I don't want easy—I want *you*," he says without reservation. "Come to my place tomorrow."

"Why?" I ask like a naïve schoolgirl and immediately feel stupid.

"Because I want to fuck you," he states boldly, sending a fire bolt between my thighs.

Realization takes shape that this won't be a relationship of romantic dates and getting-to-know-you strolls in the city. That's not what this is. We both know that when I leave, I'm going home to my husband, and until I make a defining choice, is there really any point in seeking something that might not ever be? Plus, we passed taking it slow when we were getting off together in the first week.

His cell chimes, and when he takes it from his pocket, I curse that phone for making Alec take his warm hands off me.

"I gotta get back to work," he says after checking his text. "Let me walk you to your car."

He helps me with my coat, and with his hand on the small of my back, he guides me outside. I show him where I'm parked and he walks me over to the driver's side door but doesn't open it.

With my back against the car, Alec asks, "Tomorrow?"

"Tomorrow," I confirm before he presses into me, pushing my body harder against the door.

And this time, his mouth moves purposefully with mine. His hands hold tightly on to the sides of my face as he moves me to his liking. Using his tongue, he opens my lips, and I take my first taste, getting punch-drunk as he controls every movement. Each lick is a softly spoken curse, intoxicating me even more.

My limits blur when I feel the throbbing between my legs. How could a single kiss do this to me? I want to fuck him right now, but if he fucks like he kisses, I don't know how I'll ever be able to walk away from him.

Alec abruptly tears his lips away from mine, leaving me panting. A cloud of vapor billows between us as flakes of snow float down from the low-hung clouds.

He grinds his hips against me. "You feel what you do to me?"

I drop my head to his chest, close my eyes, and savor the touch of his erection pressing against me. He's got me so wound up, I'm ready to let him fuck me right here in this parking lot. When he takes a step away from me, I take a step with him, not trusting my wobbly legs to support me. He then opens my door.

"I'll text you my address."

I slip into my car, and before I can say anything, he closes the door and walks away. Unable to catch my breath just yet, I watch him until he pulls out of the parking lot and drives away.

"Holy shit," I exhale, wondering if that really just happened or if I'm lost in a dream. The nagging between my legs is the only proof I need to know the truth. I lean my head back and cover my face with my hands as I laugh at how unbelievably happy I am right now.

I never thought I'd ever have another first kiss in this lifetime, and holy fucking hell, that was unbelievable!

chapter three

THE TOUCH OF HIS LIPS AGAINST MINE THREW ME INTO THROBBING EXCITEMENT, but it wasn't just his kiss—it was everything about him. It was the way he triggered my heartbeat with his eyes, which screamed "You've never known a man like me." My heart is *still* pounding from that look, and I can't believe that actually just happened.

I park in front of Brooke's house, blazed in excitement, and rush to her front door. I don't even knock. I just walk right inside wearing a shameless smile.

"Brooke," I call.

"In my bedroom."

I walk in to find her emptying a laundry basket of clean clothes.

"You won't believe what just happened," I blurt, and when she shuts the drawer to the dresser and turns to face me, I tell her, "I met him!"

"Met who?"

"Alec."

Her face drops, eyes wide and mouth agape. "Rewind," she says as she sits on the edge of the bed. "What the hell are you talking about?"

Her tone kidnaps my elation, slowly bringing me down from my high. I walk over to the corner of the room and take a seat in the chair next to the window.

"I called him this past weekend." My confession sparks another bout of astonishment in her eyes.

"Are you crazy?"

"Maybe I am. But I haven't been able to stop thinking about him."

"What if Landon finds out? My God, Tori, what are thinking?" she scolds harshly. "The two of you are supposed to be working on your marriage and getting it back on track."

"We didn't just slip off track, Brooke. We completely derailed," I exclaim. "I'm miserable. You have no idea what it's like living in that house with him. He treats me like a prisoner, always watching my every move. When I went to Austin, I finally felt free, and when I called Alec, I finally felt happy."

"You have to give it time. It won't always be like this, Landon just needs time to trust you again."

"That's so easy to say when you're not the one living it day by day. His distrust is driving me away, and before you say anything, I know I deserve it. And I know he has every right not to trust me, but . . ." I drift, not knowing how to explain my heart. My throat tightens, and I turn my head to look out the window. "I don't know how to explain what I'm feeling. None of it makes sense."

"Then maybe you need to press pause."

I look back to Brooke. The concern she now wears for me chokes me up, and the tears finally fall. "What if I don't want to?"

"You're playing with fire."

The fire has been burning for months now, but it's never been enough. Today Alec set that fire ablaze, and tomorrow, I'll be going to his place with a can of gasoline.

"I kissed him," I confess as my face crumples in my own self-inflicting agony, and I cry more when I continue admitting, "It felt amazing. Everything about it felt like everything I've been missing in Landon."

"You can't see him again."

"I'm going to his place tomorrow."

"Don't do it," she cautions. "You know if you have sex with him, and Landon finds out, he'll divorce you. Don't be stupid, Tori. Think about your kids."

I sit here as emotions pour out of me, responsibility and desire war within. I'm so lost, and I'm wondering if being with Alec is where I'll find myself.

"You're not this girl, Tori."

"What if I am?"

"You're not," she states adamantly.

"What if I want to be?"

"Trust me, you don't. You don't want to be the woman who cheats on her husband and loses everything."

"But what if it's already lost?"

She walks over and sits on the small ottoman in front of me. With her hands on my knees, I see her own tears flooding in her eyes. "I love you," she affirms. "And I will always love you no matter how badly you fuck up, and I'm telling you right now, as your friend, you are about to lose everything. You don't want to do this. You're caught up right now. Everything is exciting and new, but those feelings are just temporary. And when they're gone, and you're left with nothing, you'll realize that you made the biggest mistake of your life."

But what if Landon never finds out? I can keep my family intact while having Alec too. I mean, are we really built to remain with one person for our entire lives? We're ever-changing, constantly evolving. Maybe I'm not the enemy; maybe marriage is the enemy, and I'm merely its victim. Are we really expected to deprive ourselves by committing to one person, knowing that both partners will eventually grow new wants and likes? Are we supposed to deny our inevitable evolution and settle for a less than fulfilling life just because we say "I do"?

Landon used to fill the spaces in my heart that were vacant when I was in my twenties. And now, in my thirties, there are new spaces that have opened up and need to be filled, but he can't fill them. No one person is capable of being someone's everything. Landon fills the security and goodness in me, and Alec fills the need for spontaneity and this newfound desire to explore a different side of my sexuality.

But because marriage says I can only choose one, am I suppose to be forever incomplete?

"Do you love him?"

"Alec?"

"Yes."

I shake my head. "No. But we have this connection that feels . . . I don't even know how to describe it, but it's a hard feeling to walk away from."

She shrugs her shoulders. "I don't get it. It's got to be more than just this *feeling*."

"I guess it's a combination of a lot of things. He's older, more seasoned in life than me. It's the lifestyle he lives and his views. It intrigues me, and I'm wondering if I'm more like him than Landon at this point in my life. But I have to try to find out, and Alec . . . I trust him to be the one to show me and to teach me something new about myself."

"But what if you talked to Landon about trying something new and exploring it together?"

"No. Landon is nothing like that. It would just be awkward. Plus, Landon and I are so out of sync right now. It would never work."

"There's no talking you out of this, is there?" she questions with worriment.

"I don't know."

"Promise me something?"

I nod.

"Promise me when you go home tonight that you'll look at your girls and think about how it would feel to not have them all the time. Think about how it would feel to spend Christmas all alone while they're with Landon and whatever woman he'll be dating or married to, because you know he will find someone else eventually if you do this to him. He *will* move on."

I nod again, unable to speak around the knot in my throat. I don't even want to think about any of that happening, so I quickly shut it away and tell myself I will just have to be extremely careful. I'll have to cover every single track of mine because I can't lose my family, but I'm also not strong enough to walk away from what I'm about to do. The pull is much too powerful to even attempt resisting.

When I notice the time on the clock that sits on Brooke's nightstand, I realize I must get going to cover the tracks from today's indiscretion.

"I have to go."

We walk together to the front door, and when she hugs me she says, "I'm going to call you in the morning, okay?"

"Okay." But I already know I'm going to let that call go to voicemail.

I get back in my car and head over to the mall to pick up my phone and buy a couple gifts for the girls. I need proof that I was shopping in case Landon tracked me on his app today. When I arrive, I make my way through the Macy's to the garment rack that aided me in my deception today. I part the hangers to find my cell phone safely guarded by an army of slacks.

Bending down, I retrieve the phone to see no calls or texts from Landon came through. And since none came through on my disposable phone, I don't need to worry about lying to him in case he did call and there was a glitch in the call-forwarding.

As I walk out into the mall, I pass Victoria's Secret and stop. Turning, I look at the satin and lace. I can't remember the last time I bought a new pair of sexy panties. What do you need to buy this stuff for when you've been with the same man for as long as I've been with my husband? But I can't show up to Alec's in a worn down pair of panties with broken threads of elastic popping out from the seams and an unmatching bra.

I step inside, my stomach trilling with excitement, and look around. As I browse, I find myself enjoying the thought of wanting to please Alec with my selection. It's an enticing feeling to know that whatever I buy, it'll be Alec's hands that will take them off of me.

Black is too obvious. Red is too slutty. White is too innocent.

I don't want to look like I'm trying too hard, so I opt for a pair of lacy panties in a light blush color along with the matching lace bra. The sales clerk rings me up, and I pay in cash. The last thing I need is for Landon to see this charge on the credit card. When she hands me the little pink bag, I thank her, and quickly make my way back into the mall and find the nearest trash can. I take my new lingerie, stuff them into my purse, and toss the bag.

After I buy the girls some shirts and toys, I drive home where Landon is already waiting for me. I power down my disposable cell and take my purchase out of my purse before stashing them into the emergency roadside kit in the trunk.

I don't trust Landon not to search my purse.

I used to love being at home, but now, every time I walk through the door, it feels like I'm suffocating. This place no longer houses the once-happy family it used to.

"What were you doing at the mall all day?" the warden questions from the kitchen, not even trying to hide the fact that he checked up on me.

"Nothing much," I tell him as I set the shopping bags on the counter. "I tried on a bunch of clothes that I didn't wind up buying, ate lunch, and picked up a few things for Jill and Emily."

"You didn't work today?"

"I couldn't get in the right headspace. So instead of forcing the words just to end up deleting them, I decided a day out of the house would clear my head." I walk up to him and give him a hug. "I didn't think you'd be home so early. How was your day?"

"I have to go back. We are fully booked tonight," he tells me before giving me an emotionless, mindless, closed-mouth kiss to my lips, tarnishing the lingering traces of Alec.

"Again?"

"Don't act so surprised," he says as he walks over to the fridge to grab a bottle of water.

Ever since the *Times* review, Chin-Chin has been booked out for months, leaving me on my own with the kids.

"I'm not surprised. I'm just wondering when it's going to slow down enough for you to be home."

"Don't know."

"Why are you being so short with me?"

"Bad day," he snips.

"You want to talk about it?"

"It's nothing you want to hear."

"Landon," I say as I take his hand. "I want to know what's bothering you."

He leans against the counter and sighs heavily. "I've had a sick feeling in my stomach all day. The same feeling I had when I found all those text messages you were sending that guy," he says. Landon goes through waves of good weeks and bad weeks when it comes to his anxiety about me. "And then I tracked you, even though Dr. Lapinski told me to stop doing that. When you weren't at home, but at the mall, I started thinking the worst."

"Honey, I was just shopping and wandering around. That's all."

"I almost drove up there because I kept thinking you were there with that guy."

"Alec? I haven't talked to him in three months. It's over and done with, Landon. You have nothing to worry about." I assure him with my lies, feeding him my sugar-coated poison.

He then turns to me and, with growing frustration, asks me his never-ending question. "Why did you do it? And don't give me that 'I guess I was bored and got swept away' bullshit. I need to know the truth."

"I don't know. What I've told you is the truth."

"I can't get this shit out of my head, Tor. I close my eyes at night with the vision of you fingering yourself and cumming while that fucker watches you." His words come harshly. "You have no clue how you've fucked with my head."

"It was one week," I stress, trying to excuse my behavior. "You act like I had this full-blown affair or something."

"You might as well have, because it's exactly what it feels like to me."

"How long am I supposed to be punished?" I snap. "It's been three months and you still track my phone and everything. It's fucking ridiculous, and I'm sick of it."

"You're so fucking selfish."

"I said I was sorry a million times. I don't know what else to do, but I'm here. I'm not leaving you. If I didn't want you, I'd be gone."

"That's bullshit, and you know it," he shouts, his face flaming in rage. "You're too scared to leave because you're afraid of being the one to break up this family. You'd rather push me to do it so you won't have to carry the blame."

"Is that what you want? You want me to leave?"

"Do whatever the fuck you want to do."

"You're such an asshole!"

"You're lucky you have me because most men would've left your deceitful ass already," he seethes and then walks away, grabbing his coat that's lying on the couch.

"Where are you going?"

"Back to the restaurant. I came home to relax, but you shot that to hell."

He slams the door to the garage behind him, leaving me drowning in the aftermath of my destruction. I hate the man I've turned Landon into, a man who holds so much resentment for me. I asked him the other day after we fought if he still loved me.

"I care about you," he told me. *"But I will never love you the same way I did because of what you've done."*

I hate that he's still so angry. I betrayed him, I know, but how long am I supposed to live like this? Why can't we just move on? But no, I'm constantly being punished. He throws what I did in my face all the time, and I can't take it anymore. We live under a gray cloud of doom and depression, which is most likely why I'm still obsessing over Alec. He's the ray of light that filters through all the murk and grants me moments of assuagement.

He gave me relief from my life today when I saw him. I can't remember the last time I felt so exhilarated, only to come home and have Landon piss it all away with his constant gloom and accusations. Maybe we wouldn't be in such a fractured state if he could just let go of the anger and move on.

I'm no longer the only one to blame for our marriage falling apart, because when we fight like this, he's practically pushing me into Alec's arms. If only he would leave the past in the past, maybe we could have a shot at making this work.

I created the wound, but it's Landon that's pouring acid on it and driving me away. Sometimes I wish he would fuck some random woman to even the score so we can go back to being okay. That's how bad I want the peace back, even though it won't be enough to make me walk away from Alec.

chapter four

When did I lose my heart?

When did my blood go cold?

I kissed my husband goodbye this morning. I told him I loved him.

And when he left, I pulled out the bra and panty set I bought yesterday along with my disposable phone.

I now stand outside the entrance to Alec's building. My hair whips in the gusting wind as snow swirls like dust along the sidewalk. People walk past me from every direction, but I remain still. I wonder if any of them know what I'm about to do. Can they see the disgrace on me?

I look up, wondering which window is his, wondering if he's watching me.

I don't need anyone to tell me what an awful woman I am; I already know. But if there's one person that can erase the world around me, it's Alec. With him, I'm free. With him, nothing else exists.

My feet move, taking me through the doors and leading me to the bank of elevators. I step inside and press my finger against the button to illuminate number five, and when I reach the floor and the doors open, I hesitate.

I want this. I know I do. I've thought about what this would be like since that very first week. The fantasy has even crept its way into my dreams a few times, but suddenly, I'm terrified. I don't know what I'm getting into. These are uncharted waters I'm embarking on, and I'm scared shitless.

The elevator doors close before I step off, and I'm being taken back down to the lobby.

Maybe this is a sign.

When the doors open again, I walk out and over to a bench by the large windows. The people are still moving about outside. The snow is still falling. Nothing has changed, and here I remain even though I've been craving change, craving something new. Alec is my new. But I'm not a risk-taker. I'm not someone who walks into a situation blindly.

My stomach churns with monumental anxiety.

Walk out of here. Go home and find your adrenaline rush elsewhere.

Don't listen to her. Your adrenaline rush is waiting for you on the fifth floor. Go.

He's not the rush you need. He's the rush that will annihilate you.

He's the rush that will awaken you. He might even save you from a life of unfulfilled fantasies.

"What are you doing?"

I turn to Alec who's sitting on the bench with me. I didn't even realize how deep in my head I just was to not even sense him sitting next to me.

"Are you okay?"

I nod slowly—nervously.

He takes my one hand in the both of his. "Tell me what you're afraid of."

"You," I respond through the cords of my constricted throat, and when I look at our hands, I notice mine are trembling. "I'm sorry."

"Don't be sorry." His voice remains gentle, yet so self-assured. "Do you want to leave?"

Yes.

"No."

He stands with the slightest hint of a smile while still holding my hand, and as I look into his eyes, I leave my world behind, stand, and walk with him. Alec never lets go of me as we take the elevator up to five, and when the doors open this time, I step off.

"This is me," he says before opening the door to unit 502.

His cologne faintly lingers in the air as I walk into his loft. I move slowly, allowing my eyes to scan the space, aware that Alec is observing my every move.

"I'm impressed," I note as I take in the square footage of the fully renovated studio.

The place is completely open with contemporary finishes: dark gray walls, stainless steel fixtures, large windows that naturally light up the whole room. Support beams help to mark off the living, dining, and bedroom areas, which are fully furnished in a minimalistic way. Boston isn't cheap, and I definitely wasn't expecting him to have a space like this.

"Don't be," he responds, and when I turn to see him still standing by the door, he walks over to me while explaining, "My father bought this loft back in the eighties as an investment property. Got it for dirt cheap and never let it go. Being the generous man he was, he sold it to me for what he originally paid."

"Who renovated?"

"I did. I used a portion of my inheritance." I look at him, and he runs his hands over my coat, from my shoulders down to my arms. "I used the project as a way to distract myself after he died."

I don't respond as we continue to hold each other's attention, and the fear I felt down in the lobby is no longer present. This is the magic of Alec; it's his ability to overpower the entire world and become my sole focus. He's all I can see, hear, and feel in this moment.

"I'm glad you're here," he says.

I reach my hands up and run them along the coarse, dark stubble of his unshaven face. It crackles against my palms before I slightly tug him down to me because all I can think about is the touch of his lips.

His mouth hovers over mine, so close I can taste his cool breath when he says, "Tell me what you want, Victoria."

"I want you to kiss me."

With his tongue, he traces my bottom lip slowly, and it takes everything in me not to push up to him and lick his tongue with mine. We watch each other as he does this and then he murmurs over my lips, "Are you on birth control?"

His question nearly hollows my gut. It's the awakening slap in my face at the reality of this situation and what we're about to do.

"I have an IUD," I whisper.

He then gives me what I need and covers my mouth with his in a binding kiss. My hands slide up his face and into his hair, dark with flakes of gray. It's long enough for me to clench my fists around as his hands drag down the small of my back to my ass. The force behind his touch is strong as he squeezes my flesh and jerks me tighter against him.

When he dips his tongue into my mouth, the taste scintillates me to the core. He possesses my mouth, marking it with his, and I willingly allow him this delight. My coat falls to the floor when he pushes it off my shoulders, and then I wrap my arms around his neck. Before I know it, he lifts me off the ground and carries me over to his bed.

I lie on my back, and he supports himself above me as each breath of mine hits hard. With his knees, he opens my legs and settles himself between them. He doesn't speak a word, only eyes me as he slips one of his hands under the hem of my top. The moment he touches my bare stomach, my abs tremor. He feels my jitters and presses his hand firmly down on me.

"You want me to stop?"

I shake my head, but that doesn't mean that I'm not suddenly feeling every debaucherous choice I'm making in this moment. His hand slides farther up and over my breast. I can feel his touch all over my body and in the pulsating heat between my legs. He softly kneads, and my body instinctively bows up to him, pressing my breast firmly into his palm.

With his other hand, he lifts my back off the bed. He takes my arms, raises them above my head, and slips my top off. My nipples press against the delicate lace of my bra. I grow self-conscious while he shamelessly looks me over and bring my arms in front of me to cover myself.

"Don't do that with me," he says. "It's just skin."

I open my mouth to speak, but he doesn't allow me to excuse my action. "Everything you've been taught about your sexuality, let it go with me. It doesn't exist in my world. When you're with me, it's just us. Fuck what anyone else might think. Nothing we will do together will be wrong because it's between only you and me. We make the rules—not society."

"But I've never—"

"I don't care."

He then sits back on his heels, reaches over his head, and pulls his shirt off, exposing his toned chest.

"I'll tie your hands up if you don't drop them from your tits," he says, and I slowly move them away.

With him on his knees between my legs, I lie back as he runs his hands from my knees slowly up the insides of my thighs. I close my eyes when my legs quiver. I want this to happen, but it's also the knowing that the hands on my body, touching me intimately, are not the hands of my husband, and that alone is enough to freak me out. It's a storm of emotions battling, creating a war in my head and in my heart.

I want this even though I know it's wrong.

I open my eyes to see the glint of my wedding ring I forgot to take off.

This is so fucking vile.

My pulse sprints out of control.

His hands continue to move painfully slow, closer and closer to my center, and when he cups the heat of me in his hand, I startle.

"Wait," I clip, clutching my hand around his wrist. "I don't know if I can."

"Does this feel good?"

"Yes, but—"

He takes my other hand and forces me to touch his erection. "You want this?"

"Yes," I admit against my tormenting thoughts, because when you cut through all my guilt and all my fear, there's a burning desire that I can't kill.

"Are you scared of my touch?"

I nod, because I am, because it's new, because it's different.

"Are you wet?"

"Alec . . ."

"Are you?" he presses.

"Yes."

He releases my hand and begins unbuttoning my pants, saying, "I'm not going to touch you."

Dragging them down my legs, he then stands beside the bed, unhooks his slacks, and takes them off along with his briefs. His cock is rock hard as he stands entirely naked in front of me.

"I want to cum with you." His voice is heavy. He gets back onto the bed and sits on his knees, facing me. "Touch yourself."

"What?"

He takes his cock in his hand and slowly pumps it. "We've done it like this a hundred times."

"That was different."

"When I put my cock inside you, I don't want any doubts or any fear. And right now, you're feeling all of that," he tells me. "I also want you comfortable with your body. I don't want those fucking walls you brought in here with you. So if you want what you say you want, then you need to show me you're willing to do this my way. Either that, or you can go back home to your husband."

But that's the last place I want to go, so I will my reluctance to go away, and I sit myself up against the headboard. "Okay," I agree on a shaky voice. I nervously slip my hand inside my panties, but keep my eyes closed. I can't possibly look at Alec while I do this because this is beyond embarrassing.

"I want you to watch me, Victoria." And when I open my eyes, he tries to settle my nerves. "I've see you touch yourself before, I've heard you moan my name when you cum, I've heard you cry, and I've never once judged you or laughed at you."

"I know."

"Look at my cock. I want you watching me while I watch you."

I flick my eyes back to his and see nothing but a desire for me to give in to him.

"Show me," he says, and I put my faith in him to make me feel safe enough to do this.

I lift my hips and slip off my panties. If he's bold enough to be entirely naked, then I'll try to be as well.

He's right, I came here to try something new, to be someone different, but I came with walls of protection. If I want to play it safe and never explore who I might really be, then I should've stayed home. But I'm here. I'm in Alec's world, so I need to let go and trust him.

I unhook my bra and slip it off my arms, my eyes locked to his. With a swarm of butterflies in my stomach, I take a hard swallow and spread my thighs, exposing everything to him.

He smiles cagily at me before his eyes leave mine, falling to my breasts and then farther down. I slip two fingers into my mouth, wetting them, and then drop them down between my legs. His breath staggers when I start rolling my fingers over my clit, and the knowledge that I'm doing this in front of him heightens every nerve ending in my body. Every inch of my skin has reached a new level of sensitivity.

I move my eyes from Alec's face and watch him as he strokes his cock, the cock I fantasize about having inside of me. He reaches down with his other hand and grabs his balls as he continues to jerk off. His grip is tight in both hands and the veins in his forearms protrude.

Thrill conquers abashment the more I lose myself. The excitement ruptures in my chest and down my limbs. I moan as I give in to the pleasure of watching this man getting off to the sight of me doing something no man has ever seen me do before. It's a rush, and I feel like I'm floating as the world outside the two of us swims out of focus.

Taking my other hand, I drag my finger through my arousal before pushing it inside me. I watch Alec and meet his tempo as I finger myself. It doesn't take me long to find the edge of my orgasm with the intensity between us. Both of my hands drive me higher, the sound of my wet pussy blends with the sounds of his flesh slapping.

"I'm about to go," he groans.

The ecstasy in his voice, the strain along his chest and neck, his dilated eyes, all from the sight of me, sends me reeling.

"Oh, God," I whimper as my core flares in pleasure.

Alec's eyes clench shut, and with the first ribbon of cum he shoots onto my stomach, I erupt in a blinding orgasm. My vision blurs as he continues to pump himself all over me, and knowing it was me that got him off spikes my self-esteem. I ride out my orgasm, rolling my hips over my sticky hands, moaning and panting.

Time slips and suddenly we're kissing, his body on top of mine, never even allowing me a second to feel embarrassed about what I just did. The weight of him pushes me into the mattress, and I gladly welcome the pressure against my chest as he swallows my ragged breaths. His hands grip my face tightly as he holds me still beneath him. I don't even recognize the skin I'm in, I'm flying too high, and I've never felt so free in the entrapment of this man.

I want to writhe against him just to get off once more, but he has me pinned. Never have I been the one with an insatiable appetite, but there's something about how this man makes me feel that turns on my greed. I want more every time, and when he gives me more, it's never enough. It's a constant hunger pang I can't rid myself of, so I keep coming back.

Our kisses are slow, and I'm finally able to catch my breath. He rolls us to our sides, our bodies marked in each other's orgasm, sticky and sweaty.

"You make the sexiest face when you cum," he says, and I blush, lowering my head and tucking it under his chin. He chuckles. "Why are you so damn shy?"

"Why are you so damn blunt?" I counter when I look at him.

"I'm not. I'm just comfortable. Animals fuck each other in the wide open."

"So?"

"We're animals too, Victoria. But you're under the mindset that sex is this secret act that you need to hide and not talk about in case you offend someone who, probably, fucks just as filthy as you do."

I smirk with mild laughter. "I don't fuck filthy."

"Not yet," he says and then gets out of bed.

I watch his bare ass as he walks into the kitchen, grab two bottles of water from the fridge, and then return.

He hands me a water and I take a sip.

This man doesn't own an ounce of modesty, but I'm not complaining. For being forty-one, he's in great shape. My only concern is that he's going to be disappointed in me. I've only had sex with two men in my life, and Alec . . . well, I don't even want to think about how many women he's been with. Women who are assured in their sexuality—confident—uninhibited—everything I'm not. I wonder if I'll be a bore to him, because Lord only knows what his expectations are, and as much as I want this, I'm doubting myself. Hell, I'm struggling right now sitting here naked.

I adjust myself, pull the sheets out from under me, and drape them over my lap so at least my bottom half is covered.

"Why do you do that?"

"What?"

"I just saw your pussy."

"Can I ask you something now?"

"Anything," he says before taking a guzzle of his water.

"Why me when you can get anyone? I mean, why not go for someone who's more like you and less like me?"

"Because I like you. In the same sense that you see me as a challenge, I see you as a challenge"—he then rips the sheets off of me—"and I don't just want anyone"—he grabs my legs and yanks me down—"I want you"—and then he pushes my knees open.

Oh, my God. He's staring at my pussy in broad daylight.

I lift my head and watch him as he opens my folds with his thumbs—one by one. My head is screaming in self-consciousness as he examines me.

He looks up and reads my expression clearly. "Why does this make you uncomfortable?"

"Because . . ."

"Be honest."

"Because you're looking at the most intimate part of me."

"You're wrong," he says. "You're devaluing your heart. *That's* the most intimate part of you."

I lose sight, closing my eyes as my head falls back onto the pillow the moment he slides his tongue up my pussy and to my clit. He sucks my clit into his mouth, causing my hips to buck into him. He releases a pleasurable growl that vibrates against me as the pressure of his sucking builds. I reach down and grab onto the sides of his head as my body squirms out of control. His eyes dart to mine, and I can see the smile in them.

He continues to suck and lick, and when he's satisfied, he props up on his knees, and holds himself in his hand. When I see he's already hard again, I swallow thickly, suddenly scared of how raw this situation has just become. My heart thuds loudly, echoing in my ears. He takes the tip of his cock and runs it along the outside of my pussy.

"W-w-w-wait!" I frantically stutter, knowing that once I do this, there's no possibility of turning back, but it's when his eyes peer down to mine, I focus on solely him and get lost in his sea of blue. "Go slow, okay?"

He pushes into me, first the tip, and then, inch by inch, deeper and deeper. I freeze up, making it difficult for my body to adjust to the size of him. He fills me differently than Landon does, stretching me in new ways. Once Alec is fully inside me, he holds himself still and allows me time to relax.

"You're tense," he whispers.

My heart's beating beats I've never felt before, barraged with a million sensations at once. I'm too hot, too ripe, too full of life. My past fades into the back of my head as Alec becomes my only present.

"Move," I breathe, and he pulls back, drawing himself out of me without any sense of urgency.

Every part of him sliding along every part of me. He moves without rush, pushing his hips back down to me, filling me again, stretching me even more. I want to cry out because the pleasure is so intense it's nearly intolerable.

"Oh, fuck," he groans on a strained voice. His face wears the same passionate ferocity that's coursing through me.

My hands grip his shoulders as he moves inside my body, my wedding ring staring me in the face, making a mockery of me, but I can't stop. I don't want to. It's too good. It's too raw. It's the most potent narcotic of my life.

Alec watches me when I reach around and yank off my rings.

"Get rid of them," I beg, needing him even more to erase all the tension and sadness in my life.

He takes them and throws them across the room, metal clinking against the hardwood floors. I look up at my escape, wrap my legs around his waist, and sling my arms around his neck.

"Fuck me, Alec."

chapter five

BETWEEN ONE HEARTBEAT AND THE NEXT, MY ENTIRE LIFE CHANGED.

I no longer know who I am anymore. I used to be me, but that was then, and this is now.

I've lost myself completely.

I live in a constant state of quiet despair.

I'm not quite sure how I got here, and I have no idea where I'm going.

I've been sleeping with Alec for over a month now. My hunger grows the more I feed it, and I can no longer see a way out of this. I'm at his loft every chance I can get, multiple times a week. If he can only get away from work for fifteen minutes, I take it. In those moments, we fuck each other like rabid animals, fiending for our fix. Alec is inside me more than Landon. He's always on my skin. He's always on my mind.

The days I know I won't see him, I'm anxious and panicky, but he's still with me because I spend those days texting and talking to him over the phone. Somehow, we always remain connected.

With Landon, I've become good at disguising myself. To him, I'm a wife who made one mistake and is doing what I can to fix it. We go to marriage therapy every week, but at this point, it's a total sham. We talk about ways to build trust and rekindle the flame we lost. We make goals and promises, and when we walk out, we kiss before each getting into our own cars. He goes to work, and I get on my phone to call Alec.

If you asked me if I still love my husband, I couldn't answer you.

How do you know the difference between love and familiarity after thirteen years and two children? But if you asked who it is that beats inside me, it's Alec. He's the one that pulls me through to the next day.

But I can't lose Landon because I can't do that to my girls. I don't want my family to be broken. I can't break their little hearts. So I stay. I stay and I play my part.

To the outsider, Landon and I are on the mends. We fight less, and he's extending me more trust, all the while, I'm secretly drifting farther away from him.

Our therapist wants us to go on dates every week, but I spend the whole time thinking about what the date would be like if it were Alec that I was with. We talk about future plans, but what if there is no future for us?

My head is all over the place as I wander through this clandestine turmoil, and living these two lives has become so time-consuming that my work is suffering. It's impossible to get my head in the right space to write. And even if I could, there's no time between juggling two men and being a mom. I had to ask my editor for an extension, but even with the extra time, I'm so far behind that I doubt I'll be able to meet the new deadline.

And then there's Brooke. She knows what's going on with me and Alec and is beyond appalled. Our interactions have been sour at best, and as of late, she's been up my ass because she's drowning in my social media that I haven't cared enough about to keep up with. I've lost track of everything that it's now too overwhelming, so I avoid it. I can see my world slowly crumbling around me, but it isn't enough to make me stop.

Even if I wanted to, I don't think I could.

"What are you thinking about?" Alec asks as I lie in his arms, the smell of our sex still lingering in the air.

I tighten my arm that's draped over him as sadness blooms inside me. Today is a hard day. I'm emotional and clingy and dreading the thought of going back home.

He kisses the top of my head, pulling my naked body closer against his.

"You don't have to go," he says.

"I wish it were that easy."

"Tell me what you want."

Leaning my head back, I look at him through misty eyes. "I want everything to disappear, everything but you."

"You know how much I care about you?"

I nod because I can sense it without him even having to tell me.

"I'm crazy about you."

"Why can't this be easy?" I weep, and he catches my tears that slip out, wiping them away.

"Nothing good in life is ever easy."

"Is that what you are?" I ask. "Are you what's good for me?"

"What do you think?"

"I don't know. Tell me. Tell me what I should be thinking."

He shifts his body on top of mine, and I love how small he makes me feel when he traps me beneath him.

"I could be good for you," he says. "You need a man who can make choices for you, a man who will take care of you. You wouldn't be so lost with me, because I'd never allow you to lose yourself."

A few more tears fall, and as I feel the strength in his words, he grows hard between my legs.

"Who are you crying for?"

"You."

He kisses me deeply, and when he pulls back, he tells me, "I love that you cry for me."

His intensity is my elixir. "Touch me."

I watch as he cracks a subtle smirk. "I want you to do something for me." He reaches over to the nightstand, picks up his cell phone, and turns us over so that I'm now on top of him. "I want you to suck my cock."

"And what are you going to do?"

"Film you."

"Uh-uh," I say with a shake of my head.

"You know I like to watch, and when you're not here, I want to have this to watch when I need to get myself off."

I stare at him, dumbfounded, and when he twitches his eyebrow, challenging me to give in to his request, I abandon my insecurities in an effort to take another step into his world.

"Wrap your sweet little lips around me."

I slip down between his legs and wrap my fingers around his shaft. The moment I hear the beep that indicates he's turned on the camera, I drop my head over him. Knowing he'll be watching this later, I want to make it worthwhile. I take my time, moving my mouth slowly over the silky smooth skin of his thick cock, rolling my tongue over the tip before sliding back down.

"Look at the camera, baby," he directs, and I do.

I work the length of him while gazing into the lens as he watches me on the screen of his phone. My hand pumps in sync with my mouth as I bob up and down. With my other hand, I stroke my fingers along his perineum, a move he showed me a couple weeks ago.

"Fuck." He groans loudly when I touch him back there. "Put my balls in your mouth."

Alec is always unfiltered when telling me what he likes and what turns him on. He encourages me to do the same, but I still find it difficult to be so direct with him.

I continue to jerk him off while I tease him with my tongue. With every lick, his balls tighten, and then, with both my hands pleasuring him, I do as he instructs and take him in my mouth, sucking on him gently. His hips buck, but I don't relent. He's powerless in my touch, and I love that I can give this to him.

I watch as he struggles to hold the camera still, his face flushed with desire. He opens his legs wider, and I nuzzle my head deeper between them as I add more pressure to my mouth and finger. When I hear his breathing stagger, I sense that he's close. Being with him as many times as I have, I've come to know his body well and how it reacts, so I move my head and take his cock back into my mouth. It doesn't take long for him to harden even more against my tongue.

He reaches down with his free hand, and when he twitches in my mouth, he pushes me down on him. His cum shoots down the back of my throat as he holds me locked in place. I grip his thighs with both my hands and swallow all he gives me. His orgasm rages, and I relish his body as it shudders in gratification.

His hand softens on my head, and when I slide my mouth off him, he looks down at me with a smile.

I crawl up into his arms and rest my head on his chest as his heart pounds against my ear. He used to intimidate me when we first started sleeping together, but he's been able to settle most of my nerves this past month, and I've come to trust him with my body. Sex with him is a whole new experience for me. It's always different, and he has a way of pushing me and challenging me to explore new things with him.

I've never touched a man as intimately as he likes me to touch him. Landon would freak if my finger got as close to his ass as Alec likes mine to get, but Alec is completely free with his body, which helps me be less resistant with mine. I allow him to touch me in places my husband never has. And because of this, I feel closer to Alec than Landon when it comes to sex.

"I want you to watch yourself," he says, handing me his phone. "I want you to see what I see."

I hit play, and we both watch what just happened between us. I don't recognize the girl in the video who's giving a blow job to a man she isn't married to. This woman is nothing like me, but at the same time, she is me. I never would've found her if it weren't for Alec helping me discover her. She turns me on as I watch. I never knew I could be so confident to allow myself to be filmed, but that's the power of Alec. I'd do almost anything if he asked me.

When the video ends, he tosses the phone aside.

"How do you feel watching that?"

"Surprised," I admit. "That girl doesn't feel like me."

"She *is* you," he affirms.

We spend the short time we have left with each other cuddling in bed. We don't speak as Alec runs his hands through my hair while I graze my fingers lazily along his naked body. With my eyes closed, I allow myself to pretend this isn't wrong. That it's Alec I belong to, and I don't have to rush home. I wonder what life would be like if that were the case. Would he still be as exciting? Would I still feel the thrill every time we were together?

It doesn't matter though, because I'm not his—I belong to someone else.

"When can I see you again?" he questions as I pull my clothes on.

"I have a signing this weekend and won't be back until Tuesday."

"Is this the New York trip you told me about?"

"Yes."

Alec throws on a pair of pants and then follows me into the bathroom. While I touch up my makeup, he leans against the doorjamb and watches.

"What if I went with you?"

My eyes dart to him in the reflection of the mirror. "What?"

"You go to these things alone, right?"

I turn to face him. "If you're asking if Landon comes, the answer is no. But Brooke, my assistant will be with me."

"What if I got us a room of our own?"

"People know I'm married," I tell him. "What if someone saw us?"

"I'll get a room at a different hotel. You don't have to stay where the signing is, do you?"

I shake my head. "But what about Brooke?"

"She already knows about me."

"Yeah, but she doesn't approve of you or what I'm doing with you. I can't ditch her like that."

"You can't or you won't." He steps over to me, backing me up against the sink with both his hands braced next to me on the counter. "Friday through Tuesday, you could be all mine. No running off to get home to your husband. No sneaking around," he says.

"We never leave this loft for fear someone will see us, but in New York, we'd be boundless."

His offer is everything I've been wanting with him—total freedom.

"You'd seriously come?"

"I'd seriously come," he affirms.

chapter six

I feel like the worst friend for what I'm about to do. Brooke and I are about to takeoff to New York, and she still doesn't know that I won't be staying with her. It's been weighing on my shoulders, but I need to cover my tracks. If I told her before we got on this plane, she would've refused to come. If that happened, it would have gotten back to Landon through her husband that she wasn't with me. Questions would've been asked, and I'd be up shit creek.

So I kept my mouth shut, until right now.

I look over to Brooke, who's flipping through a magazine, and when the plane departs from the gate, I'm already hating myself.

"I need to talk to you about something." My apprehensive voice strikes her attention. "I know you're going to be pissed, but please—"

"Is everything okay?" she questions, closing her magazine.

There's no right way to drop this bomb, and with my gut twisted in knots, I decide to just tell her straight up—rip off the Band-Aid.

"Alec's coming to New York, and I agreed to stay with him." I brace for her reaction as she glares daggers at me. "Please, don't hate me. Be mad, but don't hate me, Brooke."

"Are you out of your fucking mind?" she seethes under her breath.

And I am. I'm *completely* out of my mind.

"He offered to come, and I couldn't say no."

"Yes, you could've, but instead, you decided to ditch me. Do you even know how much I was looking forward to this trip? I wanted to spend this time with you before the baby comes."

"I know. I'm sorry. We can still hang out."

She turns away from me and stares out the window. I keep my mouth shut, not wanting to upset her more. The plane races down the runway, and when we lift off the ground, I become acutely aware that this trip might forever change our friendship.

"Brooke, please say something."

It takes her a moment, but she eventually turns to me and, with an accusing tone, asks, "What is it about this guy that's worth hurting the ones who love you?"

"That's the thing though—I don't want to hurt anyone."

"But you are. You're corrosive to everyone but him."

Her words are truth. I hate coming face to face with the reality of my actions. It's too much responsibility for me to bear, and it only makes me want Alec more because he's the one that can make all the despair in my world disappear.

"How much longer do you plan on carrying out this affair? When does this end for you?"

"The truth?"

"I think I deserve it," she responds.

"I can't even imagine walking away at this point. I want to cry every time I leave him to go back home."

"And Landon?"

"He has no idea."

She shakes her head at me. "I don't want to judge you, but you're making it very difficult."

"I just want to be happy, but it's a lose-lose situation. If I leave Landon, then I lose the girls and crush their world. And if I leave Alec, I'll be miserable without him."

"Eventually you're going to have to make a choice or else the choice will be made for you when Landon finds out. And he *will* find out sooner or later."

I already know this, but it's easier to live in denial, so I do.

"Why do you even want to be with a guy who's okay with this whole situation? It doesn't say a lot about his character, Tor."

"It's complicated," I tell her. I feel like I understand Alec's position in this equation, but I don't know how to go about defending him.

"That's your excuse for everything these days." She opens her magazine back up, saying, "I'm done talking."

There's nothing I can say to excuse my behavior—it's inexcusable—everything I'm doing is. But it doesn't mean I don't want to justify myself. It's human nature to do what you can to reason with yourself that there's a purpose to the things you do, but I've yet to resolve what the purpose of all this is. And until I find that reason, it's impossible for me to rationalize this to make sense out of it all. I'm trapped in my self-created labyrinth of lies and betrayals.

When the plane touches down a short hour later, Brooke has yet to talk to me. She's pissed, and rightfully so. We extended the stay of this New York trip because she's now almost four months pregnant and she wanted to have a girls' getaway before she has the baby. I keep telling myself it'll be okay and that I can figure out a way to make this up to her. I know the right thing to do here, but I can't do it. I can't walk away from my drug of choice when he's down in baggage claim waiting to take me on the bender of a lifetime. My skin is already tingling in anticipation.

As soon as we deplane and head through the airport to the luggage carousel, my heart begins to skip beats. Brooke remains silent with me. She just needs time to cool down, but I fuel her fire when she sees me smiling the moment I catch sight of Alec waiting for me.

I want to run to him, jump in his arms, and kiss him, but I don't.

It's an awkward situation with Brooke here. She wants nothing to do with Alec—her loyalty is with Landon. She's known him since the first day I met him, and the two of them have always had a special friendship because of their shared love for me.

Brooke takes notice of Alec and veers away from us to wait on the luggage when he approaches me. He moves with caution, and out of respect for my friend, refrains from touching me.

Alec senses the tension. "Are you okay?"

"She's hurt."

His eyes boast concern for me and my feelings rather than hers.

After he helps me with my bags, he excuses himself to go outside and get us a cab, leaving me alone with Brooke.

"So, you're just gonna go with him?"

"I'm sorry."

"You're fucking unbelievable," she fumes as she storms off.

"Brooke." I call out for her, but she refuses to acknowledge me, walking out to catch the hotel shuttle bus.

With Alec waiting on me, I let Brooke go and make my way to the taxis. He's already loading the luggage when I spot him. I approach, and he opens the door for me, and once we get in and the cabbie starts to drive, Alec takes my face in his hands and kisses me. Despite the brick of disloyalty in my stomach, I open up to him—a kiss so deep, our souls fuck. He's my heart's emollient, taking away my stress in a split second. With my marriage in shambles, Alec has become the place where my soul can cocoon itself to find comfort and solace. He keeps me whole—free from falling apart.

Sliding my tongue along his, I taste the freedom we've been deprived of, but now it's ours to do with as we wish.

"I can't believe you're here," I gleam.

When we arrive at the W in midtown, we don't have to waste time checking in since Alec arrived earlier this morning. We make a beeline through the impressive lounge and head straight up to the room. Clothes are coming off before the door shuts behind us. We're fervid, clawing at one another as we fumble in our steps, but he doesn't lead me to the bed.

The moment both of us are stripped bare, he turns me around in his arms, facing me toward the full-length window.

"What are you doing?"

"I'm going to fuck you up against this window."

I look at the mass of people below. It's the middle of the day and the street is filled with hundreds of pedestrians.

"Alec." I resist wearily.

He moves me in slow steps closer to the panoramic window, and

I tell myself that I can do this. That this is why I chose to be with him—to explore this unfound part of me.

I gasp when he pushes my body against the cold window, my tits press firmly against the glass. My breath catches with unease, and I'm terrified to look down, fearful that people can see me.

Alec brings his head over my shoulder and rests it against my cheek, releasing a heady breath. With my forehead leaning against the window, he whispers seductively in my ear, "Open your eyes and look."

I take a deep breath, hoping to swallow a little bit of courage, and when I open my eyes, I catch a few heads tilted up. I shut them quickly and turn my head, nuzzling it into the side of Alec's neck to help calm my nerves.

"How does this make you feel, to know people are looking at you?"

"Scared," I breathe.

"You're in my hands, Victoria. You have nothing to be scared of."

He moves his head back, and I feel the loss of his comfort.

"Spread your legs."

When I step my feet apart, he brings his hand through my legs from behind and cups my pussy, kicking up my heart rate. I brace my hands against the window my breath is fogging up, and my knees nearly give out when he shoves a finger inside me. He begins pumping his hand up into me, and when I look back down, only a few people are peering up at us as they continue to rush along in pace with the crowd.

The moment a woman looks up and locks eyes with me, a rush of adrenaline floods into my bloodstream. It's an unexpected feeling that comes out of nowhere, but one that turns me on. Alec continues to touch me as my nipples ache against the frigid glass. It's the end of March, but the winter is still bitterly cold.

Alec grabs ahold of my hips, and when I push my ass out, he finally gives me what I've been burning for. He thrusts into me, pinning my body flat against the window. I know people are watching us, but the pleasure is so overwhelming that I can't find any strength to open my eyes. It's all I can do to remain standing while Alec fucks me with unforgiving passion. I reach behind and wrap my hand around the back of his neck, urging him forward.

He kisses my shoulder before bringing his lips to my ear. "I love the way your pussy feels wrapped around my cock."

"Oh, God," I moan loudly when he gives me his crass words.

"You're so fucking wet, I can feel you dripping down my balls."

"Alec . . ."

"Say my name again."

"Alec," I pant as the throbbing in my clit becomes too much to tolerate, and I beg, "Touch my pussy, Alec."

The moment I say those words, his cock twitches inside me, swelling in desire, and when he touches me with his fingers, my whole body bucks in ecstasy. I cum into his hand while he strokes my clit and fucks me. My whole body quivers as I struggle to remain standing.

Alec bands his free arm around my stomach and holds me close to keep me from falling. I cry out his name once more and he loses himself right along with me. Our bodies jerk and tremble together as we get off. I grab his hand that's still between my legs and grind down, enjoying every piece of this orgasm before we give way and lower ourselves to the floor.

As my heartbeat slows, I'm able to think coherently, and I can't believe that strangers just watched us having sex. Up until now, we've been so private with each other, but I knew it was only a matter of time until this particular fetish of his would come into play. It wasn't as terrifying as I thought it would be. I know he's been slowly guiding me to this point, never rushing me. I wear my emotions on my sleeve so it's been no secret between us how reluctant I've been with every step. But with everything we do, he proves to be a man I can trust my body with. Never once has he made me feel unsafe.

Alec lies on top of me, and when he brushes a lock of hair away from my damp forehead, he gently asks, "Are you okay?" as he always does.

I love this about him, that through his strong personality, he nurtures me. It's in these rare moments that I can feel myself softening to him. I never felt like anyone looked out for me as a child—never felt tenderness from my parents. My father left when I was only three years old, and my mother wasn't the affectionate type. And even though I know Landon cares deeply for me, I never felt as if he held my entire being the way Alec does.

"I'm okay," I murmur as my body tingles in placidity.

"You surprised me."

"I did?"

"I thought you'd resist me on that."

"A part of me wanted to," I admit.

"Why didn't you?"

I run my hands up his arms and over his shoulders. "Because I know it's something you need. And because I trust you."

He stares down at me while I continue to run my hands along his arms and back, and when he drops his forehead to mine, he asks, "Why haven't you left him yet?"

His words feel like splashes of acid on my heart. Landon is the last thing I need to be thinking about while Alec and I are lying here naked with each other.

"I don't want to talk about him."

"I do." His tone is firm, and I know he isn't going to drop this conversation.

He shifts off me and we both sit up.

"I don't want to hurt you, Alec."

"You can't hurt me," he states. "I just want to know."

"I'm scared of what it'll do to my girls if I left. My parents divorced when I was little, and I swore that I'd never put my children through that. The pain I feel for them when I consider leaving my husband is unfathomable," I explain. "I'm their mother. I'm supposed to protect them, not put them directly in the line of fire."

"It doesn't have to be as brutal as what you're thinking," he says. "I'd be more concerned with the fact that you're teaching them that it's okay to be with someone who doesn't make you happy."

"Landon's a good dad," I defend.

"But you two fight?"

"Yes."

"He yells at you?"

"I deserve it."

His eyes narrow, irritated with what I just said. "How long are you going to be his punching bag?"

I never thought of how my marriage would affect my girls. He's right. What am I teaching them about relationships? I feel so much remorse for what I'm doing that I allow Landon to throw insults my way when he's mad at me. It's a pathetic excuse for atonement, but I allow it nonetheless. The girls can hear us when we fight, and I don't want them to think it's okay for a man to talk to a woman like that. They have no idea what I've done to hurt their father, all they know is that their father spews disgusting words into their mother's face.

"I don't know what I'm doing anymore." Alec doesn't move as he watches my pain surface. "There's no way to protect my girls from having their hearts broken, but you're right, I'm setting an awful example for them. I wish I had someone who would just tell me what the right thing is to do."

"Life doesn't work that way. Sometimes we have to make hard choices, but just because they're hard, doesn't mean they're wrong."

I blink sadness away when I feel the burn of unsteady tears. Alec finally reaches out for me and pulls me into his arms.

"Do you love him?"

"I don't know."

"You don't love him." I draw back and look at him. "When you love someone, you know it. The fact that you're confused tells me that you're just scared to admit the truth that you no longer love your husband."

What if he's right? What if it's fear that's making everything so unclear?

"Are you happy?" he questions.

"No."

"Do you want to be?"

I nod. "Yes."

"Tell me what makes you happy?"

"Aside from my girls . . . *you*."

chapter seven

I RUN THROUGH THE LOBBY, FLY OUT THE DOORS, AND HAIL A CAB.

"Where to?" the driver asks, and I tell him the hotel where the book signing is being held.

"As fast as you can get me there, please."

I open my purse and pull out my compact to freshen up my face. Spending the night with Alec was amazing. We were finally able to be with each other without any interruptions. If he wasn't waking me up for sex, then it was me waking him up. We went at it all night long while drifting in and out of sleep. And this morning, I had to force myself out the door.

If it weren't for Brooke, I would totally ditch this signing just to be with Alec. Our time together is always so limited that I feel an urgency to take all I can get. But it never fails that I'm left wanting more. That's the thing about affairs, I guess. We never have each other long enough to feel satisfied, and when I'm not with him, I'm always panicked and anticipating the next time I'll see him again.

When the cab pulls along the curb of the hotel, I throw him enough cash for the ride and tip and jump out. I normally take my time putting myself together for these events, but when I burst through the doors, I'm an hour late with only a touch of makeup on.

"You're late," Brooke snaps from her chair.

She has the whole table already set up, and the guilt returns.

"I'm sorry. Traffic was really bad," I lie.

Her face is mottled in irritation. "You missed the author photo."

"I hate those things anyway."

"Doesn't matter. It makes you look unprofessional."

"I know I'm an asshole," I tell her, "but can we try to get through today without being so abrasive?"

"You're calling *me* abrasive?"

"No," I say, back-stepping my words. "I meant us."

She forces a smile. "I'll be good."

When the doors open to the readers, it's a whirlwind I'm unable to enjoy. Sitting next to my best friend and watching her work her pregnant ass off is undeserving. I screwed her over. She didn't have to show up today, she could've screwed me over too, but she didn't. She showed up for me—to support me. She's a much better person than I am, and I'm nowhere near worthy of her friendship right now.

Not one picture was taken with a genuine smile today. Everything about this signing was a lie. Every fan I met felt like a deception. They have no idea the thorns I bear under these clothes. They'd be better off to stay away from me because all I seem to do these days is hurt people. I'm a total fraud, but not one person who walked through this room today knows that fact besides Brooke.

She's knows the rot I've become.

"Let me help you pack this stuff up," I offer when she picks up a stack of books.

"I've got it," she dismisses. "Just go."

"Brooke—"

"What?" she snaps. "Is there something you want to say to make yourself feel better about being a total bitch to me?"

I bite my tongue because no matter what I say, I'm only going to make this situation worse.

Brooke grabs my purse and holds it out for me. She won't even look me in the eyes, and when I take the purse from her, I attempt to apologize, but she cuts me off. "Yeah, I know. You're sorry. But not sorry enough because we both know where you're going when you leave."

Shame and guilt sock me in my stomach, and before I break down in front of this room full of authors, bloggers, and a few lingering fans, I duck my head and rush out. I shield my face that's covered in tears with my hand as I hightail it out of the hotel. I don't even bother trying to catch a cab; I'd rather lose myself in the sea of people.

"Victoria!"

I turn back to where I just came from and see Alec pushing his way to catch up to me.

"What are you doing here?"

"I was waiting for you," he says, and when he finally reaches me, he grabs my face in worriment, asking, "What happened? Are you okay?"

Passersby zip around us, bumping our shoulders, and I'm scared that a reader or an author might see us.

"Alec, we can't be here," I panic. "There's too many people around that know who I am."

Without missing a beat, he takes me under his arm and hails a cab.

"What happened?" he asks once we're tucked away in a stale-smelling taxi and heading back to the W.

I wipe sadness from my cheeks. "It's my fault. I deserve to feel this way."

"Why are you being so hard on yourself?"

"Because I'm selfish," I snap. "I'm weak and self-centered and—"

"Enough," he halts with agitation. "I'm not going to sit here and listen to you beat yourself up. You want to do that? Do it with someone else. Because when I look at you, I don't see any of that shit."

"How can you think for one second that what I'm doing isn't selfish?"

"Because I only care about who you are when you're with me. I don't want to think about who you are when you go home to your husband. I already know you're fake as shit with that man, but that's not the same woman who shows up at my door."

I flick my eyes to the rearview mirror and catch the driver silently scorning me before diverting his eyes back to the road. Even he knows how atrocious I am.

"Look at me," Alec demands. "This situation is far from ideal, but you're not in it alone. I'm here with you, aren't I?"

"You are, but—"

"No buts. All that matters is that I'm here and that I'm fucking crazy about you. Leave all that other bullshit behind. I don't want to piss away the short amount of time we have together."

His words come out harsh, but I can understand where he's coming from. He didn't have to come to New York, but he did, and I shouldn't be tearing down what we have together by listing all the reasons why it's wrong.

"You're right. I'm sorry."

When the cab drops us off at the hotel, I'm thoroughly drained and hungry. We find a quiet spot in the lounge to settle and enjoy a drink before heading to the room to freshen up for our dinner reservation.

After applying a touch of mascara to my lashes, I walk out of the bathroom to find Alec wearing the same clothes from earlier as he sits on the edge of the bed.

"Why haven't you changed?"

He holds out my disposable cell phone and says, "Change of plans."

I cowardly take the phone from him, worried that whatever I'm about to look at has something to do with Landon, but I'm instantly relieved when I look at the screen to see a text exchange between me and Brooke.

When I look at Alec in confusion, he tells me, "I got her number from your other phone. I didn't know if your husband was still checking up on you."

I read the text he sent her, inviting her out to dinner.

"I texted her and let her think the messages were coming from you."

I'm blown away that he would sacrifice his time with me tonight so that I can try to mend my relationship with my best friend.

"Alec . . ."

"You two can take the reservation."

"Are you sure?"

"I wouldn't have texted her if I weren't."

I step between his legs, amazed by his selflessness, and run my hands over his shoulders.

"I can't believe you did this for me."

"There isn't much that I wouldn't do for you."

He pulls me into his arms, and we kiss as he holds on to me tightly. This is what I wish Brooke could see, that Alec doesn't have questionable character, that he has a good heart, that he cares for me, and that he's simply caught up in this mess that I take full responsibility for. It's only because of me that she believes Alec acts in Machiavellian ways. I'm the deceiver, I'm the wretch, I'm the miscreant.

I miss Alec the moment I leave him to meet Brooke. I arrive at the restaurant before she does, and when the host seats me, I order a glass of wine to calm the swarm of emotions that are attacking me from the inside out.

A few minutes pass before Brooke shows up.

"I didn't know we'd be meeting at such a nice restaurant," she says when she sits. "I'm way underdressed."

"You look fine."

I struggle to think of what I should say to her as she looks over the menu. I want to say I'm sorry, but I've said it too many times at this point that I'm sure it only comes across as meaningless. This isn't the first time our friendship has hit a rocky spot. We've been friends for fifteen years and have had many ups and downs, but this is the first time we've dealt with a situation of this magnitude.

Our waiter stops by, and after he presents this evening's chef selections, he scurries off.

The silence grows to an uncomfortable level, and I decide to just say the first thing that's weighing on me the most.

"I can't lose you, Brooke." Saying the words aloud hurts worse than I thought it would.

"You're not going to lose me."

"Then why does it feel that way?"

"Because this is a fuck-up of epic proportions," she says. "I want to understand you, but I just can't. You're my best friend, but I don't recognize this person you've become."

I don't respond because what can I say when I don't even recognize *myself*?

"I want to be here for you, but I'm terrified to stand by and watch you destroy yourself. I'm scared I won't be strong enough to help you pick up the pieces when this all falls apart."

I've purposely been avoiding this talk with her because I'm not ready to face the cold hard truth. Nothing good can come from this, I know that, but as long as I live in denial, I can trick myself to believe almost anything.

"Say something," she urges.

"I don't know what to say."

"Pick the first thing from your heart."

I look into the eyes of the one person I know I can trust above all others and confess the single thing I've been trying to fight off with every ounce of strength my soul has. "I think I love him."

She drops her head with a heavy sigh as if that was the absolute worst thing I could've said, and a tear slips out, carving its way painfully down my cheek. I can't believe my life right now. How did everything get so blurry? It's not like Landon and I had any major issues, but then I met Alec, and *BOOM*, everything changed in an instant. Before I knew what was even happening, I was making choices I didn't even know were choices, and I couldn't take them back. And now, I'm not sure I would take them back because of how I feel about Alec.

"He's not a bad guy, Brooke," I start to defend. "I'm the one that lied. He didn't know I was married."

"But he does now."

"Yes, but—"

"But nothing. He shouldn't be encouraging you like this if he cares about you. He'd wait until you figured things out at home."

"It's not that simple."

"Because you don't want it to be," she argues. "I think it's the thrill of sneaking around that you get off on."

"You think I like this?" My voice pitches, and I quickly bring it down. "You think I enjoy trying to juggle two completely different lives? I hate it. I wish I didn't have to lie and sneak around. It's beyond exhausting and only makes me feel like a horrid piece of shit."

"Then why do it? Why put yourself through all of this if you're so miserable?"

"Because I'm scared it might be the biggest mistake of my life if I left Landon. I'm afraid that I might never get married again and wind up forever alone. And what if I just haven't given us enough time to save our marriage? I mean, I still have feelings there for him, but they've changed, and I'm confused about what they are. But what if our turning point is right around the corner, and I give up too soon?"

"Life is full of what-ifs. There's no guarantee of anything, so if that's what you're waiting for, you're going to be waiting forever." She sits back in her chair and takes a sip of her water.

"What do I do?"

"I can't make that decision for you. I won't even attempt to guide you in that choice. But I will tell you this, Landon doesn't deserve this. His whole heart is invested into saving your marriage. He told Chris that things were getting better, Tor. You have him completely fooled and it isn't right."

"I know," I tell her. "Trust me, I know. I'm just so lost right now. You have to believe that I don't want to hurt anyone. I know I'm selfish. I know I'm fucking everything up. But I don't know what to do."

"You're addicted," she says, nailing it on the head. "You're acting just like an addict. I know you want help, but the only one who can help you is *you*."

She then reaches over and lays her hand on top of mine, a loving touch I'm undeserving of.

"Brooke, I know I keep saying it, but truly, from my heart, I'm sorry for what I'm doing and for abandoning you on this trip."

She takes her other hand and gives me pure compassion, saying, "I know you are."

"You should hate me."

"I'm mad at you—furious even, but I don't hate you." She then does the unexpected and cracks a soft smile. "You owe me. Like majorly owe me for this bitch move you made."

Her forgiveness cuts my wound of unworthiness even deeper. She's right. Both she and Alec are right. I need to make a choice here to free myself and everyone around me of the pain I'm inflicting.

chapter eight

Leaving New York felt like a lancing of my arteries, stalling my heart in treacherous misery. I woke up in tears that last morning, dreading the moment I had to leave the warmth of Alec to catch my flight back home.

Home.

Funny thing is, it's Alec that's beginning to feel like home, but it's not funny at all.

He held me, soaked up my tears into the flesh of his fingers, capturing my heart's pain that ached solely for him. Alec tells me he likes it when I cry for him. I can only assume it reassures him that, even though I'm still with my husband, it's him I'd rather be with. My tears offer a sense of security, and it pleases him to see the physical reaction my body has when it comes to him.

Alec had a later flight out, but he rode with me in the cab to the airport anyway. I felt myself splintering as we drove further away from our collusive paradise. The anguish was overwhelming, and I knew in that moment, in the backseat of that yellow cab, that my marriage was over.

The plane ride home was too short, not nearly enough time to drain all my tears. Brooke sat next to me as I cried behind my sunglasses.

"I think I'm going to leave Landon," I told her, and it was then that she dropped all her anger toward me and wrapped me in her arms. We didn't speak after my admission, but when the plane landed in Boston, Brooke assured me that whatever happened, she would be there.

Walking through the front door of the house I bought with Landon so many years ago, the house we brought our two children home to, was depressing. These walls no longer grant me comfort and serenity. I've destroyed everything our family was supposed to be.

I knew what I had to do, but the moment my girls, my life sources, came running into my arms to welcome me home, I chickened out. They are the only things that are keeping me with Landon. With their skinny little arms around me, I couldn't find the strength to rip their world to shreds.

So the insidiousness continues.

Since returning from New York, I was able to see Alec only once before he had to leave on a business trip to Dallas for a week. We've still been texting and talking, but his absence has left me hollow.

I miss him.

I spent an hour with Landon this morning in our weekly marriage therapy session. He spoke about my New York trip and how he's finding it easier to trust me while I'm away. I felt sick to my stomach when he said this, but I buried it deep as I smiled at him and gave him a reassuring squeeze on his knee.

We then talked about his need for me to be transparent with him. That if I ever felt like straying again, I should tell him so we can figure out what it is I'm needing and work together to fill the void. Landon told me to never be afraid to be honest with him even if I thought it would hurt him. But he has no clue the secret I hide.

We left as we always do, a kiss in the parking lot before he heads back to the restaurant and I call Alec while I drive home. But Alec didn't answer today.

And now I sit in my living room, lonely and dismal.

The phone rings, and I leap to life until I realize it's the wrong ring. When I pick up my regular phone, I'm consumed with dread when I see it's Tabitha, my editor. I've missed the deadline for my extension, and I've been avoiding calls from my editor and my agent these past few days.

"Hello?" I answer, knowing I can't avoid this situation any longer.

"Madilyn," she says, always addressing me as my author name. "What in the world is going on?"

"I'm sorry. I know I'm late with the manuscript. I've just been distracted and the words aren't coming to me."

"Then you need to call me, but missing two deadlines when we have a contract creates a serious situation. Every book is on a timeline, and when you throw that off by not meeting your commitment, you throw other books off schedule as well. I have to worry about the money being invested into the marketing of this book, and when you fail to deliver on contractual dates, it makes all of us look bad," she reprimands harshly. "I've contacted your agent and advised her that the contract we have on the remaining books is being reviewed."

"What does that mean?"

"It means there's a good chance we might have to pull the plug on you."

Shit!

"I've put my ass on the line for you, Madilyn, but we set contracts in place for a reason," she says. "I can't do my job if you don't do yours."

"I completely understand and apologize for the delay. I promise you I'll do whatever it takes to turn this around in order to secure my standing with you and the publisher. I've been dealing with issues at home, which has completely turned my world upside down."

"Look, we all have stuff in our lives that comes up, but you need to communicate with me when these situations arise," she says, and I agree with her. "Tell me where you are in the book. What's your current word count?"

"Around thirty-five thousand."

"Christ," she breathes in agitation.

"I know it's not much, but I can push out a good five thousand words a day and have this to you in two weeks."

"You can write this book in two weeks?"

"I'll make it happen. You have my word."

"Do what you can, but there are no promises on its publication, or at the very minimum, a monetary penalty to pay back a portion of the advance you received for this book."

"I understand."

"I'll be in touch as soon as we reach our decision."

Oh, my God. This is bad—really fucking bad. I'm losing sight of my responsibilities, and I'm now at risk of losing the financial security of being published through a publishing house. For months, my entire world has been nothing but a foggy haze with Alec being the only thing in focus. I'm in a constant state of fight or flight, and even in this moment when I know I should fight, my first thought is to run and hide from everything I'm compromising. It makes me want the comfort of Alec even more. I want to drown in him, because drowning would be so much easier than fighting my way to the surface, only to have to swim to the shore that feels like a million miles away.

I pick up my disposable phone and dial Alec. Again, all I get are unanswered rings.

Something inside me snaps, and I break down in tears, crying for someone to take my hand and help me out of this. I want a mom or a dad who cares enough to save me, to tell me what to do. I want the touch of a protector to swoop me up and take me far away from this mess I've created. Alec has that touch, Alec has the qualities of a caretaker I desperately need right now, but he's gone, and I'm so confused. I'm so torn. I'm so far from who I am.

I no longer recognize the world I wander around in.

I hear the garage opening, and I startle, quickly powering down my disposable cell that holds only one phone number. I shove it under the seat cushion that I'm sitting on and wipe my tears, but I'm a messy crier, and Landon knows I'm upset the moment he walks through the door.

"Everything okay?"

I nod.

"You're crying."

"I'm just having a bad day," I strain around the emotionally swollen cords in my throat.

He comes to sit on the coffee table in front of me—love and concern splashed across his face, and I hate myself for being the shitty wife he's clueless to. He's too good for me.

"What's going on?"

Maybe this is the moment I tell him that I've flushed our marriage down the toilet along with every dream we ever made together.

He told me earlier he wanted to know if I ever felt like straying, but can I do that? Do I manipulate the truth, not admit to my affair, but tell him I feel the need for one? Do I take a cleaver to the trust he gives me that allows me to be with Alec?

How much longer can I hold myself together?

Maybe I'll tell him my need for someone else, and *he'll* be the one to leave me, freeing me of having to own the blame of being the one who says it's over.

Pride is my enemy.

"You told me you wanted me to be honest with you even if it hurts, right?"

"Yes," he says. "We need to be completely open with each other."

I hesitate, but I've already opened the gate, so I admit my half-truth, "I miss talking to Alec."

Landon's face drops, and a new slew of tears stain me in my ruination.

"Have you called him?"

"No," I delude. "But I want to."

"Why?"

I want to say that I don't know, but the truth fights past the lies. "I used to think that all a person needed to be happy was to find that one special person, but the idea that one person can be someone's everything is impossible."

"I don't make you happy?"

"You do, but there are parts of me that you can't possibly fill."

"What was it that he gave you?"

He's being so calm, and I draw courage from it, telling him, "His personality didn't make me feel like his equal, and I found myself being drawn to that."

"I thought you liked standing by my side."

"I do, but I also like the feeling of standing behind someone. But that's what I'm saying, it's impossible for you to give me both. You're either one or the other," I explain. "Everything he was contradicted you, and he made me aware that I had these empty parts of me that I never knew were there, but now I do."

"And you feel incomplete?"

"In a way . . . yes."

He stands and walks over to sit in the chair on the other side of the coffee table.

"So what you're saying is that you're never going to be completely happy unless you have some sort of side piece in this marriage?"

His words spotlight an instant understanding of something I never thought I could make sense of, and maybe I'm just so desperate not to lose either Alec or my family, that I respond with, "Lots of people have open marriages."

I can't believe that just came out of my mouth.

He looks at me dumbfounded. "Is that what you want?"

I shrug my shoulders, unnerved by his reaction, but he stuns me when he asks, "How does this work?"

"I don't know."

"So, what, once a week we get a free night?"

One night would never suffice when it comes to Alec.

"And you'd be okay knowing that I was having sex with another woman?"

It's a frightening feeling when I realize that I want Alec so badly that the thought of Landon with another woman would be something I'd tolerate just so I didn't have to lose Alec.

"I mean, I don't think it would be something that we would talk about or throw in each other's faces," I tell him.

Landon leans forward with his hands clutched together. "That might work for some people, but that's not the marriage I want. I would never, not even for one second, consider it as an option. So, if this is something you want, then I can't be with you."

I save face, quickly responding out of fear, "It's you that I want most, but you asked for honesty. And you're right, it would never work for us."

"But you still think about calling that guy?"

"I haven't thought about him in a long time, but today . . . yeah, he crept into my head."

Lies. Lies. Lies. What the fuck is wrong with me?

"Maybe I shouldn't have said anything," I say in self-admonishment.

Landon moves back to the coffee table and sits down. "I'm glad you told me. It's not easy to hear that my wife is sitting at home in tears because she wants to talk to another man, but you didn't have to tell me. The fact you admitted that to me, in a weird way, makes me trust you even more. You chose to tell me something that most would keep secret instead of acting on your impulse to call him."

"So you're not mad?"

"I'm not happy, but I'm not mad. I need you to be honest with me, always. I need to know how you feel so I can have the chance to help you so we can work through it."

Why am I doing this to him? Why am I giving him hopeless hope?

chapter nine

"Honey, you almost forgot these." I shove the tickets he bought for the girls down into the side pocket of his overnight duffle bag. "I hung their princess dresses in the back of your Jeep."

"Thanks."

The last time Landon packed this bag was the night he walked out on me almost six months ago, but now he packs it to take the girls on a daddy-daughter weekend. They've been begging to go to Disney on Ice, but when I went online to purchase the tickets, the Boston show was all sold out. Luckily, I was able to snag seats to the Philadelphia show, so they're road-tripping it and making a weekend out of the occasion.

"Did you get the snacks for the road?" Landon questions.

"Already in the car, babe."

I walk out of the bedroom and holler up the stairs, "Girls, Daddy's almost ready to hit the road."

They squeal as they clamor down the stairs.

"Did you go to the bathroom?"

"Yes, Mommy," they say in unison.

I grab their bags that I packed earlier and get them into the car. After hugs and kisses and Mommy-will-miss-yous, I walk to the back of the Jeep where Landon is loading the bags.

"They are so excited," I tell him.

"Please tell me you charged their iPads."

I laugh. "Both are at one hundred percent and they have their headphones."

He closes the hatchback and then pulls me into his arms, an affectionate display I'm unworthy of.

"So what're you going to do this weekend?"

"A whole weekend without kids . . . I'm going to sleep in and catch up on some reality TV."

He smiles down at me, adoration in his eyes that mine don't mirror, but I do my best to fake it. Each day that passes, my heart detaches from his a little bit more, and it's becoming harder to return his affections toward me. Landon leans down to kiss me, and I keep it a closed-mouth peck.

"You better get going so you get there with enough time for the girls to rest before the show tonight."

"I'll call you when we get checked in at the hotel."

He hops into the driver's seat, and I wave them goodbye.

Once out of sight, I close the garage, open my car door, and pop the trunk. Unzipping the road side emergency bag, I retrieve my cell and turn it on. When the screen lights up, there's a missed text from Alec.

Alec: Miss you.

My blood thickens with joy, and I'm immediately dialing him.

"Have they left?" is the first thing he asks when he answers.

"Yes."

"And you sent the book to your editor?"

"I did," I tell him. "It's off my shoulders." I used Alec's trip to Dallas to my advantage, taking that time apart to work long days and pull late nights. By the time he returned, I was farther in the book than I originally thought I would be, and was able to finish it the next week without it interfering with our time together.

It's not my best book by any means, the writing is shit, but the words are there and I met my deadline. I was able to keep my contract with Simon & Schuster, but I did have to pay back twenty-five thousand dollars from the advance they gave me.

When I explained that financial hit to Landon, I told him the strain from our marriage was what caused the writer's block. He was understanding and took care of the girls while I worked around the clock. But the book is done, and I'm free to be with Alec this weekend.

"I want to take you somewhere tonight," he says.

"And where's that?"

"On Saturday nights members can bring a guest."

"Members?"

"I want you to better understand my world," he says, and I then realize what he's talking about.

"Oh, I . . . Alec, I don't think I can . . . I mean . . ." I stammer in trepidation. I could handle people watching us when we were in New York, but I was in the safety of our room. It was still just me and him.

"Relax," he calms before telling me, "You'll be with me, in my hands."

"But, are you wanting to . . ."

"Only if you want to, but that's not why I want to take you."

"Why then?"

"Because I want you to get a better understanding of who I am and what I like," he explains. "I want your eyes wide open to what it means to be with a man like me."

His words come as a warning of sorts, but I've been with him for months now and feel I understand him pretty well. I'd be lying if I said I haven't been curious as to what these places are like. It's one thing to research it on the Internet, but to be there in the flesh is something I *have* to see.

"Okay," I agree. "I'll go with you."

"Are you sure?"

"I'm a big girl, Alec. I think I can handle it."

"That didn't take as much convincing as I thought," he says lightly. "Can you do me a favor?"

"Sure. What is it?"

"Open your garage."

"Why?" I say wearily, and when I rush to the front of the house and peek out the window, I see his silver SUV. "What are you doing here?" I fuss in unease before running to open the garage. I watch in horror as it opens and he drives in.

I quickly push the button to close the garage the moment he's completely in.

"Alec, what the hell are you doing here?" I snap when he gets out.

He wears a prideful smile as he strides toward me, and I feel like I could swallow my heart because it's lodged so damn high in my throat.

"You're not happy to see me?"

"I am—It's just—You can't—"

His hands are on me, strong and sure. "Breathe."

But how can I when he's here? In my home? Where I live with my husband and daughters?

He kisses me with a surge of confidence. My eyes remain open as a bolt of fear shoots up my spine.

"Alec," I mumble as I pull back.

"You told me they were gone."

"They are."

He stands, self-assured, and says in an even tone, "Invite me in, Victoria."

My hands tremble against his when he starts taking steps, backing me into the house he was never supposed be in.

"If I'm open enough to allow you to see my world, then I want to see yours."

I shake my head slowly as sadness builds behind my eyes, and I tighten my hands around his.

"What is it, baby?" he asks gently, dropping his head down to meet my eyes.

"I don't want you to see this world."

"Why?"

"Because it's a lie at this point."

"You think I don't already know that?" he says. "You cry every time you leave my bed."

He turns his palms against my hands and laces our fingers together before bringing them to his chest. I drop my head against him, and his heart beats steadily into my ear.

"If this world is a lie, where is your truth?"

"It's holding me," I tell him. "It's wherever you are."

He drops my hands and we wrap our arms around each other.

"Do you love me?"

"Please, don't ask me that," I beg on an unsettling whisper. I don't know if I can give him those words while I'm still married to another man. He has my body, but do I let him know that he has my heart? The moment I tell him I love him, he'll know, and there's something about giving that to him that terrifies me.

"I want to hear you say what we both know."

I draw back and look at him. "I can't."

"Why?"

"Do *you* love *me*?" I counter.

His lips lift, sexy and sly, before he grabs my ass abruptly and picks me up. I lock my ankles behind his waist as he carries me over to the couch. Setting me down, he drops on top of me, not allowing for second thoughts when he kisses me with blinding brutality. One drip of him on my tongue, and I'm a goner, drunk beyond capacity.

"Say it," he demands between kisses, grabbing on to my yoga pants and panties and ripping them off my legs when I obediently lift my hips.

"No."

I push his patience with my denial, and he scowls at me as he unbuckles his belt, jerks his fly open, and shoves his pants down his thighs.

"Tell me," he persists, yanking my hips toward him.

"No."

With his pants around his knees, and our shirts still on, he slams inside of me with primal urgency. I hold on to him as he fucks me wildly on the couch where Landon and I gather with our kids every night to watch cartoons before bedtime. His body slaps against mine as I fist the fabric of his shirt. He's ferocious, rapidly thrusting into me while we're surrounded by photos of my once-happy family. Smiling faces and beaming eyes watch Alec and I fuck, further decimating every promise I ever made them.

Colors streak along tenebrous skies as Alec drives. I stare out the window while nerves gnaw away at me. Lights eventually dim into ink as we leave the city behind.

I feel like an idiot, wearing a conservative, black, cap-sleeve, silky maxi dress. Only an amateur would wear an ankle length dress to a sex club.

"What should I wear tonight?" I asked him while I was packing my overnight bag before we left my house earlier.

"There's a dress code, so wear whatever makes you comfortable, but make sure it's something tasteful."

Excitement and curiosity abandoned me the moment we left Alec's loft. Now, all that fills me is the insecurity of walking into the unknown.

"Everything okay?"

I look to Alec, shoot him a fleeting smile, and respond, "I'm good," before turning back to my window.

The drive to North Shore feels long, but not long enough. My stomach flip-flops when Alec veers off the highway. I know we're close, and I suppress the urge to tell him to turn the car around. Alec is relaxed as he drives, dressed in gray tailored slacks and a black button-down. We look like we should be dining at a fine restaurant not going to a swinger's club.

When we finally arrive, he pulls into the back lot of a two-story building with no windows, not at all what I was expecting. From the outside, the place looks like any typical dance club.

Alec parks and kills the engine.

"Your husband may be clueless to your lies, but I'm not," he says, taking my hand in his. "I'm going to ask you again: Are you okay?"

I shake my head no. I've never been so nervous in my life.

"I need to know how you feel."

As we sit under the moon and stars, I confess, "I'm scared."

"Of what?"

"The unknown."

He takes his other hand and sweeps his thumb along my cheekbone. It's a tender touch meant to soothe, but I'm so wound up.

"Like I said before, you're with me. Nothing will happen unless you say so, okay?"

"Okay."

He lifts my chin and kisses me softly before stepping out of the car and walking around to open my door. He holds my hand as we walk to the building's entrance.

"Don't let go of me."

He firms his grip. "Never."

We step inside, my knees wobbly, and I'm immediately relieved when I'm greeted by an upscale bar and lounge. Men and women, dressed similar to us, sip cocktails and mingle about the way I would expect from any other trendy lounge in the city. Seating areas are scattered about the large room, and after Alec checks us in, he leads me across the room, his hand never leaving mine.

A man greets Alec, clearly acquaintances, while his wife or girlfriend eyes Alec, sparking a flame of jealousy in me.

Has she fucked him before?

I swallow down the burn of spite and divert my eyes away from her, but then Alec introduces me, and I'm forced to shake hands with her. The exchange doesn't last long, and when we take a seat, Alec orders me a glass of wine. I look around the room, judging every single woman here when I realize there's a good possibility they've had Alec inside of them.

The emotional woman in me wants to lash out and make accusations, but I have no right. I've known this about him from day one. He's never hidden this side of himself from me. Maybe I should take comfort in the fact that I'm not a one-night hook-up. That Alec adores me, takes the time to comfort me, and has given me six months without ever making me feel like he isn't invested in me.

The wine comes, and I have to restrain myself from guzzling it.

"This is nothing what I expected."

"And what's that? Leather and whips?"

I laugh. "Maybe."

"I'm not into bondage or domination, Victoria. You know that."

We sit, enjoy our drinks, and Alec does his best to distract me with small talk, making me laugh and calming me.

As time passes, couples and singles find their way down the four hallways branching off the main room. Alec catches my eye, pulling my attention away from the lone woman leaving the room for one of the corridors.

"Are you ready?" he whispers, his breath ghosting along my ear.

I draw bravery from the alcohol and give him a slight nod.

Hand in hand, we walk down the long stretch. He opens a door that leads to several rooms that hang off a web of hallways. His pace strolls along slowly, and when we pass the first room, I turn my head to see a man fucking a woman up against the wall while another woman is squatted down behind him, her face buried between his ass cheeks.

Oh, my God.

Alec peers at me with a smirk on his face as doubt begins to chill my blood. The sounds of moaning and slapping flesh fill my head. My palm sweats against Alec's, and when he guides me into a large room, I stall in my step.

A handful of people are fucking on beds, couches, and even on the floor while others watch. Some are masturbating in corners, and some are only inches away from those having sex. But this isn't the sexy image I've held in my head. I could easily romanticize this if I were writing it in a book, but this is reality. Stone. Cold. Reality.

My gut churns at the sight before me. It's perverse and sickening. I turn to a young couple, the man fucking the woman like a dog—rough and filthy. An older man, hairy with a protruding beer belly, stands in front of them as he yanks on his flaccid dick, stretching the skin with every tug. He steps closer and reaches his other hand out under the woman's jiggling breasts. He hardens when she grabs his hand and places it over her tit. He immediately blows his load on the floor next to the hand she's using to prop herself up.

Alec releases a throaty moan, and when I look at him, his face is marked in arousal.

This is disgusting.

I can't do this.

Feeling dirty and gross from what I just witnessed, I pull my hand from his and bolt out of the room.

"Victoria!"

I rush through the dark halls and dimly lit lounge filled with perverts dressed in gossamer.

"Victoria, stop!"

I throw my hands against the doors, forcing them to slam open as I run out into the frigid night. My heart bruises my ribs, and I panic.

What the fuck are you doing, Tori?

Alec flies out the doors after me, and I burst into tears, crying loudly.

"What the fuck, Alec?"

I'm hysterical when he grabs me and bands his arms around me.

"No," I fight, jerking my body to break his hold. "Don't touch me!"

"Calm down!" he shouts, his voice pure gravel, but I won't—I can't.

I wail, thoroughly freaked to have seen those grotesque acts right in front of my face. I want to run far away from this place and pretend this night never happened.

"Let go of me!" I continue to thrash in his arms, and he finally relents, releasing me from his hold. Once free, I hunch over, tears falling freely while I try to catch my breath.

"Talk to me," he commands. "What happened in there?"

I stumble back on my feet, needing more space between us, and suddenly, I feel like I don't know Alec at all.

I look at the man I thought I knew and shake my head in disbelief.

"I need you to talk to me," he presses.

"I can't do this."

"Tell me what scared you."

"*You*," I tell him before my voice turns sour. "Is that what you like? Watching those disgusting people?"

"Watch your mouth!" he reprimands harshly.

I take another step back, my chest heaving. "That was sick. I feel like throwing up."

"That's me, Victoria."

"No, it isn't."

"That's what I like."

"No," I deny as I belly-over and cry.

His hands wrap around my arms and pull me up. He's a kaleidoscope of fractured beauty through my tears.

With his eyes boring into mine, he softens his voice. "This is me."

"This isn't you. I don't want this to be you."

"This *is* me, Victoria."

"Why?" I sob. "Why do you need this?"

I fall against his chest and he holds me firmly as I feel my heart breaking. I can't be one of those people. I thought I knew his needs, I thought I knew what they looked like, but I was wrong. I could never be that woman he fucks while some gross fat-ass watches and tugs his limp dick.

He kisses the top of my head before resting his cheek on me. His voice is pained, saying, "Baby, please, tell me I didn't mislead you."

He didn't. I misled myself.

He cradles my face in his hands and tilts my head back, looking down at me with such tenderness. "Why is this hurting you so badly?"

"Because," I whimper, "I'm in deeper than what I ever expected. I've completely fallen for you, but I can't be what you want. I can't be this."

"Be *you*," he stresses. "Find out who you are and stop trying to be what others want you to be."

"But I want you."

"You have me. I'm not running from you; I'm right here."

"But I can't give you this. I can't give you what you need."

"You're scared," he says as he watches more tears freefall down my face. "I didn't expect to bring you here without some sort of reaction. This is new to you. It's going to take time."

"What if I never get there?"

"Then we will deal with it. I won't rush you. I'll push you, but I won't rush you. I'm not going to force this on you."

"I wish I could give this to you. I want to, I do . . . I just—"

"You're enough. What you give me is enough. I know you're trying," he affirms before pulling me back into his consoling arms.

I hold him, pressing my fingers into his back, needy for him to take care of me. And in this moment—desperate and scared—I hand him my heart.

"You were right," I tell him as his heart lulls the tears away.

"About what?"

"I've fallen in love with you."

part three

"Sometimes I sit alone under the stars and think about the galaxies inside my heart and truly wonder if anyone will ever want to make sense of all that I am."

~ Christopher Poindexter

chapter one

Winter melts into spring, bringing the city back to life. Magnolias bloom pink blossoms all along the streets of Alec's neighborhood. He picks rogue petals out of my hair on the windy days.

In April, I run the Boston Half Marathon while Landon and the girls cheer me on. Later that afternoon, I meet Alec in the Public Garden while my family thinks I'm at the spa getting a massage. It's one of our many stolen moments. We sit under a cherry tree, amongst the budding tulips, while he fingers me beneath the jacket draped over my lap.

I'm head-over-heels attached to Alec, but when spring burns into summer, I'm utterly absorbed in him. I love yous are anemic because we are beyond love—we're fanatically dependent on each other for survival.

It's been nearly a year since Alec and I started texting, and not once has predictability crept in. This man lives by no rules and has swept me away, birthing inside of me a constant pang of wanderlust. I dream about the day I can freely hold his hand while he leads me through life. To get to that point, I have to battle my way through fear and pride, a war I'm much too weak for—so I continue to dream.

"It's only twelve days."

My gut pits with dread and loneliness. Twelve days feels like a prison sentence. "I'm going to miss you."

"You'll be having too good of a time to miss me," Alec says, his cock still inside me as I straddle him on the couch.

Tomorrow, I leave for Australia with Landon for a book signing, but today, I snuck away so I could have Alec one last time before I left.

"I'd rather be going with you," I tell him.

The last thing I want to be doing is traveling with my husband for two weeks with no escape—with no Alec. My cheap disposable phone I still use to talk and text with him will be of no use to me while I'm gone, and I'm worried about leaving him cold-turkey.

He palms my breasts as I remain on his lap, his cum slowly seeping out of me between our melded bodies. "Tell me what it's like when he's fucking you."

"Miserable," I respond while he squeezes me in his hands. "He feels nothing like you. I hardly ever orgasm, but when I do, it's you who owns it because it's the thought of you that drives me to it." The words hurt to admit because I deeply care for Landon, but he no longer has my heart. I've given it over to Alec.

"Grab my shoulders." When I do, he holds me as he slides off the couch and onto the floor. He picks his shirt up, which is lying next to us, and instructs me to stand over him. He leans against the couch with his head tilted back onto the cushion as he looks up at my pussy. Using the shirt, he wipes me clean of his cum before tossing it aside. "Sit on my face."

My stomach flutters in excitement. When I settle my knees onto the couch on either side of his head, he wraps his hands around my thighs and lowers me down to him. His mouth opens, taking my delicate flesh against his soft tongue. I grip the back of the sofa to steady myself. My body rocks back and forth as he teases my clit with feather-like sweeps.

He moves slowly—blissfully torturing me with his light touches. With my hips in his hands, he forbids my greed, holding me in place when I want to grind down on him. His tongue slides along my slick flesh, dipping only the tip of it inside me, causing my walls to clench and spasm. But he deprives me of the penetration my body is begging for, screaming for, practically crying for.

His beautiful face is buried between my folds, and I manage to create a moment of friction when he moves his hands from my hips to my ass, allowing me to rub my clit along the bridge of his nose. Tilting his head slightly, he captures the bundle of nerves with his mouth, sucking on me hard while he laughs at my eagerness. His lips vibrate against me when he does this, and my body quivers in response.

"Alec, fuck," I moan, my voice lacerated between ravishment and deprivation.

I need more.

I reach between my legs with one hand, grab a handful of his hair, and pull his head up into me. He squeezes my ass, spreading my cheeks apart. Vision blurs when he swipes one of his fingers between my wet pussy and his tongue and then drags it to my back hole. He circles his finger around my rim, slowly easing his way into the one spot that's only ever been touched by him.

I once told Alec, when we first started talking, that I wasn't into ass play. But when he convinced me to let him touch me there, we both discovered the truth that was suppressed within me.

Tingles surge through me, prickling along my skin, and my head falls against my arm that's clutched to the back of the couch. I'm blinded by heat, my head swimming through a foggy haze. Alec strokes his finger knuckle deep in me as he works my clit, sucking and licking.

"Oh, God," I mewl, growing dizzy because I'm unable to fill my lungs through fractured breaths.

He picks up the pressure, building the intensity. Beads of sweat roll down my back, and when the tingles warp through my veins, I pinch my eyes shut and bear down. Alec pushes his whole finger inside me, and I fucking lose it. Screaming, moaning, body writhing, cumming in Alec's mouth.

My skin no longer belongs to me; I'm too wild, too carnal.

Lights flitter behind my eyelids as my orgasm thunders deliciously through my core and down my thighs. I continue to hold on to Alec's head with my one hand, and as I slow my pace, calming down, my body jerks a few times with pulsing aftershocks.

I crumple onto my side, muscles weak, as Alec gets off the floor and sits next to me. He scoops me into his arms, cradling me like a child, and I melt into the sensation it gives me. The feeling of safety, of juvenility, of knowing this man will tuck me into his protective hands and forever nurture me. He makes me feel fragile when he's standing next to me, so strong and sure. I never thought of myself as a person who would want to feel that way, but with Alec, it's the best feeling in the world.

He rests his forehead against mine, and I smell myself all over his face. I take his cheeks in my hands and kiss him, sliding my tongue along his, tasting what he tastes when he loves me so intimately. I'm wrapped warmly in his arms, no longer capable of knowing where my breath ends and his begins as I take him into my lungs for survivorship.

Unwilling to drag my lips away from his, I mumble against him, "I love you"—he kisses me harder—"so fucking much."

We don't stop, and when the emptiness returns and hollows me, knowing I have to leave soon and that I won't be seeing him for two weeks, I cry. He bands his arms more firmly around me when I shudder against him. Never taking his lips from mine, he swallows my sadness.

I stay until the very last minute, and when he walks me to the door, I cling to him with a somber heart.

"Be safe and try to enjoy yourself."

"I will."

"Call me as soon as you get back, okay?"

With one last kiss, I tell him, "Be good," before I leave.

The excitement of being in Australia masks the loneliness of being away from Alec. Landon and I ride on my jovial mood of being somewhere new with so much to explore. We laugh, we sightsee, we take pictures to create memories he'll one day want no memory of.

After the first few days, the mask wears thin, and I struggle to keep myself together. I find myself thinking and fantasizing about what this trip would be like if it were Alec I was with. I think about how much more fun it would be, how passionate it would be.

After a day of kayaking yesterday, we came back to the hotel to freshen up. After our showers, Landon wanted to have sex. I wanted to lie to him and tell him I was too tired, but I didn't. In a weird, fucked-up way, having sex with my husband these days makes me feel guilty, as if it's Alec I'm cheating on and not the other way around. I laid on my back while Landon moved above me, but it was Alec I was thinking about. I barely lasted ten minutes before I faked my orgasm just so he would get off me.

Another day passes, and I have to force myself to not pull away when he reaches to hold my hand. I have to force my affections, and even at that, they're weak and generic: short hugs, quick pecks, fleeting glances. He asks what's wrong, and I tell him I think I'm about to start my period and must be PMSing. I promise not to let my mood interfere with our vacation, but it does anyway.

We video chat with the girls, and they are always so excited to see our smiling faces, to hear about our adventures, and to get the scoop on the souvenirs we're buying them. What they don't see is the unhappy woman inside me who's slowing dying. A woman who's ready to break down and leave her family. A woman who'd give anything to run away as long as it didn't hurt her children.

This morning I cried in the shower. I don't think it's possible to hate myself more than I do. The misery I feel being with my husband every day on this trip is taking its toll on me. I should want to spend time with the man I'm married to. I should want to hold his hand. I should want to make love to him. But I don't. There is no more connection between us, and I'm not sure how much longer I can keep going on like this.

I'm so grateful when we near the end of the trip and grow closer to the book signing. I need the distraction of other people. Brynn and Erin are the first of my author friends to arrive. Erin didn't bring Gabe with her, so she's sharing a room with Brynn. After Landon and I eat dinner, I ask if it's okay to go to their room that's two floors above ours, and he says yes.

I couldn't have rushed out any faster. Thrilled to finally have space, I hurry to their room, and when Erin opens the door, we squeal and hug each other.

"You're finally here!"

"How long have you been here?"

"A little over a week," I tell her and then turn to give Brynn a hug.

Brynn is a hybrid author like I am, but she doesn't do very many signings, so I'm thrilled to get to spend time with her.

"Where's your husband?" Erin asks.

"He's down in the room. He's tired so he's just watching TV and relaxing," I explain. "We've been non-stop busy since we arrived." I flop down onto the bed next to Brynn. "I haven't seen you in almost a year. What have you been up to?"

"Just pumping out books for my publisher and trying to get something out on the indie market. It's been over six months since my last self-pubbed book."

"Well, that's because of you-know-who," Erin says as she lies on her bed.

"Don't even get me started on that bitch."

I look to Brynn and ask, "What am I missing? Who's the bitch?"

"It's a long story."

"I've got the time," I tell her.

"I'm gonna need a beverage," Erin chimes in as she walks over to the mini fridge. She grabs a tiny bottle of vodka and a can of cranberry juice. "Want a drink?"

"No, thanks." I turn my attention back to Brynn. "So, what's the story?"

"You know Ashley, right? The blogger at All Spines?"

"Yeah. She reads and reviews all my books."

"Well, she's one of my beta readers," she tells me before Erin hands her a drink. "She's been reading for me for a couple years now, so there was no reason for me to not to trust her when she asked what my next project was about." She takes a gulp of the vodka and cranberry. "Did you hear about the book called *Pressing Stones*?"

"I think so," I lie so I don't sound completely out of the loop. Let's face it, my life in the book world has been nonexistent this past year because of Alec.

"Well, I decided to pick it up and read it when the blurb sounded close to one of my stories."

"No way."

"Someone needs to cunt punch that heifer," Erin says with a sharp tongue.

"She stole your fucking story?" I exclaim.

"Uh huh. I knew it was no coincidence, so when I confronted her, she admitted to the pen name she wrote under but claimed she didn't steal the story idea. She insisted she had been writing the book before I even told her about the story, but she's full of shit."

"Wait. How did she have the time to write and publish it before you?"

"Because I was still in the middle of working on my previous book when she asked about my next idea."

"It's such shitty writing," Erin says. "I still think you could write it and nobody would know," she tells Brynn.

"No way. I don't want to be accused of copying since her book came out first."

"Did it do well in the rankings?" I ask.

"I mean, for a no-name author coming out with her first book, she almost broke the top one hundred on Amazon. But I assure you, if I wrote it, it would've hit the *USA Today* because it's a great story and I'm a much better writer than she is."

"Has she come out on her blog that she's writing under a pen name?"

"No," Erin tells me. "People have speculated, but she denies it's her because she wants to keep blogging."

"Unbelievable," I sigh. "There's not a damn person you can trust in this industry. Everyone is trying to climb to the top, forgetting that we need to support one another. I can't tell you how many girls I used to be friends with, and then the minute they get a successful book under their belt, they think they're hot as shit and their whole attitude changes."

"If only the readers knew how vindictive half these authors were," Brynn remarks. "I mean, it makes me sick when Kristen posts on social media under her pen name and readers gawk all over her. I want to put her on blast so badly."

"Well, I won't be sending her any more of my books to review."

"Same here," Erin adds. "I'm glad I have a good circle of authors to run with. There's too much drama out there to get mixed up in."

"Which is why I'm not going to say anything about what Kristen did. The last thing I want to do is create another scandal on Facebook. There's enough of that going on."

"I agree," I tell Brynn. "As much as it sucks, it's best to just avoid it." I see the frustration on her face and reach over to give my friend a hug. That story was income, it was lunch money for her kids, it was food on the table. No one deserves to get ripped off like that. "I'm so sorry this happened to you."

"I'll get over it," she dismisses, but I know it'll weigh on her shoulders for a while. How could it not? Our stories are our hearts, and when people shit on them, tearing them down and leaving nasty reviews, it hurts deeply no matter how thick your skin is. But to have someone steal that story and publish it as their own, that's beyond wrong.

We quickly change the subject and enjoy the rest of the night and before I know it, it's after one in the morning. I say good night and head back to my room to find Landon sound asleep, but I don't feel bad because I needed this time away. So much so, that I ditch Landon for the girls the following night after the signing.

By our last night in Sydney, I'm alone at a random bar down the street from the hotel. Landon and I went out to dinner and got into a nasty fight. I couldn't even tell you what started the fight because we've been bickering so much these past few days. One thing led to another and he called me frigid and unloving, so I called him an asshole. But it was when he threw my week of unfaithfulness in my face, I burst into tears and stormed out, leaving him to eat alone—if he only knew that my unfaithfulness has spanned far beyond just a measly week.

I've been sitting in this bar ever since—drinking and missing Alec. Alcohol curbs my anger with Landon, allowing guilt to take over. I've never ached for a man as much as I'm aching for Alec. There's not a second that goes by that I don't wish I were with him. I know my heart's choice, its been screaming it to me for months. I've been lying for so long, staying in an unhappy marriage and forcing every single emotion with him. I'm depleted and have nothing left in me to give.

I order another shot, pay my tab, and head back to Landon.

If I'm going to do this, I have to do it now because tomorrow we head home and the moment I see my girls, I know I'll chicken out again. And I can't do that. I can't go on like this.

With a good amount of alcohol in my bloodstream, I feel numb when I walk into the room where Landon is packing. I go over and sit on the edge of the bed next to the suitcase and look at the man I fell so madly in love with when I was younger. The man I made my life with. The man that gave me two of the most beautiful children in the world.

"I don't make you happy, do I?" I ask.

He sets the suitcase on the floor, sits next to me, and we start the conversation we should've had a long time ago.

"If you're asking if I'm happy, the answer's no. This isn't the relationship I want. You're my wife, Tori, and you can't even hold my hand without making me feel like I repulse you."

His words tear me wide open. I thought he couldn't tell. I thought I was doing a good job at faking it.

"You just lie there while we're having sex. Like all you want is for it to be over with."

"I'm sorry," I say as a year's worth of hidden pain falls from my eyes.

"I haven't felt your love in a really long time." His voice cracks as his own tears spill over. "Tell me what's going on because I've been feeling you drifting for months now. I've been scared to say anything for fear that you'd run. But I feel like I'm the only one trying to hold us together, and I'm so tired, Tor. I'm so fucking worn out."

We've been slowly slipping this whole year, and now, we're no longer lovers—we're roommates.

I need to be honest and selfless, so I dig deep and grab on to what little strength I have left, and tell him, "You deserve to be with someone who can make you happy."

"I want to be with *you*, Tori. You're my wife." His voice is thick with emotion.

"But you're not happy."

"Because I don't feel your heart is in this anymore. I don't need much to make me happy, just you. A wife who lets me touch her. A wife who wants to make love to me. A wife who wants to sit next to me on the couch instead of running away to be alone in the bedroom. I don't think I'm asking for much, but I need to feel that you love me."

Heartbreak drips from my chin and falls onto his hands that are now holding mine. I can't even bring myself to look him in the eyes when I admit, "I know, but I . . ." I take my hands from his because he shouldn't be touching a monster like me. "The thing is . . . I don't want to try."

Landon's head falls into his hands. His cries are painful to listen to. "Why are you doing this to us? What is it that you need? Just tell me and I'll give it to you."

"I'm sorry."

Lifting his head, he looks at me. "What are you trying to say? Do you want out?"

And here it is, my moment to give him the words I've been too afraid to say for all this time. I take attempt to take a deep breath, but I can't. The hurt is too much. "I think another woman could make you happier than I can."

"I don't want another fucking woman. I want you!"

"I wish I could love you like you deserve to be loved," I cry, hating myself for doing this to him.

His eyes widen in horror. "You don't love me?"

"I do." I'm quick to soothe—to do what I can to take this pain away from him. "I love you enough that I can't be selfish with you anymore. I want to keep you because you're so damn good to me and I love our family, but I've changed and so has the love."

"You're not willing to fight for this? You're my goddamn life."

"How long do we hang on? We've been falling apart for a year."

"One year of fighting after we've spent thirteen years building this life together, and you're ready to walk away? I'd fight for you till the death."

What do I say when I don't feel the same? I don't want to lie to comfort him, so I don't respond.

Neither one of us speaks for a long time, we only cry, filling the room with the most astounding sadness that could possibly exist. He doesn't touch me, and I don't touch him. We're two individuals, no longer melded as one. I see how badly he's hurting, and I wish I could change my heart's desire, but I know I can't. I've lost the love I once had for him, and the chances of finding it barely amount to anything.

It's gone.

Eventually, he lifts his head from his hands, eyes swollen and bloodshot, wounded from the bullet I just fired into his heart. "Where do we go from here?" he finally asks, breaking the silence there's no glue for.

I wipe my face—the face of a villain—and drop the guillotine on our marriage. "When we get home, I'm going to leave."

chapter two

It's been two days since I told Landon I wanted a separation. We haven't spoke about it, but there's no need—it hangs low in the air between us. When we arrived back in the States yesterday, I went ahead and booked reservations to stay at a hotel. Just another safeguard to protect myself from Landon finding out that I'm with someone else, because if we are going to get a divorce, I hope to do it as amicably as possible.

There are no words for what I'm feeling as I continue to pack my suitcases. I'm about to leave this house and walk out into the unknown. There's no plan, there's no direction, there's no security, and that in and of itself is frightening. But at the same time, it's what I desperately need. Along with my urgency to be with Alec, there's also been an underlying urgency to run away and escape from this life I've created with my husband.

As I empty my drawers into my luggage, I do what I can to focus on Alec to protect myself from the debilitating emotions that threaten to break free from the cage I've built around them. I tried calling him last night when Landon drove to pick up the girls from his brother's house, but all I got was his voicemail.

A chill razors up my spine when I hear Landon return from dropping the kids off at school. I hate that I'm inflicting this upon him. He doesn't deserve any of this, but my heart's been screaming at me to run to Alec for nearly a year now. I thought it would eventually fade and I'd grow tired of him, but I only want him more, so much so that it's created a constant ache inside my chest.

"You're really leaving?"

I turn to Landon, who's standing in the doorway of our bedroom. He looks at me with indifference in his eyes, a result of my constant back and forth game this year. I led him to believe we were good and happy, but when I grew tired of pretending, I pushed him away. I've done nothing but jerk him around, and I know he can easily find someone that'll treat him better than I can.

"Don't you think we should talk about this?"

This is the part I want to hide from, but I know I can't, so I give him a nod. I follow behind him when he walks into the living room. He takes a seat on the couch, the couch Alec fucked me on, and I sit in the chair across from him.

There's an awkward silence that bleeds between us before he finally speaks. "What's the plan here?"

"I don't know," I respond with a cowardly shrug of my shoulders.

"I need to know."

"I don't know, Landon," I maintain. "It's not like I've ever done this before."

"You can't keep stringing me along. If you're done with this marriage, there's no need to separate. It's only wasting time."

Again, doubt surfaces, and I question if I'm giving up too soon.

"I don't know."

"You can't keep saying that, Tor. This is black and white. Either you love me or you don't."

"It's not that simple," I tell him. "We have thirteen years of life together—"

"And?"

"And I'm confused. I need to get away and clear my head because there's so much tension in this house that I can't even think straight any more."

"I can't go on like this. I can't keep fighting for this marriage on my own. Love me or leave me, but don't waste my time because you're confused," he says with irritation before adding, "I want to be with someone who loves me. I want a family, and if that's no longer something you want with me, then tell me so I can find someone who does."

But it isn't black and white. If he only knew what was really going on, he'd see the gray, he'd see the blurred lines. I've blinded him to believe that I've had a flippant change of heart. This is anything but flippant though. This runs deep in my marrow, which is why I keep this battle alive.

And now, the thought of him remarrying and having a family that I'm no longer a part of scares me, but for selfish reasons, because what if I never get that? What if Landon was my one shot? There's no doubt that he will find someone to love him. He's too good of a man. But me? I'm garbage. I'm a horrible woman who does horrible things.

"I just need space," I tell him. "I need to find a way to get some clarity."

"How long am I supposed to wait?"

"I don't know."

His jaw ticks as soon as I say those three words, the same three words I say over and over and over, because I feel like I don't know anything anymore.

"I'll give you one month to figure out if you want to be a part of this family."

"And what if I'm still confused?"

"Then we're done," he says coolly while my neck burns with fear and sadness. "It's either yes or no. If you tell me that you're still unsure, then it's over. I won't be married to a woman who can't figure out if she loves me or not."

A big part of my heart wishes I could snap out of this. I want to love him—everything would be so much easier—but it's not something I can force. And the thing is, I'm in love with Alec. Everything about this is so fucked up. It's too much to deal with, which is why all I want to do right now is run. Run far away from the reality I've created while living in my fantasy.

"What about the girls?"

"If you're leaving, they stay with me." His words are firm, a tell to the unbounding love he has for them. "You want a separation to see what life will be like divorced, then that's the way it's going to be."

"What are we going to tell them?"

"Honestly? I'd rather you stay away for a week or so. I don't even know how to look at you right now." His voice grows unstable and thick. "I'll tell them you're away for work."

I watch as he leans forward, elbows on knees, head in hands. I should walk over and comfort him, but it feels forced. He sniffs and my tears break free. When he looks up, his face is streaked in heartbreak.

"I don't understand you." His words crack. "I give you everything I can."

"Landon—"

"I don't want to lose you. I don't want my girls to not have both their parents under the same roof." He stands and walks over to me before dropping to his knees—a man desperate to keep his world intact. With tears falling down his face, he grips my knees in his hands and pleads, "I love you so fucking much. Everything about you, I love. Don't do this. I swear to you, I'll do everything I can to make you happy and to make you love me again."

Comfort him. Reach out and at least touch him.

No, you'll just give him false hope.

He's your husband, for Christ's sake!

You can't lead him on when you're about to leave him for Alec.

He's never been in this kind of agony before. You need to console him.

Console him with what? More lies? Just tell him you're sorry so we can go see Alec.

You're such a fucking bitch! Your husband is crying on the floor, begging for you to honor your marriage and fight for him! Give the man a goddamn hug!

Don't give him hope where there is no hope to be had—it'll only make you a bigger bitch.

"You're what makes my heart beat. I love you most and more, Tori. I always will."

I jump out of the chair, needing to put space between us. When he stands to his feet, I tell him, "I can't do this right now. I need to figure this out on my own instead of making a choice out of guilt for how upset you are."

Anger flares, and I walk back to the bedroom. I hate that he just did that to me, trying to force me into staying.

Why did he have to do that?

How am I supposed to even respond?

I toss the rest of my belongings into the luggage, moving quickly because I need to get out of here and away from all this tension. As I'm packing, I hear Landon leave. Relief washes through me now that I can walk out of here without having to face him. I load my bags into the trunk of my car, retrieve my disposable phone, and then hit the road.

The moment I drive away, I feel the weight of the world lift off my shoulders. I'm finally free, and the thought alone is enough to rid me of my guilt for leaving.

Me: I have a room at the Copley Square Hotel. Call me when you can and I'll explain everything.

I need this.

I needed this for a long time.

This is the escape I've been yearning for. I can now be with Alec without the sadness constantly looming overhead. I can be with him freely without the constant sneaking around and scheming up ways to see him. And as much as I love my girls, I need a break from being a mommy.

I stop at the hotel in Alec's neighborhood of Back Bay and check in.

Me: I'm in room 604.

When I get to my room, I begin to unpack. I'm not sure how long I'll be staying here because I didn't expect to be gone a month, but Landon gave me the time, and like the selfish woman I am, I want to take every last second of it. But a month at a hotel like this is more money than I care to spend. If Brooke weren't about to give birth at any given moment, I'd stay with her, but since her due date is fast approaching, I didn't even tell her about this separation and stress her out. Even though I expect to be with Alec for the most part, I still need a point of reference so Landon doesn't suspect anything.

Once I have my belongings settled into their new places, I turn on the television and mindlessly flip through the channels before landing on an entertainment news show.

A knock on the door startles me, but when I walk over to look through the peephole, my heart finally settles. I fall into Alec's arms when I open the door, and I want to cry. I haven't seen him or spoken to him in the two weeks since I left for Australia.

He backs us into the room and closes the door, never unwrapping his arms from me.

I nuzzle my head against his chest. "I've missed you."

He draws back slightly, looking down at me, and asks, "What are you doing here?"

I stare at the man I never should've fallen in love with, but did. The man who's been able to soothe my heart's ache this past year. The man who's brought me to life and has helped me discover this new side of me. "I left him."

His eyes soften when I tell him this, his hands moving to cup my face. "Are you okay?"

I nod. "Australia was a disaster."

He takes me and moves us over to the bed. We sit and I continue, "As soon as it was just us and there were no distractions, I knew it was over."

"What happened?"

"We fought a lot," I tell him as I struggle to hide my tears. I know he doesn't want to see me crying for another man. "Before we left to come back, I told him he should be with someone else. I told him my heart was no longer in the marriage and that I was going to leave, and here I am."

"Did you tell him about us?"

"No. He can't know. It'll only make everything worse, and I don't want things to get nasty for the sake of the girls."

"Does he know where you are?"

"It was bad before I left this morning. I didn't even get a chance to tell him."

He runs his hand down the side of my face, but it isn't enough comfort for me, and when I drop my head, he pulls it back up, unwilling to allow me to hide. "Talk to me."

"I don't want to upset you."

"You won't," he assures. "You left him. What could you say now that would hurt me?"

"I'm sad," I reveal. "This is what I want, *you're* what I want, but I'm scared. And even though you're here right now, I feel really lost inside." My words strain around the glumness of this whole situation. "I just need you to hold me."

He leans over and slips off my shoes before kicking his off, and when he stands to pull the sheets back, I slip in. Tugging his shirt over his head, he tosses it aside and lies down with me, covering us with the sheets. Alec scoops me into his arms and holds me tightly. My fingers press into his back as an overwhelming surge of neediness takes over me. Our legs tangle, and when he tucks my head under his chin, I cling to him even more.

"Tell me what you need from me."

"Safety," I whisper against his heated skin.

He kisses the top of my head. "You're always safe with me."

I want to melt into him, hand myself over to be taken care of the way he does so perfectly. I want to follow him through life, a life I've yet to explore. I want him to lead me, teach me, protect me. I want to give him whatever it is that he needs because I want to please him.

Time falters as we hold each other, and before I know it, our bodies are slowly moving together. His hands run beneath my top up to my breasts, and when he teases my nipples with his thumbs, I drape my one leg over his hip. He pushes himself against me, he's hard where I'm soft, and I grow wet for him.

Taking his time, he peels the clothes off my body, stripping me bare.

"Does it hurt? Leaving your family?"

Our eyes connect, his steady, mine un. "Yes."

"Does it make you want to cry?" he questions with his palm pressed between my breasts.

I swallow painfully. "Yes."

"Cry."

I wrap my hand around his wrist as his hand remains on my chest and stare into his dark blue eyes, knowing I'll never be naked staring into deep brown again. Landon has always been a huge piece of my heart, and now he isn't. No matter how much Alec consumes me, there's a hollowness where Landon used to be.

I trust in Alec to guide me through this turmoil. His face is one I doubt I'll ever tire of looking at—strong and sure—but his request fractures his lines and curves. He bleeds into a prism of colors on the other side of my tears.

"Take my pants off."

With slow-moving hands, I quietly weep as I remove his pants.

He opens my legs and lowers himself between them. Holding his thick cock, he slides it along my most tender flesh, tugging at my opening. "Don't stop," he says. "I want to be inside you while you're crying."

"Why?"

"Because I want your deepest everythings all at once."

And when he pushes himself inside me, I give him what he needs. We're skin to skin, mended as one. He's never moved this slowly with me. With every roll of his hips, he pulls more and more sadness and ache from my heart, driving my soft whimpers into painful sobs.

Shifting us to our sides, he wraps my leg over his hip. He then gathers me completely in his arms and holds me closely against his chest as he continues to stroke his cock tenderly inside me.

And for the first time ever, I feel us truly making love.

And I cry as my heart tethers safely to his.

chapter three

ALEC CARRIES MY BAG ACROSS THE THRESHOLD OF HIS LOFT. I LEFT MOST OF MY belongings back at the hotel in case Landon decides to show up for whatever reason. Paranoia still runs rampant, reminding me that I have to continue to cover my tracks with every move I make.

I walk over to the large windows that wrap around the perimeter wall and look down on the magnolia trees below. Pink blossoms hover over the sidewalk, providing a whimsical shield between me and those that wander below. It's the dividing line between me and them—good versus evil. I wrap my arms around my middle and wonder if I'll always be marked in this shame, if I'll ever find my way back across the line that separates my rotten heart from virtue.

Strong arms cover my weak ones.

Warmth penetrates my ice.

Goodness cradles my disgrace.

"You're not misplaced," my protector says, his words licking my hidden wounds. I turn in his arms and see the look of compassion for the lost girl who stands so unsteady in his hold.

I never thought I would need so much from one person, but I do, and he's able to give it. He's the culmination of everything I've been lacking: a father figure, a guide, a protector—a man who can break through my carefully constructed walls and burrow himself into the core of my soul.

Why couldn't I have met Alec first? If we only would've crossed paths sooner, I could've saved so many people from the pain I'm now inflicting upon them.

My eyes silently plead for him to baby me, lead me through this difficult time, to guard me with his strength, and to never let me fall. He grips me tighter, his growing erection pressing against my stomach. He loves me weak and dependent on him, and I love that he allows the dependency. There's no expectations of having to be strong, of having to take care of responsibilities, of having to make decisions. He provides that for me.

With no more restrictions on our time together, with no more sadness of having to leave and rush back home, I release a heavy breath of tension, close my eyes, and rest my head against his chest. Unbinding my arms from his waist, I unbuckle his belt. He stands confident when I shove my hand down his pants and wrap my fingers around his thick cock. The heat of his silky flesh sears my palm. I drag my thumb through droplets of precum and smear it over the tip of him before pulling my hand out. His heavily hooded eyes watch as I slip my thumb into my mouth and capture his taste on my tongue. He's peppered tang, flavored nothing like the man I left to be with him.

Dark blue eyes bore into mine as I lower myself before him. Kneeling at his feet, I hook my fingers under the waist of his slacks and pull them down along with his boxer briefs. His cock juts out proudly in my face. My body is still reeling from the orgasms he gave me at the hotel earlier today, but it's not enough. It's never enough.

I tip my head to the side and crane my face up between his legs, taking his balls into my mouth. I steady my hands on his thighs and he widens his legs, allowing me better access. I swirl my tongue over his delicate flesh, sucking gently, pulling one bundle into my mouth completely.

"Oh, fuck," he strains, dropping his head back.

His hands grab my skull, fingers clutching around wads of my hair. He bends his knees, lowering himself down to me even more, and my heart flutters at his neediness. Sliding one hand around his cock, I slip my other between his broad thighs and deeply stroke my finger along his perineum. I continue to suck while my hands tease and pleasure. With every rough moan that grits through his throat, I grow more wet.

My clit swells, pulsing and begging to be touched, but my desire to be covered and consumed by Alec surmounts my body's ache.

He leans forward, taking one hand from my head and bracing it on the window behind me. My finger presses deeper into the sensitive tissue, and his balls tighten in response, lifting off my tongue, pulling away from me.

"Christ, baby," he growls. "Put my cock in your mouth."

Drawing my head back from between his legs, I meet Alec's eyes when I plant a wet kiss onto the head of his dick before wrapping my lips around him and sucking him deep into my mouth. His hips meet my tempo, blurring the lines for a moment as we shift control, and in the slip of a second, Alec holds my head still, fisting my hair as he fucks my mouth.

I grab on to his thigh and maintain my other hand between his legs—pressing, stroking, teasing.

"Deeper," he commands, and I push against his flesh even more, building the pressure for him.

His cock tears into my mouth with urgency, tipping me off balance and driving my back against the window. Saliva drips from my chin as I breathe heavily through my nose. My eyes burn with pricking tears as he takes my mouth hostage, spurring little gags from his deep thrusts.

I love when he loses control with his body, unable and unwilling to restrain himself.

"I'm about to cum all over your tongue," he grits through a sharply jagged breath, and I give him a look of approval. Sweat beads roll from his temples and down the sides of his face. His cock swells, twitching when he reaches the spiked edge of his orgasm. "Fuck," he strains, dragging out the curse. "Deeper, baby. Put it in me."

His cock leaps when I push my finger past the ring of muscle and into his ass.

He explodes.

A feverish groan rips from his chest as the first stream of cum splashes on my tongue. I flick my eyes up to him to see he's watching his cock as he bucks into my mouth. His face, twisted in blissful ferocity.

My lips melt around his cock as cum erupts from his tip. He buckles as ribbons of his semen fill my mouth and shoot down my throat. I take everything his body offers me, swallowing his life source. With one last thrust, his muscles lax, and he unknots his hand from my hair to brace it alongside his other on the window. His sated form hovers over me as I take my time and use my mouth to clean off the lingering traces of his orgasm from his body.

Dragging my lips away, he falls from my mouth. I look above me where his body slacks against the window. His chest heaves in splintering breaths as he comes down from his climax. I allow time to drift before I stand, and when I do, he pushes off the glass and pulls his pants up. Shoving his cock inside the fabric, he zips and buttons before taking my face in his hands and backing me up to the window. He stares at me, no words, only a ghost of a smile tilting his lips.

In this moment, words aren't needed. His touch alone is enough to make me feel safe. He drops his lips to my forehead, and I cling my hands around his wrists as he holds me still.

"I love you, Alec."

"Say it again."

With his forehead resting upon mine, our noses touching, the air from our lungs blending, my heart betrays my husband's words, "I love you . . . most and more."

Thoughts of Landon invade as I twirl my fork in the bed of pasta Alec prepared. I feel like a criminal as we eat our dinner. This is no place for Landon to be, even if it is only in my head. I take another bite of the bland noodles and feel the tug of my gut as I wonder what delicious dish he prepared for the girls tonight.

I need to call them. Tell them I love them before they go to bed, but I know Landon will decline the call when he sees my number. He needs a little time before hearing my voice.

"What did you do while I was away?" I ask before taking another bite of pasta.

"Mostly worked, but I managed to spend some time with my oldest brother and his family." He takes a swig of beer. "I got to watch my nephew play in his soccer game too."

"Did they win?"

"No, but he did score a goal," he says proudly and I smile at his love for the kids I know he wishes he had.

"And what about last night?"

"Last night?"

"I tried calling you," I tell him, remembering the agonizing anxiety to hear his voice after two weeks of being apart.

Taking another pull from his bottle of beer, he swallows before casually saying, "I went to North Shore."

North Shore.

My chest seizes in disbelief, sending a blistering chill through my veins. I do what I can not to show the hurt and jealousy that engulfs my lungs, drowning me in emotions that mark me as a hypocrite. That's exactly what I would be if I accused him of anything, but the thoughts still afflict me, shooting off in rapid-fire.

"You okay?"

No!

I nod, scared my voice will crumble if I speak.

"You're a shitty liar, Victoria." He wipes his mouth with his napkin before saying, "Tell me what you're thinking."

"I have no right to say anything."

He scowls. "Right or no right, I need to know what's going on in that head of yours. I need to know what you're feeling."

How can I tell him that I'm hurt and feel betrayed when I'm the one guilty of betrayal? I have no right to feel this way, but I do.

"I don't want to repeat myself," he says in a mixture of irritation and concern.

"I just . . . I didn't think you were still . . ." My words fall short when my ache bubbles to the surface.

He reaches out across the table and takes my hand in his. "I thought you understood that this is who I am."

"I did—I just thought . . . with everything between us that . . ." I drop my head, suddenly doubting his feelings toward me.

"I need you to look at me because I need you to understand." I lift my head to see the seriousness in his eyes. He softens his voice, telling me gently, as if I might break if not handled with care, "I am who I am, and I never wanted to mislead you into thinking that my lifestyle was something flippant—something I could turn off and on. That's not how fetishes work, which is why I've always sought like-minded people.

"But you knew I wasn't like-minded."

"Yes, I know, which is why I never hid myself from you. I came to you and laid it all out there for you to make the choice whether or not you wanted to get involved with me." He stands and rounds the table to sit next to me. "I can't force myself to change who I am for anyone. It isn't fair to ask me to. But at the same time, I have conformed for you. I know parts of my lifestyle make you uncomfortable, which is why I've never pushed you to go back to the club after I saw how upset it made you," he explains. "This isn't easy for me, you know?"

"I've pushed myself so far with you. More than what I've done with anyone. I've let my walls down and—"

"I know you have, but even with you breaking through your own boundaries, what we have is still very vanilla for my taste."

Feeling as if I've completely let him down, I shrug my shoulders in defeat, wallowing in insecurity.

"I'm okay with what we have, Victoria. If I weren't, I wouldn't have hung around for so long. But I'd be lying if I told you I'm completely satisfied, because I'm not." He drops his head.

"I'll go back," I tell him, not wanting to disappoint him.

"It's not just going. I need more than that. I need to fuck you bare while people watch. I want to see their eyes on us, see them getting off on what I do to you. I want to watch other people fuck while I jerk off or while you suck my cock." His voice exposes his unyielding need. "My other fetishes have always come second to my affinity for voyeurism.

Fucking random people and swinging . . . I can bend on that. Impact play, breath play, and those things, I like exploring them and don't doubt we can explore those things together, but I can't bend on watching and being watched. I need that, and I'm sorry if I misled you in any way."

Our eyes remain locked as I struggle with wondering what last night looked like. He just laid his expectations on the table for me, and I want to do everything I can to give him what he needs. But knowledge is what I need, so I take a hard swallow and ask, "Last night . . ." my voice trembles, "Did you just watch, or . . .?"

"Are you asking if I had sex?"

I nod, and he doesn't beat around the bush when he answers truthfully, "Yes."

His honesty is a dagger to my heart, slaughtering it into the pit of my stomach. A sob latches on to my lungs, digging its claws into the tender sheath of tissue. But I don't cry, I don't allow myself to guilt him with my tears. How could I when I've been fucking Landon? I shouldn't feel what I'm feeling, but that doesn't stop me from asking one more question I have no right asking.

"Have you been doing this all along?"

Again, he answers me in complete honesty. "Not often, but yes."

Pressing my lips together, I fight against the splintering pain of knowing he's been having sex with random people this whole time. I stupidly thought he was being faithful to me.

Faithful.

What the fuck is wrong with me?

There hasn't been one day that I've been faithful to him, so why am I so hurt to find out the same in turn? Why do I feel betrayed? I'm the worst double-standard hypocrite. I'm selfish and oh-so-fucked-up.

His hands have been on other women just as mine have been on another man, but one thing I've never shared was my heart. Never did I love two at once.

"Don't confuse sex with intimacy, Victoria. You can't hide your hurt from me," he says when he takes my hand. "I can feel you shaking."

I want to cling on to his beliefs to protect my heart, but I can't change what's been embedding into my head in a matter of a year.

"Sex with you *is* intimate," I tell him. "When you touch me, I just don't feel it on my skin, I feel it everywhere. My heart beats all over my body when I'm with you."

"That's because you love me. But there's no exchange of feelings with the others. It's just me getting off."

"And what about you?"

His forehead furrows. "What do you mean?"

"Do you feel what I feel?" I question as my mind traces back to all the times I've told him I loved him.

He's never said it in return.

Bracing myself, I ask, "Do you love me?"

I watch his smooth edges fracture into barbed temper. His eyes narrow into a scowl. "Do I not show you every fucking time we're together?"

"But you've never given me the words," I argue with trepidation, not wanting to piss him off more.

"Words? They mean more to you than actions, than sacrifice, than stability? Words are petty and frivolous, Victoria. Just look at the words you use with your husband." He drops my hand and pushes out of his chair. Standing over me, he adds angrily, "Words are nothing but shit. They mean nothing."

"You're right," I respond on a pitched voice, growing passionate about pursuing this argument. "My words this past year to my husband were meaningless. I lied to him over and over only to lie to him more. I even lied to you in the beginning." I stand, meeting him chest to chest. "But when I tell you that I love you, it's the fucking truth, Alec. I've never felt for anyone what I feel for you. There was no stopping my heart from falling in love with you." My words come with so much honesty, I can taste them.

"Is it not enough that I'm here? That I've been here for the past year, licking your tears while you cry in my arms? That I've never made you feel guilty or ashamed knowing that when you slip off my cock you go home and slip onto your husband's?" His voice booms against the walls.

"Yes, you've shown me love!" I yell in a storm of rage and passion, slamming my hands against his chest to gain distance between us. "But I need the words, Alec."

"Why?"

Balling my hands in a fit of turmoil, I lash out and scream, "Because I left my fucking family for you!"

Getting in my face, he lowers his voice, seething, "I never asked you to leave anyone for me, so don't you fucking guilt me into saying what I've already shown and proved to you."

I stand frozen as he turns his back to me and walks across the room. Time slips between us, and with every *tick, tick, tick,* my soul wavers on uncertainty. Is this real? Does he love me, or have I only convinced myself that he does? Are we together or have I only created the illusion of a fantasy that now lives in my head?

A million questions fall in fractals all around me, a glittering, shimmering kaleidoscope of colors that gives no answers. Are the brilliant flecks sparks of the love and desire that burn so blissfully under my skin every time I think about Alec? Or are they sparkling illusions reflecting the lies off their mirrored facets to blind me from seeing the truth?

My heart pounds wildly against the ribcage that's supposed to protect it. My body fighting against itself.

"Alec," I call out, and when he turns to face me from the other side of the loft, the wild beast that is my heart snaps every single one of my ribs. I stand here, fully exposed and ask, "What are we doing? Tell me what I am to you."

He strides across the room, so sure, so in control—arrogant even. Taking my face in his strong hands, he says, "You're everything I never thought existed for me."

"Tell me you love me."

"No."

"Say it," I beg on a voice that shatters around our feet. "Please, Alec. Give me something to settle my unease. Tell me you love me."

He takes my hand and slips it under the hem of his shirt, pressing my palm over that which pumps life into him with every beat. "You feel that?"

His heart hammers just as erratically as mine does.

It's passion and lust and utter chaos—it's love.

I drop my head to his chest, my hand remaining under his shirt.

"No words will ever be more powerful or more truthful than these beats that bruise me every single day I have you."

chapter four

For the first time in five days, I slept in my hotel room. And for the first time, I've been able to think without being blinded by Alec. When I'm with him, I can't see clearly because I'm too consumed by the overpowering high he gives me. I'm quick to accept whatever it is he tells me just so I can feel good again. When doubt begins to infect me, I push it away as fast as I can for fear I'll ruin what we have together.

Now, I sit in bed, sip my coffee, and question.

Why won't he tell me he loves me? Why is he so damn stubborn? How many women has he been with this past year? Will he ever stop? Can I take us outside of this fantasy—into reality—and be okay with what this is?

My stomach burns with the bile of insecurity thinking about his words: *"I'd be lying if I told you I'm completely satisfied, because I'm not."* Ever since he said that, it's lingered in the back of my head, but now that I'm here in this hotel room, alone with my thoughts and free from my drug, it tortures me. But at the same time, it's hard for me to judge him when I feel the same way about Landon. Sure, he satisfies me, but not entirely, which is why I was so drawn to Alec when we first met. It was the realization that I was missing something that I needed. But if Alec already feels that with me, then have we been doomed from the start? Was it over before it began?

I'm saved from my tormenting thoughts when there's a knock on the door.

She's finally here.

I jump out of bed and pad across the room, Alec's oversized pajama pants dragging beneath my feet.

"Happy release day!" Brooke singsongs when I open the door.

I fold my arms around her, her massive belly preventing the closeness I wish I had on this anti-climactic day. She walks in with her laptop, ready to work as blue devils dance on what should be a happy occasion.

The book that almost cost me my publishing deal just went live. The book that I wrote in less than a month. The book that will forever be marked in my selfish contamination—the book I couldn't write because I was too busy cheating on my husband. *Yeah, that book.*

"Have you checked the rankings yet?"

Slipping back into bed, I grab my coffee mug from the nightstand and shake my head. I normally live and breathe the rankings on release day, but truth be told, I'm afraid to with this book. It's the shittiest story I've written, and I'm scared to come face to face with failure.

Getting straight to business, Brooke takes a seat at the desk in the corner of the room and opens the lid to her computer while I battle my internal depression that's shrouded in barbed wire.

I look out the window at the weather that parallels my mood. Dark clouds hang low, coloring the city pale. The gray sky weeps a faint mist, staining its gloom over anything and everything.

This is all wrong.

"You're number thirty-seven on Amazon's top one hundred."

Her cheery voice darkens my world even more. Just another reminder of how everything has changed. With every book release, I've always woken up to a proud Landon. *"Congratulations, Tor. Another one for the win,"* he'd say. A bouquet of flowers would always show up midday, and when evening fell, we would all go out as a family for pizza at Basta Pasta, a little Italian joint in Cambridge. Release day has always been steeped in traditions, traditions I've destroyed. And now, I celebrate alone with Brooke in a hotel room.

Realization crystalizes that all the traditions Landon and I created for our family will no longer be. Birthdays, Christmases, first days of school, family movie nights, Halloweens—nothing will ever be as it was. Everything will be split, severed, and forever changed.

When I feel the sting of threatening tears, I take another sip of my coffee.

"Number thirteen on Barnes and Noble and sixty-one on iBooks," she says as I blink melancholy back. "I can't believe it's doing so well."

She's read the book; she knows it sucks too.

Looking at me from over the top of her computer, she asks, "What's wrong?"

"How is that even a question?" My words come out thick, exposing pain.

With eyes filled with sorrow, she pushes herself clumsily out of the chair and joins me on the bed. I toss the sheets back and make room for her. She lies with me, our backs resting against a mound of pillows stacked against the headboard. Neither one of us speaks for a while as we both mourn my vile choices. But it doesn't feel like choices we're mourning, it feels like lives—it's the death of so many years our families have shared, so many memories, so many joys.

Everything that was no longer is.

"He came over for dinner last night," she eventually says, killing the silence. "The kids played upstairs and he finally opened up to me and Chris."

"What did he say?"

"He's scared of losing his family, Tor. You have thirteen years, two kids, and a home filled with countless memories. He doesn't want to lose all that."

My face crumples as my back trembles, and I finally cry in the safety of my best friend, of my sister. I drop my head into the dip between her chest and pregnant belly, and she wraps her arms around me while the salt of my wounds bleeds into the fibers of her shirt.

"I'm scared for you," she says, her own voice breaking in sadness. "I don't think you'll find another man who will love you as much as he does."

"But it's not fair to him if I don't feel it in return," I whimper. "It would be so much easier if it were the both of us who fell out of love, but it's just me." I wipe my wet cheeks. "I wish to God that I felt for Landon what I feel for Alec. I don't want to lose my family either, Brooke. Everything he doesn't want to lose are all the things that have kept me with him for this past year."

"Do you love him? Alec?"

"I do," I tell her. "I've never felt anything as strong as what I feel for him."

"And he loves you?"

I waver.

He claims he does without words spoken, but with action and doing. It troubles me because I've always been a words person. I need them to reassure, to validate, to seek comfort. They say actions speak louder than words . . . maybe they're right. After all, he's always been there since day one. Why would he deal with a woman like me for so long if he didn't love me? I came to him with more baggage than most men would want to take on, but he took it, bore it for the both of us, and has never judged. I can see how I must've hurt him the other night when I demanded what he's already consistently shown me.

"He does. He loves me and takes care of me," I respond.

"And he's worth leaving your family for?"

"There's no way to answer that." I run my hand over the top of her belly and let it rest there. "I've been searching for certainty, but it doesn't exist. Every choice we make is out of hope. I hoped I would marry Landon and it would be forever. I hoped I would find success as a writer. I hoped I would never wind up being the person I've become. But no matter how much hope I had, never did I have certainty. But I do believe that Alec is worth the risk of putting my hope into."

"So, you've made up your mind?"

A *thunk* to my cheek startles me, and I pop my head up. Staring at Brooke with wide eyes, my mouth tugs in a warm smile, a smile she mirrors.

"I think she's trying to knock some sense into you," she teases.

Emotions blend as a soft laugh breaks through my tears. Life and death, sadness and joy—life is just as confused as I am.

I turn my head back to her belly, splay my hand over the baby girl Brooke has given to me as a goddaughter, and voice through my remaining tears, "I pray to God that you never feel a pain like this. I pray that you don't rush through life, that you take your time to discover who you truly are before giving yourself to someone else. And I pray that you're just like your mommy and nothing like me—"

"Tori." I look to Brooke whose eyes are welled.

I shrug my shoulders, owning what I've done. "I'm not a good person. Don't even try to tell me I am."

"Yes, you are," she counters. "You're in the middle of a shit storm that you created, but you're still a good person." She places her hand on top of mine and smirks, adding, "You're just a good person who makes the *worst choices ever*."

Laughter returns. "You're such a bitch," I joke.

She cocks her head with pride. "So I've been told. Now, go bring me my laptop so I don't have to roll out of this bed like a two-ton hippo. And you need to get your ratty ass in the shower and pull yourself together. I refuse to let you sit around and mope all day."

I get out of bed and hand her the computer, taking her orders like a trained monkey because she's right: I can't let this situation drown me. I have to keep on moving.

When I get out of the shower, Brooke is voice messaging Erin about making a few social media posts about the release and organizing a giveaway for her to run in conjunction to the posts. The day moves on, and so do I. I do what I can to busy myself in an attempt to dissipate the ever-hovering clouds above. I take my time with my makeup and fix my hair before getting dressed. Brooke sets the computer up for a Podcast interview I have scheduled with one of the bigger blog reviewers out there. Once live, I discuss the book and answer questions that come in real time through Twitter, all the while wearing the mask of deception. I smile and beam as I talk excitedly about the book I couldn't have cared less about, because all I care about is myself, but

I deceive the fans well. If only they knew the person who lives behind Madilyn Kline.

The day goes on with phone calls from my editor and agent, both thrilled about the rankings that have improved from earlier this morning.

"This baby just might secure a spot on the *New York Times*," Tabitha says with a tone of relief, and I apologize again for my unprofessionalism.

Facebook messages roll in from bloggers and fans, and I do my best to respond while Brooke talks to a few more authors she's become close with through book signings. I'm truly lucky to have found a small group of author friends who refuse to get caught up in egos. We stick together, no matter what successes and failures we have. We're always there to help and support, and today is just another example of our sisterhood.

Publishing is a game of strategy and luck. Some say it's purely talent, but I say that's bullshit. I'm now ranked number twenty-two on Amazon's overall top one hundred with a crappy book with even crappier writing. This book has about as much talent behind it as an auto-tuned boy band. But the cover is good, and I've got great contacts with book reviewers, columnists, and authors who promote me. Most of all, I've got the greatest fans out there. They are loyal and loud, creating the best buzz one could ask for. I have an agent with balls of steel who fights hard for me, and an editor who refuses to give up on me. But most of all, I have Brooke. She busts her ass for me every single day. She's my secret weapon.

Even though I have all this goodness, my world continues to crumble around me. If it weren't for Brooke, I'd still be in bed sleeping the day away, because when I don't have Alec, the hours are too much to battle on my own.

I tried texting him earlier, but he hasn't responded. He told me he'd be in meetings all day, but it's nearing three o'clock and a part of me was hoping for some acknowledgement from him in regards to my book publishing.

We order room service as another hour passes. I'm now ranking eighteen on Amazon, the powerhouse of all the bookselling platforms.

Brooke is stuffing a wad of fries in her mouth while telling me what she's going to be spending her bonus on. It's always been our deal: if I make the *New York Times*, then I pay her a hefty monetary reward.

I call room service to deliver a pot of coffee when I start to lose steam. Another phone call comes in—an old friend from college who I still keep in touch with. She congratulates me, and after a few minutes of chitchat, we hang up. I take the last bites of my salad when room service knocks on the door.

"I have to pee!" Brooke announces for the fiftieth time today, and I roll my eyes at her need to make the announcement each and every time.

I walk over to the door, drained and exhausted and in need of caffeine, but what I get is so much more. A current of electricity sparks through muscle, tendons, and bone. Alec looks amazing in a suit with an unbuttoned collar, holding a much too expensive bottle of champagne.

"You're here," I beam with an obnoxious smile.

I sling my arms around his neck as he walks us into the room and shuts the door behind him. I nip his neck with a soft kiss and breathe in the spice of his cologne. In an instant, the gray lifts, and I'm catapulted into a realm of euphoric joy.

God, he makes me so happy.

He holds me tightly in his arms, the scruff of his five o'clock shadow bristling my cheek when he whispers gruffly in my ear, "I plan on pouring this entire bottle of champagne over your naked bo—"

"Tori," Brooke snaps, driving bliss into a dark hole.

Alec and I unwrap ourselves from each other as she glares at us with her arms folded across her chest.

"I'm sorry. I didn't know he was coming."

She walks over to the desk and snatches up her laptop. "I don't want any part of this."

"What's that supposed to mean? You already are a part of this."

"It's one thing for us to talk about *him*," she says, directing her arm toward Alec. "But I don't want it thrown in my face when your husband is—"

"Don't go there!" I yell.

Alec sets the bottle down on the coffee table and takes a step toward Brooke, saying, "I never would've come if I had known you were here, and I can assure you that Victoria didn't mean to throw us in your face. She was just excited to see me."

Brooke's eyes are practically glazed in acid and disgust as she glowers at Alec, and I can't take the disrespect. "Stop looking at him like that."

"He calls you *Victoria*?" she ridicules.

"You have no reason to not like him. You want to hate him because you don't know him, but I'm the one you should hate."

"He knows you're *married*! Don't act like he's innocent in all this."

"You're right," Alec says to her. "I'm not innocent. I'm just as guilty as she is."

"Why are you guys doing this?"

"I love him," I defend. "Eventually you're going to have to get to know him, because I can't keep hiding him as if he doesn't exist."

Brooke shakes her head, and I'm torn between the two of them. I hate that I'm hurting her, especially in her fragile state. The last thing she needs is to be getting angry with her due date right around the corner.

"Landon is one of my best friends," she says, sticking up for the man who doesn't have a voice in this since I've blinded him from the truth that lurks right under his nose.

I'm a monster.

But I won't defend another man in front Alec. I won't disrespect him like that, so I keep the focus on the here and now. "Alec's a good guy too. You keep telling me and assuring me that I'm not a bad person, that I'm just making bad choices. With me, you're forgiving. Why is Alec any different?"

"I don't know. It just is."

"It's fine," he tells me before turning his attention to Brooke. "Put it all on me because she's been through enough this past year, and I refuse to allow her to carry this burden on her back any longer. You want to hate me because it's easier? Then hate me. Blame me. Take it all out on me because there's nothing I won't do to protect her from any more heartache."

"You want to protect her?" Brooke sneers, stepping up to him. "Then leave her alone."

Alec turns to me. "Is that you want?"

"No." My answer is firm when I walk to stand by his side.

Brooke keeps her focus on me. With sadness in her eyes and anger on her tongue, she seethes, "I'm so mad at you." Her strong façade cracks, and a tear fights its way down her cheek.

I don't respond, because what can I possibly say? I love Brooke and I hate that I'm hurting her again. I hate all of this and wish I could make it all go away, but that's no longer a possibility. This has spun too far out of control that it's past the point of stopping. I've fallen for another man, and now I have to carefully calculate how to end things with Landon without him finding out about this affair until we're officially done. The last thing I want is a bitter divorce even though I know I deserve it.

Brooke pushes past us and walks out, leaving Alec to mend the unmendable. But somehow, he manages, because that's how powerful he is—he's a force to reckon with. He's the antidote that intoxicates and heals, refusing to let me break. Licking my wounds, he frees me of guilt and misery and takes me as I am, faults and all.

chapter five

The sound of my cellphone ringing pulls me out of a deep slumber. I reach out my arm and fumble my hand over to the nightstand. The light from the screen nearly blinds me. I pinch my eyes shut before I can see who's calling and answer the phone with a groggy, "Hello?"

"Tori, it's Chris."

"Chris?" I blink my eyes open. "Is everything okay?"

Alec stirs from behind me.

"Brooke just went into labor. We're on our way to the hospital."

"Oh, God. Okay, I'll—I'll get myself together and head that way."

"I'll text you the room number when we get there," he tells me.

"Okay. I'll see you in a bit."

"Is everything okay?" Alec questions on a sleepy rasp as he slips his arm around me.

I roll over to face him, the warmth of his body consuming me. "Brooke's in labor. She's on her way to the hospital."

I haven't spoken to Brooke since she stormed out of my hotel room. It's been almost a week, but no matter the tension between us, I wouldn't miss the birth of her daughter for anything.

"Are you leaving?"

"Yeah. I need to be there."

His arms band around me, tugging me flush against him as he lets out a sleepy growl. "You have to leave right now?"

"I have a few minutes."

"That's all I need."

A giggle falls from my lips when he flips me over. I quickly shimmy out of my pajama pants as Alec yanks down his boxers. I'm already wet for him. He spreads my legs and pushes my knees down into the bed, opening me up wide for him. Bending down, he takes a taste before sinking his cock inside of me like he has perfect right to be there—and he does.

"What do I taste like to you?"

Rearing back slowly, a smile twists his lips. "Like sin," he says, thrusting dangerously hard back inside me, kicking the air out of my lungs.

With my arms around his neck, I hold on to him as we fuck each other urgently, desperate to rip the other apart to find our release.

I've never had as much sex before in my life, but with Alec, it's all I seem to think about. Even in the beginning, I couldn't talk to him on the phone without mindlessly slipping my fingers down my panties. He's just as eager as I am though. He made it clear that, even early on in his adolescence, he had a high sex drive. I'm seeing it more since I left Landon and have been spending most of my days and nights with Alec. The smell of our sex is always in the air, but still, even with all the orgasms, I want more.

I wear the scent of Alec on my skin, the phantom pressure of his hands on my body lingers, and the orgasm he gave me still echoes deep inside. Contentment wraps around me like a blanket as mirth paints itself on my heart.

The sliding doors open to the women's hospital, exchanging warm obsidian night for the fluorescent chill of sterilization. With the birth of my two girls and Brooke's son, I know my way around, so I quickly hop in the elevator and head up to the labor and delivery rooms.

Opening the door, I find Chris standing next to the bed, holding Brooke's hand. I ease quietly into the room, and when Brooke leans her head to look over her husband's shoulder, I speak softly, saying a simple, "Hi."

"Can you give us a couple minutes?" she asks Chris, and before he leaves the room, he gives me a hug.

When it's just the two of us, I immediately apologize. "I'm sorry about the other night."

"I'm sorry too. I shouldn't have exploded the way I did."

"It won't be this way forever," I tell her. "I'm just trying to figure everything out."

She nods and I walk over to give her a hug.

"How are you doing?"

"I got my epidural."

"That was fast."

"I labored at home for a few hours, so by the time we got here, I was dilated enough to go ahead and get it."

"Lucky you," I say in jest, remembering how both my girls came so fast there was never enough time for drugs and I was forced to have them both naturally.

"I'm so ready to meet her." She smiles, cradling her belly in her arms.

"You girls good?" Chris questions when he walks back in, but the joy dampens when I see Landon follow in behind.

I slip off the edge of the bed when his eyes meet mine, my heart tangling with my stomach. I haven't seen or spoken to him since I left two weeks ago. His eyes flit from mine to Brooke's as he approaches her.

"How are you doing?" he asks her.

"I'm drugged," she jokes, and he laughs a laugh I haven't heard in such a long time, sinking my heart even deeper into my gut.

I sidestep away and walk over to Chris who's standing by the door.

"Are you okay?" he asks from under his breath, and I hate how awkward this is when the four of us have always been so close and so united, now only to be divided.

I nod and he wraps a supporting arm around my shoulders as I watch my husband and best friend talk.

"Shh! Oh, my God, you two are so loud," I whisper as we creep around the side of Brooke's ex-boyfriend's house he shares with a few of his frat brothers.

Holding the flashlight, I shiver against the midnight bite of winter. Patches of snow crunch beneath our feet as Landon and Brooke give a pathetic attempt to contain their drunken laughter.

The plot for revenge came about after too many beers at the bar we just left, and even though I was against the idea, I wasn't about to let these two intoxicated idiots out of my sight.

Brooke bellies over and muffles her laughs with her hands when Landon's foot gets tangled in a hose and he trips to the ground. "Who the fuck has a hose strung out in the middle of winter?"

"A penis face, that's who," Brooke slurs as Landon finds his footing. "That's his window."

I look in the direction of where she's pointing and shake my head. "Are you crazy? His room is on the second floor."

She jumps up and lands with her legs in a wide stance, chopping her hands like a ninja. "You doubt my skills?"

Landon laughs at her.

"You two are completely wasted."

"Come on, Landon. Give me a boost."

I turn the flashlight off and watch the two of them climb onto the air conditioning unit. Landon squats down to allow Brooke to sit on his shoulders. Their hands latch together, and when he moves to stand, he stumbles and they both break out into a fit of laughter. Once calm, she manages to grab on to the gutter and the two of them look like buffoons as he hoists her up to the roof. Her feet use Landon's shoulders as leverage to kick off and boost herself up onto the roof, sending Landon flying off the metal box and falling ass first onto the ground.

"Brooke, you're gonna fall," I scold, straining my whisper as she fumbles along the snowy roof.

"The fucker broke up with me on his Facebook wall for everyone to see," she snaps before crawling up to his window on hands and knees.

Walking over to Landon, I hold out my hand to help him up. "Are you okay?"

"Brooke," he calls out on a breath, ignoring my question. "You forgot

the bag." He reaches into his back pocket and pulls out the handcuffs and lacy panties we bought at a kink shop on the way here.

He tosses the bag up to her, and we both watch as she opens the window and crawls in. As soon as we hear the loud thud of her ass hitting the floor, a barrel of laugher forces its way through Landon, but I keep an eye on the commotion above. Loud voices, the flash of Brooke's camera, her ex shouting curses. Brooke crawls back through the window, slips on her feet, and slides down to the gutter, fucking it up and bending it as Landon runs over to help her down.

We bolt, making our escape. The two of them clamor into the backseat, drunk and crazy as I start the engine and make our getaway.

"Revenge is a bitch!" Brooke says before giving Landon a high-five in which they both miss.

The good times seem light-years away from where we stand now. I don't even know how we got to this place filled with so much heartbreak. The three of us used to be bound tightly in friendship, love, and happiness. We were young and free and so full of life. And now . . . everything has unraveled.

A nurse comes in to check Brooke, and when I excuse myself, she tells me to stay. I inhale the familiar smell of Landon when he walks past me and leaves the room, his eyes remaining downcast. He's my husband, but he feels like a stranger. I know everything about him, but nothing at all. I've drifted so far from everything, and now I stand here and feel like an outsider. This past year has changed me so much, so beyond recognition, that now they are the ones who look different.

When the nurse finishes up and leaves the room, Brooke tells me, "You should talk to him."

"It's not the right time. You're about to have a baby."

"We're going to be here all night. Are you really going to spend the next how-ever-many hours avoiding him?"

I turn to look at Chris, and he adds, "She's right. Now's as good a time as any."

Instead of protesting, I make my way down to the waiting room where Landon sits.

What do I even say? It's not like I have an answer for him or anything.

He looks at me when I slowly walk over and take a seat in one of the chairs facing him.

"Hey," I say awkwardly, as if it were the first time we'd ever spoken.

We stare into each other's eyes, and I release a silent prayer for God to reignite the passion I once had for Landon. If I could just get it back, I wouldn't have to lose everything we've built. I sit and wait, hoping a higher spirit takes pity on me and saves me. But nothing happens. There's nothing left between us except for the pain I've caused this man who never deserved an ounce of pain. I'll forever crucify myself for what I've done to him, for the life I'm taking away from him.

"I miss you."

I wish he wouldn't say things I can't say in return.

"How are the girls?"

"They miss you too," he says.

"It's killing me to be apart from them."

"And what about me?"

"Landon, don't."

"Don't what? Don't ask my wife if she misses me?"

I drop my head, hating every second of this. I don't even know how to talk to him anymore. All the tension and hollowness I used to feel every time I left Alec for Landon returns. It pits my heart, chilling my bones, and my soul screams at me to run to Alec for warmth and safety.

"Is there someone else?"

"What? No." I respond quickly, fearing he can hear my lying heart pounding the truth against my chest.

"So what have you been doing these past two weeks?"

Getting defensive, I tell him, "Releasing a book, Landon. I've been working and trying to figure out the next step for us."

"And have you figured it out?" His words drip in irritation and hurt.

I stall, letting my eyes drift from him.

"Can we at least talk?"

"Isn't that what we're doing?" I respond.

"I want to talk away from all this," he says, gesturing to our surroundings. "Will you come home and talk to me?"

Home.

I don't feel like I have a home anymore.

"I don't think I'm ready to come home just yet."

"Your hotel room then?"

The hotel room your wife has been using to fuck the man she's fallen in love with? I'm the worst type of disgrace.

"Okay."

chapter six

Brooke wound up having a C-section that night. Even though it was uncomfortable, Landon and I didn't leave until after we had the chance to see the baby and check in on our friend to make sure she was doing okay after the surgery. As much as I wanted to be there for Brooke, I was happy to get back to Alec—get back to the world that's just ours, and ours alone. A world that feels so far away that it must be in a different universe altogether.

It's been three days since Anabelle was born, and Brooke is going stir-crazy while she waits to be released. She called me this morning, begging me to come and keep her company, and since Alec will be tied up in client meetings all day, it's the perfect opportunity to get some snuggle time with my goddaughter.

When I arrive, I laugh at the image of Brooke sucking down a miniature box of chocolate milk as if she were hammering back a shot of alcohol.

"That must be some good chocolate milk," I tease.

"Don't even with me," she groans. "Please tell me you brought some real food."

When I hold up the to-go bag from Tossed, she throws her head back in exaggeration. "Thank God."

I pull out the two salads I ordered, and she's eager to devour it. Setting mine aside, I walk over to the clear plastic bassinet and scoop up the tiny bundle. She sleeps deeply as I cradle her and walk over to the rocker and sit down.

"So, where's Chris?"

"He's spending some father-son time with Ryder."

"Have they said when you can go home?"

"I told them I wanted to go today, but I think it'll wind up being tomorrow," she answers before shoveling a forkful of leaves into her mouth.

"How are you feeling?"

"My incision hurts like a bitch, and I'm terrified it's going to pop open when I have to poop, but other than that, I feel glorious."

I laugh at her sarcasm and look to Anabelle. "Your mommy is off-the-rocker crazy."

"Speaking of crazy, what's going on with you and Landon? I haven't talked to him."

"Nothing," I tell her. "He's coming to the hotel to talk later this week."

"And Alec . . .?"

"What about him?"

"Is he really what you want?"

Ever since I found out that he's had sex with other women, I've been struggling. Countless questions taunt me, and I wonder what our future will look like. He couldn't be more opposite of Landon. Everything about him, right down to his values and beliefs, contrasts everything I thought I wanted in a man. There's no denying how much I'm drawn to Alec, but he's stubborn and stuck in his ways. He still won't tell me the words I'm desperate to hear, leaving me to trust in action alone, but I'm not sure its going to be enough to reassure me. I need the comfort of his words, but I also need to know that he can be monogamous.

"Tor." Brooke's loud voice crashes through my thoughts, and when I look to her, she shakes her head, asking, "What's taking you so long to answer?"

I open my mouth to speak, but words fail me.

Setting her food down, her tone shifts to seriousness when she asks, "Is there something you're not telling me?"

Yeah. There's a lot I'm not telling you because I'm too damn prideful to admit that I'm having doubts.

"I know I came down on you and Alec the other day, but if there's something going on . . . if something's happened . . ."

"You wouldn't understand," I defend, scared of what she'll think if she knows the truth.

"You want to know what I think?" she questions without any intention of letting me answer. "I think he's shady."

"That's not surprising."

"I'm serious. I mean, how much do you really know about this guy?"

Growing annoyed. I stand and place Anabelle back in her bassinet before turning to Brooke and snapping, "What's that supposed to mean?"

"Don't get mad. I'm saying this as a friend and because I care about you, but I'm worried that somehow he's gotten you so swept away that you can't see the red flags."

"What red flags?"

"I guess the first that comes to my mind is that he seems to always be available to you. I mean, you said he's a partner at an advertising firm, right?"

"Yeah, so?"

"Yet he's able to come and go as he pleases, and when he's at work, he's able to constantly text and call you. I dunno . . . seems a little shady."

"He's not calling or texting me now," I refute.

"I'm serious, Tori," she says, softening her voice in concern. "Have you been to his office? Seen where he works? Met any of his co-workers?"

"No. We keep ourselves hidden for obvious reasons."

"Look, I know you say you love him, but I can see in your eyes that I'm not the only one who's doubting him."

And now, all of those questions that were plaguing me before have just multiplied. She's right—with a job like his, how is it possible that he's able to text me for hours on end? I never bothered to wonder about this because I'm always blinded by intoxication. All I've ever cared about was having him around and having his attention. As long as he's with me, in one way or another, I let everything in the world go so it's only the two of us.

"I hope I'm wrong," she says. "But if you're planning to leave Landon like you say you are, then you need to make sure this guy is who he says he is."

"He is. Now can we drop it?"

I can't let what Brooke said go. She planted more seeds of doubt, making me sick to my stomach. I don't even want to entertain the idea that Alec isn't who he says he is. I *know* he is. I've been with him for a year, and from the beginning, he's been straightforward with me. When I asked him the other night if he's had sex with other women, he could've easily lied to me, but he didn't. He told me the cold hard truth knowing it would hurt me, knowing it could possibly drive me away.

My phone buzzes with an incoming text as I sit in my hotel room. Brooke's name pops up, and I open her message.

Brooke: Don't be mad, but I Googled the firm he works at and his name appears nowhere on the site. So, I called and asked for him and was told that no one by the name Alec works there.

With icy fingers, I close out her message and drop the phone onto the coffee table. Disbelief rankles through my chest, unlocking a cage of anxiety.

What the hell is going on?

Limbs tremble as I walk over to my purse and pull out my disposable phone. Flipping it open, I quickly text him.

Me: Are you still at work?

While I wait for his response. I do my own research and look up the company on my main cellphone. I click on the Directory tab and scroll through, looking for Alec's name when my other phone chimes.

Alec: Left an hour ago. At the gym now.

The anxiety thickens, and an overwhelming urge to find something incriminating about him floods all of my senses, taking me hostage. Tapping on the address bar I type in *www.fetlife.com*, but I no longer have access to the site because I deleted my account after I met Alec.

I've never bothered to question him about still being on the site, because let's be honest, I haven't been thinking straight since the moment he entered my life.

I click to register a new account, and just like before, I keep my details vague, and unlike before, I select my fetish as "Vanilla". Entering a different username from my previous, I'm ready to submit the information to gain access to the site. Once everything is approved, I do a search for his username, and his profile pops up.

I'm taken aback to the first time he messaged me—everything seemed so innocent and harmless.

I click on his profile and scroll down to find recent activity. A wave of nausea hits me as I read the messages from women who have posted on his wall.

Nice photos. You looking for a play partner?

It was great seeing you the other night. Stop being a stranger and come out to play more often.

Did you talk to David yet? I still think he has tickets to the concert you mentioned wanting going to.

Check out my pix and message me if interested.

Jealousy flares, pricking its thorns through my overly sensitive flesh.

Who the fuck are these people and why is he talking to them when he has me?

I scroll up, unable to stomach reading any more posts and see the timestamp that notes his last login.

Active 5 hours ago

What was he doing on this site five hours ago when he was supposed to be at work?

Tension mounts, and I feel I'm on the brink of a panic attack. I look to his profile picture and see his relationship status is *Single*.

My thoughts run rampant, creating a monsoon of noises in my head as my pulse spikes. Exiting from the site, I jump off the couch and bolt out the door.

On the verge of a catastrophic breakdown, I rush through the hotel, and run the few blocks it takes me to get to Alec's building, in dire need of answers and explanations.

When I hit the fifth floor, I walk down the hall to his door and knock, hoping he's back from the gym, if that's even where he really is. But there's no answer.

Out of breath from my racing heart, I lean my back against his door and slide down to the floor. Wrapping my arms around my legs, I drop my head to my knees and cry, wondering if I've destroyed everything for a lie. I'm so confused and hang on by a thread that I've handed over to Alec to hold because I trusted him.

Tears soak through my jeans as I think about all my lies and all my betrayals. Have I fallen in love with a fraud?

Time passes as chunks of my heart break away for the family I walked out on, but my heart also breaks for Alec because I love him. Because I have a year invested in him. Because I risked everything to be with him.

"What are you doing on the floor?"

Lifting my head, my cheeks burn against the salt of my dried tears.

He rushes over to me when he sees my swollen eyes. "Are you okay?" He reaches down and I hold his hands as he helps me to my feet. "What happened?"

He's wearing long gym pants with a sweat-soaked shirt, and I find comfort in at least knowing he was where he told me. Needy to trust in all he's led me to believe, I throw my arms around him and bury my head against his chest. The wetness from his shirt seeps into my pores and I succumb to his power to soothe and console.

This year has taken its toll on me, and I'm so desperate for solitude and peace that I battle with the urge to just let go of what Brooke texted me and what I saw on his profile. The temptation to accept him as is—whether it be true or not—is profound.

He kisses the top of my head before tucking me into the crook of his arm and unlocking the door. Walking into the loft that has become my ivory tower of safety, I grow even more desperate. I need him, and all of this, to be true. I need it so badly because I can't be without him.

I continue to cling to him, balling his shirt in my hands. He drops his gym bag to the floor and pulls me into his arms. "Baby, what's wrong?"

"I need this to be real."

"You need what to be real?"

Lifting my head from his chest, I look into his eyes, saying, "*You*."

"What are you talking about?"

Digging deep, I find a shred of strength and step out of his hold because there's no way I can think straight when he's touching me. I need to silence my fears by finding answers to the unknown.

Taking a deep breath, I ask, "Where do you work, Alec?" but my voice comes out weak and scared.

His forehead furrows in confusion. "What?"

"Just tell me."

"You know where I work," he says and then adds in frustration, "What's this all about?"

"Edelman, Vanksen, and Partners, right?"

"If there's something you want to say, just come out and say it."

"I got a text from Brooke today," I tell him. "She said that you don't work there. That you're not listed in the company directory."

"Is that so?" he responds through tight lips. "Well, I guess if she says it's true then it must be."

"Alec—"

"And when she told you this, did you just take her word?"

"No," I admit. "I got on the website and looked as well."

"Then I guess you know she's full of shit."

His statement catches me off guard and confuses me. Shaking my head, I say, "Alec, your name wasn't on there."

"No?" He walks over to the office space on the other side of the room where he keeps his laptop. I watch as he leans over his desk and works his fingers over the keyboard. "Come here."

I make my way over to where he stands and look at the screen where he's pulled up the directory.

"Do you see a Harrison Demry on that list?"

The moment he says his last name, I kick myself. In my state of panic, I only scrolled through looking for his first name, scanning the list for A's in search of Alec. And I know Brooke did the same because I've never told her his last name. She would've called, asking for Alec—just Alec.

"But who's Harrison?"

Anger splashes in his eyes, and he slams the lid closed. "Me," he barks. "In business I go by my middle name."

"Alec, I'm sorry."

"Have I not proven myself to you? First you question my feelings for you and now you question my integrity," he lashes out at me, scolding me like a disobedient child, but I don't cower.

"I'm sorry, but my world is spinning so out of control that I'm desperately searching for something secure and finite to hold on to."

"Then fucking hold on to me!"

"I want to!" I cry out. "But I'm scared."

"Why are you so afraid of me?"

"Because you can hurt me more than what I could ever hurt you. Because I'm putting everything on the line for you—I'm risking it all." I brace my hand on the edge of his desk when my emotions surface and explode. "It's so simple for you, but it's not for me. I'm married. I have a family and thirteen years of a life I've built with someone else that I'm walking away from."

"Then go home!"

His voice barrels through the room, bouncing off the wooden floors and echoing against the walls.

My heart stalls while he glares down at me, his nostrils flaring with every threatening breath of his.

"If you can't trust me, then what the hell are you doing with me?" he seethes. "If you're so terrified to leave your family, then don't."

"So you're just going to let me go? It's that easy for you?"

"You wouldn't believe me if I told you no, so why fucking bother?"

"Then prove me wrong, Alec," I plead. "You see my stress, you see everything that's on the line. All I'm asking for is reassurance."

He stalks away from me, raking both his hands through his hair before turning back to me and losing his shit, shouting, "God dammit! What the fuck do you want from me?"

"Tell me you love me!"

"You think my saying those words will secure me to you? Christ, Victoria, they're just petty words!"

"Not to me. And you should want to reassure me with them if I tell you that's what I need, but you're such a fucking hard ass and refuse to give them to me. Why?"

He turns his back to me and stands there with no response, with no answer, which only fuels my madness. I want to hurt him like he's hurting me, so I go ahead and piss him off more, asking, "Are there others just like me?"

"What the fuck are you talking about?" he says to the wall, refusing to look at me.

I carve the truth into a lie, placing all blame on Brooke when I tell him, "In Brooke's quest to check up on you, she got onto the fetish site where we met. She told me your page was filled with messages and that you had been logged on earlier today."

"You girls act like children." He finally turns around, a look of disgust on his face.

"Is it true?"

"How dare you try to make me into the villain here. What? You thought you'd be the one to change me?" he sneers, twisting his features. "You wanted to step into *my* world, remember? You knew who I was. You knew what I was about and what I was into, and when you chose me, you chose to accept me *as is*. And for your information, I have friends on that site. In case you haven't noticed, I don't function as easily as you do in this world, and that site provides me a place to go where I don't have to pretend to be something I'm not."

"So it's a place where you can be completely honest?"

"Yes."

Walking over to him, heart scorching in a fury of flames, I ask, "Then why does it say you're single?"

He grabs my chin forcefully, digging his fingers into my face, and fires his words. "Because why the fuck would I give my all to a woman who can't even give me hers?" Pushing my face away, he snaps, "Get out."

I've never been so furious and heartbroken in my life. "I hate you."

"Funny. I thought you loved me," he says. "And yet you swear those words aren't cheap, but you just shit all over them, didn't you?"

chapter seven

I'M IN THE FROST-KILLING HOUR, MY PETALS WITHERING ON A SLOW-DYING FLOWER, turning them into puce flakes before they fall from the heart that once provided the sustenance of life.

My hands have never been so dirty. They're stained in the blood of so many from all the wounds I've inflicted upon them. Contempt hates the silence, but here I sit, trapped in a prison of wretchedness.

I'm alone.

My biggest fear teeters on a knife's edge, tormenting me.

Did I just lose everything for a cheap thrill?

No. I won't allow myself to reduce what Alec and I have—had.

No matter how much I hurt right now, I can't deny that he sparked a fire in my soul. But the ignition sent me into flames, blazing, burning—burning—burning, giving me no choice but to cinder until all that remains are ashes on the ground. And now I have to ask myself: Was the ride worth it when in the end we just crashed and burned?

Is it even the end though?

God, I hope not.

Picking up the phone that connects me to him and no one else, I send yet another text.

Me: Please, Alec. Text me back. Call me.

And again, just like the past two days, I get nothing in response.

I haven't left this hotel room since Alec threw me out of his loft. I can barely stomach food, I haven't showered, and I refuse to take off the pajama pants that I took from his closet the other week.

Brooke calls and texts me just as much as I've been calling and texting Alec. And just like Alec does with me, I ignore her messages and decline her calls, sending them to my voicemail.

I can't face her.

I'm too embarrassed to admit that not only did I fail with my marriage, but I've failed with Alec, the man I thought I was so sure of. I can't let this happen. I have to find a way to make this work, to save face, to stitch us back together—to keep my pride intact, what little pride I have left.

Me: I was so stupid and out of line. I love you. Please, you have to believe me.

Another groveling text. I've sent so many, I'm sure he can smell the stench of desperation.

Looking at the time, I drag myself out of bed and force myself into the shower. I cry when the spray hits my skin, washing away what was left of Alec's last touch. Water marries with tears, taking my agony down the drain and into the sewers where they belong.

I'm unworthy of heartache.

Taking my time, I do what I can to rid myself of the sadness before Landon arrives, but it's all for naught. Nothing can release me from this—nothing but *him*.

Shutting the water off, I shake the thought of Alec out of my head—again, another useless feat.

That man owns me.

With a towel wrapped around me, I walk out of the bathroom and turn on the television in an attempt to drown out my thoughts with a little white noise. Landon is on his way over to talk. Before my fight with Alec, I thought I knew what I was going to say, but now that everything has blown into shards of chaos and confusion, I don't know what I'm going to tell him. I try not to think too much about it, after all, it's *him* that wants to talk to *me*.

I fix my hair and do what I can to hide the dark circles under my eyes and cover the redness from too many tears shed. Tucking Alec's sleep pants into one of my suitcases, I turn off my affair phone and hide it away too. My eyes sweep the room for any traces of Alec that may remain from the time he's spent here.

When Landon's knock hits the door, anxiety from not knowing what's about to happen strikes a corded nerve, shooting a rippling of anxiety up my spine. Only one week remains on the deadline he gave me. In one week, if I can't make a decision, he'll make it for the both of us, and that'll be it. We'll be divorced and starting new lives on our own.

"Hey," he says in a dank voice that reflects everything we've become.

"Hi."

He walks in slowly and looks around the space he assumes I've been living in for nearly a month. I grow uncomfortable, nervous that somehow he'll see the smear of sex all over this room. The bed, the couch, the desk, the shower, the walls. Alec has fucked me on top of and against every surface of this room.

Can Landon see it? Does he sense it?

Turning around, he looks at me with decaying hope. "Do you know how hard this has been on me?" I stand motionless and unresponsive. "Three weeks of coming home to the kids and no wife, wondering what I could've done better. I lie in bed every night and think about you." He steps toward me and touches me for the first time in so long. As he cups my face in his hands, my heart softens a little. "Tell me I'm not the only one, Tor. Tell me you lie in bed and think about me too."

Don't comfort him with lies.

Don't hurt him with the truth.

Closing my eyes, I avoid speaking and take in a deep breath. His scent fills my lungs, reminding me of everything I stand to lose. The absence of Alec has ripped a hole in the very fibers I'm made of. He refuses to respond to my every attempt at contact.

What if I've lost him? What if what's standing before me is all I was ever meant to have?

I've never been alone.

In high school I had Trey, and then I had Landon, and then there was Alec. I've always needed a man in my life to fill the void of my father leaving after my parents divorced. I never felt the love of a man as a child, and now I cling to it, cry for it, and need it for survival.

In one hand I have Alec, a man who threw me into a turnstile filled with a blazing passion of love that's so powerful and so hot it threatens to sear me if I'm not careful. But he shoved me out. He didn't even fight for me.

And in my other hand I have Landon, a man who built his world around me, gave me two beautiful girls, and gave me a life most would dream of. A life I *once* dreamt of but no longer do because all the excitement and desire we had has been snuffed out. But unlike Alec, this man fights for me. Unfortunately, it isn't him I want fighting.

I slip my hands around his wrists as he holds on to me and look into the eyes of what just might be my consolation prize after losing Alec.

"Say something," he requests, a plea for me to return his sentiment, but I can't, because when I lie in bed at night, I'm not alone, and it's not Landon that fills my mind.

When I say nothing, he drops his head to mine, and the closeness tugs at the bloody gash Alec left me with.

I'm so lonely.

With broken hearts and battered souls, our lips touch. Victims in this game called love, we kiss, moving with uncertainty into a gray fog where no understanding resides. Motions happen without choice or approval.

Time slips from existence and we're on the bed. My hands press into Landon's back, pulling his weight on top of me.

I'm adrift, wandering aimlessly inside my head of vacancy.

Slowly, our bodies move together, the ache of my broken soul begging to be healed. Clothes fall to the floor, leaving nothing between us except bared flesh and hidden lies. Landon sits on his heels between my open thighs and looks at me with sadness. His eyes drop from mine and drift over every detail of my body, melting time as if he's locking my every curve into his memory.

A whip lances my heart, slicing a singeing wound into vessels and nerves when his body lowers to mine.

Suddenly, I'm aware of everything.

He slides his cock along my slick pussy.

This is it.

I hold my breath, complete with understanding, and pinch my eyes shut as he takes his time pushing himself inside me. He savors every inch gained until we're completely coalesced.

This is his goodbye.

Without urgency, without rush, he makes love to me. His hands gently glide over my body while I hold on to him to keep from drowning in pain and regret. Everything about the way he's looking at me, the way he's kissing me, the way he's stroking his cock inside of me, it all screams that this is the last time the two of us will ever be together like this.

Landon whispers kisses along my neck and murmurs against my skin, "I love you," giving me the words so easily, and I choke on my tears. "You're so beautiful."

His adorations tear me apart, and I can't believe this is actually happening. Our broken bodies sway and rock together, sealing the fate of finality with every kiss, every lick, every breath of pleasure. Tears slip from the corners of my eyes, rolling down the sides of my face and into my hair.

"Tell me you love me," he says.

"Landon, please . . ."

"It's been forever since I've heard you say it." His voice is heavy, weighing me down in dissension, and when he says, "You don't have to mean it. I just want to hear it one last time," everything I've been holding back, claws its way out.

I cry.

It's ugly and honest and brutally painful.

He kisses trails of salt and then slips his hand between my legs.

A moan erupts through my sobs when his fingers find my clit. With feather-light touches, he drives my body closer to an orgasm I shouldn't indulge in.

"Say it," he urges as he continues to move inside my body.

"Landon, oh, God." My body jerks up to his, the sizzle of ecstasy electrocuting my bones.

He begins to thrust his hips, and before I throw myself on the sword, I feel him thicken, and that's all it takes to send me over the edge. I cum as our bodies lock firmly together. We hold each other more tightly than we ever have before, with bone-breaking strength as he spills into me. I spasm around his throbs, and in the hurricane of emotions swarming between us, I cry out through my orgasm, "I love you, Landon."

Sometimes lies soothe.

He pushes into me again, shuddering through his climax, and I comfort him one last time, holding him against my chest. "I love you."

Collapsing on top of me, his heart beats against mine, a thumping reminder that this is it—we're finished.

I'm torn with the impulse to wrap my body around him and keep him forever. But I can't. I know this feeling to cling is because, no matter how far we've grown apart, it's terrifying to let go of security. No one likes saying goodbye, especially me.

Landon rescued my faith in trust when I had lost it with Trey. He was my best friend, my lover, my everything, and to watch it all dissolve into this moment—in this hotel room—is heartbreaking.

He rolls off of me, and I watch as he grabs his pants from the floor and pulls them on. And just like flipping a light switch, we go from so much to nothing at all. A few minutes ago he was telling me he loved me, and now he's empty. He won't even look at me.

"Landon?"

Nothing.

He shrugs his shirt on and then sits on the edge of the bed for a silent minute, his back facing me. He then stands and walks to the door.

"Landon," I call out, and he stops with his hand on the door handle. "You're not going to say anything?"

He turns his head, and I see why he's been keeping his back to me. Tears stain his face, falling like death from his eyes. My own well up, taking away my ability to breathe.

"The only way I could get you to say you love me was by telling you to lie to me." He speaks through the bullet hole I shot through his heart. "There's nothing left. I can't pull on your heartstrings when they're no longer attached to anything."

chapter eight

THE DOOR CLOSES, AND THERE'S NO DOUBT IN MY MIND THAT LANDON CAN HEAR my sobbing wails as he walks down the hall to the elevators. I'm sure everyone on this floor can hear the excruciating pain ripping out of my chest.

I fist the sheets that are covered in our sex—covered in our goodbye—and lose myself in a dark well of debilitating agony.

This year has been a slow walk to the grave I knew I would ultimately land in. And here I am, naked and all alone, waiting for someone to shovel the dirt on me.

Grabbing a pillow, I shove my face into it and use it to muffle my screams. The sadness hurts too much, and I do what I can to replace it with something else. So I scream harder than I ever have before, shredding my vocal cords. My face burns as I release another piercing shriek, welcoming the razors slicing their way up my throat. I yearn for more of this blistering pain to overshadow the agonizing suffering afflicting me.

Nothing can save me though.

Hurling the pillow across the room, I fall onto the bed, curl into a ball, and allow the misery to suffocate me.

Why even try to dull what I should feel?

I deserve the crucifixion.

I've been nothing but a silver-tongued devil, lying and deceiving to indulge in self-fulfilling pleasures. Pleasures I had no right to partake in, but did, regardless of morals and vows. I handed my soul to sin, allowed its infection, and ultimately fell in love. To think I deserve anything more than losing everything would only sharpen my horns.

Minutes fade into hours, fading into darkness, fading into hollowness, turning me into a corpse. My naked body shivers as I stare at the ceiling, limp and lifeless. I barely have enough energy to blink, only doing so when the burning becomes too much from the loss of moisture. And then, like sandpaper to an open wound, I blink.

I feel on the verge of death, and I'm scared. I don't want to be forsaken. The thought alone terrifies me, triggering the need for nourishment and consolation. It's the longing to be taken care of that continues to follow me through life. Because even though I want to give up, I know I can't. I'm not strong enough to do this on my own. I need to breathe, to fight my way up to the surface's edge, but these waters are dark and bury me under their weight.

Rolling to my side, my muscles ache, but I absorb it as I push myself off the bed. I look to the floor at the pile of clothes Landon peeled off of me. The thought of touching them doesn't seem right, so I make my way over to the closet and toss on a pair of jeans and a top. I don't give a shit what I look like, I just need to be saved.

Even though I know I shouldn't, I can't stop myself from looking in the mirror. My whole face is puffy, splotched in redness with swollen eyes that are bloodshot to hell. I run a brush through my hair and eventually tie it up in a knot. I leave everything behind, taking only my hotel keycard.

With my blurred vision, I have no business getting behind the wheel of my car, so I walk. It's after three in the morning—the witching hour—and the streets are eerily quiet. The darkness cloaks me in its ink, but I need light, I need warmth, I need Alec. He's all I have left, and I'll do anything to get back into his graces.

Steps fade behind me and soon I'm standing in front of his door, not even remembering how I got here.

Pressing my palm against that which separates me from him, I ball my fist as fear and loneliness strangle me, and I knock.

I knock and knock and knock.

I refuse to allow him to ignore me, so I continue to knock until I hear the click of the lock. The door opens, and there he stands with sleep-stricken eyes, wearing nothing but a pair of pajama pants.

"What are you doing here?" he questions with dullness in his voice.

"You won't answer my calls or return my texts. Please, Alec, just let me talk to you."

He swings the door open, and I step inside the secret oasis he's welcomed me into for this past year. We've shared so many memories here, happy ones and also tristful ones, but no matter good or bad, I cherish them all. The thought of losing all that we've worked up to terrifies me, because I don't know how to survive this on my own.

I need him and all that he gives so badly that I'm willing to turn a blind eye to the things I know I can't change in him. I just lost the life I spent thirteen years creating—I can't lose Alec on top of that.

"What do you want to talk about?"

Alec stands across the room from me, and I curse the distance. I need this tension and this feud to disappear so we can be good again. I look into the eyes of the man who's managed to change the trajectory of my life, and I feel my blood thaw from the ice Landon left me with. Whether it's turning a blind eye or forgiveness, in this moment, I'm willing to let all my doubts and hesitations go. Maybe he's changing me, or maybe it's fear that's changing me, but I no longer care.

I dig down deep, searching for the right words to say, but there's no script when it comes to Alec. With everything that's been stripped from me, I give up the fight and let my heart do the talking.

"I read a lot of poetry," I tell him softly as he stands firm with his arms crossed over his chest. "I don't think I ever told you that."

"No. I didn't know that."

"I don't know why, but looking at you right now reminds me of something Rumi once wrote. It's been years since I've read it, but . . ."

My words drift as I hang on to my emotions, needing him to hear me without any distraction.

"Will you tell me?"

"He said, 'Somewhere between right and wrong there is a garden. I will meet you there.'"

Alec's arms fall to his sides, his whole demeanor changing. He walks toward me, stopping a breath away, standing close enough for my body to soak in his heat, and says, "'When the soul lies down in that grass, the world is too full to talk about,'" finishing Rumi's quote.

"How did you know that?" I ask in surprise.

"You're not the only one who has a thing for poetry."

He finally touches me, running his hands over my shoulders and down my arms. A touch I wasn't sure I'd ever feel again—a touch that heals.

I stare up into his eyes, needier than ever. "Why can't that be us?"

"It can be. But we can't be in that garden if you don't trust me. It only exists in the gray where there's no questioning or reasoning. It's accepting things as they are and being at peace."

"I was so stupid. And I'm so sorry. I never should've doubted you." My voice, soft but fervent.

"You hurt me."

"I know. And I feel terrible. I had no right to make assumptions or to judge you when you've been nothing but transparent with me from the start." I reach out and brace my hands around the sides of his chest. "I won't ever question you again."

"Are you going to trust me?"

"Yes."

"I'm sick of your fucking walls."

"They're gone," I promise, willing to do whatever he asks in order to keep him. "I made my choice."

"And?"

"It's over with Landon."

He takes my face in his strong hands and releases a heavy sigh.

"I love you, Alec," I affirm. "And I don't care if I never hear those words from you. It doesn't matter anymore because I *know* you love me."

"Every fucking day," he responds before grabbing me in his arms and kissing me.

I sling my arms around his neck and he lifts me up, carrying me over to his bed. I'm barraged with a million sensations at once, kissing him open and deep, thieving the breath from his lungs to feed off of. He's a savage, ripping my shirt off and yanking my bra down. His mouth wraps about my nipple, and he sucks—hard. I lift my hips off the bed when he rubs my pussy roughly over the denim of my jeans.

His touches are merciless.

He needs no permission and he knows it. Exultant in his sexuality, owning every piece of it unforgivingly.

I never got this from Landon, but I have it with Alec, and it's everything I've ever needed. He's woken the beast in me but also knows when I'm in need of his tenderness. He reads me well without my having to tell him. And right now, he knows I'm in need of viperous passion after our tumultuous fight, and he gives it to me.

I push into his hand as he continues to palm me.

"Greedy," he says gruffly as I claw at his bare back.

He rips open the fly to my pants and jerks them off my legs, tossing them across the room. He then grabs me and pulls me up to my knees with him. Our chests heave as he stares at me. "You want my dick?"

"Yes."

"Take it out," he instructs, and I grip the sides of his pants and shove them down to the bent crook of his knees.

He's rock fucking hard, tinged in deep pink, ready to bury himself inside me. I can feel the wetness building between my legs, my clit pulsing as blood rushes to my core. Alec's cock hangs boldly between us, and I can't take the stalling any more.

"Fuck me, Alec. Don't make me wait."

His lips curl, and the next thing I know, he's flipping me over on all fours, slapping my ass, and shoving two thick fingers inside my pussy.

I cry out in bliss, happy to just have any part of him inside of me, but he doesn't stay long.

"You want me to fuck you?"

With my head hanging down, I beg, "Yes, please."

"You want it here?" he questions, thrusting his fingers into me in one swooping force. "Or do you want it here?" he asks as he drags his fingers out of me and slides them up to the pucker of my ass, pushing just the tip of a finger inside me.

Euphoria washes over me, taking away my ability to think straight. I'm completely lost to ecstasy.

"Have me however you want me," I moan, desperate to have him fill me and erase everything I lost when Landon used me and left me. "I'm yours, so take me."

His cock lies heavily on my back above my ass as he continues to touch me so intimately. Hunching his body over mine, he takes his finger from me and says with a throaty whisper in my ear, "I'm going to fuck your pretty little cunt, and I want you squeezing my balls when I do."

"Alec—God, please," I mewl.

His fingers sink into my folds and down to my clit. "You're so fucking wet."

"Yes."

The strokes of his expert fingers cause my body to lurch and tremble.

"Are you done fucking your husband?"

"Yes," I respond because I can't stomach this charade going on any longer. "It's over. I only ever want your hands on me. It's all I've ever wanted."

"No more sneaking around?"

"No. It's just you."

"Why?" he goads, needing to hear the words for himself.

I move past my pride, knowing I'll never get those words from him. Alec isn't someone I can force to do anything he doesn't want to do, so I relinquish the expectation that I can somehow change the unchangeable. Because he's right, I have to trust him—I have to trust that maybe he knows what I need better than I do. So without reservation, I tell him, "Because it's you that I love. No one else. Just you, Alec."

He takes his cock and holds himself against my opening. "Say it again."

"I love you, Alec."

Bucking his hips, he forces his way inside me, knocking me forward with unforgiving force. I fist the sheets in my hands as he draws back and then slams himself into me again. With his hands holding on to my shoulders, he fucks me with one powerful thrust after another, grunting like an animal while talking so filthy to me.

With every penetration, with every word spoken, with every drip of sweat that falls from his body to mine, he stitches me back together. But this time, he uses *his* threads, knowing he's strong enough for the both of us.

Reaching my hand between my legs, I hold him in the palm of my hand. I squeeze and tug with just enough pressure to seesaw between pleasure and pain the way he's taught me. And I know he'll continue to teach me and guide me in all aspects of life—always two steps in front of me.

He wraps an arm around my stomach and pulls me down on top of him. He sits on his heels and leans back, with his hands braced on the bed behind him.

"Fuck me, Victoria. I want to watch my cock sink in and out of your pussy."

Leaning forward with my hands on the mattress, I rise up on my knees before falling down over him.

"That's it," he encourages, and I pick up the pace, bouncing my ass up and down, fucking him as he watches from behind.

It's a new position for us, one that I never experienced in all the years with my husband. Alec has turned me upside down and inside out. I can't even imagine going back to what I used to be before him, because with him, I'm higher than what should be humanly possible. But he makes it possible.

My body begins to stagger in uneven rhythm as I draw closer to my climax, and I know Alec can feel me when he tells me, "Don't wait for me. I'm nowhere near done fucking you."

"No?" I pant breathlessly.

"No, baby. Go ahead, I want to feel you cum all over my cock."

His words are the same as they were when we first met, when all we had was spending our days masturbating over the phone together. I never would have thought I'd be where I am a year later. Me, head over heels in love with Alec, bent over his dick and exploding in a mind-numbing orgasm. This was never supposed to be me. I was never supposed to be this woman. But I am, and I can't go on punishing myself for it.

Before my heart rate can slow, Alec tosses me onto my back, throws my legs open, and covers my pussy with his mouth. Licking, sucking, nibbling. Shoving a finger inside me to lube it in my arousal, he then drags it out of me and pushes it in my ass before taking me back in his mouth.

My vision swims out of focus, and I close my eyes when they begin to roll in the back of my head.

"Jesus!" I cry out as I pull fistfuls of his hair.

He darts his tongue out and begins fucking me with it. The combination of both my holes being filled throws me into the flames of another orgasm, another one that Alec doesn't join me in. He doesn't allow me to ride this one out before feeding his cock back inside me.

"Alec, please—Oh, fuck!" It's too much intensity building, too much for my body to handle. "Slow—I can't." I can't breathe as another quake erupts, shattering my lungs as I struggle for air when I cum again.

He doesn't relent, doesn't slow his pace. I'm captured beneath him. I can no longer see him behind the sparkling fog, and I panic. I try to push him away, but he's quick to grab my wrists and pin them down next to my head. "Trust me to know what I'm doing. You're going to fucking love this."

His voice cuts through my panting moans that teeter on agony. As much as I need him to stop, I need him to keep going even more.

He releases one of my hands, and I cling my arm around his neck, forcing his head down onto mine. "I can't see you," I stress but my voice doesn't sound right.

"Just a few more minutes. Hang on to me."

Every sound hollows into a faraway tunnel, and the moment his fingers are back on my clit, my body convulses in another climax, sending tingles that don't subside down all four of my limbs.

Both our bodies are slick with sweat, but it's no longer me inside my skin.

"Fuuuck," Alec grunts before rupturing in his own orgasm, shooting his semen into my body, filling me, warming me. I hold him close, my eyes remaining closed, and time warps from all around me.

"I need you to focus on my voice, Victoria."

All I hear is a ringing echo deep inside my head. Warmth cocoons me, and I feel myself being lifted.

"Let me know you can hear me, okay?"

I nod.

Is he rocking me?

"Are you warm enough?"

I nod. The numbness in my face begins to wane, and I start to feel the heat of his chest against my cheek. He continues to talk to me, asking me questions that require me to respond. Unrelenting tingles prick my hands, and I curl them into my chest.

"Are they bothering you?"

This time, when I nod, I'm able to voice a hum, answering with a dreary, "Mmm hmm."

I can feel him taking my hands in his and rubbing my palms, eventually releasing the needling pain.

I'm lifeless in his arms, crumpled in a ball. With muscles depleted, I don't even try to move. Slowly, I regain my senses, and I nest in the comfort of being cradled in his lap. I take deep, relaxed breaths, savoring the musk of his sweat. Alex lulls me with gentle swaying and fingers massaging my scalp.

"Are you still with me?"

"Yes," I manage to whisper.

"Can you open your eyes and look at me?"

They flutter for a moment before I'm able to blink them open. Light filters in, and the first thing I see is that he has me wrapped in a blanket. When I tilt my head up to him, his hair hangs haphazardly, a lock of it fallen onto his forehead.

"How are you feeling?"

"Tired."

When I attempt to sit up, he stops me, saying, "Don't try to move too much on your own right now. Just let me take care of you."

"Why?"

"Because you're coming down from subspace, and it's going to take your body a while to recoup."

I repeat his words in my head, still feeling a bit flighty, but I'm able to recall the word "subspace." It sounds familiar, and I close my eyes, hoping it'll help me remember where I've heard it.

After a few moments pass, I look to Alec and ask, "You had that on your profile, didn't you? That's why I know the word."

"Did you like it?" His lips lift in a subtle grin.

I shake my head, slightly confused with what subspace actually is.

"Do you understand what happened?"

I shake my head again.

"It's an altered psychological state you can push people into. I started learning about it and experimenting with it when I was in my early thirties. I've never done it with someone who's been emotionally attached to me though."

"Why would that make a difference?"

"They say it's more intense and quicker to take hold, which is what you just experienced," he tells me. "But it can wreak havoc on your system if you don't get any aftercare."

"Aftercare?"

"This," he says, strengthening his hold on me for a brief second. "Affection, touch, keeping you warm, talking to you until you regain lucidity. It all helps with bringing you back down."

"I didn't even know this was a thing. It scared me."

"I'm sorry, baby. I got carried away," he says, to which I counter, "It's okay. You don't have to apologize."

Alec lays me down in bed next to him. With both of us on our sides, I stare into his eyes, feeling closer to him than ever before.

"Did you like that?"

"Yes," I respond, and he kisses me, sealing what I never want broken again.

He's all that exists for me right now. Somehow, in the eye of the impossible, he's taken the anguish of my marriage ending and magically made it okay. With Alec, I'm no longer in pain. I'm soothed, tucked safely in his arms, right where I'm meant to be.

chapter nine

Me: We need to talk. I called and scheduled a session for us to meet with Dr. Lapinski this Thursday at 10am. Text me back and let me know if this time works for you.

In three days, what was implied the night Landon left my hotel room will finally be voiced. In three days, there will be no turning back. In three days, we will write the closing sentence to our story.

Our marriage therapist is also a divorce mediator. It's my hope that Landon and I can keep this process as amicable as possible. The last thing I want is for this split to turn nasty. We don't need anymore pain than what I've already caused.

Landon: I'll be there.

We haven't spoken since that night. And since that night, I've been staying with Alec. I came back to the hotel today because I needed to get some work done, and I'd left my laptop here with all the files I need.

I've spent the morning getting updated sales numbers together for my agent on my self-published work. And now that it's drifting past lunch time, I hop on social media to make a few posts. Filtering through my private messages, I respond to the ones that require my immediate attention. My inbox is completely flooded with the success of my latest release. Surprisingly, I've maintained excellent rankings, which should secure me a spot on the *New York Times* when the list comes out next week.

After thirty or so messages, I grow tired, close out my Facebook, and open my email—another obscene inbox awaits me.

Before I start reading messages, I scroll through and delete all the crap that's nothing but advertisements for marketing products and garbage of the like.

Delete.

Delete.

Delete.

STOP.

I freeze when I come across an email from FetLife with a notification that I have a message waiting for me. But it's not *me*, really, because I set up that fake account for the sole purpose of spying on Alec.

When I open the email and click on the link, I'm taken to the log-in screen. I quickly enter my information and then go to my inbox tab to open the message.

Holy fucking shit!

My hands fly to my mouth as everything inside me goes numb.

It's Alec.

I look at the timestamp to see that he sent the message this morning. Freaking out, I wonder if he knows it's me, but when I think about it, I come to the conclusion that, *no*, he couldn't possibly know. My last account was set up through my personal email, and this new one is set up through my business email. I even altered the profile information, changing my user name and age. Plus, it's not like he would ever know that this account had been looking at his page.

ALEC107: Why so secretive?

I question whether to respond to him since I know how important it is to him that I give him trust, and the last thing I want is to take another step back with him when we just made up from our fight. But he will never know it's me, and Brooke is right, I should know who I'm dealing with if I'm going to leave Landon. And now that only three days remain before we move forward with ending our marriage, I go ahead and respond.

I decide to go about this differently than before and take on a new personality that's nothing like mine.

BOSTONXGIRL: Got your attention, didn't it? So, I guess secretive works.

He responds immediately, and it upsets me to know that he's on this site right now, seeking out other women after I told him I'm leaving Landon. He's led me to believe we're together and that he loves me. He told me he could let the casual sex go, but here he is, messaging a dupe.

ALEC107: It's a nice change from the women who get on this site and put everything out there without regard to their safety. I like that you're protecting yourself.

What the hell?

These are pretty much the same things he said to me when we started talking. If I hadn't deleted my original account, I would go back and read through our first exchange, but I don't need to. I can remember that conversation as if it happened yesterday.

BOSTONXGIRL: No need for me to put it all out there. I'm not a desperate woman seeking attention.

ALEC107: Then what are you seeking?

It's not what I'm seeking, Alec. It's what you're seeking, and I'm determined to find out.

BOSTONXGIRL: Someone who can teach me something different from boring vanilla.

ALEC107: Anything in particular you'd like to explore?

Clicking on his profile, I quickly read through his fetishes again, and pick one without having to go for the obvious choice of voyeurism.

BOSTONXGIRL: Sensory deprivation intrigues me.

ALEC107: Anything else?

BOSTONXGIRL: A lot of things intrigue me, including you.

I need to go for blunt because I don't have time to waste building this fake relationship to get answers to the questions I have right now.

ALEC107: You have a picture? I'd like to know what you look like.

Shit.

BOSTONXGIRL: Hold on.

Without wasting a minute, I hop onto Facebook and quickly scroll through my list of friends until I come across the most decent and attractive person I can find. It only takes me a minute or two before I'm saving the photo. Clicking back to our message thread, I upload the photo and send it to him.

Yeah, I'm that low that I would swipe one of my fan's photos to send to Alec, but desperate times call for desperate measures.

ALEC107: Fucking beautiful.

"That's what you say to me, dick face," I seethe under my breath. I can't believe that he's doing this—that he *has* been doing this.

I try not to think about how many women he's sought out since I've been with him, but even if it were only this once, which I know isn't the truth, it's enough to make me question every damn thing about him.

BOSTONXGIRL: You're not so bad yourself. But if I'm being honest, I'd like to see more.

It doesn't take but five seconds for him to send a file through. I click on it, waiting for it to download, and when it's done, my stomach convulses in a putrid wave of nausea.

A picture of him lying in the bed I woke up in this morning appears. It's a selfie of him holding his erection, but I know he didn't just take that because he's not even at his loft right now. This fucker has nudes stored on his phone, most likely for occasions just like this.

My body chills in horror when I contemplate the idea that I've been nothing but a game to him.

But why? Why me? Why a year?

Maybe this is his real fetish—seeking out inexperienced women, vanilla women, and getting them to fall for him while filling their naïve heads with lies.

Fucking lies!

And from a man who has given me so much shit about not trusting him.

BOSTONXGIRL: Nice cock.

ALEC107: Your turn.

I go balls to the wall because I need to know the truth about this man I've allowed myself to fall in love with, the man I'm about to divorce my husband for, the man who has pulled the rug out from my whole world.

BOSTONXGIRL: I don't send nude photos of myself to anyone, but if you'd like to take a peek, why don't you meet me for a drink.

ALEC107: When and where?

Through the storm of fury that's raising my blood pressure to an all-time high, tears flood my eyes. The thorns I bear suddenly turn on me, puncturing my own heart, killing what I thought was so real. Because he made me believe in him. God, am I that fucking gullible?

BOSTONXGIRL: You free tonight? Eastern Standard?

ALEC107: I have I prior commitment, but I can manage a quick drink. 5:30?

That prior commitment is me. I can't believe he plans on meeting a girl before coming home from work to have dinner with me.

BOSTONXGIRL: Looking forward to it.

I don't even wait for his reply before I slam my laptop closed. I want to send it flying across the room. I want to fucking scream and cry. I want to throw my fist into his face that's so beautiful it should be sculpted in marble.

Who the hell is this man?

I don't want to believe this is true. I want to believe he is exactly who he claims to be. I want to trust him, because to not trust him is to not be with him, and I want to be with him because it's too painful to imagine *not* being with him.

I have a couple hours before Alec will show up at Eastern Standard, and I can't allow time to spiral my emotions out of control. I need to distract myself or otherwise I'll do nothing but drive myself crazy in a panic of unthinkable outcomes to this situation.

Grabbing my car keys, I force my body to move, because I have no other choice. I make my way down to the parking garage, get in my car, and head to Cambridge. Music blasts through the speakers in an attempt to muffle my thoughts as I drive to Brooke's house.

"What are you doing here?" she says when she opens the door with Anabelle tucked into her arms.

"Thought I would surprise you," I tell her, feigning my good mood because I'm too damn prideful to let her know that maybe she was right about Alec all along. "And I wanted to see this little princess."

I hold out my arms, and Brooke hands over the swaddled bundle of perfection. I follow Brooke when she heads into her bedroom and take a seat in the chair by the window.

"You want to use this opportunity to take a shower and clean yourself up?"

She flops listlessly onto the bed. "Are you saying I look like shit?"

With her unbrushed hair and several spots of spit-up staining her shirt, I shake my head. "Have you looked at yourself lately? Or for that matter, *smelled yourself*?"

"That girl has the worst acid reflux."

"I can tell by your sour stench. But seriously, I'm here, so get yourself cleaned up while Anabelle and I have a little girl talk."

Brooke rolls herself dramatically off the bed and drags sluggishly into the bathroom, leaving me alone with angelic peace. Nesting her in my arms, I stare down into her purity and wish for the world to delay its tarnishing upon her. I close my eyes and allow her innocence to console me. It's an even exchange of pacification—a give and take—a shared need for comfort.

The sound of the shower soothes even more, but it's short-lived, and I know my moment of assuagement is over when Brooke shuts off the water.

Wrapping up in a towel, she walks into the bedroom to grab some clean clothes. "You never told me what happened with Alec. What did he say when you questioned him about the whole job thing?"

Losing all the relief I had just gained, I'm pulled right back into my miserable reality.

"It's him. He does business under his middle name, Harrison."

"What?" she calls out from the bathroom where she's now applying moisturizer to her face.

"Yeah, I questioned him and he pulled up the directory on his computer to show me. You didn't know his last name, but it's there, only with Harrison listed, not Alec."

"And you believe him?"

She starts getting dressed when I respond, "Why shouldn't I?" even though I know I shouldn't at this point.

"Didn't you say he has brothers?"

"Yes."

"Any of them named Harrison?"

Her question splinters the elasticity of trust I have in him even more.

He's never told me his brothers' names—I never even asked. How is it that I've been with this man for a year and I don't know the simplest things about him? It was just the other night when we discovered our mutual love of poetry. Have we just been so blinded by passion and excitement and living life one stolen moment at a time that we've skipped steps along the way?

I lie, unwilling to admit all that I've missed to learn, and tell her, "No. None of them share that name. It's him."

But what if it isn't?

The quiver of anxiety quickens, and the urge to find an excuse to leave builds.

"I hope you're right," she says and then changes the topic, asking, "Did you and Landon ever talk?"

"There wasn't much talking."

"What was said?"

I don't immediately respond, because I'm scared to say it out loud. It was one thing for me to tell Alec, because I needed him so badly, and I knew with his touch on me that it wouldn't hurt me to say it. But he's not here to salve my aching plight.

She senses my unease to her question and takes Anabelle from my arms before setting her in the bassinet. Brooke sits in front of me on the edge of the bed and coaxes me with a compassionate tone.

"What happened?"

With my fingers tangled in knots, I finally speak. "It's over."

"Did you tell him about Alec?"

I shake my head. "No. He came to the hotel and we wound up having sex. It was awful. I knew from his kiss that it would be the last time."

"I'm so sorry."

"Do you hate me?"

"For what?"

"For *everything*." My voice breaks around the words I shamefully own.

Because *I* did this.

It was by my own hands that I destroyed everything around me.

This is all my fault, which makes it all that much worse because I have no one to blame but me and me alone.

She leans forward and takes my hands in hers with eyes that shine brightly with harbored tears. "Life isn't perfect. *We* aren't perfect," she says with compassion. "You're not the first person who has found themselves in a situation like this, and you're not going to be the last. You made vows to Landon, and I know you meant them at the time. But there's one thing you never factored in, something I never even factored in when I married Chris—it's the awareness that we're not in control of our destiny. And sometimes we break promises to the ones we love the most." She pauses for a moment, and I bear the excruciatingly painful knot that lodges itself in my throat. "The thing is, when emotions are involved, all hell breaks loose. It's the single most powerful thing we have no control over. We can't tell our hearts what to do or how to feel. They do whatever the fuck they want—good or bad—right or wrong. They are what lead us through life. I'm not saying you couldn't have made better decisions, but I could never hate you for following your heart. And if it's telling you that Alec is what you need, then I'll do my best to be there for the both of you. But one thing you can always count on from me is that I will always have your back, no matter what."

I sit next to her on the bed and pull her into my arms. We hug. We cry. She just reassured me of what was there all along: that no matter what happens with Landon or Alec, she will be there to catch me if I fall with no judgments.

"I love you so much, and I'm so sorry I've dragged you into this mess."

"It's okay."

We continue to hold on to one another until familiar voices echo through the house. I jump back and deadpan into Brooke's eyes that are startled wide.

My heart jackknifes. It's been almost four weeks.

"What are they doing here?"

"They've been staying the night when Landon has to work late," she responds, and I can't hold myself back when I run out of the room and toward the biggest loves of my life.

"Mommy!"

Oh, my God!

I drop to my knees as they run and barrel into my open arms. The meaning of life returns to my soul as I hold my babies. I've been away for so long and have been so distracted and consumed with everything going on that I allowed myself to detach as a mother.

How could I let that happen?

Another pile of guilt dumps heavily on my heart. Even though Landon didn't want to put them in the middle of this horrific situation, a decision that I too agreed with, I realize in this very moment that I not only abandoned my husband, but also Jill and Emily.

Why am I so selfish?

"I've missed you two so much."

"I missed you too."

"Me too," Emily says before giving me a kiss. "Don't ever go away for that long again."

"Never again," I assure. "Mommy promises. Never again."

"Wait." Jill pops her head up. "Does this mean we can't spend the night here?"

Looking between the both of them to Brooke, I hesitate. They think I'm back, but I can't go home. I can't be in that house with Landon knowing we're over.

"Girls, your mommy is really tired from her trip and—"

"So we can still stay over?"

I laugh, relieved by their innocence, that they're more concerned about their slumber party than my so-called return. "Yes, you can stay the night."

"Yay!"

"Thanks, Mommy!"

Not two seconds later they are out of my arms and running upstairs with Ryder, leaving me on the floor, drenched in the worst mommy guilt.

"How could I leave them for so long?" I ask, looking up at Brooke.

"Every mom needs a break."

"It wasn't a break. I left them and sometimes went days without thinking about them," I tell her sadly. "What kind of mother does that?"

"A mother whose world is falling apart," she says, reaching her hand down to help pull me up to my feet. "Don't beat yourself up."

"You've been there for them more than I have this past month. I didn't even know you had been watching them."

"Landon needed help, Tor," Chris says from across the room. "On the nights he has to be at the restaurant, I've been picking the girls up on my way home from work."

I turn back to Brooke. "But you just had a baby."

She shrugs her shoulders. "You guys are a part of our family."

"But—"

"You'd do the same for me," she says, and I would. In a heartbeat, I would scoop up her family and take care of them.

I feel extremely disconnected, not realizing that while I've been in my own world, living life with Alec, my old world never stopped moving. I left, leaving them to go on without me, leaving them to band together in the wake of my absence. My self-centeredness creating such selflessness in the ones I left behind.

"You staying for dinner?" Chris asks.

"What time is it?"

"A quarter to five."

"Crap," I exclaim under my breath. "I have to get going. I have to be somewhere," I tell Brooke. "I'm sorry to rush out, but there's something I have to take care."

"Don't worry about it."

I go upstairs and give the girls hugs and kisses goodbye before heading back downstairs.

"Tor, you got a minute? There's something I wanted to show you."

"Yeah, I have a few minutes. What is it?"

I follow Brooke back to her bedroom. She goes over to her nightstand and picks up the book that lies next to a picture of her and Chris on their wedding day.

"I've been reading this and came across a quote," she says, handing me a copy of *Corelli's Mandolin* by Louis de Bernières. "Open it to the bookmark."

I crack the spine, allowing the pages to separate from the grocery list she used to mark her spot. With her finger, she points to the passage, saying, "There. Take your time and read that."

We both sit in the same spot on her bed where we just shared our tears, and I read:

And another thing. Love is a temporary madness, it erupts like volcanos and then it subsides. And when it subsides you have to make a decision. You have to work out whether your roots have so entwined together that it is inconceivable that you should ever part. Because this is what love is. Love is not breathlessness, it is not excitement, it is not the promulgation of promises of eternal passion, it is not lying awake at night imagining that he is kissing every cranny of your body. No, don't blush, I am telling you some truths. That is just being "in love" which any fool can do. Love itself is what is left over when being in love has burned away, and this is both an art and a fortunate accident.

Everything silences inside me, and I shut the book. There's no more good conscience versus bad conscience arguing what's right or what's wrong inside of my head. It's only me and myself.

"Do you believe that's what love is?"

"I don't know," she says softly. "I read it last night and thought . . .

maybe this is a sign. Maybe I picked up this book for a reason. Or maybe my mind is slipping from the lack of sleep, but for whatever reason, I knew I needed to share it with you."

"What about those couples who've been married for twenty, thirty, forty years and say they still feel the butterflies?"

"They're full of shit," she says with a smirk on her lips and seriousness in her eyes. "Eventually, those butterflies you feel for Alec will fade as well, just like they do for all of us. And that's where your life together will truly begin."

chapter ten

I SIT AT THE BAR AND SIP FROM A MARTINI GLASS FILLED WITH THE COURAGE I NEED to keep myself from running from what I fear will be the truth. I'm not strong enough on my own, and if he walks through the door and I'm without my liquid shield of bravery, I'll succumb to whatever he tells me. I'll wash it away and convince myself of whatever I need convincing of just to keep him.

We're powered by a magnetism that is far beyond the realm of usual.

Taking another sip, I check the time on my phone when my affair phone chimes with a text.

ALEC107: Tied up in a meeting. I'll meet you at the hotel as soon as I'm done. Miss you.

I don't bother responding when I turn in my seat and see him slipping his cellphone in his suit jacket. I take a hard swallow as a swell of nerves pulses through my blood. My pulse races while I watch him scan the room, looking for the girl in the photo I sent him. Turning around, I shoot back what's left of my cocktail, biting against the burn as it flames its way down into the pit of my stomach where my heart now lies.

I don't want this to be over just yet.

"Another drink, Miss?"

I shake my head and then slip off the barstool onto weak knees. Taking my purse, I turn to spot Alec, and will myself to put one foot in front of the other even though everything is telling me to spare myself of the heartache and run.

Walking toward sinful love as he stands so confidently in his suit, erotically dignified with perfectly placed age lines on his face and hair that boasts flakes of silvery gray. But it's what lies underneath that has captured my soul and brought me to life in a world that never existed before I met him.

Remember, he's here to meet another woman.

As I close the distance between us, he turns his head and spots me.

My heart stammers.

His face shifts in an array of emotions before eventually relaxing his eyes.

"I can't believe you," I sneer under my breath.

"What are you talking about?"

"What do you think I'm talking about?" I snap. "Why don't you tell me who you're here to meet?"

Staring down at me, eyes dripping in the bile of annoyance, he responds, "You."

"What?"

"Don't play coy when you're the one who set this trap up."

I shake my head.

There's no way he knew.

"I don't believe you."

"Why is that not surprising? Your trust in me continues to be an issue."

His demeanor is ice cold, so cold it sends a shiver up my spine, and I'm about to blow. Turning my back to him before I cause a scene in this place, I rush through the people, bumping elbows as I weave my way out of the busy lounge consumed with the city's white-collared workers.

As soon as I'm out the door, I feel breathless in my panic, but there's no respite when a heavy hand grabs me and jerks me around. With Alec in my face, I fume, "You're a liar. I don't believe you!"

"Why is it so damn hard for you to see that the only untrustworthy person here is *you*?"

"Is this a game to you? Because it's not for me!"

"It was you who created a fake account. It was you who sent me a fake photo. And it was you who invited me here," he says harshly. "This isn't my game . . . it's yours."

"You're lying. You're only twisting this around because you got caught. I didn't message you; you messaged me, remember? This was all you!"

"You're right. I did message you. All along, knowing it was you with a barely-there vague account with no photo, just like the one you originally set up. Except this time you marked yourself for what you really are—vanilla."

Maybe he's telling the truth.

"Who's Harrison? Huh? Is he your brother?"

"You're fucking crazy."

"If I called the office right now, would Harrison Demry still be there? I mean, he's partner at the firm, surely he works long hours, unlike you."

Grabbing my arms, he shakes me, seething through clenched teeth, "What the fuck is wrong with you? Why are you so self-destructive?"

"Let go of me!"

His fingers bite into my skin, breaking capillaries, bruising me, hurting me.

"Tell me it's not the truth!"

"I don't owe you a goddamn thing," he barks, pushing me out of his hold. "A year I gave you. A year of dealing with your bullshit just to wind up here."

"Just tell me the truth, Alec."

"You wouldn't believe the truth if it were God himself telling it to you."

"Then make me believe!"

"It's too late for that. I'm done with your childish games," he says before walking away from me.

"I gave up everything for you!" I scream with my hands balled into fists, tears springing from my eyes, blood dripping from my heart.

Turning back to me, he says with a frost-bitten tone, "Go home, Victoria."

"No," I cry out because I need him. I need him to want me more than I want him. I want him to hold my hand and prove me wrong. I want him to fight to keep me because he loves me like I love him.

But he does none of that.

Stalking his way back to me, he holds out his hand, demanding, "Give me your phone."

"What?"

"The phone you use to talk to me. I want it."

"No."

He grabs my purse, yanking it out of my hand.

"Alec, no!" I fight to get it back, wrestling with his hands, but he's quicker.

Snatching the phone, he shoves the purse against my chest.

"Give it back to me."

"I don't think so," he says before flipping it open and breaking it in half, severing that which connects me to him when I can't be with him. He holds the two pieces out for me, and when I take them from his hand, his words are definitive. "It's over. Go back to your husband."

"Alec, wait! I'm sorry," I call out as he walks away for what I know is the last time. People stare and whisper as I cry for him to come back, but he never does. He just keeps walking until there's nothing left but razor-sharp fragments of what used to be my heart.

When I make it back to my car, I'm at my lowest low. No more pride exists for me—I've pissed it all away. I toss the chunks of phone Alec left me with and pull out my other cell to call the only person I have left.

"Hello?"

"Brooke," I wail. "He left me."

"Who?"

"Alec. It's over."

"Where are you?" Her voice is panic-stricken.

"It's all over. I've lost everything, and I don't know what to do."

"What happened?"

"It doesn't even matter anymore." Tears drip from my chin. "He hates me. They both do."

"Landon doesn't hate you."

"He does."

"Tori, you need to ask yourself what it is you're wanting. What the hell are you doing all of this for?"

Taking a deep breath, I begin hiccupping through serrated sobs, doing my best to quiet myself down.

"I'm serious," she says. "You need to figure this shit out and fast."

"I don't know what to think anymore."

"What do you want?"

"I. Don't. Know!"

"Erase whatever happened tonight. You and Landon divorce and you're with Alec—what's the dream? What's your ultimate-ever-after?"

Wiping my tears, I take in another deep breath.

"Stop thinking too much and just answer it," she pushes.

"Marriage," I spit out, completely unfiltered. "I want to be married. I want to have a family. I want to be loved and cherished and taken care of. I want a home that *feels* like a home. I want a man who'll hold my hand when I stumble, a man who'll fight for me, and man who has enough love for me that he won't ever give up on me." The words spill out in a heap of sadness. "I just want to be happy."

"Then go to your fucking husband, Tor! Stop this mess and go to him because he gave you all of that. And before you got so damn blinded by Alec, you *were* happy!"

"But it's over with Landon."

"You're still his wife."

"He doesn't love me anymore."

"He does," she states firmly. "He's been fighting for you for a year. That man loves you, Tori. But if you go to him, you better be willing to do everything in the world to save your marriage and to find your way back to loving him, because I know that love for him is still inside of you."

"I don't know what to do."

"Listen to that stupid heart of yours."

I hang up, and I don't know if it's my heart guiding me or fear, but I wipe my face and drive.

Brooke's words echo in my mind. What if she's right? What if everything I've been searching for was everything I already had. Did I let the spark of Alec dim what was right all along?

I told Landon that it was impossible for one person to be another's everything, but if it's one person that I ultimately want, I'm going to have to make that sacrifice. If it's too late with Landon, I'm going to eventually want to remarry, even though I know I'll always be left with empty pieces. And if that's been the main issue plaguing me with Landon, it's not a reason to let our marriage fail, because with him or without, in the end, no one will ever be enough to complete me.

But the real question is: Do I love him? And if not, is it possible to fall back in love after love has already died?

Regardless, the safety net is no longer there. Alec is gone, and if I don't have Landon, then I have nothing. The fear of being alone in this word is too much for me to bear. I can't do it. I'm not strong enough. So I'll fight for Landon and hope with everything I've got in me that we can find our way back, that we can save this marriage and move forward. I don't know if we even have a chance, but two things I do know are that I'm not entirely ready to throw away thirteen years of a life I've created with Landon and I'm not ready to walk away from my girls.

I pull up to Chin-Chin, the valet opens my door, and I keep my head down, hiding my blotchy face. I walk in, and the place is packed. I didn't think it would be this busy on a Monday night, and I immediately feel stupid for coming here. There's no way he'll be able to talk to me—the kitchen has to be crazy with this many people.

"Tori! Hey!"

I turn around to see Chelsea, one of the bartenders.

"Are you here to see Landon?"

"Yeah, but—"

"I can go get him."

"No," I say, stopping her when she starts to walk off. "It's fine. I didn't realize it would be so busy."

"Ever since that four-star *Times* review, it's been a packed house every night."

How did I forget that?

"Right. Well, I better get going."

"It was good seeing you," she says before sauntering off with her blonde locks flowing behind her.

I decide to wait for Landon at the house since I won't be able to sleep if I go back to the hotel. There really isn't a point to the hotel anymore. It was just a façade so that I could be with Alec.

Alec.

The thought of him tightens my chest. I'm going to have to find a way to deal with this pain because there is no doubt he's done with me. His words left no room for misinterpretation. But in this moment, I can't deal with the pain. I'm in shock right now and my world is spinning faster than what I can keep up with.

Walking through the door and into the living room, it feels like it been years rather than weeks since I've been here.

It still smells the same.

With backpacks hanging in the mudroom and artwork on the fridge, I'm reminded that this house holds more good memories than bad. It was easy to paint this world in dull colors when Alec shone so brightly. It was the thought that because everything was so great with Alec, then everything must have been not so great with Landon.

Did I convince myself of that or was it actually that way?

When I enter the bedroom, I recall all the nasty fights we had in here this past year—all stemming from Alec. We never fought like that until I allowed myself to fall for another man.

I shake the thoughts from my head because I'm not willing to deal with them right now.

I go to the kitchen and pour myself a glass of wine.

It's unsettling to feel like a stranger in your own home.

I take a few big gulps before topping off the glass. It's quiet and dark, much like my heart at the moment. This day was a total shit storm, and I'm in dire need of comfort, but I no longer know where comfort resides. This last year it's been Alec that I could count on finding solace.

I shake him away again.

Taking my wine into the bedroom, I pass the time by taking a long hot shower. And then settle into bed with mindless reality television playing in the background. With the stress of the day, it doesn't take me long to doze off.

The sound of the garage door closing awakens me. I sit up in bed nervously and look at the clock that reads three in the morning.

Where has he been?

When I see his shadow stumbling into the bedroom, I flick on the lamp.

"What are you doing here?" he slurs with his hand bracing him upright against the doorjamb.

He's completely wasted.

"Did you drive home like this?"

"I took a cab."

He pushes himself off the side of the door and barely makes it to the bed before falling face-first onto the mattress.

"Are you really here or am I seeing things?" he mumbles with his face buried in the sheets.

I place my hand on his back and immediate recoil when he flinches against my touch.

"I'm really here."

"Mmmm," he groans, and I know there's no chance he'll remember anything I say by the time he wakes up in the morning, so I give up on the idea of talking to him until he's sober.

Crawling to the end of the bed, I take off his shoes and decide to just let him sleep in his clothes. When I turn off the lamp, he rolls onto his side, giving me his back.

Lying in the same bed with my husband after a month is awkward, but if there's a chance to save this marriage, maybe its worth taking. I don't expect for it to be easy and painless, but I don't think it could be any worse than the agony I've already put myself through. Perhaps the passage from the book is true, and if so, then I must love Landon. I just need to work my way back to being *in* love.

I lay my head on the pillow next to my husband and stare at the back of his head. Silence fills the room, and for some reason, it allows me to breathe peacefully, giving me hope that maybe this is the end to our nightmare.

"Tor." Landon's voice is loose and uneven.

"Yeah?"

A long pause spans.

"I fucked Chelsea tonight."

conclusion

"And in the end, we were all just humans . . . drunk on the idea that love, only love, could heal our brokenness."

~Christopher Poindexter

afterword

(Two Months Later)

I once swallowed a bottle of pills. I was a freshman in college. Trey found me hours later passed out in my dorm and rushed me to the emergency room. I was forced to drink activated charcoal. I'll never forget that night. But it's not what happened that night that I won't ever forget—it's what didn't happen.

You see, Trey had called my mother when we arrived at the hospital. He told her what was going on. He told her the campus police were there along with the hospital's psychiatrist. He told her I was scared and crying. He told her that her only daughter tried to kill herself by downing a bottle of pills.

And you know what she did?

Nothing.

She lived fewer than ten minutes away from the hospital, and she never even bothered to come.

Instead, she tucked herself in bed and went to sleep.

It's one of many examples of how I was neglected.

These are the things I've been discussing with my new therapist. Along with marriage therapy with Landon, I see another doctor for individual sessions. It's the only way I can work on myself without lying.

I've never told Landon about Alec, and I've never questioned Landon about Chelsea. We both woke up that next morning and told each other that we wanted things to work between us. We said that we would leave the past in the past, we promised to never look back, and vowed to move forward. Needless to say, Chelsea no longer works at the restaurant.

I never understood why I did what I did, but after two months of intensive therapy, I've come to realization that I'm an attention seeker.

We focus on my past, talking about what life was like for me as a child, as a teenager, and as a young adult before my mother died. I grew up in the shadows of my big brother, the one who made straight A's, the one with determination and lofty goals everyone knew he would accomplish. He was praised and bragged about by so many.

I was always jealous of him—I resented him in many ways.

I yearned for someone to take notice of me, so I rebelled. I did what I could to get the attention I was lacking, but nothing worked. I would break curfew, and nobody said a word. My sweet sixteen came, and my mother skipped town for vacation, leaving me home by myself. I dated an asshole who threw his fist into me more times than I can count, and nobody saw. I excelled at sports, but nobody ever came to my meets. And in my most desperate cry for attention, I swallowed a bottle of pills, and nobody even cared.

When life became all about the kids and Landon's restaurant catapulted into success, I turned to the first thing that fell into my lap and showed me a little attention. Alec gave me more than what I could handle. He overloaded me with attention and took care of me the way one would with their child—he was the protector and guardian I'd been missing my whole life. It's no wonder I became utterly and soul-consumingly addicted to him.

With each revelation I make in coming to understand why I made the choices I made, I think about how I used Alec for attention and ask myself: Had I fooled myself into thinking I'd fallen in love with him or was the love I felt genuine? It's the constant debate of reality versus fantasy.

Were my feelings real or illusory?

Regardless of the answer, they were intense.

I've been trying not to compare Landon to Alec, which is a struggle I deal with daily. I do what I can to push Alec out of my mind as

Landon and I work to rebuild our marriage. We read books, we go on dates, and we try new things in bed, but often my mind drifts back to my time in the loft.

Alec's not someone I'll forget, but a part of me wishes I could. I often pray at night that his face will fade away because it hurts too much to know he actually existed, and that for a moment, he was mine.

Or was he?

I guess I'll never know the truth behind the fantasy, and because of that, it's the fantasy that will live on within me. He imprinted my soul, and no matter what I do or how far I tuck him into my memory, he'll always be a part of my past, a part of my story—a part of *me*.

But I made my choice, and I chose Landon.

I don't know if we'll make it, if we can survive all the damage we've done, but we take it day by day.

It's my hope to fall back in love with my husband, and I'm committed to doing everything I can to fix myself and mend my heart back with his.

after afterword

(Six Months Later)

Leaving the drugstore, I rip the packaging open and toss it into the trash can before getting into my car.

It only takes a few minutes to complete the activation process.

Endorphins burst in my veins, sending a current of electricity through my bloodstream.

My heart races with each button pushed.

I listen to the rings as my skin pricks with anticipation.

"Hello?"

I'm already high.

"God, I've missed you."

"I've missed you too, Victoria."

Everything I've been missing, the rush, the excitement, the sparking ember in my heart, it all erupts in a blazing fire from his voice alone.

Neither one of us speaks, only the sounds of our breaths filling the space between us pass the seconds by.

"I can't do this," he says, extinguishing everything he just set ablaze. "I can't go down this road again. Whatever phone you're calling me from, throw it the fuck away."

"Alec, please."

"I loved you, Victoria. I really did."

And then the line goes dead.

the end

I do not love you except because I love you;
I go from loving to not loving you,
From waiting to not waiting for you
My heart moves from cold to fire.

I love you only because it's you the one I love;
I hate you deeply, and hating you
Bend to you, and the measure of my changing love for you
Is that I do not see you but love you blindly.

Maybe January light will consume
My heart with its cruel
Ray, stealing my key to true calm.

In this part of the story I am the one who
Dies, the only one, and I will die of love because I love you,
Because I love you, Love, in fire and blood.

-Pablo Neruda

FROM THE AUTHOR

Thank you for reading *Lost in the Affair.*
If you enjoyed this book, please consider leaving a spoiler-free review on Amazon.

Follow
e.k. blair

Instagram:
www.instagram.com/ek.blair

Facebook:
www.facebook.com/EKBlairAuthor

Twitter:
twitter.com/EK_Blair_Author

Goodreads
www.goodreads.com/author/show/6905829.E_K_Blair

Bookbub:
www.bookbub.com/authors/e-k-blair

acknowledgements

First and foremost, thank you, Anonymous! Thank you for trusting me with your darkest secrets, thank you for choosing me to be the one to tell your story, and thank you for believing in me. Getting to know you through this process has been a joy and an honor and an experience I will never forget.

Now, let's keep this short and sweet:

My husband, thank you for your never-ending support.

Lisa and Ashley, my amazing editors, thank you for continuing to help me grow as a writer and encouraging me as an artist.

Sally, you are my left hand and my left brain, and I don't know what I would do without you!

Jennifer, thank you for never shying away from being honest.

Nina, I'm sure you thought I was crazy when I asked you to represent Anonymous by being on the cover. You are stunning on the outside and simply beautiful on the inside. I couldn't have asked for a more perfect book cover. THANK YOU!

Adrianne, Kathryn, Veronica, Lisa, and Andrea—you know exactly why!

To the bloggers, fans, and my Little Black Hearts, none of this would be possible without your consistent support. "Thank you" will never be enough for what you give me, but it's all I have, so THANK YOU. From the bottom of my heart—THANK YOU!

A Dark Erotic Thriller

#1 Bestselling Romantic Suspence
#1 Bestselling Erotic Thriller

"What E.K. Blair achieved was thrilling and shocking. This series was un-put-down-able, and the end result was nothing short of brilliant!"
-Totally Booked

"E.K. Blair's boldest, most daring work to date. Twisted and completely brilliant. You're in for a wild ride."
-Vilma Gonzalez, USA Today

"WOW! This was one of the craziest book rides I've ever been on."
-Maryse Black, Maryse's Book Blog